Pearl Weaver's Epic Apology

Pearl Weaver's Epic Apology

Rachel Keener

The characters and events portrayed in this book are fictitious. Any similarity to real persons, living or dead, is coincidental and not intended by the author.

Printed in the United States of America

First Edition: May 2017

ISBN 978-0-692-83740-5

For contact information, visit www.rachelkeener.com

For Mattie

Part One
Characters

I

I wished for Persephone.

Red pomegranate seeds in my palm, like a fistful of rubies. *Persephone, Persephone,* I begged.

Daddy had recently finished reading the Greek myths with me. When I asked for a second round he smiled and handed me the book.

"If they mean that much to you, you should read them yourself."

"But were they real?" I asked.

He nodded. "These stories live, and that makes them real to people like us."

It was Persephone that lived for me. I read her story, about being kidnapped from her mama's arms and then sealing her doom by eating six pomegranate seeds, until I no longer needed the words. I could see it all around, whenever I wanted. I saw Hades, the thieving god with his mocking smile. Persephone, as beautiful as the flowers in the fields where she danced. I saw the Underworld like a pomegranate prison.

And then one morning I walked in on Loretta, our housekeeper, decorating the dining room table. Her back was turned and she murmured softly, "Maybe one more ... perfect."

She stepped back to admire her work. I looked at the table and held my breath. Mama's crystal bowl was in the center. Matching red candles on either side. And nestled in the bowl, six pomegranates.

"Like it?" she asked as I reached out to touch the fruit's skin—smooth and waxy, like polished leather. "Got the idea from *Better Homes*." She turned her head to the side and stared at the bowl. "Don't know that they're pretty, but there's still something to 'em."

I picked one up as Loretta's hand clutched against her chest. "You've messed up the balance. If you're hungry, grab some of the banana loaf I baked. You don't wanna eat these, too much seed for just a bit of juice."

"I need this."

"What on earth for?" she demanded.

I shrugged. No matter what I said, I wouldn't convince her—how with one glimpse of that fruit, I did more than hear words or see characters. I felt the myth inside me.

That night, in the fields behind my house, I cradled six pomegranate seeds in my palm and made my wish. Then I crunched the seeds between my teeth and fell headfirst into the myth.

I danced across fields in full bloom. I stomped yellow blossoms and twirled until I was dizzy. I dared Hades to try and slow me down.

But soon the flowers wilted and the moon hid. Darkness coiled around me, and my dancing fields turned foreign and dangerous. In the distance my home glowed brightly, nearly every light was on. Daddy's voice called through the darkness, too, but I huddled on the ground and shivered because of the taste that lingered on my lips. That soft, sour insult of my pomegranate prison.

The next morning I woke up warm in bed. Daddy sat in a chair next to me, thumbing through my book of Greek myths. My earliest memories of him were just as he was then. Eyes focused on the pages of a book, large hands grasping a worn out cover.

"Mornin'," I whispered.

He looked up. "Nearly noon. You happy to be found?"

"I'm hungry."

He snapped the book closed, stood up, and walked to the window that overlooked the fields where I had spent the night. "I searched until I found you asleep on the ground at dawn. You were half frozen. I know you could see the house lights through the dark. I know you heard me calling. I was so worried I even…I even searched the pond."

"It was Persephone," I said. "She…I ate the pomegranate."

His dark eyes sparked with amusement, but quickly dimmed. "Pearl, when I said the myths live, I meant on the page." He held up my book. "I'm taking this back. No more myths. But here's something that will help." He handed me a spiral notebook.

I flipped through the blank pages.

"I understand wanting to live the story. That's why I write." He placed his palm on the top of my head, smoothed down the mess of curly hair that was my mama's gift. "You are such a character."

He walked to the door and called over his shoulder, "Come eat while I soothe Loretta. She's completely riled."

But Loretta was never easily soothed. Soon after she was hired to clean, she became our only compass. She kept the home on track and pointed in the right direction, but her task wasn't easy.

"Just a bunch of highfalutin poetry," she'd growl to the pan she rinsed. "Not a lick of common sense between 'em."

So common sense was her mission. She fried the cabbage and scrubbed the dishes, but she also dispensed wisdom without filter or warning. I listened carefully. Not because I believed her, but because I could never decide whether she was a fairy-tale stepmother or an old Aesop's crow.

She didn't weigh a hundred pounds, was all bone and dentures, yet her iron convictions, her absolute judgment filled a room. Her voice hovered just above a whisper, always ladylike, as she heaped fire upon my head. And in case words alone weren't enough to shame or scare me into behaving, there was always the threat that I might kill her if I didn't straighten up.

In her early sixties, Loretta had suffered a mild heart attack. More than a decade later, whenever something really upset her, she'd grip her hand over her heart and pound it. It was her way of letting me know I had grieved her until her heart was *on the verge.*

"I won't stand for it, Tom," Loretta whispered in the dining room.

I was in the kitchen, wolfing down a second bowl of Rice Krispies, even though in her anger, Loretta had refused me sugar. Daddy was whispering too, trying to keep me from hearing. They didn't realize my ears, not yet muffled by age, were sharp, seeking things. Their powers reached far beyond what adults anticipated—through walls, down hallways, and even up the stairs.

I heard a thump, and knew that Loretta's fist had found her heart. "She could've froze to death!"

"You act like it's February," Daddy said.

"I've known animals to freeze in spring!"

"She's no mouse."

"Well some crazy man could've grabbed her. Who knows if we'd have gotten her back."

"She's so young, with fire for an imagination. I talked to her, and took away her book. No harm's been done."

"No harm?" Loretta gasped. "You've filled her head full of things she's too young to make sense of! All these *stories,* the same ones you're always grumbling that your college students don't understand. There's only one worthy book, though you won't be bothered with it anymore."

She was talking about the giant coffee table Bible displayed on a desk in her bedroom. Every time I was caught misbehaving, she'd warn that I had better hurry and read it cover to cover.

Daddy groaned. "A person's never too young to feel beauty, to know tragedy."

"Oh save it for the classroom!" Loretta snapped.

"Let's calm down ..."

"She isn't like other little girls, because you've never let her be. She's thirteen, with a room full of books, yet never held a Barbie. She's never attended a slumber party or begged us for the latest fashion. She'll start a new school this fall but has no clue how to be like the other girls. Surely you haven't forgotten *why* she has to leave her old school? Thank heavens you convinced them not to put that kidnapping mess in her file. Just imagine if the sheriff hadn't accepted your donation. Her permanent record would be ruined!"

A spotless permanent record was the high prize in Loretta's eyes. She made sure every illness that caused me to miss a morning of school was excused with a doctor's note. All my library books were turned in on time. I was never tardy. And my homework folders, report cards, and field trip slips were always signed and returned the next day.

"I hope you're not implying what happened was all her fault," Daddy said. "If that group of bullies had just once invited her to play..."

"It was your fault," Loretta cried. "She's never been taught how to be normal. She has a chance for a fresh start at a new school this fall, but will she take it? No! She'll go in there play acting again and get torn to pieces. And guess who'll be the one to pick up those pieces? Not you. You're too busy reading poetry and touring conferences."

"But she wasn't acting. She has this—" Daddy stopped quickly, and sucked in his breath. "She can make things come alive."

Silence.

I paused and held my spoon in midair. We were all thinking of the person Daddy wanted to bring to life.

II

Since I was already in trouble, I helped myself to a heaping scoop of sugar over a bowl of fresh cereal. I looked around while I ate. Mama's treasured rolling pin was still laid next to the coffeepot. Her favorite jade cactus still leaned toward the window where she'd first placed it. Her best cooking kettles dangled on the pot rack above the island where she last left them. When Loretta cooked, she used the newer set, hidden in the pantry.

I had no memory of Mama in the kitchen. But I knew that this room was not like any other. It required a soft voice and a light step. Going to the kitchen was like visiting a cemetery.

Daddy tried his best to share memories of her, to plant them in my mind so that they could grow and become my own. He liked to tell a bedtime story about the day he met her. How she was the prettiest baker at Dewey's, a shop known for cake squares and paper thin ginger cookies.

He was a worn out doctoral student when he stumbled into her store. It was the week he would defend his dissertation. His thoughts were jumbled, his heart raced, and he had a twitch in his right eye. He sat, brooding over a cream cheese danish, papers scattered around him when Mama walked to his table.

"Oh," she said as she picked up his pastry. She took a small bite and shook her head. "No wonder you look miserable. Let me bring you something better."

She woke me up, he would always say. Showed him there was light outside of his own shadows. She carried him a pink lemonade cake square.

"Now this," she said with a smile. "Won't disappoint."

He took a bite. Fell in love.

And he expected the same thing would happen to me. I would fall in love with Mama through bedtime stories and weekly visits to Dewey's for pink lemonade squares.

I would eat one and enjoy it, but then I'd ask for seconds and always order a vanilla square. I wanted him to do the same, to just *try* the vanilla square. But it was only little pink cakes for him.

And always pink cakes for Loretta too. She said it was a shame we never visited the cemetery. Never took flowers or went to speak a few nice words over Mama's grave. So Loretta worked hard to defend her memory in other ways. Like ordering pink lemonade birthday cakes for me every year, even the year that I specifically asked for a teddy bear cake from the grocery store.

"It's what your mama would have baked for you. She'd never allow an old grocery store cake for her baby girl," Loretta explained as she carried a sugary pink rectangle to the table instead of a teddy bear.

I knew then, that although the number of candles might change, the cake would not. Mama couldn't buy a present or watch me blow out candles, but she was still our Sugar Queen. And if her life inspired cake, then it was her death that inspired most everything else in our home. The hours Daddy spent behind a wobbly desk. The stories he chose to teach. My obsession with Persephone.

"Oh, Tom..." Loretta sighed, as the iron in her voice melted. "Men don't know how to raise little girls. You've done an excellent job making sure Pearl is smart, but what about good?"

"What do you mean?" Daddy asked.

"Pearl has all the book learning anybody could want. But if she doesn't know how to be good, how to make right choices, what's the point?"

I stopped chewing and waited for Daddy's sharp retort. Of course he knew I was good. I was his shadow, his best friend, his only baby girl. We were so *good* together.

"Maybe you're right," Daddy mumbled.

I dropped my spoon into my cereal bowl.

"Of course I am. Let me bring my grandniece Katie to play. She's about the same age as Pearl. It'd be nice for Pearl to have someone real to play with. And let me give her a firm talking-to about all this. I can help with more than dishes around here."

Daddy muttered a weak agreement and called for me to come into the dining room.

"Apologize to Loretta. You scared her too."

I looked at him. "But you said *sorry* means I want to change and I won't..."

Daddy groaned and I bit my lip.

"Sorry you got scared," I muttered to Loretta.

"Don't you know, Girly, every lawless deed must be judged?"

Her chin was raised, her eyes narrowed. Her voice was breaking with the effort of restraint. I stared at her as she went on and on about how I had failed to heed her warnings and appreciate the wisdom she had poured into me. I couldn't help but wonder what she would sound like, what she would look like, if she stopped holding back. If the dam broke and the yell came forth. Could anyone stand before it? Would her own heart?

Loretta brought her hand to her chest like she knew my thoughts and moaned. "I've got to lie down. I'm needing some aspirin."

The next morning I found Katie in my seat at the breakfast table nibbling a blueberry bagel. I sat across from her and studied her hair, yellow as the honeysuckle in our fencerows and straight as a pin. I stared into her green eyes flecked with gold and steadied my nerves. I had read enough stories to know that good girls are sometimes beautiful. True villains always are.

"Hey," she said. "I'm Katie. Auntie says I've gotta help you stop being weird."

I narrowed my eyes.

"I bet you go to Sycamore Day, don't you?"

"How did you know?" I asked.

"Folks that live in a mansion like this don't sign up for the public bus route."

I grabbed a bagel and carried it outside to the front yard. I tried to see my house like Katie did. It was old, built of weathered brick stacked three stories tall and smothered with ivy.

Katie came and stood next to me. "No bus driver would like coming all the way out here just for you anyways. No neighbors for miles, all that driving for one kid. Believe me, you get a grouchy bus driver, your whole year can be ruined. Sure is pretty though. Like some magazine cover."

I shook my head. "It's a storybook page. I see it in watercolors, with a burning sunset smudged across the top."

Katie laughed. "I ain't gonna be able to help you."

Loretta called us inside to finish our breakfast, and as we walked through the front door Katie nudged me. "I gotta storybook page, too, you know. It's all shimmery and white. Has big icicles in the corners."

I stopped, surprised. "What is it?"

"Alaska. I ain't been farther away than Myrtle Beach, but Alaska is the first place I'm going when I grow up."

After breakfast Loretta ordered us to play in the backyard. I'd never had a friend over and instinctively felt that it was up to me to provide the entertainment. But Katie wasn't interested in pretending Greek myths, and she had never heard of Persephone. So I acted fascinated as she explained her charm bracelet and told me about each little dangling piece. I nodded when she told me about the boy she had a crush on. And I stared dumbly when she asked me about the boys at Sycamore Day.

Katie looked back to the house with bored eyes.

"Tell me about Alaska," I said, a last effort at being a decent host.

She grinned. "The glaciers are full of worms."

"No way." I laughed.

"Ice worms. They crawl, easy as pie, through thick walls of ice. One day I'm gonna catch one." She held her hands wide apart, showing me the size of the worm she planned to catch. "And during the summer the sun don't set for nearly three months. This is what midnight looks like in Alaska. But winter is even better. The whole sky is a swirl of color. Not a rainbow, but blue and green and red trails of light all over. And the best part," she said as she took a deep breath, "is spring. That's when dead things come back to life."

"What?" I asked, suddenly very interested in Alaska.

"Frogs. Their hearts stop in winter. They're nothing but frozen chunks of slime. But in spring, they thaw and their hearts beat again. Alaska is full of magic like that."

"Girls," Daddy called from the back door. "I'm fixin' to get some barbecue if you wanna join me."

Katie rolled her eyes. "Some poet genius. Auntie told me he's a big shot writer, but he sounds just like my redneck cousins that argue about who builds the best tree stands during deer season. You'd think he'd have learned to talk smart by now."

I shook my head. "That talk is a part of his setting."

Katie smirked. "You talk funny too."

Daddy could have dropped his accent, let his tongue slither out of it like an old skin. But as he rose through the ranks of academia, as he stood before scholarly panels giving defenses and lectures, he preserved it. Making sure that at no point did his ambition separate itself from the language of his people. He believed it marked him, like a drawing on an ancient crest. To most, that mark simply said he was born to a Southern family. But to him, it said much more. It said he was *linthead.*

Daddy had never worked cotton a day in his life. Never heard the mill whistle, except in his dreams. But his grandfather, Abel, had gone to work in the mills at age seven, when the wages were pitiful and the cost high. Abel lost a brother, two fingers, and the chance to learn how to read. But he gained something too. A miracle that would become the house Daddy and I loved. A tongue that knew how to tell a perfect story.

It was at Abel's side, listening to linthead stories, that Daddy learned the importance of his accent, the importance of settings. At the same time that Abel told him about falling in love with the mill owner's daughter, about the baby born on the floor by the spinning machines, Daddy was reading through the county library. Book after book, written story stacked upon the spoken, and he decided *it was all the same.* Whether from his grandfather's mouth or Shakespeare's pen, it was always love and fear and the war between them. Only one thing separated the stories, giving them flavor. *Setting.*

Daddy collected settings like I collected characters. He believed a good story wasn't possible without an interesting place to cradle it. So when he told stories, he highlighted accents, regional foods, the clouds of cotton dust floating through the air and settling on the caps of little lintheads. And he raised me to despise generic Dixie pride. Our family was Southern, but so was everyone else in at least seven other states, ten if we were generous. So while I was given sweet tea in my baby cup, what I really remember is my first gulp of Cheerwine, a cherry-flavored coke that made my eyes water it was so fizzy. And while I certainly enjoyed Loretta's fried chicken and biscuits, my tongue was trained to prefer barbecue and hushpuppies, the true feast of my Carolina home.

That afternoon, as Katie and I sat finishing our chopped pig plates, she motioned to the McDonalds across the street. "Their sundaes are so good. You can get 'em to mix the hot caramel and fudge if you ask."

Daddy smiled. "We'll go there for dessert."

I took a vicious bite of my hushpuppy. "But we always get banana puddin' here."

"Right. We always get banana puddin'. Since Katie is our guest, let's try something she likes. Can't be half bad, hot caramel *and* hot fudge."

Ten minutes later, my spoon scraped the bottom and announced my empty sundae cup.

"Good, huh?" Katie asked.

I nodded. "But I like banana puddin' better."

"But this has chocolate. It has to be better than banana," Katie insisted.

I wouldn't budge. "That puddin' is part of my setting."

She laughed. "No wonder you can't make friends!"

Daddy cleared his throat. "Pearl is defending her lines. It's a small step, preferring banana puddin'. But in a world where all the lines are blurring, where the hay bales are stacked next to the cluster subdivisions, small steps matter. If things keep up the way they are, the whole world will look the same one day. There'll only be one setting. Stories will all sound the same. Everybody'll prefer McDonalds."

Katie turned to me with wide, serious eyes. "Well for heaven's sake, don't talk about this 'lines' thing at school. And when you're with other girls, you've gotta pretend you love chocolate more than banana. It really is like a rule, okay?"

Daddy laughed and then groaned. "You're right. School's not the best place for drawing lines. Why don't you come back to our home later in the week? Pearl can give you a tour."

Katie shrugged as we pulled into a townhome parking lot.

"I'll have Loretta pick you up ... maybe Thursday?"

"Okay," Katie said. "Later, Pearl."

I waved and watched her walk through the parking lot. She came to a sidewalk where a big green trash can blocked her path. She grabbed the handle and rolled it behind her until she reached her front door. As we drove away, I thought about her face as she stared at my home. I thought about her storybook, shimmery white with icicles framing the page.

Later that night, as I lay in bed thinking about the events of the day, Daddy came and sat on the edge of my bed.

"I want you to give Katie a chance," he said.

"At what?"

"Teaching you things you don't know. Things that I don't know either."

"You want *her* to tutor me?"

I remembered the kids who stayed after school to drill math fact flashcards. I felt sorry for them as I sailed away, free for the day, in the afternoon car line. I felt superior too.

Daddy sighed. "Don't shrug off everything she says, just because she's not like us. Some of it might help at school this year. All right?"

I nodded.

"And be more thoughtful to Loretta. Just because she don't like poetry, doesn't mean she can't feel things deeply. She cares a great deal about you. I suppose, after me, she loves you most. There are things that, if you let her, she can teach you too."

Daddy kissed me on the forehead, then stood to leave the room.

"Wait!" I called.

"Yeah, baby?"

I wanted to tell him that I was good. I wanted to convince him that Loretta was wrong, I was more than smart. But as my mind reached for proof, I saw the ropes and the tree on the playground. I heard police sirens. I remembered Daddy's eyes, and how they stopped shining when he looked at me.

"I never meant to…I want you to know that…Just…tell me about our house. Tell me about the miracle."

"Not tonight, baby. I gotta get to my writing."

He was telling the truth. There was a story he'd been chasing for months and I knew by the way he hurried to his library, rather than meandered as he'd been doing each night, that he was pinning it down.

"Tell me *something*," I demanded, eager for a distraction from my thoughts. "Or I won't sleep at all."

And I knew he would, he must. In our home, words were as real as rooms—places we would go together to settle into something comfortable and familiar.

"You go first," he said.

"Someday, we're going to Alaska."

He grinned. "Really? You know I'm not much on snow."

"Dead things come to life there."

He raised an eyebrow. "What sort of things?"

"Frogs."

He laughed. "Well, how 'bout that."

"Your turn."

He whispered my favorite poem.

I closed my eyes, thankful for the thousandth time for the place I was born, and the daddy I belonged to. Alaska had midnight suns and resurrected frogs. But I had poetry.

Daddy was reciting a famous British poem, full of meaning beyond my abilities. Oh, but the way he said it, with that ancient tongue of his people. Not like a redneck arguing about a tree stand in deer season, but like a song, like a lullaby. His stretched syllables and softened suffixes made the words sink to the floor of my heart and glow like a lost treasure ship.

Every time I heard him say it, I knew all good poems deserved at least one Southern voice. I pitied the poems read only with clipped, hurried syllables. I pitied the poets, too, who'd never heard their poetry read Daddy's way.

He turned the light off, crooning in perfect Carolina pitch, "Tiger, Tiger, burnin' bright."

III

The next morning, Loretta met me at the breakfast table.

“Where’s Daddy?” I asked.

“He left a note on the fridge for us to have a girls’ breakfast and ... well, talk,” Loretta answered.

I carved a slice of country ham into tiny bites. “You mean you’re gonna tutor me on how to become good again.”

“Again?” Loretta smiled dryly. She picked up a bowl and swirled a spoon through it. “I warmed up some molasses. I know you like a bit of something sweet with your meals.” She drizzled dark brown syrup across my plate. I dunked a corner of my biscuit into it and sucked the sweetness out of the bread.

“*Mmmm.* Gimme one more spoonful,” I begged.

Loretta pressed her lips together and closed her eyes. “Good girls aren’t greedy. And they don’t talk with their mouths full.”

I sat back in my chair and swallowed my bite in one gulp. “That’s your lesson? I just need to give up sweets and take smaller bites, and I’ll be good?”

“Mercy no! There’s much more to it than that. You’ve missed so much training ... all your foundational years where the groundwork is laid." She leaned forward and held her head in her hands. "You should *know* right from wrong by now."

Five minutes into our first tutoring session, and my badness had overwhelmed Loretta. I smothered a grin and reached for the molasses to help myself, but my hand paused in the air as I remembered Daddy's response when Loretta said that I was smart, but not good. *Maybe you're right.*

My hand dropped into my lap. I craved his approval more than any sweet thing on earth. "Make me a to-do-list to study," I suggested. "I can memorize anything."

Loretta brightened. "A list..."

"Let me get the notebook Daddy gave me so that I can write it down."

When I returned to the table, Loretta was gone. I sat down and wrote the rules she'd already given.

1. *Don't ask for extra sweets.*
2. *Don't talk with a full mouth.*

Loretta returned and heaved her enormous Bible onto the table with a loud grunt.

I gulped. "I don't have room to write all that."

"Not all of it," she said. "Just the most important list ever."

She flipped through the pages, cleared her throat, and began to read. As I listened, I realized she'd overheard some of Daddy's lessons after all. She tried to use expression and convey emotion. Her voice soared over each *shall not* before plunging into a hissing whisper.

"Thou SHALL! NOT! m-u-u-u-r-r-r-rder."

I crouched over my notebook and couldn't bring myself to look at her. My face burned with strange heat. The way Loretta read her list made it seem like she really thought I might be a murderer. And an adulterer.

When she finished, she slammed her Bible shut with dramatic flourish. I studied what I had written.

"Well how 'bout that," I whispered with wonder. "I *am* good. I don't murder. I don't covet. I don't steal or tell lies. And really, Loretta, it's hardly appropriate for you to put adultery on my list."

Loretta exhaled slowly through puckered lips. "Remember that fit you threw for me to trade in my Oldsmobile and drive a Thunderbird like that one mom in the car line?"

I grinned. "Loved that car. It was so shiny and—"

She pointed her finger at me. "Covetous. And now you swear some story forced you out in them fields?"

"It was Persephone ... she really did—"

"False witness!"

She pointed to the crystal bowl in the center of the table. The pomegranates had been thrown away. Brittle pinecones replaced them.

"And what about the pomegranate?" she asked. "Was it yours to take? I bought that with my own money."

"But it was just a piece of fruit."

"Child, a piece of fruit was Eve's downfall."

Loretta thumbed the pages of the Bible, as though she shuffled a deck of cards. "Don't you want to make up for what happened at school? Don't you want your daddy to quit worrying about you?"

"I do!"

"Then it's time you chased down something that ain't make-believe."

I closed the notebook and held it to my chest. Loretta's mouth twitched into a half smile. "Praise be," she whispered. "You've been given the right tools at last."

I carried my notebook for rest of the day as Loretta coached me on what to add to my list. I wrote: *Don't slump. Don't stare out windows and grin. It makes folks uneasy.*

I was relieved when it was Thursday morning because it meant that Katie was coming and I could take a break from Loretta's list. I hoped fashion, TV, and boys—the things Katie wanted to teach me—would come more naturally. I remembered that Daddy had promised her a tour of our home, so I met her at the front door.

"This way," I said, grandly.

I'd half-heartedly given tours to Daddy's colleagues at his annual Christmas open house, but Katie was *my* guest. I wanted her to see that my home was more museum than anything else. A place where the rooms weren't for dwelling, but were for dividing us from a world that wanted everything to be the hot-fudge-sundae same.

It hadn't always been so. Abel and Stella had moved there from a falling down mill shack. To them, the home's beauty was in the deed paid, the solid roof, and the clean floors for their little boy to romp across. Years later, when their daughter-in-law moved in, she declared the empty rooms looked poor, and hired experts to stuff the home with fancy things.

After Daddy inherited the house, he didn't change the style right away. But one day he went into the attic looking for an old fireplace poker. What he found was all our family's things. Treasure lying unwrapped on a dusty floor. Linthead pictures folded and crammed down into old shoe boxes. Stella's violin.

Soon, all the rooms changed. History was prized above style. Stories more than seasons. And when he married Mama, she brought her own heritage to showcase. They worked together, designing each room like a well-written setting, to showcase our quirky family history.

I began Katie's tour in the hallway off the foyer that led to the dining room.

"This hallway belongs to Daddy's cousin, Crazy Henry," I told her. "He died before anybody liked his work, but now his paintings are almost famous."

I watched Katie stare at the paintings and resisted the urge to explain them. Daddy said that was rude, because different eyes see different things and that's the point of art. But nobody could ever see the whole thing when they looked at our paintings. Because Henry didn't paint hills, trees, or old red barns. He painted pieces of these things. The front corner of a barn, so detailed I could see where the wood bees bored. The middle of a hickory trunk, right where it begins to stoop over.

Katie stepped closer, laid her hand against a painting. "What made him crazy?"

It was a question I'd never been asked. The grownups who had taken the tour seized on the fame and skipped the crazy. But it was the one question about Henry that I most wanted to know too.

I gave Katie the same answer Daddy always gave me. "Keep looking at his art. He wants to tell you."

I motioned her to follow as I led her to the great room. I watched her stare at the walls in wonder.

"This room belongs to my great-great-granny on Mama's side. She ran away with the circus when she was fourteen and worked as a dancer, an elephant charmer, and a clown. These are all her things."

Sideshow banners, clown shoes, and elephants' sequined masks decorated the walls with faded color and flash. I pointed to a picture framed on the mantel. "That's her."

The woman in the picture was grinning and sassy, wearing a tutu that stood out perfect and straight like it posed for the camera too. Other pictures of tired dancers and collared animals surrounded her.

Katie studied the photo. "She's so cool."

I felt a surge of pride. "I know."

We passed the staircase next. "This is Walt's. He was a collector."

The floor by the first step all the way up to the ceiling was covered with shadow boxes and old tins. If it was rare, if it was old, if it could be held in your palm, then Walt prized it. Things like thimbles, spoons, coins, and postcards. My favorite collection was the Civil War tintypes. They all looked the same at first glance. Unsmiling soldiers with cold, gray gazes.

"This one's the best," I said and pointed to a tin in the center of the stairway. I was breaking one of Daddy's rules, but there were so many little things in the jumbled display. I didn't want Katie to miss my confederate soldier. All the other soldiers held their swords or stood with empty hands. Mine gripped a piece of paper.

"It's a letter," I told her.

"Oh and how do you know?" Katie smirked. "It could be anything. A map or the measurements to a new suit..."

I glared, but I didn't say that I knew because the soldier *told me so.* Loretta was correct when she declared I wasn't like other girls. But it wasn't just because I'd never held a Barbie or attended a slumber party, and it wasn't because I didn't have any friends. It was because I'd made best friends out of the characters inside my home. I'd sat for days letting Henry paint my portrait only to discover he painted one curl on my forehead. I'd charmed elephants with my circus granny. Once, an elephant got spooked by the lions and tore the room to pieces. Loretta nearly died that day from the pain in her heart.

But the soldier and his letter were the best. He was weary and afraid, and the only thing that soothed him was a well-told story. I whispered all my favorites to him and always ended by begging him to read me his letter.

"You gonna scowl all day or is there more to see?" Katie said.

I turned toward the kitchen, the least interesting room in the house. "This way."

Loretta had just pulled a loaf of poppy seed bread from the oven. We ate a slice as I explained how the kitchen belonged to Mama and that nothing had changed since her death and nothing ever would.

"But there's nothing special about it," I said. "Except pie." I pointed to a framed picture on the wall. Birthright pie, Mama's specialty. Daddy said it was absolutely perfect. After she died, he framed a picture of it and hung it on the wall. But nobody knew the recipe, and I had never tasted it. Of all the characters inside my home, Mama belonged to Daddy. For me, she was simply the missing one.

On the second floor, I led Katie to the Oriental Room. It was designed to honor Mama's daddy, who served in World War II and became obsessed with Asian arts. I pulled a sword off the wall and showed Katie the ninja moves I'd perfected from spending time in that room.

"Sheesh. Remind me not to tick you off," she said, grinning.

We went to my room next, boasting great green walls straight from my favorite baby storybook. Katie stopped in front of a picture framed on my dresser.

"Your mama?" she asked.

The picture was a black-and-white photo of a young woman with long hair tossed over her shoulders and a beautiful, wide smile.

"Great-grandma Stella. I'll show you her room."

I led her to the room at the end of the hall. "This is the Linthead Room. It was Abel and Stella's, but now it's our guest room," I said, even though I couldn't ever remember having an overnight guest. Still, there was an effort for comfort—a tall bed piled with too many pillows, a bottle of lily hand lotion on the dresser. The walls were lined with linthead pictures that Daddy had restored and enlarged. Most of the people in the pictures were scrubbed up with fixed, serious mouths, but there were some candid shots too. Photos full of cotton dust and gray eyes. A violin bow was mounted and centered on the wall among the pictures.

There was nothing dazzling about the room, but it was Daddy's favorite. He let Loretta handle all the details for his Christmas open house, from the invites to the menu, except for the Linthead Room. In the weeks before the party he'd rearrange the pictures and lay one of Abel's old caps across the corner of the bed.

"Is that it?" Katie asked, as she leaned against the bedpost. "The whole house?"

"There's one more room," I answered. "The best."

I led her up the small staircase at the end of the hall. This was always the last stop on the tour, a sort of punctuation mark to end it in a perfect spot, a writer's library.

On the night of Daddy's Christmas party, the room would be glowing with warmth and light from the fireplace and the reds of Pinot and Cheerwine. The scent of old books would mingle with the spice of gingersnaps arranged on a platter. The room whispered of magic and everyone that stood inside it listened.

Except for Katie. "The circus stuff was way cooler."

She wasn't impressed by the walls that sloped in odd angles, matching the lines of the roof. She barely glanced at the handcrafted shelves filled from top to bottom with books. She didn't notice that unlike other rooms, this was not a finished exhibit. This room grew richer and more interesting every day, as the piles of writing around the desk either grew or shrank.

The one thing that caught her eye was Daddy's desk. It was placed in front of a large twenty-four-pane window that faced west to frame sunsets and storms.

Katie stood in front of it with her arms crossed, looking amused. "I got one of these," she said and grinned.

"His desk?"

She laughed. "That ain't a desk."

Katie wasn't the first person to question Daddy's desk. His colleagues expected something grand, something that showcased the words, the moods, the pure electricity that its wood had supported. But Daddy's desk was a dime store purchase. A salvaged piece, covered in scratches and too many coats of varnish. With a small, flat top made of three boards nailed together, no drawers and four skinny legs. One of the legs had to be propped up with a book to make it stable enough to keep the desk from tottering back and forth.

I pulled a book from the shelf. "Daddy wrote this on that desk."

Katie reached under the top and pulled out a small wooden wing from each side. "This is an old towel rack. Your genius daddy writes on a table built to keep wet towels from mildewing." She saw my frown and shook her head. "I'm not making fun, it's just my grandma has one of these in her basement. When I was little I'd roll out Play-Doh on it."

She took Daddy's book and flipped through it quickly.

"Five hundred and twenty-seven pages," she groaned. "I'd get bored out of mind trying to read a book that thick."

The girl had gone too far. She had already deprived me of banana pudding and irritated my stomach with the over-the-top richness of hot caramel *and* hot fudge.

And now she had the nerve to laugh at Daddy's desk and shrug off the importance of his novel.

"At least he's not been stuck in Carolina his whole life like you," I said. "He roams the whole world through his pages."

Hot sparks flashed in her eyes and her face flushed pink. She moved around his desk, sank into his chair, and picked up his pen like it could take her someplace too.

"It's like that?" she asked.

I nodded.

"How do you know?"

I thought about all the nights I'd watched Daddy as he huddled over that desk. There was no door to the library. Instead, I spied around a heavy curtain that hung in the doorframe.

Katie snapped her fingers. "How do you know it's like that for him?"

"Cause I've watched him write," I said, simply.

"Can anybody do it? Write themselves someplace different?"

"Of course not," I smirked. "It's a gift."

"But what if they tried to learn?"

I laughed loudly, like she had when I said banana pudding was a part of my setting.

"What if they were willing to work as hard as it takes?" she persisted.

"They'd need an excellent teacher."

"You could teach me. You're always making up stuff."

Her eyes burned with envy. No one had ever envied me anything other than my good grades. And the result of that had never been glowing eyes or a longing look. It was only name-calling on the playground.

"I only *read* stories," I said.

She twirled Daddy's pen between her fingers. "But you know the man that makes them." She picked up Daddy's novel again. "Five hundred and twenty-seven pages... Hey, Auntie said he has a class later today. She said you usually go."

I nodded.

"Can I?"

I wasn't going to give Katie another opportunity to mock something I adored. "No. You don't even like to read. You'd hate it."

She crossed her arms. "You wanna learn how to fit in? You want Loretta and your daddy to think you're fixed?"

"Well... yeah."

"Then give me writing lessons. I don't work for free."

I sighed. "Fine. Come to the class. Just don't blame me when you die of boredom."

Excitement stirred in her eyes.

"Look, no matter how good a teacher is or how hard somebody works, it doesn't click for everyone." I was trying to lower her expectations, soften the blow that would come the first time she touched pen to paper.

But Katie raised her chin, just like I'd seen Loretta do so many times. "Betcha ten bucks I catch on quicker than you."

"Oh yeah? You think becoming a writer is easy?"

"Of course I don't." She pressed Daddy's novel against her heart. "But I've got a head start. I've got the right kind of desk."

IV

I was in kindergarten when I started attending Daddy's classes. He coaxed me there with a bribe of warm doughnuts and chocolate milk to enjoy during the long drive to campus. Seven years and countless doughnuts later, and my attendance rivaled Daddy's best students.

I sat near the back of his classroom so that I could watch everyone. Some students were in awe of him and took pages of notes. One girl either had a crush on him or was trying to charm her way into a good grade. She smiled at everything he said, even "Where did I put my notebook?" Most of the students kept turning to look at the clock.

Daddy was an excellent teacher. He was not fun, like my sixth grade science teacher who took her classes outside to observe nature. He was not sympathetic, like my gym teacher who never made anybody run laps if their heel had a blister. Daddy didn't care how many tears a girl cried over her grade, he would not budge. But he was consumed. For the hour he stood before his students, he offered up every scrap of wisdom he had.

The day that Katie came with us, Daddy kept bringing up settings in his lecture. I guessed this was for Katie, because of our banana pudding conversation. But then he said *Persephone,* and I knew he was speaking to me.

"Poor, pretty, Persephone. What makes her myth live?" he asked.

No one answered.

"Don't say love! That's a one note tune that thousands of writers sing and repeat." He turned to write his statement on the board. "Fine," he yelled out. "You'll change the words? You'll make the characters strange? Crazy?"

A few students squirmed, like he spoke to them. Like he knew of all those half-finished, midnight scribblings stuffed under dorm room mattresses.

"Still the same tune," Daddy continued. "It's the setting. A setting can save the story. It *is* the story. Bring me to the mountain, the desert, the ocean—put me in the war, the disaster. Take me *where* love is, because if you do... if you pull that off... it'll save your story. And I'll keep reading the love that you need so badly to write."

I thought of all the stories Daddy had not saved. His poetry was a prized thing. His novel was full of music. But there were others. Half stories burned in the fireplace. I had a guess about who was inside them, about who he couldn't save.

"Pearl, why's your myth got such a hold on you?"

He had never called on me in class before. I shook my head and stared at the floor.

"Not love!" he boomed. "It's the doom of the Underworld, compared to the beautiful golden fields. Without that contrast, without that setting, would it even be a myth?"

Students turned and stared at me. My face burned with heat.

"Well?" he demanded. "Parents misplace children every day. If Persephone was lost in the Walmart parking lot while her mama roamed the cat food aisle, is her story beautiful? Pearl? Anybody?"

Silence. Daddy sighed. "Since nobody wants to speak, let's write five sentences on the subject."

He went to his briefcase and pulled out my notebook. I had left it on my nightstand. He passed it down the row. "You, too, Pearl."

Katie turned around. "Lemme borrow some paper."

I gave her a page and watched as she bent over it, biting her nails. She looked back at me. "Ain't you gonna do it?"

I shook my head.

She turned to her paper and wrote quickly, without stopping. When she sat up she read over her lines, her mouth silently forming the words. Then she grinned at me and whispered, "It ain't hard."

Daddy was watching, waiting for me to begin. But he wasn't the reason I did. Katie had looks that I could never measure up to, and she knew all about clothes and TV and boys. There was no way she was going to outshine me in Daddy's class.

I flipped past Loretta's be-good list and found a blank page. When I was finished, there was time left and I wondered if I should edit my sentences. But I'd done what he asked, written what was on my mind. It was a clumsy shadow of what I thought, and that's why I hated writing.

He asked for volunteers. Several hands went up. The students read their sentences and Daddy nodded appreciatively. He was never critical, as long as he sensed effort.

"Pearl," he said gently.

I took a deep breath, knew I didn't have a choice.

"You are wrong about love. Maybe it is just one note. It's still the whole reason for the myth. And you are wrong to call on me in a college class. I'm just a kid."

He laughed. "Good." His eyes found mine and he nodded. "Perfect."

Wait, I wanted to shout. *Now I'm good?*

I stared at my lines. Daddy had a way of overlooking my flaws, or even making them seem desirable. My mischief was prophetic of a gifted future. My unruly hair, a tribute to Mama. And my five awkward sentences, an unlikely witness that I was like him.

The bell rang, but Daddy had trained his students to hold steady until he dismissed. I looked up from my lines to see the delay.

It was one last hand, waving furiously in the air. I saw chipped red fingernail polish, heard her charm bracelet jingling. I leaned over her shoulder and read her lines. *Katie wuz here.* Just like what bad girls scribbled on the bathroom stalls, complete with the idiotic spelling. Underneath, like four staccato shouts:

Alaska.

Alaska.

Alaska.

Alaska!

V

I obeyed Loretta's list and happily discovered that I was still *good* when I hid in my room and ate a sleeve of cookies. True wickedness was when I walked through the house with a stuffed mouth, leaving behind a trail of crumbs.

Loretta beamed when she tested me and I rattled off her rules. She declared to Daddy that I was cured, and she was able to cut her aspirin dose in half. But I didn't feel different, and Daddy wasn't so easily fooled. He knew I could still see Persephone whenever I wanted. He guessed that I still ate too much sugar and still longed for a faster car. The only thing the list had made good was my ability to hide. My true proving ground would come when I started school. To Daddy, goodness was making a fresh start. Good girls had friends.

Katie visited nearly every day, and under Loretta's supervision she taught me how to be cool. She brought a Caboodle, a small trunk that looked like a hot pink tackle box. It was filled with all sorts of makeup and hair accessories. We sorted through dozens of colorful creams and potions, but the only thing I was permitted to do was paint my nails. Loretta said I was too young for anything else, but that it would benefit me socially to have a basic understanding of makeup. Katie didn't wear much makeup either. The Caboodle belonged to her mama who was a glitzy show skater down at the Skatey Lady. Cheerleaders, like Katie, preferred the natural look of lip gloss and lots of bronzer.

Katie also brought tapes of songs she had recorded during the Top Forty countdown. Each song began with a deejay's voice introducing it or the jingle of an advertisement. Katie had handwritten the lyrics to her favorites and would sing along as the tape played. Then she'd slide the sheet of notebook paper to me. "*That* is true poetry."

She brought videos of soap operas and would shush me whenever I scoffed at the thin plot lines. Loretta started offering brownies and milk as we watched, and soon the plots didn't seem so simple.

My favorite lessons were from the stacks of fashion magazines. I would scour the pages filled with tidbits about award-winning mascaras and how to have a flat stomach, while Katie bent over her notebook and practiced her novel writing. Once she was finished—she never wrote more than a page—it was my turn to teach. I'd resist the urge to correct even basic mistakes, because I knew if I made just one edit, I'd kill the whole thing. So I'd draw a smiley face at the top and whisper, "Nice."

Katie would beam, "I know!"

Late one afternoon, when I thought Daddy was writing, I curled up with a stack of magazines and read them all cover to cover. I was embarrassed when he suddenly spoke over my shoulder. "*How To Tell What My Guy Is Thinking*... What on earth are you reading?"

I blushed. "The new lessons you ordered."

Daddy pulled the magazine from my hands. "Not this."

Katie was on the couch next to me, reading a magazine too. "We've been working on this all summer. Auntie said we gotta teach her how to be cool so she can make a fresh start. Truth is, I'm such a good teacher that by the time I'm done she won't need that fresh start. She could go back to her old school and they wouldn't even know it was her, she'll be so different."

"I can't go back," I said.

"I know, I know." Katie nodded. "Auntie said something awful happened to you on the playground."

"No. I got expelled."

Daddy groaned. "We quietly withdrew. There's nothing in your file anymore about being expelled."

The phone rang and Daddy hurried out of the room as Katie crossed her arms and grinned. "Ain't you full of surprises. Got yourself kicked out of the most expensive private school in town? How does such a good girl—"

"I'm not good," I interrupted.

"You make straight As and have never had a crush." She laughed.

"I'm smart, but that's not the same thing."

Katie stared at me, eyes wide. "What on earth did you do?"

"Tied Gretchen Hollings to a tree and left her there. They put out a county kidnapping alert. It was a pretty big deal, but Daddy thinks if the kids had been nicer to me I would've made better choices."

"Well, did you do it because you were bullied?" Katie asked.

I thought for a moment. "I don't think I was bullied. If anything I was always left alone. When I was little, I was invited to birthday parties because parents invited the entire class. But by fourth grade, girls were picky about who could attend their parties, and at lunch empty seats sprang up around me. Teachers warned Daddy that I seemed antisocial. One day last year, my teacher ordered Gretchen Hollings to play with me during recess. Now, you know that seventh grade recess isn't about swings or seesaws. For boys it's all about kickball. For girls, it's all about clubs. Gretchen told me to hurry up and play something so that she could get back to the FFM. It stands for Future Fashion Models."

Katie groaned. "I hope you told her that's a horrible name. FFM? That reminds me of the farm boys that meet to discuss milk cows. They should've called themselves the Runway Riots."

I nodded, surprised. "That's actually not bad..."

"See?" Katie winked. "You ain't the only one that knows words. So what happened? What did you all end up doing?"

"I gave Gretchen her choice. I even offered to play kickball with the boys. But she just rolled her eyes. That's when my eye caught the bucket of jump ropes near the swing set. I told her to stand next to the tree, on the side away from the playground. As I tied her to the trunk, I told her about Joan of Arc and how Joan couldn't have joined the FFM, but she was young and strong and smart. I showed her how to throw back her head and cry '*Light your fire*!' but she wouldn't. She just kept whining that the ropes were too tight and yelling that she wasn't 'June of Arc.' "

Katie shook her head. "Little Priss didn't even get her name right."

"Exactly! That's what I tried to tell Daddy. Then the bell rang, and my class filed into the building."

"You left her? You went back inside?"

I nodded. "After they found Gretchen, I was hauled into the headmaster's office. Daddy was there denying everything, but I confessed. They talked about my good grades, my test scores, and how sometimes intelligence is a horrible handicap. Daddy told the headmaster I'd apologize. That I'd say I was sorry and wanted to change and make better choices. Then he offered to make a donation for the new orchestra department. The headmaster thought it was a great idea."

Katie tossed her magazine down on the floor. "But you still got kicked out. Was it that girl's family? Did they throw a fit over their FFM princess?"

I shook my head. "I wouldn't apologize."

Katie stared at me with round eyes. "It's just a word, Pearl. Anybody can say sorry. Doesn't mean you really feel it."

"Pfff," I muttered with disgust. "In my family, words are as real as rooms."

Katie rolled her eyes. "Well why didn't your daddy fight harder? Not saying sorry shouldn't have gotten you kicked out. Your daddy paid them a lot of money, so why didn't he just demand they let you stay?"

"He got too distracted keeping me out of jail."

Katie gasped. *"Jail?"*

"When they put out that county-wide kidnapping alert, dozens of deputies were called to search. The news truck came to the school too. Once they found Gretchen, the cops threatened to charge me with kidnapping. They were really riled up. One of them got in my face and swore I'd do hard time. But Daddy told the sheriff that if they'd just let it go, he'd pay all the service hours of the men that searched for Gretchen, plus make a generous donation to the department. The news still reported the story, even though Daddy tried to pay them off too. They titled it "A Recess Gone Wrong," but they couldn't say mine or Gretchen's names since we were minors. Loretta taped it. It's somewhere around here if you wanna watch."

Daddy returned to the room and scowled over the magazines on the floor.

"If they don't like you at your new school, *I* like you," he said. "Now enough of this makeup and dating junk. Loretta is ready to drive you home, Katie. Let's go for a walk, Pearl. Summer's dying."

I whined a weak protest, but followed Daddy through the house and out the back door into the fields. There was no path to follow, just green slopes that had been cleared of trees long ago. We kept a path in our minds as real as cobblestone though, a custom observed for as long as we had been taking walks together. We began at the far left border of land, turned at an old shed, and then walked the banks of the Yadkin River.

We were sweating by the time we came to the old shed. Normally we passed it quickly, but that evening

Daddy sat down and patted the ground next to him. I tucked my legs under me and readied myself for a lecture about how I shouldn't tell people about my near miss with jail. That was private family information.

"Today's my anniversary," he said. "Twenty years."

He'd never mentioned the day before, but I knew the date from the engraving of a wedding photo that hung in the foyer. It was of my parents, paused in a waltz on the front lawn. Mama was gazing up at him, her pink sugar mouth asking for a kiss.

"We had the wedding here. I wanted to have it at the chapel on campus, hold the reception by the magnolias. She wouldn't hear of it. The service was small, neither of us had large or close families. Just fifty or so people. She walked down the staircase for her aisle."

I thought of Mama, flanked by dead Civil War soldiers and floating down the stairs.

"We had the reception on the front lawn," he continued. "I hired orchestra students from the school to play, and we danced while the sun set. I have a whole book of photos to show you." He looked at me. "She dreamed of you getting married here. She loved our house. She used to take pictures of it. It was just a hobby, but she loved to carry her camera around. Was always pulling it out to snap a photo of something that caught her eye. Somewhere there's a whole box of her photos." He sighed. "I need to show you. Sorry I haven't."

I shrugged. "It's okay."

"No. I never gave you her truth."

"You've told me lots."

He smiled. "About cake and birthright pie."

"More than that. I know Mama shopped antiques and had wild curly hair."

"She loved games."

I looked at him and waited.

"Any kind, board games, card games, but her favorites were outdoor games. She used to stretch a badminton net across the front yard every spring. I hated it, dreaded that net every year. She wanted me out there swinging that racket and sweating like a pig. Besides playing, I hated how it looked. There was our beautiful home with an old net in the yard. She said the back wasn't level enough."

He laughed and glanced back at our land. "And golf. She treated our fields like a driving range. She'd stand for hours and hit buckets of balls. We'd find a lost ball nearly anytime we took a walk."

"Did you golf?" I asked.

He nodded. "She had a way of keeping score. If you knocked it past the tenth fence post it was one point, but if you knocked it past the carved beech tree, it was two. She was so much fun."

He pressed his lips tightly together, and I knew he was hurting. It's why we stuck to bakery desserts, as predictable and painless as lullabies.

"Let's walk back, Daddy. See what Loretta's fixing for supper."

"She loved stories, Pearl."

This was unexpected. Mama loved stories.

Now I had questions. I wanted to know which of the books in his library she read. Which ones disappointed her. Which ones she returned to, again and again.

"American poetry or British?" I asked.

"Both."

"Dark Russian novels or sad Southern ones?"

Daddy smirked with mock disbelief. "Southern."

"Could she choose a favorite and keep it? Or did it change all the time like yours?"

"There was a favorite."

I wrapped my arms around myself like I could trap the wonder inside. *Mama had a favorite.* Like me. One story, out of thousands.

"Was it a myth?" I dared to whisper.

Daddy laughed. "Some call it that."

"Greek ... like mine?"

He turned his head to the side. "Parts."

"What's it about?" I pressed.

"A curse ... and the word that defeats it. She believed the story was real and alive. She could see it all around, in everything."

"Do you?" I asked.

"I did, and then she died and I refused to. But now ... remember what you wrote about your myth? How the whole reason for it is love? That was your mama's echo, the very thing she always said about her story."

"Let's read it!"

"We will, but Loretta's got supper for us and then I have to pack. I've got that conference tomorrow."

After supper I still headed straight to Daddy's library and begged.

"It'll keep us up most of the night," he explained. "I hadn't planned to mention it to you until I got back, when we could have time to read it together. But on our walk I got all caught up thinking about your mama and how she'd have given you her favorite story long ago. We'll read it first thing when I return. Promise."

I started to insist. He would have given in, too, but there was something different about him that night that made me hesitate. I looked at him, and the thought burned through me that he was suddenly old. I wished it away. I told myself I was just sensing his sadness about his anniversary. Still, there was a gray cast to his skin, a paleness I didn't recognize.

He pulled my spiral notebook from his professor's satchel and scanned Loretta's be-good list.

"She's a tough tutor, huh?" He turned the page and found where I had written my five lines. "Sit at my desk while I'm gone. Do some more work on what you started."

"Bunch of junk," I answered.

He stared at my lines, his mouth moving as he read the words. He shook his head and smiled. I gave him my crinkled funny face, to prove my disgust.

I hadn't learned yet, the thing Daddy already knew, the thing he learned from Abel and lived out with Mama. Sometimes words are beautiful just because they happen. Just because they are spoken, cried out, at the very last minute.

VI

When Daddy left for his conference, our good-byes were quick and casual. Neither of us knew it was our final scene together. If we had, there would have been edits. He would have read me Mama's story, no matter how tired he was or how much packing he had to do. I would have let his paleness mean something. Let it fill me with inspiration to write him a hundred pages, each an original note of everlasting love.

But that's only the way it goes when I close my eyes and redo things. The true memory is of me raising my hand in a good-bye salute as I walked down the hall. I didn't even turn and face him.

"Bye, Pearl, love you."

"You, too, Daddy."

Three days later, I was sitting cross-legged on the floor of the Circus Room when Loretta came to me. I had pulled a purple sequined mask off the wall and tied it around my face. If I turned my head the right way, Loretta shimmered with old circus shine.

"I've got bad news darlin'." Her voice quivered.

"You burn the chicken? I'd just as soon order pizza again."

"Honey, I've got real bad news."

"For who?" I asked, curious as to why I was Loretta's *darlin' honey.*

She cleared her throat. "Both of us."

No one ever had to tell me that Mama had died. I was so young when it happened the knowledge was absorbed rather than spoken. When Loretta told me about Daddy, big tears, alive with the room's glow, rolled down her face. I sat masked in old sequins and blinked furiously. But Loretta did not disappear and her tears did not dry up, and her *honey baby's* would not hush.

My house filled with visitors, but I don't remember their faces. Buckets of chicken and trays of potatoes smothered in cheese lined the kitchen counters. But I don't know what I ate, or even if I did. I don't know if I cried or screamed or whispered.

Only one thing is clear from those first dark days: I never lifted my purple circus mask. Loretta didn't mention it until the morning of Daddy's funeral.

She came to my room and held up a new dress. Katie appeared behind her and grinned.

"I had to guess at the size," Katie said. "But I think I got it right."

The dress was cut two inches above my knee, fitted at the waist with darts and hems instead of a doll-like ribbon. The neckline was shaped like a heart and sewn with tiny silver beads.

"It's way too old for you," Loretta said as she helped me into it. "You know Katie though." She chuckled. "I really should've exchanged it, but didn't have the time with all the plans to make."

Katie rolled her eyes. "This is what teens wear. That's why you brought me here in the first place, to teach her stuff like this. I'm gonna get one if they go on sale."

Loretta's hands trembled as she tried to lift my mask. "Let's do something with this." I shook my head furiously and she stiffened her arms to force me. "Just ... take ... it ... off," she grunted as she tried to catch my wildly swinging head.

"Stop it!" Katie yelled. "See how those silver beads at the neck match? I picked this dress to go with that mask."

Loretta choked back a sob, but moved her hands to my hair. She smoothed it back so tight it was hard to blink. Katie stepped forward and pulled some curls loose around my face. Loretta handed me a pair of panty hose, and though I despised the tight itchiness on my legs, I knew I had to let her win something. Katie pinned a white rosebud to my chest, reached into her pocket, and pulled out a tube of lip gloss. She smeared it across my lips while Loretta protested. My mouth tasted of strawberries.

Katie turned me around so that I could see myself in the mirror.

"You look nice," Loretta said.

Katie nodded. "She's smokin' hot."

Loretta's eyes widened. "This is no time for hussy talk."

I stepped closer to the mirror. I didn't recognize the girl I saw, with her sophisticated black dress and the white rose that matched the paleness of her skin. With the shine of old purple velvet, the same color the sky turns when the light first leaves it.

A car horn honked outside.

"That's our ride!" Loretta said. "A friend offered to drive us, and I thought it was a good idea to start saving gas money now that there's no wage earner in the house."

Loretta hurried us outside and into the back seat of the car. I bit my lip as we rolled in reverse. I was on my way to Daddy's funeral.

"Do you know the way to the chapel?" Loretta asked her friend. I heard the disgust in her voice as she spoke the word *chapel.*

Daddy and I didn't go to church. This was a glaring omission in my education on Southern settings. Little churches dotted the hillsides every mile or so, yet we never found ourselves inside one on Sunday morning. Daddy was intentional about showing me other details of our homeland—foods, music, even Nascar—but we always drove past the churches.

Literature is crammed with Bible, but Daddy disconnected the stories from anything divine and plugged them into something more general. He'd say, "This Abraham and Isaac bit just symbolizes sacrifice..."

In my mind, the Bible was Loretta's book. And going to church was Loretta's hobby. She went every Sunday morning and evening, and attended the widows' prayer circle on Wednesdays too. Only *most* Wednesdays, because sometimes she'd be too tired and her heart would be acting up. Or she'd be knee-deep in making strawberry jam, frying pies, or canning tomatoes. On those evenings, she'd fuss and worry all night about how she was cheating the Lord. If I acted too happy about her fresh jam, she'd shake her head, run her hands across the ruby jars, and call them her "thirty shekels of silver."

For a long time, I thought that was the name of the jam, like a recipe. One day at breakfast, I nibbled a dry biscuit and whined, "Sure could use some Thirty Shekels Jam."

Daddy roared laughing. Loretta was horrified and assumed I was mocking her. Later, Daddy explained that "Thirty Shekels" wasn't the name of a recipe, but a metaphor for her guilt.

My first reaction was shock over Loretta knowing how to use metaphors. My next was curiosity. I asked Daddy why she felt guilty for making jam.

"Cause of her setting," Daddy explained. "We live in the thick of the Bible belt. And that's why she keeps a two-ton Bible in her room, goes to church on Sundays, prayer meetings on Wednesdays, and feels guilty if she misses."

"Well I've got the same setting," I said. "So how come I don't have a giant Bible? Why don't we pray on Wednesdays?"

"Because I draw your lines, and I quit all that when your mama died." He looked at me with sad eyes. "Do you wanna pray?"

From my perspective, the question presented a choice between a guilt-driven Loretta or my sweet daddy. It was a choice between ruby red jam or cold dry biscuits.

"I'd rather have jam."

But after Daddy died, Loretta was newly horrified by our lack of church membership.

"I told him a thousand times he needed to get back into church," she grumbled to her friend. "I mean, Anna Pearl's been to college but not Sunday school. And now he's gone and died, and there ain't no place fit to mourn."

It was the Dean of Humanities that offered the campus chapel. Loretta told anyone who would listen that it wasn't proper to have a funeral in a place that also held questionable modern art lectures. My unchurched daddy left her no choice.

Inside the chapel, teachers from my old school came and hugged me. But no family attended. Daddy didn't have any family left that he kept in touch with. Mama had some, but Loretta said she'd been in such a fuss trying to get all the arrangements made that she hadn't contacted them yet. The pews were filled with people he worked with or taught.

Loretta led Katie and me to the first pew. She handed me a hymnal to flip through and slipped a green Jolly Rancher into my palm. I looked up and saw a large photo on an easel to my left. It was Daddy's only publicity photo. A black-and-white three quarter profile, with squinted eyes and smirking mouth. The one for his books. The one for his funeral.

Loretta took my hand. An organ began to play a slow sad song. I decided right then that I hated organs. The sounds coming from it were like a factory, vibrating and mechanical. As the song dragged on it seemed like music was dying, too, and I guessed that was the whole point. They were setting the mood.

When the organ solo finished, Daddy's friends lined up and read his best poems—the ones critics loved.

None of them knew his real favorites like I did. Ones that reviewers skipped by but meant the most to him. As they read, their voices broke into jagged syllables, leaving words hanging and lines unfinished, ruining the rhythms that Daddy cherished. And when emotion didn't overwhelm them, they still didn't know when to pause, when to take a breath to let a line kiss us. I sat in my pew thinking, *Come back.* Teach them how to read a perfect line. *Come back.* Show them the right way.

A chaplain spoke next. He said something about how we had gathered together to comfort one another and especially "sweet Pearl" in her time of great sorrow.

I don't remember standing up. I don't remember Loretta grabbing my hand or trying to pull me back to my seat like she swears she did. I just remember feeling surprised by the sound of my voice as I cried out "You mean this is for me?"

The chaplain blinked, said something about giving me peace and comfort.

"I thought this show was for my daddy. That's why I put on panty hose. But this is to make me feel better? By listening to that dead music? By hearing y'all kill my daddy's poetry?"

I hadn't meant to call it a show. I wasn't trying to have a smart mouth or disrespect the chaplain. But it was my first funeral, yet another failing on Daddy's part to raise me Southern right. Besides stories, I had grown up without any context for the art and ritual of mourning.

So everything seemed wrong. Not just the music and poetry, but the pews were so hard I could feel the knobs of my spine rolling against them. And the awkward flower arrangements, roses turned into large blooming hearts by wires and Styrofoam.

Loretta stood and pushed down on my shoulders till I collapsed in the seat. The chaplain cleared his throat, glanced at his notes, and continued his peace and comfort speech. My spine rolled crazily against the wood behind me and I searched hard for my own comfort. It rushed inside me like the Yadkin when it breaks over the banks.

"Tiger, Tiger, burnin' bright," I whispered. *The right way.* Loretta jabbed me with her elbow. I sucked in my breath and said louder, "In the forests of the night." I closed my eyes and heard Daddy teaching me *Pause now, Pearl. Breathe, and let the next two lines come together.* "What immortal hand or eye could frame thy fearful symmetry?"

Loretta sobbed and patted my knee. The organ started playing and everyone stood and flipped through their hymnals. *It is well,* they sang. *It is well, it is well, it is well.* Did they know? Could they not feel the storybook lie sitting inside their mouths? Even Loretta sang it, her soprano voice all shaky and fragile.

Once, not long ago, I could have joined them. Like on that last summer walk with Daddy. Or during those sweet trips for warm doughnuts. I could have hummed it all those days while Daddy and I sat for hours, lost in a book together. If I had known it then, if someone had taught me, I would have sung that song. I would have believed it with my whole heart.

But not at Daddy's funeral. Nothing was well. So I sat in my seat while everyone around me sang and I did the only thing that felt true. I cried *Tiger.*

I ripped off my purple mask and slung it toward the Styrofoam hearts. I locked my gaze on my black-and-white Daddy. I kept my heart near his dark squinted eyes. And I cried, with all the love and madness that blazed inside me, "*Tiger, tiger burnin' bright*!"

VII

"Feels like I'm stuck in a nightmare," Loretta repeatedly moaned. And one of Daddy's friends leaned over and said, "You must keep thinking you'll wake up and this will have been an awful dream."

But Daddy's death never seemed like a dream to me. Dreams suspend reality, allow the impossible to occur, the dead to rise. And most importantly, dreams end. Sometimes with a terrifying shout, but always with open eyes and a foggy memory of stories played out in the dark. Death is a different creature. It accentuates the real. All the innocent, overlooked details of a mundane life, suddenly become piercing, cutting things.

Like pocket change. Thirty cents in the bowl where Daddy emptied his pockets. Three dimes dropped from the tips of his living fingers that he'd never spend. Or his walking stick leaned against the back door, waiting—forever waiting—for him to come and carry it through the fields. There was his bookmark, frozen in place, inside our latest read. He'd never turn another page. All of these things seemed suddenly brighter, louder than any celebrated art or relic in our house. And they cried with me, *Come back, Daddy*.

I touched each of them, desperate to absorb any piece of him. And while Loretta complained of nightmares, reality seared my heart. *If only I could hear his voice. If only I could hold his hand.* Nightmares would have been mercy.

Katie still came every day. I assumed Loretta forced her, but one day I overheard them whispering.

"You give your grandma the money I sent?" Loretta asked.

"Yep."

"She get some groceries?"

"I wrote a list and Big Jamie came over to drive her," Katie answered. "But all she came home with was dog food, toilet paper, buttermilk, and antacids. She acted like I was crazy for wondering what happened to all the things on the list. I should've gone with her. She still gets her Meals on Wheels though."

"What about the rest of the money? Surely she didn't spend it all?"

"I don't know what happened to it. She can't keep track of anything. And she keeps calling me by your name."

"What about your mama?" Loretta pressed. "Isn't she gonna buy y'all some food? Last time I looked in your pantry there wasn't but a handful of cans. Your fridge was bare."

"Maybe..." Katie's voice trailed off in the way that meant *Probably not.*

So Katie was coming for the funeral food. She was getting her three squares a day compliments of my daddy's death. I thought back to the day we took her home. Maybe Katie was poorer than I realized.

To her credit, she tried to earn her food. She could have eaten all she wanted, watched TV, and roamed the house. But she carried her plates to my room and sat, flipping through magazines while I dozed. Sometimes she'd hold up a photo for me to see. "That's the kind of jean jacket I want." Or she'd gasp after stuffing her mouth with a huge bite of cake. "Have you tried this coconut cake? It's to die for."

To die for was a painful cliché and yet the right one. She was eating death cake. The only reason somebody made it for us was because Daddy was dead. I couldn't bear to eat that food. Just the sight of those KFC buckets turned my stomach.

One day Katie carried her plate to my room and grinned shyly. "I got you something." She handed me a small cup and a spoon. "Banana puddin'. Cause you're the only girl I know that likes it more than chocolate."

I held the cup in my hands, stirred the pudding, and forced myself to try a small bite. Katie noticed the effort and nodded. "If you crave anything else, just let me know."

"Thanks," I whispered.

We both jumped at the sound of my voice, and I realized it was the first time I'd spoken since crying "Tiger" at the funeral.

"Well, is there anything?" She leaned closer and whispered, "You craving stories?"

I flinched and Katie smacked her forehead. "Stupid question. People die all the time on soap operas, but I still have no idea how this works. Just last week Raquel's husband died when his yacht sank and yesterday she was out on a date with somebody new."

"It wasn't stupid," I said.

"Really? Cause I know it might be too soon. But yesterday when I was getting that puddin', I thought about how everything you and your daddy talked about came back to stories. I figured you might be missing them more than puddin'." She looked down into the cup and smiled to see that it was nearly empty. "I knew you'd eat if we gave you the right thing. Just wait till Auntie hears this. She's been wringing her hands over you not eating. I told her, 'Auntie, you got to feed her the right thing.' But heaven help her, she won't budge for nothing. She says 'we got all this chicken and potatoes. No sense in wasting money when there's no wage earner.' Shoot. I paid a buck for that puddin' but it was worth ten dollars to see you eat."

"What about..." I whispered. "Stories?"

"You miss 'em?"

Never in my life had I gone so many days without a poem or story. I had tried to read, but the words were jumbled and confusing. I read the same paragraph over and over, but nothing made sense.

"I can't read," I said. "My eyes are messed up..."

"Well, geez, you don't think I can? I mean, I'm here all day anyway, why not put me to work? Is there a certain book you're wanting?"

I reached beneath my bed and pulled out a book.

Katie looked at the cover. "Jane Ear."

I winced.

"All right, smarty pants." She flipped past the title page, not checking for a dedication or author note.

"Looks like you picked a doozy, but I'll do my best." She noticed Daddy's bookmark, marking our last page together, and pulled it out. "Might as well start with page one." I gasped, but Katie cleared her throat and began to read, "There was no possibility of taking a walk that day..."

She didn't pause in the right places, and I guessed that she was skipping words she didn't know how to pronounce, but she had marvelous expression. Especially the parts where young, tortured Jane began to fight her abuser. I listened intently, as this new Jane asserted herself with a strong Southern voice that rose with heated emotion, yet couldn't manage a single hard-edged suffix. For a few blissful moments, I forgot myself.

Loretta called from the stairs. "Pearl? Time to drink your vitamin shake."

Katie snapped the book shut. "I'm gonna like this kid. I mean the part about the birds went on way too long. And everybody talks too hoity-toity, but when she attacked her cousin, I mean just flew at him in that rage, I wanted to high-five her."

"Don't make me cart you off to the hospital," Loretta called. "I talked to your doctor and if you don't drink at least one shake a day..."

Katie stood and opened the door. "Lemme go tell her about the puddin'. She can be such an ol' hickory stump." She stopped suddenly and turned toward me. "So why'd you choose *Jane*, anyway?"

"I didn't."

Katie looked at me strangely. "You're still weird, you know, even after all our Caboodle lessons." She tossed me the book and I pressed it tightly against my chest. I didn't know how to explain that I had never picked Jane. She had found me, in a moment of blind panic, soon after Loretta handed me an old copy-paper box.

"Take this," Loretta had said. "Now he's gone, things will eventually get moved around, boxed up, sorted. So right now, while his memory is fresh, take this and fill it with the things you want to keep."

It was an act of kindness that only someone who lived with us would know I needed.

She was giving me permission to build my own little exhibit, a portable one that I could reach down and touch during the long hours of the night.

I found it easy to skip over priceless art that Daddy loved. I walked past historic relics that he told me were one-of-a-kinds. Daddy was my one-of-a-kind. I wanted things he touched. Broken things, used things, things he wore out. I wanted his smell. Coffee mugs and sharpie pens. I wanted his sound. The strong words, commas, and question marks.

There was so much to choose from and the box was small. As I stared at stacks of his papers, I struggled with whether to choose the things he'd read to me, the things we'd laughed about together—or take things I didn't know, things I'd yet to learn. I couldn't decide which was the greater loss, letting go of things I knew and loved, or losing the chance to ever discover something new.

I grabbed his favorite coffee mug. The one with the crack and the broken handle that he said held heat better than any fancy insulated mug. I grabbed his favorite pen. The one that graded term papers and signed his books. The picture he kept on his desk, of him and Mama smiling like fools without fear. His favorite anthology of poetry, full of notes in all the margins. I grabbed his galley, the first one his publisher mailed him. Just inside the cover was another gem. His signature with letters so slanted he joked his name was worn out and trying to lie down.

I grabbed the notebook he had given me, still open and waiting on top of his desk. I flipped through piles of his writing that he'd never shown me. I chose a slim stack of papers, not because I wanted less, but because I knew Daddy was careful with his words. The fat stacks were probably filled with research.

And then my eyes fell on his unfinished novel. That summer, he'd been more pleased with his work than I could remember. Hurrying each night to his desk, looking haggard in the mornings. And there it sat, all that it would ever be. It was too cruel, the pointlessness of all his long nights, the futility of that half stack of pages. *Come back,* my heart demanded. *Come back and finish.* And for a moment, it seemed like he would. What writer would ever leave a half-written novel behind?

"Anna Pearl!" Loretta called.

"Coming," I yelled. But as I stepped out of the room, I looked down into the box and saw that half-finished novel. There was space behind it, room for all that should have been written. And the sight of that space, the black emptiness of an unfinished novel, broke me.

Loretta came running. I fought her embrace and wise words and started swinging blindly for a bookshelf.

Books came crashing to the floor, but the one with the frozen bookmark fell perfectly into my palm. As Loretta pulled me from him, as she pulled me from the room that held all that I loved and so much about Daddy that I didn't yet know, I held on to that book. I crammed it deep into the emptiness of that box and begged it to fill my heart.

"Jane!" I screamed. *"Jane Eyre!"*

VIII

By the end of summer, Katie had moved into the Oriental Room. Her clothes, magazines, and lip glosses decorated the room more than Asian artifacts. As the start of school rapidly approached, she refocused her efforts on teaching me. Only this time she skipped the Caboodle and soap opera lessons. *Jane Eyre* was our instruction manual.

"It's us against them," Katie said after reading about Jane at the school for orphans. "No matter how uncool you are, any kid will rally around you against a mean teacher. Remember when Jane breaks her slate, and that nutjob teacher forces her to stand on a stool in front of the whole class for hours as punishment? What's she thinking the whole time? Everyone hates her. Everyone thinks she's a rotten liar. But what does she discover? Nobody liked that teacher, and all the kids were rooting for her. It's like the banana versus chocolate law I told you about—there are some things a girl always has to choose. And if the choice is between a teacher or another kid, they have to side with the other kid. So if you get in a situation where you don't know what to do—let's say you get called on for an answer but you forgot your homework and your face is getting hot and you're thinking everybody will laugh at you for being a big dummy—you turn those tables against the teacher. You make it out to be an us-against-the-powers-that-be situation, and I promise you, nobody'll laugh. They'll just get mad at the teacher with you. It's the law of school. Recorded as truth more than a hundred years ago by Jane Eyre."

Nobody had taught me books like this before. *Jane Eyre* was supposed to be discussed in literary terms. Although Daddy never overwhelmed me with technical discussions, he at least pointed out the book's settings and plot choices. And he certainly loved to discuss the author's story-laden bloodline. *Stories run in families, Pearl, just like blue eyes and curly hair.*

But if Daddy was a gentle and wise professor, Katie was a mad one. She skipped words she didn't know. She added in slang to spice things up. And she was committed, even obsessed. She reread each chapter several times before moving on.

"It's too hoity toity," she declared. "But when I read it over and over it gets easier. If I know what's coming, I can quit trying to pronounce all the words and just let it roll."

Let it roll, she did. With a Carolina tongue, Katie read page after page, throwing in an occasional *I'd cuss him!* when an enemy harassed Jane. Each reread was better than the last. Katie started looking up the unknown words and replacing them with something more familiar. "Repast" became "breakfast." Jane's "inanition" became her "crazy hunger, bad as a bear in the spring."

Part British orphan, part Dixie vixen, Katie's version of Jane was fast becoming my favorite character. While she read, I stopped obsessing about the walking stick leaned against the back door. I quit whispering the thousand *Come backs* my heart cried. I embraced Jane, hungry for her like a bear in the spring.

The day before school began, Katie armed me with a list of do and don'ts. The most important rule was hidden in chapter five of *Jane Eyre*. Katie read it to me three times, growing more animated with each version, before snapping the book closed.

"I only hope you caught that wisdom," she said with a solemn voice.

I stared blankly.

Katie groaned. *"Burnt porridge is as bad as rotten potatoes!"*

I laughed, but Katie glared. "I am heart-attack serious. You just sit and think on that line."

It was from Jane's first breakfast at the school, when the porridge was burned. None of the girls could eat it and they all whispered together how disgusting it was. I tried to make the connection to my life.

"School stinks like rotten potatoes?" I guessed weakly.

Katie shook her head in disgust. "There is one thing that can always break the ice for a new kid, one thing that always puts every kid on the same team. What is it Pearl? I can't do all the work for you. Think!"

I sat in silence for a few minutes, thinking. Then I realized what the porridge did for Jane, how it took the focus off of her, and I knew what Katie was teaching.

"Cafeteria food is gross," I shouted. "That puts kids on the same team."

Katie sighed with relief. "Listen to this line: *'The whole conversation ran on breakfast, which one and all abused roundly…'* Hear that? *One and all!* If you were at that table, that would include you. The hardest thing tomorrow will be lunchtime. You head to the empty table and you'll sit alone all year. The first day is when patterns are set and groups are formed. It's the day you gotta jump straight in and break the ice."

"I don't know how," I whined. "I've never—"

"Well, one thing is for certain, if you start talking about banana puddin' lines, *you* are what'll be served for lunch. Huh-uh, you talk about how gross school food is, how unfair it is to expect you to eat it, especially with that new "healthy hot lunch" program that makes everybody get a tray. Every single kid in school wants to rebel against it. That's a line we all stand behind. The only foods you can ever admit to liking are the rolls and the pizza. When you walk into that cafeteria tomorrow, you carry your tray to a full table and you remind yourself that '*burnt porridge is as bad as rotten potatoes.*'"

When I went to bed that night, I thought about Katie's lesson and how she was teaching literary themes after all. Only hers were different than anything I'd been taught before. I remembered what Daddy said about art. Different eyes see different things. But he'd left out the part about how usually, we see ourselves. I saw myself everywhere in Jane. As the struggling orphan. As the angry, hungry child. As the scared new girl. And on my first day of school, the real challenge was not the assignment to memorize the periodic table by Friday or conjugate the Latin verb *sum.* It was to fulfill Daddy's wish and make a fresh new start at school. I had to resist my old, solitary habits. That meant I had to eat lunch with somebody. It meant I had to approach a stranger and talk to them.

The next day at lunch, I carried my tray to a table filled with girls. Most of them ignored me. A couple glanced up and then quickly turned away. I looked at the girl next to me. She was stirring her plate of ziti and seemed annoyed when I sat down next to her. She scooted her tray over a couple inches, sighed loudly, and took a sip of lemonade. *Burnt porridge... burnt porridge...* I reminded myself.

"They make that in hardware buckets," I said.

She raised an eyebrow. "Hmm?"

"The lemonade. They have five-gallon buckets they dump the powder and water in. Then they stir it with a paint stick. Who knows what used to be in those buckets. Paint or antifreeze. Maybe old nails."

I had no idea how they made the lemonade, but hardware buckets seemed like an interesting theory.

The girl pushed her tray back. "Disgusting. I can't believe we're required to buy this stuff."

I nodded. "I'm just glad they served rolls today."

"I know, right? Tomorrow is hamburger day and there won't be anything worth eating then."

"So gross," I said.

"I'd do anything for some Yoplait."

"Or chocolate cake," I said and resisted the urge to shout a preference for barbecue and banana pudding.

"Oh, chocolate cake!"

When the bell rang to signal it was time for class, we picked up our trays and carried them to the trash.

"I'll be in the same place tomorrow if you wanna sit with me," she said with a shy smile. "I'll try and sneak some crackers in for us."

I grinned and nodded. *Victory!* I had passed—excelled!—the hardest test of my new school. Katie was going to be so proud. Loretta would insist we celebrate with ice cream and oh, Daddy would finally see that I—

I sucked in my breath and brought my fist to my chest like I'd seen Loretta do so many times. *Thump, thump,* my fist pounded against my heart, like I could strike away the pain. For a moment, for a brief flash when my new friend smiled and offered crackers, *I had forgotten.*

Daddy couldn't hear about my first lunch buddy. He couldn't roar with laughter over my hardware bucket tall tale. He wouldn't know that I was passing his test. He wouldn't know that I was becoming *good* again.

Kids pressed around me, pushing their way out of the cafeteria. I stood stone-still in the buzzing crowd and choked over my sobs. I didn't care whether I seemed nerdy or weird or ugly. I didn't care if the other kids laughed, or if they noticed me at all. There was only one person that mattered. And he wasn't there to see me.

I cursed myself. How silly I had been. To think a lunch buddy could make everything better. To think I could be good. *Nothing could be good again!* Old, sweet joys, like the first bite of a warm doughnut, would sour my heart with longing. New victories, like a lunch buddy or a fresh start, could only give trophies of pain. And holidays—Christmas mornings and birthdays—would just be one more way to count off how many years Daddy had been gone. Everything would always hurt.

A teacher saw me standing in the middle of the empty cafeteria. "Are you lost, dear? Do you need some help finding your next class?"

I shook my head.

"Then hurry on. The tardy bell will ring soon. Don't want to miss any of the first-day tours."

I spent the rest of the day aimlessly following teachers to view the science labs, the computer corridor, and the orchestra chamber. A year earlier, I would have been impressed. I would have stood in line to stare at a plant cell through one of the microscopes in the science lab. I would have been excited to tell Daddy that I could learn to play the oboe. But nothing caught my interest until the very last stop on the tour. The art room.

I was not an artist. Even as a young child, I preferred words on the page to pictures. What had me trembling with excitement was the enormous art closet. Piled inside were stacks of supplies, boxes filled with tools and buckets of paint. On a bottom shelf, lined up like pomegranate seeds, were quarts of glossy red paint.

I hurried to find Katie by her locker.

"I need some help," I told her.

She rolled her eyes. "Can't find your locker?"

"I'm gonna steal the red paint from the art room."

Katie's mouth fell open. "What on earth for?"

"I need it." I couldn't explain it to her any more than I could explain the pomegranate to Loretta.

Katie shook her head. "No way."

"Please," I begged. "Please!"

"You'll get kicked out of here too. This was your last chance at leaving the old you behind and making your fresh start."

I worked hard to lock away my tears, so that I could sound strong and brave. So that I could sound like someone who knew exactly what she needed, and how to go about getting it.

"But Katie. That is exactly what I'm going to do."

IX

"I know how to rob the art room," Katie announced, after reading more of *Jane Eyre.*

"So you'll help me?" I asked.

"I didn't think I would, but now I know what to do. Listen closely, you'll hear it too."

Katie read aloud about Jane becoming a governess at Thornfield Hall, a gloomy mansion owned by the brooding Mr. Rochester. I was smitten by the budding love between him and Jane. But Katie sped through the love pages, and her voice quickened with excitement as she read about the sound of fingertips brushing against the wall, eerie laughter down a midnight hall, and the smell of smoke rising. The staff of Thornfield Hall declared it all the mischief of a drunken servant, but Katie had her doubts. "They're lying to Jane," she insisted. "Every story needs a monster. Sometimes that's the best part."

After reading about Jane finding the master's bed blazing with fire, Katie lowered the book. "And that's how we'll rob the art room."

"I don't..." I paused and thought about how Jane put out the fire and rescued her love. "We'll find a way to look like heroes?"

Katie groaned. "Jane's a good girl, not a thief. We can't think like her. What does Jane tell us in this chapter? She hears laughter, smells smoke, says that somebody was trying to kill Mr. Handsome. But I don't believe her."

Blasphemous! I thought. "This is Jane's story. We have no choice but to believe her."

"Says who? Some teacher? Jane is only telling her side. Imagine if the monster was speaking, what would it say?" Katie lowered her voice into a husky garble. "*If I wanted him dead, he'd be dead.*"

"This has nothing to do with the art room," I scoffed.

"The fire was a distraction. If the monster had wanted to kill him, he'd have been killed. Jane and Mr. Rochester were all bound up with worry over the fire. In the meantime, who knows what the monster was really up to ... it could've done anything it wanted. Even rob an art room."

"So you're saying ..." I began.

Katie nodded. "We need to create a distraction."

The next day, I sat in art class counting down the minutes. When the bell rang I went to the science hall to meet Katie. We waited for a few minutes until the hall was clear, and then while Katie posted lookout, I walked to the red fire alarm lever. With thumbs-up from Katie, I pulled the lever in one swift motion.

Sirens wailed. Teachers herded kids out of classrooms and toward the exits. We ducked into a bathroom and hid inside stalls by pulling our feet up on the toilets. A teacher opened the bathroom door and yelled "All clear!" We waited another minute, peeked into an empty hall, and stepped out to hurry to the art room. Suddenly, the sirens stopped.

"False alarm!" a voice around the corner said. "Call everybody back. Last thing we need is to let them stay in the parking lot much longer. No telling how many have already snuck off."

The voices were headed straight toward us. Katie grabbed my elbow and pulled me into the cafeteria. We crouched behind a row of garbage cans.

"It's okay...we'll just stay here for a couple minutes," Katie whispered. "Once everybody else is back inside we can blend in."

"But the art room, we can still—" I began.

"No. They're calling teachers back. If we go now, we'll be busted for sure."

"But my paint!"

Katie squeezed my hand. "Shhhh! There just wasn't enough time. Who knew they'd give the "all clear" after a couple of minutes? Least we didn't get caught pulling the alarm."

What would the monster do? I asked myself. I peeked around a garbage can and saw the lunch lady's purse tucked beneath the register. Nearly every morning I saw her smoking in the parking lot. I crawled toward the register.

"Come back! Somebody might see you!" Katie whispered.

I dug through the purse until I found a lighter. Then I reached up and grabbed the napkin dispenser and crawled back toward Katie.

"What are you doing?" she demanded.

I struck the lighter and stared at the golden flame. "Monsters don't give up. They always have a Plan B."

"Don't you dare. Prank pulling is one thing, but... Pearl Weaver, stop it!"

I twisted the napkins into tight ropes, lit them, and tossed them into the trash cans. Soon, thick, dark smoke filled the air along with the smell of burned casserole. We began to cough and gag. We crawled to the far exit and ducked into the stairwell. Just as the door closed, we heard panicked shouts of *Fire!*

The halls were still empty, and the sirens wailed again. We raced to the art room, hurried to the back closet, and crammed brushes and quarts of red into our backpacks. We were headed to the nearest exit when the sirens silenced and the art teacher, Mrs. Deacon, rounded the corner.

"Girls!" she shouted. "What are you doing inside?"

"I'm... we just..." Katie stammered.

I glared at Katie. "I knew this was a bad idea. They better let us join after all this trouble."

"Who? What idea? What's going on here?" Mrs. Deacon said.

"The FGP," I answered. "Before we can be members, we have to prove that we are willing and able to hunt for evidence."

"What's FGP?" she asked.

I sighed. "Future Ghost Patrol. I know it's against the rules to have unofficial clubs—"

"But when you're a girl, everything's a club," Katie interrupted. "And the Runway Riots wouldn't take us... said I wasn't tall enough and that she needed a better tan. So, we're trying to join the FGP."

I nodded. "They ordered us back in, to try to get evidence about the ghost. I'm sure you know the one, since he was killed on your hall."

Mrs. Deacon scoffed. "Nobody's been killed on my hall."

"The night-shift janitor was," I insisted. "Years ago, before you taught here. Folks found him killed on the art hall with a wet mop still in his hand. The murderer was never caught. But every once in a while, people say they can still see the janitor cleaning that hall. It's why it's shinier than the others."

"It *is* shinier!" Katie whispered in awe.

"Mrs. Deacon, you know how hard it can be for girls to fit in," I pleaded. "We *need* to join the FGP. That's why we came back inside. This is our best chance to see the hall when it's not full of kids ... our best chance to finally see the ghost."

Mrs. Deacon's eyes searched the art hall behind us. She shook her head, like she dusted away ghostly suspicions. "This isn't a drill," she said. "I just came to get my purse. Go outside and find your home base. They're doing head counts. We'll talk more about this club thing later. Non-sanctioned clubs are absolutely forbidden."

"Yes ma'am," Katie and I mumbled.

Mrs. Deacon watched us exit the building. Once we were safely outside, Katie panicked.

"She's gonna remember!" she cried. "She's gonna discover the paint is gone and remember seeing us. She'll know we're thieves."

"But she won't be able to prove anything," I said. "We didn't use the flimsy lies of being lost or going to the bathroom. We were on ghost patrol. That's so weird she can't question it."

Two fire trucks turned into the parking lot just as security pulled the garbage cans out of the building. The cans had been hosed down, but were smoldering. Ashes floated aimless in the air. The principal held up his bullhorn to call for everyone's attention.

"Someone endangered the entire school today," he barked. "Arson is a serious offense that requires jail time. So whoever you are, be on notice, your little stunt is not taken lightly." He sighed. "Due to the risk of smoke and fume inhalation, school is dismissed. Please report to the bus lot."

Cheers erupted all around us, but Katie's face was flushed and she was gasping for breath. "We're arsonists. You got the whole school dismissed."

"I know," I whispered. "Amazing."

She grabbed me by the shoulders and shook me until the jars in my backpack rattled. "What's wrong with you? You're a sinking ship and I ain't going down with you."

"You said it yourself," I replied. "The monster is the best part of any story."

"Well I'm not a monster."

"Don't worry," I said, smirking. "We all know you're the pretty, popular cheerleader who has never had a single real problem."

Katie pointed her finger in my face. "You don't know everything like you think you do. You don't know *stories*!"

I gasped. "*I* don't know stories?"

"You don't know Persephone."

I laughed loudly. "Oh really, Miss-I-can't-read-this-word-so-I'll-just-skip-it. Please tell me all about Persephone. Have you even read it?"

"I looked it up in the library that day after class when your face went all hot over it. Persephone knew not to eat those seeds. And of all the things to sink her ship over, not a chicken pie or chocolate cake, but pomegranate seeds? Have you even tasted them? And we're supposed to feel sorry for her. What a joke. Let me let you in on the secret of girls like me and Persephone. She wasn't trapped in the Underworld. She was escaping. Maybe she loved her mama, but your daddy was right about one thing. It takes more than love to make a story work."

Her words tumbled with the myth inside me. Katie's face, Persephone's dance, a pomegranate prison like a long gray sidewalk leading to an empty fridge. And the mama once longed for, now... dreaded?

"You think you're so smart because everyone's always made a big deal out of your As," Katie said. "You think you got me all summed up. I'm just a pretty, dumb cheerleader. Well the truth is, I'm jealous green of you. I'd trade places with you in a skinny minute."

Her revelation took my breath. "But why?" I whispered. "Cause I'm richer?"

She locked eyes with me. "I'm jealous of how your heart broke at your daddy's funeral."

My hand itched to slap her. Blood rushed hot and red to my face.

"Ohhhhh, look who's the angry one now," she said coolly. "It's true. I sat next to you through that whole service, saw you staring at his picture, heard you shout that poetry, and all I could think was how unfair it is that some folks get to love like that. Mama says Daddy moved to New Hampshire when I was two. He got himself a new Yankee wife and new daughters. I don't even get a card on my birthday. He could die tomorrow and I won't know. I've never had a parent worth crying for. But you? Your daddy was worth weeping over. You had him for almost fourteen years, and *that* is something to envy."

Pain ripped through me like Katie had punched me in the gut. I sat on the ground, scared to move or breathe lest I burst.

"And if we get caught because of your stupid stunt, I won't be allowed to try out for cheer. The one thing that makes me who I am...and I won't even have that anymore. Thanks a lot, Pearl. I hope it was worth it." She tossed her backpack by me on the ground. "You keep the evidence. I'm going over to stand with my real friends. I'll see you back home."

I watched her walk away, past the smoldering garbage cans. Bits of ash scattered through the air and across the students, in their hair, on their clothes, over their skin—like lint. Memories, burning like new blisters, swelled inside me. I remembered Daddy and his cotton talk. All the pretty stories. I slumped forward and pressed my forehead against my knees as my breath exploded into jagged gasps. *Oh yes, I had a daddy worth weeping over.*

Kids started boarding the busses. Mine would soon pull away. I had to find the strength to stand up, in spite of my pain. I had to find the will to move and breathe and *live* with the wreckage inside of me.

And the only thing that soothed me, the only thing that helped me stand and board that bus, were the backpacks next to me. I lined up quarts of red paint inside the darkness of my mind. Shiny, like fool's gold. Glowing, like pomegranate promises.

X

The paint was watery and dribbled red trails across the floor. The walls drank the color and absorbed it deep, leaving the surface blotchy with patches of white peeking through. When I used an extra thick coat to get a deep crimson, the paint pooled on the wall like drops of blood.

Fortunately, most of Daddy's library was lined with bookshelves and books. There were only two walls with significant white space to paint. But by the second wall, I was nearly out. I was cursing the inevitable pale rosy hue, when I heard footsteps coming down the hall.

Katie pulled back the curtain in the doorframe. "I'm headed to Mama's. She wants to highlight my hair before cheer tryouts."

Things were still tense between us, so I didn't turn and face her. "Have fun."

She stepped inside and looked around. "Auntie is going to freak out when she sees this."

I waved away her concern. "She never comes up here anymore."

Katie stared at the wall that was a deeper shade of red. "I know this ..."

She reached into her purse, pulled out *Jane Eyre*, flipped the pages, and nodded. "*I resisted all the way...*," she began, as she read about young Jane being locked inside the Red Room as punishment for defending herself against abuse. The chapter ended with Jane collapsing unconscious in a fit of horror.

Katie closed the book and looked at me with worry. "I'm telling Auntie. I don't care how much trouble we get in for stealing that paint."

"What's got you so riled up? It's just some new paint on the walls."

"You're making the Red Room," she cried. "The Red Room was for dying."

"Pfff."

"But it's where her Uncle John died. Who are you planning on dying in here?" She whirled to leave. "I'm getting Auntie."

"Katie Monroe! If I wanted to die, I'd just go down to the pond."

Her mouth fell open and then she snapped it shut. She stared at me, waiting for me to explain.

"There's a pond at the back of our fields, near the Yadkin. I almost died there when I was six," I told her. "There was this old, rickety canoe on the banks. I'd beg Daddy to row me across. He'd always say no and blame the mosquitoes. So one day I went to the pond alone. Pushed the canoe in the water, crawled in, and rowed out a bit. It began to sink. I tried to row back, but it's impossible to row a sinking boat. Soon I was sinking too. The water was dark and heavy. No matter how much I kicked, I just kept sinking."

Katie shivered. "How'd you make it out?"

"A hand reached through the water and dragged me to shore. One of the yardmen. I survived because of him, but I never learned how to swim. Ever since then, I've always been too afraid."

Katie crossed her arms and studied the walls again. "So if this room ain't for dying, what's it for?"

"Who did Jane think she would see?" I asked. "Who would return?"

Katie thought for a minute. "Her uncle's ghost."

"Exactly. The Red Room is not for dying. It's the room for meeting ghosts."

Katie's eyes widened. "Is that supposed to make me feel better? Cause it don't."

"I ain't planning on dying. I'm gonna resurrect the dead."

Her lips pressed together in a thin, straight line, holding back the lecture she wanted to give. "Fine." She pointed her finger at me. "But you have a fit in here like Jane, and there'll be nobody to help. Auntie's knee-deep in baking pies to raise money for new church pews." She looked at the red walls again. "Gives me the willies just thinking about it." She stepped through the curtain and into the hall. "I'm off to get blonder. You best save me some of Auntie's pies."

I finished painting and spent the rest of the day sneaking nibbles of pie while Loretta swatted me away. Later that night, once Loretta was asleep, I returned to the library and sat on the cold floor. The room was dark and silent. There was a bit of moon shining outside, but the window broke the light and scattered it into small bursts across the floor. It reminded me of the part of my pond story that I didn't tell Katie. About how from the banks, the water seemed like an empty black pit. But as I was sinking, I saw there was much more. The pond was a world where dead things, bits of swimming scum, thrived. The light above could still be seen, only it was bent and crooked.

"Come back, Daddy," I called.

And alone in that Red Room, just like Jane had been, it wasn't hard to see ghosts. Hadn't I already seen him in that library thousands of nights? He was there at his desk, lighting a candle. He was standing by the window, watching a sunset. He was over near the shelf looking for a lost masterpiece.

Now he was my lost masterpiece. I heard him reading, laughing, singing out my name. I watched him write, watched him edit, watched him throw a bad story into the fire. He smelled like coffee, like ink, like glazed doughnuts wolfed down before they got cold. He was every mood—surly and withdrawn because a character turned flimsy, vibrant and warm because the words were too, sweet and wise as he welcomed and taught me.

A roar surged inside me. A whole wilderness of pain stormed the gate of my heart.

"Daddy!" I cried.

It was the cruelest trick of grief. The idea—the *lie*—that if I could only see him once more, I would feel better. I had promised myself that I wouldn't be greedy. If I could only hear his voice again, if I could just have a chance to say good-bye the right way, it would be enough. But what is the right way to say good-bye? And how can there ever be enough?

I needed more than a circle of old memories to loop over and over in the dark. Just empty ghosts dancing like lint in the air.

"Choose," Daddy said, with his arms open wide like he could embrace the world. I remembered the moment. It had happened just a few months ago at his college class. I looked to my left and right as the ghosts of bored students sprang up around me.

"Don't just stare at blank pages. Don't leave your character in limbo. You don't like something? Cross it out and choose something better. Want something different? Write it that way. The power is yours. But you have to be brave enough to make the choice. Pearl?" he called and I jumped, because he wasn't supposed to call on me in a college class.

He motioned around the room and I followed his stare as new ghosts arrived. *Me.* I was tying Gretchen to a tree. I was running from the deputy that swore I'd see jail. I was sitting in the Circus Room, wearing a purple velvet mask while Loretta sobbed *Honey darlin'*. I was at his funeral, shouting "Tiger!" while everyone else sang lies.

I shivered with disgust. *I hated my story!* I'd been raised on words of beauty. Why was my own plot a dark pit, swimming with dead things?

I raised my hand and drew a big X in the air.

"I cross you out," I whispered to the ghost that tied up Gretchen. "I cross you out," I said to the ghost in purple velvet. "I cross you out!" I yelled to the orphan that was forever crying "Tiger."

I snapped my eyes shut and exhaled slowly. When I opened them again the room was nearly empty, my ghosts had disappeared. The only one left was Daddy. His back was to me and he was scanning the massive bookshelf.

"Did I ever tell you about Abel and the ghost mill on Brown Mountain?" he asked.

"Shhhhh," I replied.

Daddy looked over his shoulder, his eyebrows rising in surprise. I raised my trembling hand high in the air. I drew a slow, painful X. Daddy's mouth parted and he was about to speak, so I spoke first.

"I cross you out."

I collapsed into a heap on the floor so that I wouldn't have to watch him disappear.

"Your ghost isn't enough," I sobbed. "And everything hurts. I've got to make a fresh start."

I began whispering Jane's first line, "There's no possibility of a walk today. There's no possibility of a walk today. There's no possibility of a walk today..." until I fell asleep. When I woke up, sunlight beamed off red walls. Sure, drips of paint were scattered recklessly. The trim work around the shelves was smeared. But the mess had been edited, and the walls seemed darker now, the color of old blood.

I was no longer just a Southern-tongued orphan. I had crossed out Pearl Weaver and her sinking story. Jane was my fresh start. I would resist all the way!

XI

Katie and I became friendly again, but it was clear that we saw each other differently. To her, I was no longer a nerd who needed help. I was a wild card who would force my own way. And to me, she was no longer the picture of teenage perfection. She was Persephone.

Despite the return of a calm routine, the small details of ordinary life began to fade away. I forgot my bus number and walked by a whole row of busses trying to remember which was mine. It wasn't until I saw Katie step on board that I knew where to go. And just before English class, I stared at the dial on my locker unable to recall the first number of the combination.

I should've skipped, but there was something about English class that made me want to show up, even when I was unprepared. Maybe it was that my teacher, Mr. Stanley, called out lines with passion. Maybe it was that he was kind and sympathetic. He had already extended the deadline for turning in my essay on a Robert Frost poem. "I'll give you a couple more days," he said. "Because I really do want to hear your thoughts."

But when I showed up to his class without my poetry book, he wasn't forgiving.

"Go get your book," he ordered. "Never come to class without it."

"I can't," I said.

He misunderstood and thought I'd lost it. "Look, I know you don't get the point of this class. I know you'd much rather be reading *Teen* magazine about pop stars and makeup, but what I wish you could see is that these books mean something *Teen* magazine never will. If you let them, they can change you. So don't... don't just toss them anywhere like they're trash. For crying out loud, show some respect for the writers."

I heard a chorus of giggles. Mr. Stanley glared at the class to silence them. "Let's move on. How about we begin with a pop quiz over last week's material?"

But I couldn't move on. I couldn't lower my head and scribble hateful words across my paper like any other misfit. Because Mr. Stanley was wrong about me. I treasured books. I revered writers. At that very moment, I was letting stories change me.

I remembered when Jane was falsely accused by a teacher and forced to stand on a stool for hours. My hands curled into fists and I climbed on top of my desk. I stood straight and tall, high above the rest of the room. Kids all around me gasped and whooped.

"Get down," Mr. Stanley yelled. "Before you fall and hurt yourself."

"This is what it looks like to let a story change you," I shouted.

His eyes grew wide. He was a veteran teacher, used to handling rebellious middle schoolers. But he was also a reader. So I let my eyes hold his gaze and my heart begged, *See me.* But my character flashed like lightning in the middle of his room and he missed it. He passed over the magic, too scared of the madness.

"Class, we'll have to take the quiz on Wednesday. Right now I want you to go straight to the library. Tell Miss Hardy I'm sending you for study hall. Jessica, please take the names of any students who don't report to the library. Don't forget, quiz on Wednesday." He looked up at me. "I'm going to call the office."

As the class filed out, a few kids stared at me with wide, curious eyes. Others gave me grins, joyful that I'd freed them from a pop quiz and an hour long poetry lecture.

The office was slow to respond. I stood for more than twenty minutes on top of that desk. My legs began to tremble with the task of balancing three feet off the ground on a slanted square that wobbled from a rusty hinge. My calf muscles began to cramp.

Stories were fire and passion and electricity. They were sunsets and storms, framed in Daddy's window and twisted together. But standing on top of that wobbly square, I was numb. So numb, I forgot to breathe.

One minute I was counting the linoleum tiles and the next I was lying down in the school clinic. My forehead throbbed and I brought my hand up and pressed an ice pack across my brow.

"There, there," a nurse whispered. "You had a bad fall. Let the ice do its job. Can you sit up and drink a bit of ginger ale?"

She propped pillows behind me and held a straw to my mouth as Miss Claudia, the guidance counselor, entered the room.

"That didn't go how you planned, did it?" she said and winked. "Can't trust these desks. They're too rickety. Gotta remember we're public. No fancy private school desks for us. So..."

She pulled two packs of M&M's from a tote and handed me one. "Mr. Stanley told me he fussed at you just before this happened. I'm betting you thought you were in big trouble. And it stressed you out. So..."

She had the curious habit of ending her thoughts with a drawn-out *so.* It made everything she said seem like she was still figuring it out, and therefore it was open to debate.

"Stress can certainly make people react oddly. So..." She reached out and squeezed my hand. "It's okay. You aren't in trouble. I just want to chat and have a chocolate break. What do you think about school? Being in the eighth grade can be a pill. More homework, more tests, more hormones."

I took a sip of ginger ale. Felt a boom of pain inside my head and groaned.

"And in the past week you've missed some class. You've stopped turning in your homework. I've had reports that you sleep during lunch and seem withdrawn. And then today you stood on top of your desk."

I tried to rearrange the ice pack.

"I know what happened this past summer. So..." She squeezed my hand again. "I'm sorry. Do you want to talk about it?"

The room was spinning. I closed my eyes and saw quarts of red paint dancing in the dark.

"Daddy died of typhus," I said.

She cleared her throat. "I don't think folks get that anymore, dear."

"They get it on the moors."

"It says here he was traveling...and you said he was on the moors...so he was in England?"

I nodded.

"Huh. Well maybe what's going on here is that you're making connections between your stresses. A new school, losing your English book, losing your father in England...you're connecting all of those together. It's not an uncommon reaction. The mind starts to try and make patterns and predictions out of our pain." She smiled. "Or there's also the possibility that you're an average teen girl. Attention is never a bad thing at your age. Why *not* have English class dismissed? When I was your age I wore fake, bright red glasses to school. Wore them every day because a pretty television reporter wore a similar pair. Nobody but me and my mom knew they were fake." She poured a handful of M&M's into her palm and only ate the yellow ones. She looked at my file and read for another minute. "How are things with your guardian? Says here you've known her your whole life. So..."

I shrugged my shoulders. "She's forced to raise me."

Miss Claudia frowned. "I'm sure it's a big adjustment for everybody. These things take time."

She waited for me to comment more, but when I didn't she started writing notes in my file. After a few minutes she looked up and smiled. "Okay, here's the plan. And I say every plan should begin with food." She laughed brightly. "You finish these M&M's. Then rest until it's time to go home. And next time you start to feel overwhelmed, come find me, okay? I promise I'm more fun than falling off desks. We'll grab some chocolate and take a break. And if there's any way I can help—"

"There is one thing," I interrupted, maybe too eagerly. The wish came to me while standing on top of the desk, when I locked eyes with Mr. Stanley and he missed the magic. I didn't want a secret story inside a secret Red Room. I wanted Jane to come home to Carolina. "You'll think it's silly."

She shook her head. "Promise I won't."

"I had a nickname ... before ... Loretta won't call me by it and I miss it."

"Well I'll call you by it. My big brother called me Sissy growing up. What's your nickname?"

"Jane."

"Pretty. You can use appropriate nicknames at this school. Lots of boys go by Bo when their real names are something more formal like Robert. You only have to use Anna Pearl on your state exams."

I smiled. She noticed and seized upon it. "Tell you what, I'll send a note around to all your teachers to let them know to call you Jane." She picked up her pen and drew a dark line through Anna Pearl on my file. I reached my hand to the bruise above my brow and pressed it tenderly. A hard won trophy.

"Weaver ... that's an unusual last name. Can't say I know any other Weavers. I'm always interested in tracing family histories. Do you know if that's an Irish name ... or maybe Germanic?"

"It's Carolina," I answered.

Miss Claudia chuckled. She figured I was ignorant about European legacies and complicated family trees. But Weaver was a Carolina name and nothing more. I wasn't the first in my family to choose a better story.

The Heart-Shaped Museum

Abel Weaver was born Abel Thomas Cunningham. He spent the first six years of his life playing in the fields behind the mill village. If he was hurt or hungry, he was tended by whichever mill mama was home with a new or sick baby. Once he turned seven, his own mama declared him ready for work. He was too young, even by mill standards, but she promised things like a bicycle and a baseball glove once he earned his own wage. Even at seven, Abel knew she was lying, knew he'd never own a bicycle or use a new glove that hadn't been broken in by some other boy's hand. Ever since his daddy died of lint lung, they'd lived just two steps from starving. Abel would be working to earn his own biscuit.

Just before Abel joined his mama and brother Jack at the mill, the Boss declared a new rule. Large families dominated the pay lines, with a daddy, mama, and seven or eight kids all collecting a wage. So the Boss announced that for every additional child after the first, the pay for a full day would be one dime less.

But a hungry mama is a crafty one. Abel's mama left him alone in the new hire line. She told him when the Boss asked his name, not to dare say Cunningham.

The Boss came and stood in front of Abel with a pencil and a clipboard. "Name," he grunted.

"Abel, sir."

"Abel what?"

Abel stammered, he hadn't thought that far ahead. Then his mind went to the last thing his mama said just before she left him in line. *You gonna be a fine little weaver-man. You got the cotton in your blood.*

"Weaver," Abel answered.

"How old are you?"

"Thirteen, sir."

The Boss winked. "Of course, the law says you must be thirteen."

"Yes, sir."

"You sure is a runt though," he laughed. "Your family in the mill?"

"No, sir. Mama's home sick."

"Can you sweep?"

"Yes, sir."

"Can you work a knife with them runt fingers?"

"Yes, sir."

"All right." The Boss nodded. "You head back with Big Ronnie. He'll get you set up cutting bales loose."

Abel began his first days in the opening room, where raw cotton bales were delivered, opened, and fluffed before processing. He and other unskilled workers used a small blade to cut through the ropes that held the bales together. If there was still time left on their shift once they finished, they took brooms and swept the floors of lint. It was because of his broom that the Boss first noticed Abel.

"Your pile of lint is always twice as big as any other boys. How come Runt?"

"Cause of that redheaded baby," Abel answered.

There was a tiny girl, not much older than a toddler, who ran up and down the halls of the mill. Abel could tell by looking at her spotless white leather shoes that she wasn't linthead. But every week or so her mama came to the mill for some unknown reason and brought her along. The little girl always managed to escape. She'd run, mouth open and laughing, up and down the halls with her hands swatting through the air trying to catch the floating lint.

"I had to sweep around her one day and keep my lint pile moving or else she'd run through it," Abel continued. "I wanted to smack her. But by the time she left, my lint pile was bigger than it'd ever been. So I got to wondering why. It's cause the lint don't go in a straight line. It zigzags around corners, behind machines, under the chair. And if you leave it be on the floor while you go sweep somewhere else, it'll just float away again. You got to keep the pile moving as you sweep. Now I always sweep like that little girl is running down my hall."

The Boss laughed. "You're addled in the head, Runt, but you sure got an eye for doing things right. Why don't you run down to the picking room. It ain't so different from sweeping a floor clean. See if you can get the cotton as clean as you get the floors."

The picking room was where the cotton went after it was opened and fluffed. In this room the workers cleaned the cotton and picked out all the dirt, grass, and weeds that clung to the white fibers. Abel's little fingers were quick, diligent things. He liked searching out hidden flaws and fixing them. His mama liked the wage increase that came with his promotion. She didn't buy him a bicycle, but she did treat him to a dish of ice cream. Abel's cotton work was always clean and thorough. After four years the Boss sent him to the carding room.

Abel's mama blamed the carding room for killing his daddy because it was the dirtiest room of them all. It's where big machines pulled apart the fibers of the cotton. Carders stood by the machines feeding sheets of cotton into them while clouds of lint billowed as the fibers were torn and twisted. Abel's daddy spent years as Head Carder, until the cotton dust filled his lungs so much there wasn't any room for good air.

Abel was standing in line waiting on the mill whistle one morning when his mama approached the Boss.

"Sir, us spinners need another doffer. One with quick, nimble fingers, please. The bobbins are getting behind and that makes for less spinning."

The Boss grunted and then motioned to a boy nearest him.

"Take Max," he said. "He's fifteen but been cutting bales for years now. He'll make good use of the chance."

She walked to him and asked him to hold out his hand. She frowned back at the Boss.

"These are calloused, fat man's hands. No way they can learn how to be quick and nimble now. That season's done passed this child." She glanced over at Abel. "But you there, you have fine little fingers. Hold out your hand." Abel glanced nervously at his mama but did what she asked.

"He's in the carding room," the Boss said. "Just trained him there three weeks ago."

"But sir," she pleaded. "You can train anybody to be a carder. This boy would be a fine doffer. I can spot 'em by their hands."

The Boss shrugged. "Whatever helps you spin."

And with that, Abel was moved to the spinning room. This room held prestige among the younger workers because it's where the change happened, as sheets of cotton were turned into thread. His mama was a spinner and stood for hours each day, watching the machines and making sure the threads didn't break. Whenever one did, it was her job to tie the ends back together. Abel and his brother Jack were doffers. When a bobbin was full of spun thread, they quickly exchanged it for an empty one. They had to be fast. There was always the threat of the spinning machine catching a finger.

Abel loved the spinning room, not because of the prestige it held, and not because it's where the change happened. He loved it because of Jack. The brothers chased each other all around the giant machines. It was like that in all the mill corners. Every room had pockets of boys romping with wild magic in their bones.

The bosses would bark at them to stop. Send some home early to be whipped by their daddies for laziness. But the romping never ended. It didn't matter how hard the work, how awful the whipping or how dangerous the machines, the mill boys always managed to make a game of their days. They were always inventing new ways to race and hunt and *win*.

Tag was a favorite sport for Abel and Jack. Whenever the Head Doffer stepped out of the room, the boys ran laps. One morning Jack snuck up behind Abel, landed a solid punch in the arm, and yelled "it!" just as Abel reached for a full bobbin. The punch knocked his arm down, which pulled his hand into the machine. Abel didn't feel a thing. He just heard his brother scream and saw the threads turn red with his blood.

Two months later, when Abel's hand was healed enough to return to the mill, he had to convince the Boss that he could still switch bobbins even though he was missing two fingers on his right hand.

"Go back to the opening room," the Boss ordered. "That paw ain't fit for doffing."

"I'll be even faster, sir," Abel promised. "I don't have to worry about the machine catching those two fingers no more. I can reach right in without thinking about it. I'll be able to grab the bobbins even quicker now."

The Boss made him prove it, and even though Abel was secretly terrified to use his wounded hand, he performed well. He spent the next two years switching out bobbins and playing tag with Jack.

Then one afternoon the Boss came to the spinning room looking for extra hands to unload a cotton delivery. Jack raised his hand in a pick-me fashion. Abel did, too, and frowned when the Boss picked his brother. As Jack rounded the spinning machine to leave, he slugged Abel in the shoulder. Abel was mad that the Boss had picked Jack and returned the punch with all his might. It was a mean punch, not a play one, and boys always know the difference. But Jack just rubbed his arm. "Whoa, where'd my little brother go?" He grinned. "Who's this strong man standin' here now?"

Minutes later, a group of women ran and grabbed Abel's mama and pulled her out of the room. The machines were too loud to hear what they were saying, but Abel saw the horror on his mama's face. He followed them outside, carefully keeping his distance because his mama always worried the Boss might find out he was her child and dock his pay. Jack was lying face down. A colt tied to a post had gotten spooked when a carding machine inside broke with a grinding shriek. Jack had never owned a horse, and their daddy hadn't lived long enough to teach them not to walk close behind one. One swift kick to the head, and Abel's fists-flying brother was dead.

But it wasn't true. Abel knew the whole thing happened too fast to be true. He had watched his daddy wither away from lint lung. He knew that death was a slow, drawn-out thing. It was months of gasping for air. It was Mama twisting her apron behind the door, begging the hurt to hurry up and be done. Jack could never die in an instant. He was far too wild and strong.

But then the morning of the funeral came and as Abel stepped out the door of his shack he turned and looked over his shoulder for Jack. He expected his brother to come dragging along like always when Mama ordered them to church. But Abel stared back into an empty house. There were no footsteps behind him. No shadow overtaking him. Nobody slugged him on the arm. Abel sucked in his breath, leaned forward, and held his stomach like he'd been punched. *My brother.*

At the funeral, Abel looked around at all the lines. They were everywhere. A line of lintheads, stretching down the road, on their way to pay last respects. Lines in the graveyard dirt, a cold rectangle dug into hard red clay. Lines in a pinstripe print down the preacher's pants. Lines, impossible to cross, between him and his mama.

He was standing alone, just like he always did before the opening of the mill. His mama was surrounded by her three sisters. She leaned against them with her eyes closed.

"Mama?" he sobbed. "Mama?"

She flinched and opened her eyes. She held her finger over her mouth to let him know to hush. He nodded, but he couldn't stop sobbing. The preacher started talking about halos, ten thousand years of a gospel choir singing, and robes of fine *linen.*

"He was linthead," Abel yelled. "Jack wouldn't stand for no fancy linen. He had the cotton in his blood."

The preacher blinked rapidly, cleared his throat, and smiled. "I'm just trying to remind everybody that all things work together for good. Even something as sad as losing this poor boy."

This poor boy. They didn't know him. They didn't even know him. Never once in his life had Jack been some *poor boy.* Jack was a cotton king. He could change the bobbins quicker than anyone in the mill. He was a boy whose curveball made every batter tremble. A boy who knew all the best fishing holes. He was—Abel paused and choked back the scream in his throat—*my big brother.*

The preacher prayed while Abel stood pounding his fist into his palm over and over. The lintheads stepped forward and tossed raw cotton bolls across Jack's grave as they left. The red dirt turned white, and a mound of cotton soon covered Jack.

The next day, Abel returned and found a tombstone marking the grave.

"What's this?" he asked the preacher, who had just wrapped up another funeral.

"Mill owner bought that. Heard about the poor boy and how his mama couldn't afford the tombstone. Ain't you glad to know there's saints like that left in this world?"

"What's it say?"

The preacher walked over to Jack's grave. "Jack Cunningham. And then right beneath it is the words I picked out," the preacher said proudly. "All things work together for good."

Abel was just a scrappy boy of thirteen, but he landed a grown man's punch on the preacher's nose. The preacher smacked him so hard it sent him flying back.

"Varmint," the preacher yelled, as he tried to compose himself. "Now I got blood all over my new shirt. And I got a revival tonight." He stormed off trying to rub the stains from his shirt, while Abel sat crouched by his brother's grave with his lip throbbing and bloody.

"It ain't ever gonna be good again, Jack. And I ain't gonna stand for nobody saying it."

He ran his hand over the cotton bolls covering the grave. Everybody called Jack a *poor boy* now. Even his mama had wept *my poor boy*.

"You ain't no poor boy neither," Abel sobbed. "Don't they know you? Don't they remember all the ..."

What? What would he always remember about Jack?

Abel swallowed hard. *War.* Over an invisible line drawn down a too small bed. If Abel's foot crossed an inch onto Jack's side, he'd get a swift knee in his gut. Sometimes Abel would fight back and they'd end up rolling onto the floor slugging at each other. They fought over most things, really. Like who got the first turn to cast the new fishing pole or who got the last bite of cornbread.

Abel had noticed it was that way with most brothers. A constant round-and-round over who was King. But inside the battle lived a willingness to play and romp and find some brave new adventure. On an ordinary day, a brother was a guaranteed playmate. On a good day, he was a best friend.

Still though, there was something more about Jack, something Abel knew other brothers didn't always have. Jack taught him his most basic skills. Like how to open a knife and close it without catching his thumb. How to climb to the top of the poplar tree and get back down. How to throw a good punch. How to find the best night crawlers for fishing. How to jump out of a barn loft without twisting an ankle.

Jack had taken care of him too. Anybody that called Abel "runt," except for Jack or a boss, could expect a black eye. When Abel had a cough that wouldn't go away, Jack searched the woods for a honey tree to soothe his throat. And if Abel was sent to bed without supper, Jack would sneak him biscuits in the dark.

Jack had never disowned him, even in the mill lines. Most of their buddies thought Abel was Jack's half brother, since they didn't seem to share the same mama. It didn't hurt as much to be disowned by his mama, because Abel always had his brother. All the mill boys knew they belonged to each other.

Abel fell forward into the cotton covering Jack's grave. "I'm orphaned."

And it was true. When Jack died, Abel lost more than a best friend. He lost his mama and daddy too. Jack had met so many needs, taken care of him in so many different ways, that Abel lost his whole family with one swift kick from a spooked horse.

He remembered Jack's last words. *Where'd my little brother go? Who's this strong man standin' here now?* Jack had meant it for a joke. But those last words were a gift now, the last lesson his brother would teach him. He whispered them over and over. *Where'd my little brother go? Who's this strong man...?* It was like the world split in two before him, and all he had to do was choose on which side he wanted to live.

Jack was the only person who treated Abel like a Cunningham. And now all of their boyhood dreams, Cunningham dreams, lay orphaned under a cotton-covered grave. The Cunningham story was too hard, with lint lung, near starvation, missing fingers, and dead brothers. So that day, Abel dusted it away like lint in the air.

He was a Weaver for keeps. There was no telling what a Weaver's story might hold.

XII

A name is far more than a grammar teacher's proper noun. A name is a verb too. It's a word of action that calls forth a character, breathes life into a simple daydream. I had wished on names and captured glimpses of great characters before. But now, the magic was outside of me. Other people called me Jane, and she became flesh and blood.

Jane, they said. *Good job on your quiz.*

Jane, they called. *Finish up your lab.*

I no longer secretly met Jane inside my mind. She was whisked off the moors of my imagination. Jane Eyre came to middle school.

Loretta scanned my school progress report and smiled over the grades. But then her eyes fell to the name printed at the top.

"What's this Jane nonsense about?" she mumbled. "I've watched you scrawl it on your homework too. Now here it is printed on top of a school report. You don't reckon this is the name on your permanent record now?"

I shrugged. "It's no big deal. It's just school stuff."

"Your records follow you your whole life."

"This is my fresh start," I explained. "Girls always joked about Pearl, said it's an old lady name. Nobody makes fun of Jane."

Loretta frowned. "My name's been changed three times. The first two because of what other people thought best, but the last one is the name I picked."

"Loretta Elinore Mason," I said slowly, as I considered the idea of her choosing that name. "What was it before?"

"Loretta Elinore Richards at birth, but everybody thought it was too serious a name for a little tadpole like me. They called me Lori when I was a girl. When I got married, I wanted to be called Loretta. I think it's a classy sounding name. I had to go by Elin though, because of my husband."

"Why?" I asked.

There was an answer I expected, already forming inside my mind. It was something about how her husband knew another Loretta, a mean nasty woman who treated him cruelly. Perhaps an old lover, teacher, or even grandmother. But instead, Loretta said something unexpected.

"He was ... he was a ..." She stopped and lowered her head. "Look, you don't have to throw away your name just cause other people don't like it. Who cares if they laugh at Pearl?"

The conversation returned to my name, but I was stuck on hers. I was still waiting for her to finish her answer. *He was a ...* what? What was this man who died just two years into their marriage? What kind of man couldn't stand the sound of his wife's pretty name?

Daddy said that sometimes one perfect sentence sums up a whole book. Loretta hadn't given me a whole line, only a piece of one. But in that half uttered sentence, I realized a world of old stories was locked inside her heart. Maybe that's why it always hurt.

"I'll give you a thumbs-up for your grades though, Girly," she continued. "They took a dive for a bit, but you've managed. You deserve a treat. Maybe ice cream?"

"I just want you to call me Jane."

I knew it would be a tough sell. Loretta had a hard enough time giving up stale potpourri. The scent could have been gone for years. It might be nothing but dyed wood curls in a bowl, but it would still grace the coffee table. She believed throwing something away was the same as saying it had never been good.

"I'm not saying Pearl isn't a nice name," I reasoned with her. "I'm just saying that I've changed."

She looked at me tenderly, but shook her head. "Even if the whole world calls you Jane, I'll be the one calling you Pearl."

"Why do you always have to be like that? Why can't you do something that will make me happy, even if you don't understand? You might as well go ahead and beat the nonsense out of me."

Loretta's eyes widened in surprise. Just a few days before, I'd overheard her talking on the phone. "These Weavers are such an odd breed. I loved Tom. Lord knows I did, but I didn't understand him and I don't understand his girl. Half the time I can't decide whether to beat the nonsense out of her, give her a hug, or just sit down and bawl. This summer, I thought I was doing her some real good. She was even taking notes on what I taught her, but ever since Tom died..."

"Of course I won't beat you," Loretta answered. "But think of your daddy. What would he say?"

"He'd say I have fire for an imagination. And he'd say that you were getting all riled up over nothing. This doesn't have to be such a hard thing."

"What's hard?" Katie said as she walked in the room. She had been an easier sell.

Loretta bowed her head and mumbled with frustration.

"Ooookay," Katie said as she glanced back and forth between us. "Y'all wanna go shopping? There's lots on clearance right now."

"We hate shopping," I muttered. "That's the only thing me and Loretta agree on."

"Well tough. I need some new jeans," Katie insisted. "One of those little plaid skirts with the pleats too. Some clogs. I'm kinda itching for a whole new look."

Something biting and cruel had been on my tongue to say, about the rotten luck of being stuck with an old widow with no imagination and a teenager obsessed with looking cute. But then Katie said *whole new look.*

The idea captured me. I glanced down at my gray sweat pants and old YMCA T-shirt. This would never do for Jane. I looked at Loretta. She was sitting with her head in her hands, looking defeated.

"Maybe we should," I said, my mood suddenly cheerful. "Might be good to go out for a bit. What do you think, Loretta?"

She shrugged wearily. "Fine."

We spent the day combing through department store sales racks. Katie found plenty of good deals. I was disappointed though.

"You can't find anything?" Katie asked. "What on earth are you after?"

"Something vintage."

Her face brightened. "Why didn't you say so in the first place? I know exactly where to go. Mama has to find all sorts of vintage things for her skating shows. She's been a disco dancer, a hippie chick, and a flapper. She found most of her clothes at the antique store. They have a ton of things and super cheap prices." She scooped up her shopping bags and ran to Loretta. "One last stop, Auntie, and then I promise we're done."

The antique store had an entire back room filled with old clothes. I scanned the racks and began to piece Jane together. I found several dark skirts that trailed the floor. Followed by blouses with lace at the collar. A pair of button up ankle boots in my size. And I pinned a large brassy brooch beneath my chin.

"You'd do better to stick with some pants and a T-shirt," Loretta advised. "Penney's was having an awfully good sale if you wanna go back."

Katie came out of the dressing room wearing a pair of denim bell-bottoms and a fringed leather vest. "Mama would die for this. She'd invent a show just to get to wear it."

Loretta rolled her eyes and groaned. "If only I'd held onto all my worn-out stuff. Could've made a fortune selling it to you ninnies." She took another look at me in my floor length skirt and high-collared blouse. "Least you get points for modesty."

I twirled around and studied myself in the mirror. I loved the weight of my new skirt, the feel of it swishing against the floor. I loved the way the fabric gathered in my hands as I lifted it off the ground. I loved the way people stared at me as they walked through the store. I no longer just felt like Jane. I looked like her too.

"I want all of it."

"But you gotta get some basics for school," Loretta said. "Your jeans are getting too short on you. You've been growing so much."

I shook my head. "These are my school clothes."

Loretta frowned. "School won't allow it."

Katie disagreed. "They'll just be glad she's not indecent. Girls get sent home for that all the time." She stepped close to me and whispered, "It's a risk, you know. Odds are you'll be an outcast the first day you wear this. Undo any good progress you've made."

I didn't flinch. "It takes a first person to start a trend."

Katie turned back to search the racks. "Look," she shouted. She held up a large, puffy coat. She tried it on and pulled up the hood. It had a thick layer of fur that extended in a bushy frame around her face.

Loretta scoffed. "Look like an Eskimo."

"I know," Katie squealed. "And look at these." She held up galoshes, trimmed with fur at the top. "They're my size too. Bet they come all the way up to my knees."

"You must not have noticed the woolly worms," Loretta said. "They had wide brown bands across their backs. That means a mild winter."

Katie shook her head. "No way you're gonna talk me out of my Eskimo coat. And look at what was right next to it. Like they were meant to be together." She held up a floor-length ball gown in dark green velvet and winked at me. The collar rose high and ended with a flourish of lace. The back was gathered tightly, ending in a bustle at the waist.

Loretta frowned. "Where on earth will she wear something like that?"

"Middle school dance is coming up. Everybody's going," Katie answered.

I took a deep breath as she handed me the dress. I cradled it in my arms, felt the pull of its heavy fabric, the weight of its antiqued story.

"What are you waiting on?" Katie asked. "Go try it on."

Inside the dressing room, I ran my fingers across the soft green velvet and remembered the purple circus mask. *What is it about velvet,* I wondered, that could make a girl so brave. That could make a girl do the unthinkable. Go to her daddy's funeral. Go to a middle school dance. Each of them so terrifying.

I stepped out of the dressing room. Katie brought her hand to her mouth. "Wow."

Loretta looked miserable. "You've grown up on barbecue and puddin', but you wanna dress like the Queen of England. I get that 'you have fire for an imagination,' but Girly, you always carry it too far."

I started twirling her words away. I twirled and twirled in front of the mirror until the only thing I could feel and see was a soft blur of green.

"Look at you," Loretta muttered. "I don't even know you anymore."

It was the finest compliment she could have given me. I walked across the room, grabbed her hands, and squeezed them.

"She's lovely," Katie said. "Surely you can see that."

But Loretta jerked her hands from mine and stared at me, with eyes full of worry and dread. I longed to ask her, to beg her, to finish the line that summed up her story. *Was he a hard man? A foolish man? A man who never saw the beauty hiding behind the mess?*

"I don't know what I'm supposed to do," Loretta whispered helplessly.

I bent down and kissed her cold, wrinkled cheek, and didn't care that she flinched. "Loretta Elinore Mason ...just enjoy the story."

XIII

My long skirts trailed the school hallways. My high-collared blouses were hot. I poured sweat during PE, even though I tried to take it easy. Teachers raised an eyebrow or cracked a hidden grin when I entered their classrooms. Plenty of kids laughed. Some called me Grandma or Pioneer Girl. But a few saluted me. Gave me a nod when they passed. Soon they began to ask questions.

Maybe it was my bizarre style that drew them in—the dark skirts, my pale skin, and the bit of tattered lace around my collar. Maybe it was my new confidence, my refusal to blend in, the thing that so many were desperate to do. I was scorned by most. But slowly, I began to earn respect as a freethinker, a rebel, a bold misfit. Not from the cheerleaders or the athletes or the student leadership council. The kids who didn't laugh or jeer, the kids who soon became *my group,* were on the fringe too. We were an odd mix of readers, math club geeks, strange girls who drew fake tattoos on their calves, and boys who couldn't manage the nine-minute mile. These were the kids who welcomed Jane to middle school.

These were the kids who soon decided they'd rather be someone else too.

We started hanging out together under the stairs in the few minutes before the first class bell. Soon, I was Jane Eyre among elves, hobbits, time-travelers, galactic warriors, medieval maidens, and a native. We were middle school losers. We were star novel winners.

When the night of the dance came, I sucked in my breath as Katie pulled the laces tight in the back of my ball gown. I spent an hour twisting my hair into what I imagined was a classic Victorian updo.

"Wow," Katie said when I was finished. "You look sorta beautiful."

Katie wore my black funeral dress and spiky high heels. Her lips were crimson with lipstick, and her eyes lined with smoky shadow.

"You think it's too much?" she asked, when she saw me staring. "I don't normally wear makeup like this but I grabbed Mama's Caboodle and—"

"Your mama would be real impressed," I said.

Katie smiled with relief, stepped close, and put her arm around my waist. There was a mirror nearby and I gazed at our reflection. Katie looked so young and modern in my funeral clothes. I looked like a tintype ghost, standing with perfect posture and no smile.

Katie jabbed her elbow in my side. "C'mon. Party's waiting."

At the dance, we paid three dollars to enter the school gym. It was the same as always, with cages lining the walls filled with basketballs, and the air smelling of sweat and floor wax. Only now, the lights were turned low and a deejay was announcing hit songs.

Katie shouted, "I love this song!" pulled off her heels, and ran barefoot toward the dance floor. Most of the girls were dancing in a group together. The boys were shuffling around in the hallways, or running and jumping to see who could touch the Exit sign hanging above the door.

Katie stopped and turned back. "Ain't you coming?"

I shook my head and stepped toward the bleachers. "I'm gonna wait for my friends."

I sat down and looked around the gym. All the other girls looked like Katie, with cute dresses from the mall, pink blush, and black eyeliner. I smoothed the long folds of my dress and wished I had opted for something more understated. The velvet seemed a bit much.

Then an elfin girl arrived. She nervously searched the room and when she saw me, she smiled and hurried over. She wore a long tunic, leggings, and thin knee-high boots. Her hair was twisted into several different size braids with glittering jewels wrapped around the ends. On her ears she wore long feather earrings, and had velvet points—the same color of her pale skin—arching from the top. A wizard showed up next, wearing a cloak that shimmered with gold dust. A couple of galactic warriors joined us, with armored chest plates gleaming under the dimmed lights. And then the native arrived, with face paint that was a work of art. We sat wearing our storybook finest, watching cool girls dance and poking fun at them. It was marvelous.

Katie found me, grabbed my hand, and tried to pull me up.

"You've got to come out," she said as she pulled on my arm. "C'mon!" She looked at my costumed friends and sighed. "All of y'all. This is a dance, not some sit-in."

I groaned. "I don't know how."

"Just jump around and move your arms a bit."

She dragged me to the middle of the floor, took my hands, and pulled me side to side. "See," she shouted. "It's not hard."

I closed my eyes and listened. The music grew louder and louder. I began to move.

"Watch Grandma go," a girl squealed. "She's got funky granny moves."

I opened my eyes and saw the girl that mocked me. But soon I noticed other characters all around me. I smiled at them, raised my hands, and twirled around and around.

My hair, so perfectly pinned in my Victorian updo, came undone and twisted free. I reached up to smooth it down, but just as I did I heard a loud pop and all the girls squealed.

"This is it," Katie said. "Look up."

Confetti, tiny bits of gray and purple, floated down from the ceiling to the beat of "Purple Rain." Katie grabbed my hands and we laughed and twirled together, around and around through a cloud of confetti. When the song ended I walked to the bathroom to re-pin my hair. I looked at myself, still grinning and giddy in the mirror. Tiny pieces of confetti were scattered through my hair.

"Jane-Eyre-Linthead," I whispered to my reflection.

Katie appeared behind me and began twisting my hair back into its updo.

"You're having fun. Admit it," she said.

"Yeah." I smiled.

"It's a shame these dances only happen twice a year. I could party like this at least once a month." She tossed her hands up to show she had done her best at corralling my curls. "Hurry, there's just a few songs left."

We danced with wild abandon. My green velvet gown swished across the gym floor until the hem was lined with gray dust. I was sweating and my curls kept twisting free, but the songs kept coming. I looked at the throng of dancing characters around me and felt completely transformed. Pearl Weaver didn't dance. Pearl Weaver didn't have friends. I raised my hands and twirled and laughed. I had a better story.

The deejay announced the final song. Everybody groaned. Some yelled for more. I wanted the party to last forever, too, and I knew something that the other kids didn't. We weren't helpless. We could cross out the bad and write in the new. I ran to Katie's purse and pulled out a piece of paper and a pen. I sat down on the bleachers and began to write.

"What're you doing?" Katie asked as she down next to me to catch her breath.

"I'm gonna throw a party. I'm not waiting till spring to feel this way again."

She raised her eyebrows sharply. "Like a Halloween party? Or a slumber party?"

"A story party."

"A ... story ... party ... ," she mumbled. "Lame."

"Won't be," I said, defensively.

"What'd you have in mind, like a read-a-thon in the library or something?"

"The library! That's a great idea. Loretta would go nuts if I had it at home, but the school library is open till nine p.m. this week to host study groups for quarter exams."

Katie rolled her eyes. "Oh my word, you really are planning a read-a-thon. Sounds like a wild and crazy time."

"It'll be wonderful. I went to this party once with Daddy where everybody read their favorite part of a story. Only the best parts were allowed, the one passage that grabbed them most or made their book truly worthy. Some people didn't even introduce their story. They just read their favorite words and left us all guessing. There were candles and key lime tarts and plenty of *Moby Dick* lines and then this one lady kept quoting Dr. Seuss—"

"Okay, I get it. Sounds awesome," Katie said in a tone that was meant to hush me. I bent down and finished writing. Katie peered through the dim light to read my paper.

Keep the Party Going!
Come to the Best Parts Party
Tomorrow at the library
6 p.m. till close
*Come share the Best Part of your story.
Don't just tell *Who* you are ... tell us *Why*.*

"You think anybody will come?" Katie asked.

"They will," I said, and nodded toward my friends.

The music ended and the lights blinked back on. The janitor appeared and began sweeping up all the scattered confetti. I walked over to the elfin girl, handed her my paper, and told her to pass it around.

Katie grabbed my elbow. "C'mon. Loretta's waiting in the parking lot." As we walked away together, she giggled under her breath. "Yep, that's some party crowd all right."

I turned to look. I tried to see my friends the way Katie did. The bright fluorescent glow of the gym lights showcased their awkwardness. They laughed uneasily and too loud. They glanced shyly at the popular kids, but carefully avoided making any eye contact.

I beamed with pride. "They're such characters."

XIV

I couldn't get away with candles in the library, but I gathered a couple of rainbow afghans that would make colorful tablecloths. There wouldn't be any key lime tarts either, but I stuffed a box of Chips Ahoy and a bag of Doritos into my backpack.

It was easy to convince Loretta to take me back to school when I told her I needed to research a science paper. Katie wouldn't come. She couldn't see the difference between my party and a read-a-thon.

"Besides," she said. "My best part is more ice worms than words. I wouldn't have anything to say."

I walked into the library wearing my velvet ball gown. I hurried to the nonfiction section tucked in the back corner of the room. A row of computers blocked the natural line of sight to the reference desk. If we were careful, we could eat without being noticed. We could recite our stories and it would seem like we were simply calling out questions or reviewing flashcards.

I wasn't the only one who dressed up for the evening. Most of my fellow characters wore their finest. A dozen of us gathered around the afghan covered tables. The other students studying in the library stared at us with curiosity. The librarian raised her reading glasses to take a better look.

I stood in front of the group. I had prepared a list of important things to say, but my mind went blank, and I stumbled over a simple "Good evening." I looked down and saw the cookies and chips on the seat of a chair. "For your refreshment," I said too fancily, as I pointed to them.

I took a deep breath and thought about how calm Daddy seemed at his readings. He hated to be without a podium though. He said he needed something to lean against, something to hide just a bit of himself behind. I turned a chair around so that the back was against my legs. My hands gripped the top board.

"Thank you for coming," I began again. "The other day I overheard Mr. Stanley talking to another teacher about us, how we've bonded together, made our own way down these halls. Some call us freaks, misfits, or losers. But we know words and love them. We can choose our own name." Several heads nodded, and a maiden began to clap. I smiled. "Any proposals?"

"I like guild," a knight said. "It's a group that together, collectively, has real power. I propose that we're the Character Guild."

"Who's in favor?" I called.

Every hand raised in silent agreement.

"Good. Then this is our first official meeting. And as you know from the invitation, it's a Best Parts party. We all have one. Some passage or scene that's captivated us, held us inside our stories. So tonight, let's share our best parts. Who's first?"

For a long minute, no one responded. I stared straight ahead and waited until one hand slowly rose. "I'll go," said a girl in the corner.

She was new. Lately, a new face joined us every couple of days. She was small to be in middle school, the top of her head barely came to my shoulders. She was dressed simply, with a sweater and knee-length skirt. Her brown hair was tucked behind her ears, and she didn't wear any makeup. The only interesting thing about her outfit was a small glass bottle—like a chemistry tube with a corked top. It was tied with thread around her throat like a necklace.

"My name is Lucy," she began. "And though I didn't see this part, I'm connected to it. It's the beginning." And then that tiny girl opened her mouth and began to sing. She sang about trees and rivers and animals. About waking and rising and breathing. I had no idea what the song was all about.

But I wanted to know. Not because she sang well. It was not her voice or words that captured my attention. It was the way she calmly stood, a runt-middle-schooler wearing a test-tube necklace, and sang about beautiful things. Like she knew them. Like they were a part of her that nobody could take. Like the fire in her eyes was born of that very song.

A hobbit went next, as we discreetly passed a sleeve of Chips Ahoy among us. Then Aquaman, wearing dripping wet clothes that made a damp circle in the carpet, introduced himself. He spoke of villains and vengeance, with a voice full of flash and boom. Jo went next—*Jo!* And she read from the sweetest part, when Beth is still alive and it seems fated that Jo and Laurie will marry. When Scout stood up in her ham costume and talked about her brother Jem and the play and how her costume got all crushed, I hugged myself to trap the joy. An energy began to build. Where earlier we were timid about speaking, now we were hungry to be heard. More than once I urged the speakers to lower their voices when I noticed the librarian looking at us. The galactic warrior was our doom.

I should have guessed and been better prepared. A battle will always be the best part for a warrior. But I gasped in surprise just like everyone else when he flashed a twelve inch blade and began to demonstrate a final death scene.

After a couple of minutes of bizarre wrestling and cursing, the warrior plunged the knife toward the carpet. A tiny dent was left in the gray shag rug from the tip of the blade.

"Johnny Maddox, is that a weapon?" the librarian shouted. The warrior stashed his blade as the librarian ran toward us. She stood in front of the group with her hands on her hips. "When I saw you all come in, I knew there'd be trouble. Dressed up like you're doing a conjuring. But I thought maybe, just maybe, they can be decent and do some studying. Well, we'll see what the principal thinks about this tomorrow."

"A conjuring?" I asked. "You're a librarian. You don't recognize us?"

"Oh I know all about kids like you," she answered. "Y'all get mopey about nobody liking you, about not being popular, but you don't take responsibility for it.

There's a reason people don't like you. There's a reason you're made fun of. Don't y'all see it?"

I hadn't had a chance to give my best part yet. Since it was my party, I thought it would only be polite for me to let others have their turn first. But as the librarian stood there spewing venom, my best part surged without hesitation.

"I am Jane," I announced through gritted teeth as I rose to my feet. "And this is why I will always, always, always, love Jane Eyre." I turned and stared at the librarian. *"If people were always kind and obedient to those who are cruel and unjust, wicked people would have it all their own way. They would never feel afraid, and so they would never alter, but would grow worse and worse."* I turned to my group and held my arms in a wide embrace so that they would know Jane's words were meant for each of them. *"When we are struck at without a reason we should strike back again very hard; I am sure we should. So hard as to teach the person who struck us never to do it again!"*

The librarian's mouth fell open. My heart raced and my hands shook so that I gripped my skirt to keep them still. But I felt invincible.

"I'm calling security," the librarian announced as she hurried away. "If you don't want a formal escort out, you best be leaving."

I grabbed the blankets and swept away the cookie crumbs. We marched out of the library in a blazing assembly and headed to the parking lot where we yelled our lines into the night. We were characters on parade. We were stories gone wild. And I was smiling and smiling and couldn't stop even when I saw Loretta's car pull up to take me home.

I knew that if my life was captured in words, I'd re-read that night a dozen times. I'd hear test-tube Lucy's song. Taste the cheap cookies. See the silver blade dent the gray shag carpet. Shout my lines all over again.

Yes, it meant war. The night would haunt me fiercely. But I would not change a thing. Any good reader knows this much: never skip a best part.

The Heart-Shaped Museum

Three days after Jack's funeral, Abel asked the Boss to send him to the weaving room, where the bobbins of thread were turned into fabric.

The Boss paused to consider it. "I reckon I'll give you a chance. You ain't let me down yet. I worked this job long enough to know some folks understand cotton and some folks is just working a job. You the first kind, son. I bet the old-time Weavers were cotton men from way back."

The weaving room was a miracle, but nobody but Abel noticed. As he took the bobbins of thread and wove them through the looms, he never forgot it was all still cotton. He'd worked it now, in all its stages. If he held a patch of raw cotton and a strip of fabric, he could name the steps that it took to get from one to the other. He never got over the fact that such a thing was possible.

Whenever he saw curtains in a window, he thought, *I could make that.* When he saw a pretty girl in a sky-blue sundress, he thought about how his hands might have touched the fabric against her skin.

Abel's mama moved to a mill near her sisters, so Abel spent his teen years sleeping in bachelor shacks and working any extra shifts the Boss allowed. Games and war and romping were gone with his old life. Instead, he spent his free hours roaming the hills and woods behind the mill town. Before, the land had been a playground. But now, as he wandered it slowly and quietly, Abel studied its secrets. He knew the exact spot on the tree line where dawn would break through. He knew where the hawk nested, where a doe hid her fawn, and which rocks the snakes curled under.

Every year brought new creatures to watch, new stories to tuck in his heart about them. He learned that the earth is lavish, with more beauty than can be measured. Like seasons. There were far more than just four. Spring itself was a collection of seasons, a whole bouquet of tiny blooming winters. His favorite was redbud winter in late March, when the redbud trees lit up the forest with pink fire. Always along with the pink came a surprisingly deep cold. Other lintheads would groan about how winter was supposed to have ended, as they gathered extra firewood. But Abel knew it was more than a cold snap, it was a lesson, put on display by a teaching earth. He didn't understand it yet, but his heart took note—*It takes a little cold to make the good things bloom.*

If he wasn't in the fields or woods, he was working at the mill. By the time he was eighteen he was Head Weaver. By twenty-two he was helping the Boss oversee the whole mill.

His only companionship came from other young lintheads. They would meet behind the warehouses every Sunday night. Sometimes there'd be music and whiskey. Other times they'd just eat watermelon and talk. Abel went for the watermelon and whiskey, and occasional mill gossip. He couldn't remember how to be friendly or what having a friend felt like. One girl frowned when he wouldn't dance with her and told him he was as much fun as a corpse. Abel didn't disagree. Inside, his heart was as numb and absent as the place where his chopped off fingers belonged.

One Sunday Abel was just about to leave a party when the conversation turned to cotton thieves.

"Y'all hear there's thieving going on?" a lanky boy asked. Abel recognized him as a worker in the carding room. "I bet it's the bosses from the next mill. They can't get their cotton shipped to 'em cheap enough, so they let us ship it and then come steal it from us."

A girl from the spinning room shook her head. "Way us spinners hear, it ain't no thieving at all. We hear somebody, er ... something, just goes in the warehouses and turns everything all around. Sounds like a haint to me."

"Bosses wouldn't offer no ten-dollar reward to catch a haint," the lanky boy answered.

They turned and looked at Abel. He was the only one of them with a foot in each camp. He was a young linthead and a junior boss too.

"Course it ain't a haint," Abel said. "But I don't know that it's a thief neither. Nothing ever seems to be missing. Big Ronnie knows where every bale is set at the end of the day. When he comes back in the morning, things are different."

"Haints," the girl said. "How else would someone get through the locked door?"

"Well I sure could use ten dollars," the lanky boy said.

"We could go walk by the warehouses and take a look," the spinner girl offered. "Maybe we'd get lucky and get the money."

They begged Abel to go with them as a witness. If they caught the culprit, they'd have a boss right there to see their good deed and later reward it. Abel went because the path was toward his shack. He didn't expect that the first warehouse they came to they'd find the door unlocked and slightly ajar. It was already dark outside, and the young lintheads huddled by the door and pleaded with Abel to go first.

It was too dangerous to carry a lantern inside. One spark could ignite the dry cotton. So Abel stepped into the warehouse and tried not to think about all the times he'd seen snakes wriggle out of raw bales. He hoped Big Ronnie had just forgotten to lock the door, but knew him too well to think it was a real possibility.

After a few steps he heard something. He stood still and listened. It was the low, whispery sound of someone breathing.

The spinner girl heard it too and whimpered.

"Shhh," Abel ordered. Just ahead he could see that bales had been arranged in a circle.

"Ain't nothing there," the lanky boy laughed. "Don't be a 'fraidy cat." But he stayed back while Abel pressed ahead.

Abel's eyes fell upon the center of the cotton circle. There was a hint of moonlight falling through cracks in the warehouse walls. It shined across a curious patch of red that glowed like a dying fire. The corners of Abel's mouth turned up in the slightest smile, until he remembered the reward seeking lintheads behind him.

"Don't move," Abel warned.

"What... what is it?" the lanky boy asked.

"Y'all ever hear 'bout the Mill Granny of '87?"

The Mill Granny of '87 was a story told to keep mill children working hard and on task. It was about a spinner who had never married, but loved to tend the mill children. After she was swept away in the great flood of 1887, Mill Granny was said to roam the workrooms looking for lazy children to steal and keep as her own. Supposedly, the mill wouldn't notice as much if lazy kids went missing. *Better work quicker*, a boss might say to some eight-year-old sweeper, *Mill Granny's around the corner.* Every kid who ever worked Abel's mill had heard about Mill Granny. They'd all dreamed of her, at least one awful night.

"Oooh ...," the spinner girl squeaked.

"What color hair was she supposed to have?" Abel asked, his voice low and ominous.

"Was-wasn't it ...," she stammered.

Abel turned and looked at the two young lintheads. He held his hand up in warning for them not to come any closer. Then he reached and put his other hand on that patch of red glow. He gave a vicious tug as he whispered "Red?"

Someone bolted up from the middle of the circle with a panicked, nightmare scream. Her red hair was tangled around her face. The moon shined on her cotton white skin and her wide open, screaming mouth.

The two young lintheads matched her scream and ran as fast as they could out of the warehouse. Abel pretended to run with them a few steps until they were out the warehouse door. Then he turned and grinned at the redheaded girl he used to sweep around. He remembered her wide-mouthed laugh as she ran up and down the halls, lint sticking to her strawberry curls. Fat baby hands grasping for magic dust in the air. He had seen her a few times over the years coming to visit her daddy. She was Stella, the mill owner's youngest daughter.

"How dare you," she gasped as she stood and smoothed her hair and straightened her dress. Bits of cotton fuzz clung all over her. "How dare you assault me like that."

Abel sat down on a cotton bale and laughed until he lost his breath.

"You stop it," she commanded. "There is nothing funny here. Have you no manners at all?" She put her hands on her hips. "Why are you laughing like a loon?"

But Abel couldn't stop. He laughed until tears streamed out of his eyes.

"This is entirely unacceptable," she cried. "I will not be treated in this manner. Just wait till my daddy..." She whirled toward the warehouse door.

"I wouldn't do that," Abel called after her. "Those other two might be watching for you. There's a ten-dollar reward for whoever catches the warehouse thief."

"Thief? I'm not a ... I never took—"

"I don't think it'd go well for it to be the owner's daughter."

"You know who I am?"

"Of course I do, Stella. That's why I pulled your hair so hard."

"Because I'm the owner's daughter? Because you hate my daddy?" she asked, confused.

"Because it wouldn't do for the owner's daughter to be the warehouse thief. And when I saw you sleeping there, and had those two reward hungry lintheads behind me, I knew I had to get them outta here. So I told them you were the Mill Granny and made you wake up with a scream to scare 'em."

"Mill Granny?"

Abel turned his head to the side. "You mean, you never heard..." He stopped when he noticed her green silk dress. If only it had been cotton, she would have known about Mill Granny just like every other linthead. But the difference between them was stitched in silk lines.

He almost whispered, *nevermind.* It was his first thought as he stared at that silk dress. But he was sitting in a cotton warehouse with a jumpy, rich, redheaded girl who had never heard the most basic linthead story. It felt like a gift to get to tell someone about Mill Granny for the first time. A gift, to get to shape the story however he wanted, to make it his very own. She couldn't say it was wrong. Couldn't whine like most lintheads did, *That ain't how my mama told it...*

He changed all the parts that ever bothered him. Mill Granny didn't steal lazy kids. She helped them meet quotas. Her ghostly fingers switched bobbins faster than any flesh. And if a kid did disappear, it was because Mill Granny knew nobody cared for him. She only stole the mill rats, the babies nobody tended, and carried them off to love and keep at her ghost mill high on Brown

Mountain. Nobody could find the mill during the day, but late at night, if you looked up at the mountain, you'd see the cotton glow.

"Oh," Stella said and smiled. "The Brown Mountain lights! I've seen them. Last year we took a holiday in the mountains and one place we stayed had a view of Brown Mountain. At night we watched it become dotted with glowing lights. My sisters said the view played on their nerves something fierce. They preferred the gazebo by the lake. But I loved to sit out there and look for those lights. I asked the butler about them, and he said nobody knows, but there's all sorts of stories about it. And you think it's..."

"Cotton." Abel nodded.

Stella smiled. "No wonder I liked them and my sisters didn't. I always liked to visit the mills when I was little. My sisters would vomit every time Mama made them go. Something about all the snow unsettled their stomachs."

Now Abel was the one who was confused. "Snow?"

Stella blushed. "The lint. Mama says it's more like ashes floating in a burned up sky. It'll choke your nose and throat, the very same. But to me it's always been snow. That's why I adored coming to the mills when I was little. What kid doesn't love snow?"

Abel grinned as he remembered her baby hands swatting through the air. All along she had been trying to catch the snow.

"Do you think it's safe to go?" she asked.

"Better give it another minute," Abel said, though he was certain the other two hadn't stopped running until they were home in their shack. "How did you get inside the warehouse anyway?"

"I stole Daddy's keys."

"Why?"

"I like to spy on your linthead parties."

Abel shook his head. "They bore me something awful."

Stella sighed. "Sometimes y'all have banjos and fiddles. We never have nothing like that. It's all harps and organs for us. And the way y'all dance—reeling and spinning and twirling. Mama says that's the Devil's dancing. She only allows us to waltz at garden parties." She stopped and looked at him. "Do you ... do you know how to dance?"

Abel had never danced. He'd never even been tempted to dance. "Well sure I do."

"Do you think you could twirl me? Like when the fiddles are on fire?"

Stella stepped into the middle of the cotton bale circle and held out her hand. Abel took it and began spinning her until she was a blur of green silk. A cloud of lint soared above and around them as she twirled until she was dizzy. She reached for him to steady herself and laughed.

"Again!" she begged.

"You could come," he said. "You don't have to spy from the warehouses. Nobody would mind if you came."

Stella shook her head. "Daddy'd have a fit. He don't want me hanging around any place where there might be ..." Her fingers pulled a piece of lint off of Abel's shirt. "This."

"Will you be back then?" he asked. "In this warehouse next Sunday?"

She nodded.

"I could come and sit with you. I could make sure the fiddlers are there and you could twirl to music next time."

Abel saw the tempted, torn look in her eyes, and he knew what worried her. He gently tugged a piece of lint from her hair. "Snow in Dixie is always a bit magic. A bit miracle."

She smiled. "You don't talk like most lintheads."

"You don't dance like most rich girls."

"If Daddy finds out I'm the one hiding out in the warehouses..."

"I'll tell every boss I see tomorrow I found a raccoon messing with stuff."

"If Daddy finds out I'm meeting you on Sunday evenings..."

"I'll keep your secrets."

"Well you'll know two of mine, and I don't know any of yours," she said.

They stepped out of the warehouse and the moon shined down on her strawberry head and made all the bits of lint glow. He handed her his secret.

"I've been two people. I've lived two lives."

XV

A security officer pulled me from class the minute I arrived at school. He led me to a conference room where the principal, Miss Claudia, the librarian, and Loretta sat behind a long rectangle table. The principal pointed to a chair on the other side.

"Miss Mason has told me of your troubles," he said as I sat down. "And though I sympathize with your loss, there is a minimum standard for behavior in this school. You aren't meeting it. We've been observing your little club for some time now. It's a common middle school plague, this need to separate yourselves into herds. But, as I'm sure you know, unsanctioned clubs are strictly forbidden. Your group is particularly perplexing. The kids in it have never caused a problem before. But since you've started attending this school, they're suddenly dressing in bizarre outfits. Some speak in strange languages. And last night a weapon was brought onto school property."

"I brought cookies," I said, calmly.

The principal pointed his finger at me. "You threatened Mrs. Cress in the library last night. You ordered your group to strike her."

"We were studying literature. I was quoting my best bildungsroman."

He narrowed his eyes. "Your what?"

I nodded toward the librarian. "She knows."

"Coming-of-age novel," the librarian said. "She's been pretending to be Jane Eyre this whole time. She declared it herself, right before she threatened me. I skimmed the book last night until I found the exact quote. They're some kind of crazy role-playing-outcasts club."

"We're a literature club!" I shouted. I took a deep breath to calm myself. "You've got the smokers—the kids who puff out behind the dumpsters. You've got the skinnies—the girls who don't eat and keep cutting the hems of their T-shirts to show more belly. You've got the cheaters—the whole baseball team steals tests out of the history teacher's office. But the group you want to crack down on, the group the librarian fears, is the one that loves stories?"

The principal held his hand up to silence me. "You will not gather under the stairs or in the library or parking lot. No more meetings. If you want a real literature club, then you must apply for school recognition and be assigned a faculty supervisor. You are the club's leader, so I expect you to communicate my order and disband your group. Oh, and one other thing. *No more Jane.*"

I gasped. "What?"

"You are Anna Pearl Weaver. Miss Mason wants you called that. I've sent a notice to all your teachers."

"It's this Jane nonsense that started it all," Loretta griped. "You get these stories in your head, and you don't turn loose until something bad happens. I told them about the playground mess and about the Greek stuff too. Your daddy would never put his foot down. Well I will. No more playacting. You're Pearl Weaver."

"I have something to add," Miss Claudia spoke up. "I'm requiring you to meet with the school psychologist. You've had so much happen, Pearl. It may not seem like it right now, but we truly do sympathize with all you've been through. It's an incredible amount for you to have to process alone. So…"

I spent the rest of the day fuming instead of studying or taking notes. On the bus, I slumped down in my seat and pretended to read a book so that I wouldn't have to listen to Katie's happy chatter. But as the bus slowed in front of my house, she covered her face with her hands.

"Oh no," she said. "That's Mama's car. Bet she's heard I didn't make the varsity squad. Junior varsity is the same as not making it at all. She'll probably blame Loretta's menus too. Last time I saw her, she made me do a juice cleanse."

When I opened the front door I was met by Katie's mama, standing with her arms crossed. She was wearing a sweater that dropped low off one shoulder and showcased tanned, glitter-dusted skin. She tossed her long hair, one shade darker than Katie's, with the swish and style of a shampoo commercial. I knew that she was a Skatey Lady show skater, so I expected her to be gloss and glitz. But I hadn't expected such villainous beauty. It sucked the nerve right out of me.

"Well, well. You must be Pearl." She laughed as she stared at my long gray skirt and high-collared blouse. "Your clothes match your old lady name."

Katie ran up. “Hey, Mama,” she said and nervously smoothed her hair. “I ain’t told you about the middle school dance yet. You remember that “Purple Rain” show you were in a few years back? They played that song during the confetti drop. Then they played “When Doves Cry” and I remembered some of your moves—”

“Hush child. I’ve got something important to say,” her mama said.

Katie winced. “Look, I know junior varsity don’t count for nothing, but I’m gonna start doing those aerobics you want me to, and maybe by high school I can make the real squad.”

“I ain’t here about cheer.”

“Well what else is important?” Katie asked, surprised.

“I sent an audition tape into a Vegas Casino show, the biggest, most famous one. I never had the nerve to before. But now that Mama needs to go to that home, I thought, why not? And they invited me out, so I’m gonna make a go of it. I’ve already found a little house. It has a palm tree in the backyard. I’ll get to wear one of those sequined feather crowns on my head.”

“Wow, that’s amazing, Mama!”

“I fly out tomorrow to start practice for the show. You’ll join me as soon as I get things settled.”

“*Me*?” Katie whispered. “But I’ve got school...and Loretta and Pearl...”

Her mama shook her head. “I’m finally gonna do right by you and teach you how to leave these redneck roots behind. We were born for the shows. You work hard enough, and you won’t even have to worry about finishing high school. You can join me on stage. And the weather—it's never winter. We won't ever have to wear a coat. We can tan in December."

Katie's face turned pink. "No winter?"

Her mama held her palms up in cheer spirit glee. "All our dreams come true."

"Ain't my dream," Katie whispered as she blinked away tears. "I won't go."

"Quit making a fuss. Makes your eyes puffy. Just think, you'll have another chance to make varsity cheer. Better start that juice fast, cause I guarantee you, Vegas girls'll be a whole lot more competition than what you're used to. Hush your bawling, Katie." She held out a slip of hot pink paper. "You'll need this."

"What is it?" Katie asked.

"My credit card number, so you and Loretta can book your flight."

Katie ran to the Oriental Room and slammed the door. Her mama rolled her eyes and remarked on the drama of raising a teenage girl. She held the paper out to Loretta, but Loretta didn't move to accept it.

"If you're in Vegas doing hussy shows, who'll move Edith into the old folks' home?" she asked grimly.

"There's a real high limit on this card," Katie's mama said brightly. "You can get Katie anything she needs for the trip. It ain't like those other cards that just offer a little bit of money and whole lot of payment. You can get the ticket, a new suitcase if she wants it, even some of those cool jeans she's always whining for. And you can get Mama the stuff she needs for her move to the home. She might want a new cactus for her window or some magazines..."

The pink paper waved in the air, but Loretta still did not reach for it.

"C'mon now, Aunt Loretta. I picked the home out. Wasn't that the hard part? I took the whole dang tour of the bingo room and the cafeteria. I got her applied and accepted. All they need now is to go over her financials, and I never was good at math. You can find all her old tax stuff in shoe boxes in the basement. I just… I can't stay, Aunt Loretta. This is my chance. This is my shot at making it in the real shows… and they ain't hussy shows, this is real dance. I have to kick my leg up over my head for crying out loud! Most girls need years of professional training to do a move like that. You'll help me, won't you?"

Loretta's mouth was pressed into a straight line as she took the pink paper.

Katie's mama hurried toward the door. "Sorry I can't stay longer, but I can't miss my workouts these days." As she stepped out, she called back over her shoulder, "I'll call soon, and we can chat more about Mama's new home and Katie coming to Vegas. Thanks again. Knew I could count on you."

Loretta walked to the kitchen and stuck the pink paper to the fridge with a magnet. "Some women are born with too many sequins on their brain," she muttered to me. "Heaven knows legs ain't meant to be kicked over heads."

When Katie joined us at the table for supper, she was wearing her new coat and knee-high galoshes. Her pretty face was framed in fur.

"Ain't you hot?" Loretta asked.

Katie shook her head.

"Could you at least take it off at the table? Not wear it during supper?" Loretta looked around the table and sighed. "Feels like I showed up to a costume party, only no one told me to dress up. Eating supper with a queen and an Eskimo."

Katie kept her coat on even though Loretta served steaming bowls of beef stew and cornbread. Little beads of sweat formed across her brow. After supper I followed her to the Oriental Room. Dozens of homemade snowflakes, little lacy paper patterns, were hanging from the ceiling. She was a sad ice princess, framed by paper snow. She tossed me a pair of scissors and some paper. "You have the Red Room. I need a blizzard."

The next morning she wore her fur-trimmed coat and galoshes to school and joined the Character Guild by the stairs. She made quite the impression, a B-squad cheerleader who traded her pom poms for galoshes.

"Have you lost your mind?" her friends protested. "You can't hang with those freaks."

Katie rolled her eyes. "They're characters."

She introduced herself as *Katie Monroe, Ice-Worm Hunter.* I felt new strength, fresh determination with her there. I stood in front of the Guild and told them what the principal had ordered. No more meetings, no more club.

"It's not fair. We didn't hurt anybody," someone cried out.

"They can't do this. They can't tell us who we can talk to, or where we can stand in between classes," another shouted.

"What should we do?" Lucy, the girl with the test-tube necklace, asked.

"We turn pages," I said. "Become the next line, paragraph, or scene."

But in spite of my brave speech, edits came swift and fierce. Teachers broke up our group and ordered us to class. They'd been instructed to keep us separated, keep us moving along. Every time we tried to gather for even a minute—outside the cafeteria, outside a bus—someone yelled for us to break apart.

Our large group disintegrated, and smaller cells formed that wouldn't attract as much attention. Four wizards huddled in a corner. Three galactic warriors gave me a stoic nod. Two elves smiled shyly over the top of their math books.

Still, the pressure was relentless. The wizards were ordered to stop chanting. The galactic warriors could not practice their battle moves even though they were only defensive maneuvers. The elves were told their felt-tipped ears were too distracting. The native was told to quit cutting the collars out of his shirt. Aquaman was told that he could no longer wear damp clothes to school. And then I was told my long wool skirts, my high-collared blouses, were improper school apparel.

"These outfits separate you," Miss Claudia explained. "I'm sure that's the point. And I'm sensitive to a girl's need to define herself with fashion ... only these outfits mark you as the leader of a banned club. We've discussed this with your guardian and she agrees, jeans and T-shirts are more appropriate. So ..."

"You can't force me to wear jeans," I argued. "There's nothing indecent about my clothes."

"They are a distraction. If you wear them again, you'll be sent home." Miss Claudia put her hand on my shoulder. "I'm trying to help you here. These clothes do nothing but hold you out for ridicule. Life will be easier if you learn to dress a bit more like the other—"

I flung her hand from my shoulder. "If it's up to you, one day everything and everybody will look the same."

"What does that mean?"

"I'm defending my lines. These clothes are part of my setting," I cried out.

Miss Claudia shook her head. "Just dress normal, okay?"

"But I'm not normal."

"You'll be risking expulsion ... *again.* And honey, we've already got an orchestra department here. We don't need your daddy's money." She turned her head to the side and stared at me with pity. "I'm not singling you out, dear. I've already spoken to Katie. I made her hang up that big winter coat and told her she had to wear PE appropriate shoes tomorrow."

"Why? So she can play dodgeball? She was born to hunt ice worms!"

Miss Claudia shook her head. "All this anger ... Tell you what, I'm gonna bump up your meeting with Dr. Shelton. She'll help you resolve these feelings. In the meantime, go shopping. Buy some new jeans. It might even be fun."

My hands curled into fists. Jeans were more like funeral clothes than fun. The Character Guild was dying. Everyone wanted us to be losers again, with hanged heads, slumped shoulders and too-tight denim. But I knew what we really were. *Burned books. Banned masterpieces.*

And every reader knows that when stories are threatened with extinction, we have to do more than weep over the ones we love.

We have to save them from the fire.

XVI

Just before class began, Mr. Stanley slid me a folded note with my name written on it. I opened it and read the single sentence. *Please report to Dr. Shelton's office.*

When I arrived, the door was open and Dr. Shelton looked up from her desk and smiled.

"Come in, Pearl."

She stood up from her desk and moved to a couch. She sat down and tucked her feet beneath her. "I'm Dr. Patricia Shelton. You can call me Dr. Pat. Have a seat."

There was a plush recliner across from the couch, but it reminded me too much of the stereotype about patients and their shrinks. I had no plans to recline and weep my woes. I sat down in a metal folding chair by the wall.

"I'm excited to meet with you. It's truly remarkable what you've done," she began.

I startled. *What?*

"I've been given a file of some of your essays for English class. I've seen your costumes. I even chaperoned the dance. I've heard about the plots you've been spinning in our halls and the library. The cast of characters you brought to life. Nothing like this has ever happened here before."

She was a fan? Another Jane Eyre groupie?

"And all of that was because of Pearl Weaver," she said. "*You* are the one who turned our halls into a storybook. You are an absolute original."

I felt a burning sensation in my mouth and realized I was biting my lip.

"Will you tell me about yourself?" she asked. "I've read *Jane Eyre* half a dozen times. Frankly, the older I get, the less enthused I feel. But your story... that's the one I'm interested in. I want to hear from the girl who brought Jane Eyre to our school."

I shook my head, struggling to make sense of the direction she was leading us. I had expected a lecture about choices and consequences. Admiration confused me.

"You don't need to give your whole bio." She laughed. "Let's just start with something small." She leaned forward and lowered her voice. "To be honest, what I really want to know about is the first time you read *Jane.* What was that like? Did you read it alone or was it with someone?"

It was the one question, perhaps the only, that bridged my past with my present in a way that made answering easy, even compelling. Without warning, sweet memories rose to the surface of my mind. These memories were the only point where Daddy, Pearl, and Jane all shared the same page.

"I'd been stuck in Greek myths," I whispered, with my eyes focused on the floor. "Daddy'd read them twice with me and was wanting to move on to something else, but I refused. He told me I could pick anything, we'd even re-read some of my favorites. But it was only Persephone for me, all the time.

"He had this thing he would do when I was younger, to get me excited about reading a new book. He'd introduce it with a surprise. Before we read *Charlie and the Chocolate Factory*, he hid chocolates all around the house. I kept finding them in the strangest places, inside my shoe, my math book, on the windowsills. Whenever I'd ask what was going on, he'd grin and blame Oompa Loompas. When I began begging him to tell me what an Oompa Loompa was, he began to read the book.

"This summer, when I was wrapped up in Persephone and refusing to move on, I received an invitation in the mail for a candlelight tea, behind our house, at sunset. Once the sun began to fade, I walked through the back fields, almost to the river, until I saw Daddy. He was standing by a small round table. Half a dozen candles glowed in the center, covered by a hurricane glass to keep the wind from blowing them out.

"'Good evening,' Daddy said formally and bowed. He picked up a silver teapot and poured us each a cup of hot tea. He put two large scoops of sugar in my cup without me having to ask. I held the cup to my lips and felt the steam rise and warn my mouth. It was the middle of July, so muggy and hot. I set my cup down and swatted away the mosquitoes that buzzed my ear. Daddy picked up a platter and held it out to me. It was loaded with bite-sized desserts and little triangle sandwiches. He started talking about the history of English tea while I stuffed my mouth.

"When the platter was nearly empty, I sat back satisfied. Loretta never allows me to get my fill of sweets. 'We should do this once a week,' I said. Daddy grinned. 'And I've got the perfect book to go along with it.' He pulled *Jane Eyre* from somewhere under the table. I frowned and started to speak, but he held up his hand to hush me. 'Tell you what,' he said as he lifted the hurricane glass. 'We'll just read till the wind blows out the candles. That could be twenty pages or it could be two. Can you predict the wind?'

"I liked the mystery of it. I liked his challenge. So I grabbed another bite-sized cake as he began to read. As he spoke, his voice and Jane's words mingled with the sound of the river. It was darker now, and the candlelight bounced off the silver tea set onto the corners of the book. Mosquitoes bit my arms, but I didn't flinch or swat them away for fear of blowing out the candles. But suddenly, only a few pages in, the wind blew and everything went dark.

" 'Relight them,' I begged. 'You didn't even finish the first chapter.' But Daddy switched on a flashlight and tucked a bookmark into the pages. 'We're stuck.' He laughed. 'But what a magical place we've found, and what an interesting character to be stuck with ...' "

Inside Dr. Pat's office, it was quiet for several seconds. I took a deep breath to try and clear the fog of memories that had settled over me. Dr. Pat was still curled on the couch, staring at me with sympathy.

"Did you finish the book together?" she asked.

I shook my head. "That was the last time we read together."

"So you finished it on your own?"

"With a friend."

"But you're still stuck, aren't you? Pearl, you must know that your daddy preferred *you.* He didn't go to all the trouble of setting up an English tea because he was interested in Jane. He did it to spend time with you." Dr. Pat's tone began to change, from admiration to something more serious. She leaned forward. "Jane Eyre was never his daughter. She was nothing but fiction. It's Pearl Weaver that he loved."

I sucked in my breath. "Before Jane, *everything* hurt. Why can't y'all just leave me alone? Why is this such a big deal?"

"That's a good question." Dr. Pat nodded. "And I can tell you the answer. Pearl, you've suffered a great trauma. When that happens the mind can either face it and begin to process it, or it will try and escape. But here's the truth that decades of research on the human mind has taught us. *You can never escape.* The trauma stays, always there in the back of your mind, waiting to have its say. And it doesn't wait quietly, Pearl. It doesn't have any manners. It will rise up and hurt you, wound you, scream at you, sometimes at the most unexpected times or places. It pushes you toward destructive choices, as you have to work harder and harder to distract yourself from it."

"You don't know me," I argued. "You don't know my choices. Have you even looked at my quarter grades? Aren't they all As?"

"You *are* a smart girl. I am too. And I've been in this line of work for a couple of decades now. There are things that I can predict with incredible accuracy."

"Oh yeah," I scoffed. "So what's my fortune, doc?"

She locked her eyes with mine. "If you don't deal with the chaos inside your heart, if you don't face your grief instead of running from it, your troubles will multiply. Look at the trouble Jane has already gotten you in. A weapon at school, threats to teachers, disruption in your home ... it will only get worse. Jane Eyre cannot save you. Jane Eyre is nothing but fiction."

I wanted to scream something angry and revolting, but the only words that came to mind were Jane's Best Part speech, about striking back at bullies. Somehow that didn't fit.

"What will you do when Jane stops working?" Dr. Pat continued. "She will, you know. There will come a moment when she can't numb your pain. Do you have another character lined up and ready?"

I stood up, shaking my head. "You don't know that ... you don't know Jane!"

"Look, I get it," Dr. Pat said. "Everything hurts. But there are so many people who want to help you. Loretta, Miss Claudia, your teachers, me ... we are not your enemies. Let's face what hurts, together. Don't wait till you're an old woman, all scarred up from decades of horrible choices. Face it now, while you're still young and have a chance for goodness ahead of you."

I turned to leave.

"Wait," she called.

I paused with my hand on the doorknob.

"Thank you for telling me about the tea party. You spoke with honesty and bravery. My secretary will set up another appointment for you on your way out. I'd like to hear about the next time you read *Jane Eyre*, with your friend."

The secretary handed me an appointment slip as I passed by her desk. I wadded it up and crammed it deep in my pocket. The bell rang and students filled the halls. I saw the cheaters laughing outside the history teacher's office. I saw the skinnies, prancing toward their next class. I saw smoke rings rising from behind the dumpsters.

I punched the wall until my fists throbbed. My arms fell limp to my side and I glanced at my swollen, scraped knuckles. I looked at the wall, expecting to see a hole or at least a dent, but instead there was a cheerful poster printed in red and blue block letters.

TALENT SHOW SIGN UPS

What makes you special? Let the whole world know.
Share your gift at the talent show!

Underneath was a page of signatures. Dozens of girls had signed up to sing or dance. A couple were baton twirlers. A handful of boys had signed up for tae kwon do demonstrations.

I tucked my bruised hands into my pockets, and my fingers brushed against the wadded appointment slip. I pulled it out and stared at the date. Only one more week until I'd have to sit in that metal chair while the doctor picked all the locks on my heart. *Jane Eyre is nothing but fiction,* she had said.

In a blaze of anger I scribbled *Pearl Weaver, Dramatic Reading,* on the poster. I'd show Dr. Pat just how real fiction can be. I would resurrect the Character Guild.

I hurried to find the rest of my characters. "I have a wonderful plan," I promised. "It will be a new Best Part..."

I didn't realize yet, that I had done something far more drastic than sign up for a school talent show. I had canceled all future appointments.

I would never see Dr. Pat again.

XVII

I dressed in my green velvet ball gown and pinned up my hair. Loretta frowned when she saw me. "Thought this was a school function."

"It is," I assured her.

"You aren't supposed to wear clothes like that anymore."

"This is for the talent show," I explained. "Kids will be in all kinds of costumes. One girl even said she'd be wearing a halter top for her baton performance."

"But why are you ... you never wanted to be in shows before."

"If I do a reading, I'll get ten bonus points added to my final English exam. If you want me to get straight As quit worrying about my dress and take me to the talent show."

Loretta dropped me off early and left to run errands for her sister's move to the old folks' home. I sat inside the gym and reviewed my lines. I thought back to the dozens of readings I'd attended with Daddy. I knew from listening to him that a good reading is all about the pauses. If everything keeps the same rhythm then nothing presses into the listener's heart. It's about volume too. Letting the right words rise in the air, letting other words fall to the ground.

The administration started setting up chairs and testing microphones. Families began to arrive and stake out the best seats. I went to the locker room to check my hair one last time. A group of girls stormed in behind me, and I ducked into a shower stall and watched them. They wore bright pink leotards. Their hair was piled into matching side-ponytails with streaming ribbons. They took turns in front of the mirror adjusting their hair and caking on pink lipstick. Then one of them counted off "five, six, seven, eight," and they twirled in unison.

When they left, I stepped out and studied myself in the mirror. I was pale, and my hair was fuzzier than usual. The twirling girls had left their lipstick on the sink. I picked it up and smeared my mouth until it was bright pink. The principal's voice boomed into a microphone as he welcomed everybody.

I hurried to a seat in the section reserved for performers. The gym lights were dimmed and a spotlight illuminated the stage. The volume on the stage speakers was so loud the floor vibrated. I sat through dances and solos and martial arts displays. The audience was packed with adoring family members who cheered even when the performers sang flat or danced offbeat.

"And now... Pear-l-l-l-l-l We-e-e-eaver," the principal called.

My knees buckled. My hands gripped the edge of my seat.

"Go on, Granny. You're wasting everyone's time," one of the pink leotard girls hissed.

My legs carried me toward the stage, but I couldn't feel them beneath me. There were no flashing cameras aimed at me, but the Character Guild was there, every one of them, in full regalia. The native nodded. The castaway gave a salute. The felt-tipped elves grinned, and test-tube Lucy gave a shy thumbs-up.

I stepped into the spotlight circle, my eyes squinting to see past the light. And it wasn't so different from the gleam of candlelight, bouncing off a silver Victorian tea set. A soft murmur of restlessness rippled through the audience, and it sounded like the purr of the Yadkin drifting by in darkness. The dancer hissed at me to hurry up again. I swatted her voice away, like the buzz of a pesky mosquito. Daddy laughed, somewhere beyond the glare of light, because we were so stuck. *But what a magical place we've found,* he reminded me.

"Pearl?" the principal whispered. "We're waiting..."

I took a deep breath and arched my neck toward the microphone. "My... name is...," I began, but the room swallowed my voice. The principal held his hand up for me to pause, and stepped up to adjust the microphone. "There," he said. "Now try."

"My name is Jane Eyre," I spoke into the microphone. "And I love stories. But some people want to burn books. Some people like to ban masterpieces. And so tonight, in honor of every great story that's been killed, I'm going to give a dramatic reading."

The microphone amplified the fear in my voice. But the deeper I went into Jane's thoughts, the stronger I felt. I was a character again, blooming in green velvet and pink lipstick.

At the end of my reading, I lowered my voice. "Remember…," I whispered and paused. I sensed the audience waiting. I felt them lean forward to listen. "I am Jane Eyre." I raised a fist and shouted, "And I resisted all the way!"

The audience clapped dutifully. A neon tap dancer hurried to the side of the stage and began giving little test taps on the floor. But I held my finger over my lips and shook my head.

"Listen," I said.

At this signal, the Character Guild was to come alive. They were each supposed to hold a flashlight, their very own spotlight, and stand up one by one to join my show. Together, we would out-dazzle any neon or sequins, as the audience realized I wasn't a solo act. We were a novel ensemble.

Loyal Lucy stood first. Her flashlight had weak batteries though and kept blinking. She sang off-key and looked around the room like she hoped someone would join her. Her courage faded and she began to mumble before the flashlight went completely dark. She slumped back into her seat. Jo sprang up and I squinted through the spotlight and grinned. But sweet, good-natured Jo was shrill and alarming, moaning, "My hair! All my hair!" I sighed. With so many pretty scenes, why did she choose the bit about Jo and her chopped hair?

Scout popped up waving her flashlight like a beacon. She was wearing the ham costume and blubbering about how it got crushed. Even through the glare of the spotlight, I could see the looks of confusion among the audience. I scooted out of the spotlight and to the left of the stage. The whole thing seemed *different* than it had in the library. More bizarre than brilliant. I glanced at the principal. He eyed me suspiciously.

The wizards began chanting, more like lunatics than magicians. Then came the warriors. They sprang up in pairs around the audience. Silver daggers gleamed in the dark as they battled back and forth. A lady screamed.

"Put the weapons away NOW," the principal shouted.

POOF! Yellow dust burst into the air, tossed from a wizard's palm.

"I can't breathe," someone screamed. "My asthma," screamed another.

Aquaman fired a water cannon, and I felt drops of the cold spray on my face. Elves and hobbits rose up. Dummy-tipped arrows sailed with a whoosh over top of the stage. I ducked as an arrow nearly missed my head.

"Stop," I cried. "This isn't how the story goes!"

Yes, I had asked the Character Guild to join me and taught them the signal of when to begin. Yes, I was filled with rage when I told my friends about my plan. I did say, *We'll show them they can't kill our stories.* I did shout, *It's time we fought back. It's time we resisted all the way.* But I wanted flash and magic, beautiful words and everything a Best Part will always be.

People gagged and choked as more yellow dust was tossed in the air. A foul, pungent smell filled the room. Someone screamed, "Poison gas."

The lights were still off, but the audience was climbing and tumbling over one another to exit the building. Babies were wailing—so were mamas—and I could still hear the clank of the daggers as the warriors battled on. "Kill them all," one of them yelled.

The principal grabbed the microphone and pleaded for a calm exit. As the entire school evacuated, I noticed an old woman crumpled on the gym floor. Someone grabbed my elbow and hurried me outside where the parking lot began to swarm with ambulances, fire trucks, and police cars. The warriors were captured and their knives confiscated. Firemen examined the satin pouches filled with wizard dust. Paramedics carried the old woman out of the school on a stretcher. They loaded her into an ambulance and drove away. The principal pointed his finger in my direction, and a police officer stepped toward me.

And that's when I realized the truth about characters. Never put them in charge of the story. Never, ever, tell them, *just do what feels right.* Because sometimes, characters skip all the Best Parts. Sometimes, they throw themselves in the fire.

XVIII

My mug shot stared back at me from the computer screen on the police officer's desk. My frozen expression surprised me, given the panic twisting inside me. It looked like a photo of a corpse.

An officer rolled my fingers across ink and stamped them on a card. She led me to a little room and handed me a lime-green jumpsuit. I ran my inked fingers across the fabric and shuddered. There was something sickening about it.

The officer set a trash can before me and I heaved and vomited. When I finished, she barked at me to get dressed. Under her gaze, I changed out of my regal velvet.

She led me to a chair and told me to sit for further processing.

"Where's Loretta?" I asked.

She didn't answer.

"Could you let her know I'm here? She was planning on picking me up from school." The officer kept typing and didn't look at me.

"If I could just explain," I tried again. "I never meant for—"

I was mid-sentence when the officer walked away. My eyes fell to the thin, scratchy cloth of my jumpsuit. My stomach rolled again, and I realized why that prisoners' green was so revolting. *It took away my story.*

My explanation didn't matter. Neither did my intentions. I was dressed in prisoners' green, and that meant words failed me. They were no longer powerful. No longer real as rooms.

The officer returned, took me by the arm, and led me through a series of secured doors down long hallways.

"Where are you taking me?" I cried.

"Relax. Just to the holding tank for the night."

"What's the holding tank?"

"Where everybody gets tossed when they're first caught," she said. "The big fish, the little fish, the old ones, the young ones, all go to the holding tank until the judge sorts 'em." She glanced sideways at me. "Two are here because they're strung out. One was picked up for robbery, her boyfriend dragged her into a real mess. One for distribution—she's a real wildcat, won't quit hollering—and another for attempted murder. And now we've caught you. You're the baby fish tonight, so you'll get your own cell. Once you get sorted, you'll be with other girls your age."

"But I didn't do anything. I just read literature."

We came to a bolted door, and I guessed that behind it was the holding tank, full of green jumpsuits. I struggled to get free from the officer's grasp. She squeezed my arm until it throbbed. The door opened slowly, in spite of its posted warning: *Do Not Enter.*

"This is all a mistake," I sobbed.

The officer pulled me through the door and into a dimly lit hallway. Rooms built like cages lined each side. I was dragged to an empty cell at the end of the hall. It was like a dark mouth with iron teeth ready to chew and swallow. The front wall of bars slid open and the officer pushed me inside.

"But I never—," I began, as the bars closed. I bit my lip to hush myself.

Someone moaned. I dared to look and noticed a puddle of prisoner green piled on a cot in the cell next to me. I saw shoulders shaking violently. Was she shivering? Was she weeping? My eyes found a face and I gasped. She was so old, with deep lines cut across her leathered skin. I remembered Dr. Pat. *Don't wait till you're an old woman,* she warned, *all scarred up from decades of horrible choices.* The old woman's eyes found mine. We held each other's gaze until I began to think I knew her. Had we met before? Were Dr. Pat's words more than a warning? Were they prophecy?

I collapsed upon my cot and curled into my own green puddle. I worked hard to imagine myself someplace different. I heard the *Do Not Enter* door open again and another iron mouth begin to chew and swallow. The lights blinked off, leaving only the artificial glow of one fluorescent bulb flickering in the middle of the hall. Crooked shadows began to cast out from the light.

Someone screamed a forceful, panicked shriek that didn't hold back. *The wildcat?* I heard whispers too. I leaned my head toward the sound, trying to understand.

The whispers rose into a low moan of slurred speech, broken by sobs. *Help me. Help me.*

Sick laughter bounced down the hall. Then an angry shout from the same voice.

I pulled my body into a tight curl, planted my face against my knees, and covered my ears with my hands. But the holding tank was bursting with noise. The fish were all hooked on the line and screaming into the darkness. I jammed my fingers in my ears. I closed my eyes and tried to imagine silence, a world of peaceful make-believe. I tried to remember the clean, full sound of the Yadkin after a spring rain. But the screams, the cries, the twisted laughter, bounced off the walls of our tank. *Someone will come,* I thought. Surely someone will check on us.

But nobody came. People on the other side of the tank, people in the light, know better than to open *Do Not Enter* doors.

As the night dragged on, I stopped fighting. My hands relaxed away from ears, and the full force of the night's agony pressed deep into my mind. Daddy used to talk about how stretched syllables and missing *-gs* were the language of our people. But that night in the holding tank I recognized new rhythms and pitches and wondered if I'd found my true people. Maybe I was never linthead. Maybe I was always just hooked on the line.

All through the night, I listened to the symphony of screaming fish. With each rising cry, with each dark new melody, my body flinched from the lash of sound. Underneath all the mad noise remained a sad, slurred whisper. *My whisper.* Help me. Help me.

XIX

The lights blinked on and my cell bars opened in a slow yawn.

"Let's go," an officer said to me.

I followed her out of the holding tank, expecting to see Loretta outside the *Do Not Enter* door. But instead, I was handcuffed and led to a police car. The officer drove me to the courthouse, led me inside, and placed me in the back of a long line. When my name was called, a man read my list of charges.

Inciting panic, disorderly conduct, vandalism, reckless endangerment resulting in grievous bodily harm.

"In the rush to exit the building," he said, "eighty-two-year-old Louise Lawson slipped in a puddle of water that had been sprayed during the riot. She broke her hip and is having surgery today to insert pins into her bones. She will need months of rehabilitation. Furthermore one student suffered an asthma episode requiring emergency breathing treatments, resulting from the chemical dust attack of yellow powdered sulfur."

The judge scanned the papers in front of him. "Bail is five thousand, set a trial date in two weeks. Next."

An officer tapped me on the shoulder and led me back to the police car. As soon as we entered the police station again, I saw Loretta.

"Loretta," I cried. "Loretta!"

She kept her eyes on the floor.

I followed the officer back to the small room where I had first changed clothes. She took off my handcuffs and handed me my velvet ball gown. I peeled off my prisoners' green and greedily reached for my ball gown, so familiar and comforting after my long night of terror. But as I slipped my body back into that antiqued velvet, I felt its true weight. The heavy skirt dragged the ground and stooped my shoulders. Yards and yards of fabric swallowed my thin frame. I looked down at all the buttons I'd have to fasten and wondered how my tired eyes and sleepy hands would manage the task. *It wasn't beautiful anymore.* It was exhausting. It was so much work, such endless effort, being Jane Eyre.

The officer took me to Loretta. She seemed haggard, sicker than I'd ever seen her. I remembered how gray Daddy had been the night before his conference.

"All I did was give a dramatic reading," I pleaded as soon as we were inside her car. "It's no different than what Daddy did for a living."

"No different?" Loretta cried. "How about when that poor lady broke her hip? Or when the whole school had to be evacuated? Or when that boy had an asthma attack? Or when the dozens of police officers got called? Your daddy never did nothing like that."

"But I didn't think the other kids would take it so far..."

"That's the problem! You *don't* think," Loretta hissed. "It's all poetry and passion for you Weavers. You got no wisdom."

I flipped open a folder full of information that Loretta had carried out. There was a page titled Sentencing Guidelines. I choked back a sob. "Years? It was just a silly school talent show ... they wouldn't really—"

"Send you to jail?" We were stopped at a red light and Loretta leaned her head against the steering wheel. "Yes, they will."

"I was just a character."

The light turned green but we didn't move. Other drivers honked and pulled around us as we sat parked in the passing lane.

"I used to wring my hands over your library books," Loretta whispered. "I was always in knots, thinking you'd forget to pull them out of your backpack and turn them in on time. That it would go in your file that you were forgetful or tardy." She laughed bitterly. "Library books! I'd pace the floor all school day hoping you'd remember. Once I even called the secretary and asked her to remind you. I just wanted things to be perfect like your mama would have made them ... I wanted you to be spotless ... to be happy. And now ..." She slammed her fist against the seat and her shoulders shook fiercely. I remembered that puddle of prisoner green, shaking and shivering on the cot in the next cell.

"I can't go back there," I whispered. "Everybody's dying in that holding tank. You gotta help me, Loretta. You gotta do what Daddy would do. Have some meetings, make some donations."

Someone honked behind us. Loretta wiped her eyes and pulled forward even though the light had changed to red. We drove the rest of the way home in silence. We turned into the driveway and Loretta turned off the car and faced me. It was the first time she had looked at me since picking me up.

"I'll help you," she finally said. "Follow me."

She led me into the kitchen, kneeled down on the floor, and began to dig inside the cabinets. Finally she pulled out her old, enormous iron skillet. The one that she used to fry chicken and sear roasts.

"I'm not hungry," I said.

But she laid the skillet on the counter, opened the tool drawer, and took out a hammer.

"You know what makes an iron skillet special?" she asked.

I shrugged. "It gets the chicken real brown."

Crash! The hammer smashed into the skillet's center. I shivered at the horrible sound of metal smashing against metal.

"It don't break." She raised the hammer high and brought it down again. "It'll take any abuse and never show it. You can drop it, throw it, put it in the hottest oven. Iron skillets are built for hard things." She pointed a crooked finger at me. "This world took your mama. It stole your daddy. The hurts keep on coming, blow after blow. There's only one way to survive it. There's only one way to bear up and not crack or break. You gotta be an iron skillet." She handed me the hammer. "Hit it."

I tried to lay the hammer down, but Loretta's boney hand clasped mine and squeezed it against the hammer.

BAM! BAM! BAM! I smashed the hammer into the skillet's center.

"Good," Loretta cried. "More!"

BAM! BAM! BAM!

I swung for Mama and Daddy. I swung for the little girl who couldn't make friends at lunch. For the girl who sank to the bottom of the pond, because sometimes I wished that yard worker had left her there. I swung for half-finished novels. For Mama's favorite story that I'd never know or read. I swung for Persephone, because Katie was right that she ate those seeds because she needed to escape. I swung for Jane Eyre. For all the ways she had worn me out. I swung because I was home, but still hooked on the line.

Loretta wrapped her arms around me.

"Easy, Girly. *Shhh,*" she whispered hoarsely. "Your daddy said you can make anything come alive. You can be anything you want. No Greek myth will get you through the beatings. Neither will a pretend storybook. If you can really be anything, then be an iron skillet. Like I've been since I was a married girl at sixteen."

She cleared her throat suddenly and slumped to the floor. She brought her hand to her chest. "Get me some aspirin," she moaned. "Real quick now."

I ran and grabbed the bottle on top of the fridge. I kneeled beside her and popped two into her mouth. "Loretta?"

"Help me to bed. That's a good girl."

Loretta slumped against me as she hobbled to her room. I helped her get into bed and sat in the chair at her desk.

"Don't bother to keep watch. You know I get these spells from time to time," she said.

"I wanna stay a little longer."

"All right. But I can't make chitchat. Tomorrow's a busy day. I gotta move my sister to the old folks' home. I think I've finally got everything straight, but who knows what kind of tricks will come my way." She groaned softly and thumped her fist over her chest again.

"Does it hurt bad?" I asked.

She smiled. "Was there ever a good hurt?"

"Loretta, you won't let them send me to jail, will you?"

She sighed. "Your daddy paid to get you out of your last mess. He said it was a miracle that you didn't get in more trouble. But the Bible's done been writ, our world's long past fresh miracles. Best we can hope for now is a reprieve, a little rest, before the reckoning. Every lawless deed gets judged."

"I won't go back," I whispered.

"The hurts keep on coming...you're gonna have to chin up and—"

"Be an iron skillet," I whispered.

She nodded slightly and closed her eyes. She was lying on her back. Her silver hair was down and tangled across her pillow. Soon her mouth felt open and she snored softly. I slumped down on the desk and noticed an envelope. *Claudia Hensley, Jefferson Middle School,* was stamped in the left corner. I opened it.

Jefferson Guidance Intervention Report was typed across the top of the page.

Dear Ms. Mason:

This letter serves to document our meeting in which we discussed eighth grade student, Anna Pearl Weaver. Below is a summary of our discussion...

I scanned the letter. It was notes from the meeting about the library incident. Everything was recorded, including the list of my wrongdoings and proposed penalties. But at the bottom, I read something new.

You stated that given your elderly age and heart condition, you question your ability to aggressively meet Anna Pearl's challenges. We discussed the possibility of other guardianship alternatives. I have contacted a social worker, who will be in touch with you soon to discuss several good options for your present situation.

I look forward to working with you toward positive progress for Anna Pearl.

Sincerely,
Claudia Hensley

Loretta wasn't going to help me. She was planning to get rid of me. I walked to her bedside and watched her sleep peacefully. *It's not the hammer that hurts,* I wanted to scream. It's the edits. So many edits.

First, there was Daddy. Cut out of my life, like a masterpiece tossed in the fire. Next was Jane and the Character Guild. The world isn't kind to characters. Middle school deletes them.

And now Loretta was going to give me to a stranger with a stronger heart.

Daddy liked to quote the masters on how to edit. *Kill your darlings*, they taught. Only, nobody warned how much it hurts to see a darling die.

"So kill your darlings," Daddy agreed, "but always keep their bones." What he meant was if you wrote something that matters to you, if it came from somewhere inside, by all means edit it well, but don't destroy it. Save the bones. Who knows what treasure you might find in some forgotten, dusty scene.

I lived in a world of Darling Killers. My mind searched for something nasty to call them.

"Y'all aren't even readers," I whispered to a snoring Loretta.

Maybe they turned pages, but it takes more than recognizing words on a page to be a reader. It takes love and perseverance and an understanding that sometimes you have to push through ugly pages to find beautiful ones. Sometimes you have put up with cookie crumbs in the library so that middle schoolers can finally bloom.

I crept from Loretta's room but I didn't go to bed. There was no time to sleep. New edits, even jail, were coming my way.

I went to the staircase and stared at my tintype soldier. "Help me," I begged. "Tell me who to be," I sobbed as he reminded me of the truth. *Characters can't be trusted.* They're fragile, unpredictable things.

I went to see Henry next. I studied all the pieces of things that framed our narrow hall. "Then *what* could I be?" I pleaded. I wanted to be a skillet, strong and unbreakable. But I was just another screaming fish.

I ran to the Circus Room. Granny watched me from the mantel, with her fierce *dare-you-to* eyes.

"Help me," I wept. "I'm hooked on the line. Where can I go?"

I sucked in my breath because finally, I had asked the right question. Daddy had been right all along. I remembered his anthem, the one he wrote in large letters across his classroom chalkboard. I called out his words to my runaway circus granny.

"Only a setting can save a sinking story!"

The Heart-Shaped Museum

Abel and Stella met inside the warehouse every Sunday, both of them swept up in a storm of new love. But only one of them showed it. Abel just hinted at his true feelings. Love made him feel whole, but never new, so he loved purely but not madly.

Stella abandoned all caution. After four months of Sundays, she talked of weddings, and babies, and a cottage on a hill. Abel smiled and watched her with wonder. He understood instinctively that the reason she loved so freely was because she had lived a pretty and safe life. The youngest of three daughters, her days were filled with silk dresses and picnic lunches. She was a sunset gazer, a butterfly chaser, a keeper of lightning bugs trapped in a jar. But best of all was love among the cotton bales. Only now she was the one caught, another lightning bug trapped in the jar.

They made plans, a dozen "somedays" only half-believed by Abel but marked down in Stella's heart like law. *Someday I'm gonna teach you how to fry catfish,* Abel said. *Someday when we have our own house, I'll put a piano in the corner,* Stella promised.

Every other day was a chore to get through until they could meet on Sunday. Stella, whose first love was music, played sad minuets to pass her time. Abel stayed late at the mill. He supervised extra shifts and fixed any broken machine. He saved nearly every dime he earned and hid it inside tobacco cans lined beneath his bed. At night, when the mill was closed, he could no longer distract himself. It was only then, in the dark, that he would admit how much he loved her. His confession never brought relief or joy, only fear. He knew the great difference between them. He saw how easily she had fallen in love without considering the consequences.

But every Sunday, no matter how many times during the week he swore he wouldn't, Abel went to the warehouse. One night, Stella pulled a piece of cloth from Abel's pocket.

"What's this?" she asked. "Too small to be a hanky."

"Just a patch of cloth. A weaving machine was down in the mill. I went in early this morning to have a look. I finally got it up and running."

"You made this?" she asked.

He nodded.

She turned and grabbed a fistful of raw cotton bolls from the bale behind her. "From this?"

Abel shrugged. "You know it's what we do."

"But it's so smooth," Stella said as she held the cloth up to her face. "And perfect. It's amazing."

Abel smiled. "I always thought so too. Don't know how a man ever dreamed it up."

Stella tore the cloth in two, and then tore one of the halves again. "It's too pretty to hide in your pocket," she said as she tied a strip of cloth around her ring finger. She held up her hand for him to admire, and Abel watched as she flushed pink. With her strawberry hair and pink skin, she was like a redbud in spring.

"Pretty as gold," she whispered.

Stella wore her ring of cotton and never took it off, but lied about the reason.

"It reminds me of last year's Lenten fast," she said, when her mama complained again about *that old thread.* "The preacher said sacrifice isn't seasonal."

"Gracious, child," her mama laughed. "I didn't know you were preparing for the ministry."

Stella frowned. "I'm not... I just..."

"What did you give up for Lent anyway that requires such a reminder?"

"Mozart."

"Oh, Songbird. Only you know the difference between Mozart and any other fancy fella you play."

"Mama...," Stella dared to whisper. "How'd you end up marrying Daddy?"

"Mercy, it was so long ago... I reckon it was because he kept coming around. My daddy liked him well enough too. We knew he could help expand the mills Daddy was buying. That helped for sure."

"But you loved him? Did you feel like nobody ever really saw you before, until him?"

Her mama waved the thought away with a swish of her gloved hand. "The stuff of silly girl crushes. That's not what marriages are made of."

"Well, what is... what is a marriage made of?"

"Long, established family lines. Multiple streams of income. But why are you—"

Stella flushed. "Remember Jilly? She's got a crush. A silly one I guess."

"Don't get caught up in that nonsense," her mama warned. "Ruin your reputation and you'll never make an equal match."

An equal match. It was Abel's impossible wish. He couldn't get the picture of Stella twirling that cotton band around her finger out of his mind. If only he could become her equal, he thought. If only he could find a way to be worthy. Sometimes, when he couldn't sleep, he'd walk down Linthead Road in the middle of the night, all the way to the bottom of Mayfield Hill where Stella lived. He'd stare up at the mansion, with its tall white columns framing three stories. He'd never even knocked on the door of a house so grand.

I'll invent a new spinning machine, he thought. There had to be a way for the machine to spin without snapping so many threads. He bought paper and drew several sketches. He took apart a spinning machine to study all the little gears inside. But even though he could point to which parts needed improving and draw them perfectly, he couldn't label them. Much less figure out where to send his drawings once he finished them. He only read the most basic words. No matter what great ideas came to him, he was still linthead. Or worse, he thought, maybe he was a thief. Stella was a glittery jewel, and all Abel could think about was how to keep her. He despised himself for it.

He decided to tell her. He sat her down in the warehouse one Sunday night, cleared his throat, and blurted, "I ain't gonna be a thief. You was raised for better. You deserve that cottage on the hill you talk about with that piano in the corner, and we both know I can't give it to you. All I can ever give you is a mill shack."

Stella laughed. "Have I told you about Sally falling down the banks at the Connor wedding? The ceremony was by the lake and she insisted on wearing her new shoes even though Mama warned the bottoms were too slick—"

"Stella, I'm trying to tell you that—"

"Yes, but let me finish my story first, it's so funny, and I've waited all week to tell you."

But Stella didn't finish. She talked in happy circles and laughed brightly, and soon she announced it was time for her to go home. Abel gave up for the night, but determined that next time, he would not let her distract him. He would end their Sunday meetings.

But by the next Sunday, Abel couldn't go to the warehouse at all. He had to attend an emergency meeting to discuss an outbreak of labor protests erupting in mill village. Stella's daddy, Mr. Mayfield, had called the meeting.

"Bunch of Yanks behind this," Mr. Mayfield swore. "They get jealous of our money, of our gentle way of life, so they come down here and stir up trouble." He held up a yellow flyer. "This was in my house mail. Says lintheads got rights. Says they deserve better than what

I give 'em." He passed the paper around the circle of bosses. They all glanced at it uneasily, before handing it to the next man.

"Don't I give 'em a free house?" Mr. Mayfield boomed.

"Yes, sir," the bosses mumbled.

"Don't I give 'em credit down at the store?"

"Yes, sir."

"What other job does that? What other job pays a wage *and* gives a free house *and* store credit? But this paper says it ain't enough. They need *better* houses. They need *better* wages. They need education. For what? What does reading got to do with cotton? Next thing you know they'll be demanding white-gloved servants, verandas, and lemonade breaks too." Mr. Mayfield swore under his breath and held up a newspaper. "And this morning, I see this."

Abel stared at the paper. On the front page was a picture of the shack just across the street from his. It was in horrible repair, with seven children and a widow all living in the two rooms. The porch had a giant hole in it, and the picture showed one of the littlest lintheads standing down inside it, clutching a mangy cat.

"Beneath that mill rat's picture," Mr. Mayfield continued, "is a letter. *Dear Mr. Mayfield* it begins, sweet as the serpent's kiss. The whole piece is about this rat's family and how poor they are because of me. How their pay is docked for each extra child. How the husband died from lint lung and the mama can't keep her kids fed. How this rat is just eight years old but works all day same as a grown man." Mr. Mayfield glared at the bosses until the men stared at the ground. "I don't even know this boy. Yet I'm to blame for his troubles?"

"I know him," Abel spoke up. "He's a good little sweeper."

Mr. Mayfield pointed his finger at Abel. "Did you know he was just eight?"

"I never asked."

Mr. Mayfield nodded. "Even if you did, lintheads are born liars." He tossed the paper to Abel. "Read the name beneath the title."

Abel had never seen a linthead picture before. It was beautiful ... and pitiful. The boy with his lint covered hair, bright eyes, and silly smile. The hole that swallowed him. The half-starved cat. There was a page of words beneath it, but Abel studied the picture. He didn't need words.

"I said read the name," Mr. Mayfield screamed.

Abel flinched. "I never ... I can't—"

"Abraham Linton," Mr. Mayfield interrupted. "He wrote the letter and took that picture. Who is Abraham Linton?"

"Ain't that, like, a dead president?" one of the men muttered.

Mr. Mayfield groaned. "It's a fake name. But whoever is using it has gotta be hanging around mill town. So keep your eyes open for anybody who seems out of place. The man that brings me Abraham Linton gets a hundred dollars."

He dismissed the meeting with a furious shake of his fist, but as the bosses left, he called Abel back. "You manage this rat's shift, eh?" he asked, pointing to the newspaper.

"Yes, sir."

"Run 'em out."

"But she's got seven kids—"

"She let her boy pose for a protest piece!"

"Nah," Abel said. "Little frog like him, he just wanted his picture taken. I bet the mama didn't even know about the story."

"I want them gone," Mr. Mayfield demanded. "And I want everybody to know the reason why. Let it be a warning. If they cross me, I will banish them from the mill. They'll be homeless and hungry and wishing they could be one of my lintheads again."

Abel stopped in the road when he came to the widow's house. He should've fixed that hole in their porch a long time ago. It wouldn't have been hard to do, and maybe then Abraham Linton wouldn't have wanted the boy's picture. The mama came to the front door and called for her kids. A plate of biscuits was in her hands. Abel decided to let them eat their supper first. He waited an hour before knocking on her door.

The widow nodded when she saw Abel. "Figured you'd be comin' round," she said. "Saw the paper and had my Betty read it. She taught herself, you know. She's teaching my others too. It's like she was born knowing letters and what they mean. But I reckon it wasn't a very kind story for the mill."

Abel shook his head. "No, ma'am."

"We gotta leave?" she asked, her voice breaking.

Abel nodded.

She slumped against the doorframe. "Tell me one thing," she whispered. "Who is Abraham Linton?"

"You don't know?" he asked.

She shook her head. "Little Paul won't say a word. Says Mr. Linton paid him two ice cream cones and a nickel to keep the secret. But I ain't mad at him. All Paul did was tell the truth. If mill owners are ashamed by it, well then, maybe Mr. Linton is right. Maybe they oughta be."

"What will you do?"

"I got family in the mountains. We'll make our way there, somehow. Listen, when y'all find Abraham Linton, will you give him a message for me?"

Abel nodded.

"Tell him I said thanks for taking Paul's picture. It's the only picture I got of any of my babies."

Abel went home and sat on the edge of his bed and thought about the four tobacco cans beneath him. He had been saving every extra dime for the impossible dream, that one day he would buy Stella a wedding ring to replace that simple cotton band.

But he was quitting that dream. Stella didn't belong to him. He pulled the tobacco cans out, felt the weight of money inside. He walked across Linthead Road and laid the cans in a row across the widow's front doorstep. In the morning, when he woke to the mill whistle, the family was gone. So were the tobacco cans.

Mill village began to rumble. Everyone was angry that the widow was kicked out. Lintheads stood together during their lunch break and recited bits and pieces of the Linthead Letter. Since most of them couldn't read, they made up the parts that they forgot. Soon, according to their whispers, Abraham Linton encouraged strikes, riots, and a show of force. The mill closed early on Friday, when whole shifts of lintheads walked out.

New pictures covered the next Sunday paper's front page, along with another Linthead Letter. *Dear Mr. Mayfield,* the letter opened as it began a new list of linthead struggles, before urging mill village to have calm hearts and orderly actions. The closing was particularly direct. *I do not believe you have been intentionally evil, dear sir, merely ignorant. But my letters leave you without excuse. The whole Southern working class waits for you to reconcile the wretched inequality that now exists between those who spin the cotton, and those who own it.*

Abel hadn't seen Stella since their last visit in the warehouse, when he struggled and failed to end things. All of mill village spied on their neighbor now, everybody hoping to discover Abraham Linton. So Abel avoided the warehouse, and hoped that Stella understood.

But one day she marched into the mill and announced that she was there on business for her daddy. She went from room to room with a clipboard, like she was making inspections. When she finished, she stood in front of Abel. He glanced down at the paper on her clipboard. It was blank.

"Walk me home," she whispered.

Abel stared at her in surprise. They had never dared leave the Sunday warehouse at the same time.

"I can't," he told her. "You know that."

She frowned. "You've been avoiding me. And I know you're still itching to give me that sermon from our last time in the warehouse. At least do it while we walk."

It would be their last time together, Abel promised himself. He'd had enough time away from her to work up the courage to break her heart. As they walked down Linthead Road, Abel calmly explained the differences between them.

"I got nothing to offer you. No family, no promised inheritance, never been to school. If I saw your name printed, I wouldn't recognize it unless you taught me to."

They stopped at the bottom of Mayfield Hill.

"C'mon, keep walking," Stella urged.

"I've gone as far as I can. You've gotta go the rest of the way, up the hill. I can't follow you there."

Stella grinned. "What would Abraham Linton say?"

Abel spat on the ground. "He's nothing but a troublemaker."

Stella raised her chin. "He's wonderful. He's changing everything for us. Lintheads are finally being seen as people now. Have you heard that a paper from another state is going to run the letters and pictures too? We're living in a new era, Abel. People are standing up for themselves. It's time we did the same. You're right, there's a whole list of differences between us but that doesn't mean there should be. So walk me up the hill."

Abel shook his head. "I won't steal you from your family, from all that they can give you. Look at your house, Stella. Take a look, and then think of where I come from."

Stella turned and faced her home. "I see a house that's big and rich, but in the end it's nothing but brick and wood and chipped paint." She looked over her shoulder at him. "Don't you know who you are, Abel Weaver?"

"Sure. I'm no thief."

"Why do you insist on measuring yourself against something as worthless as a house? You're just like my daddy."

"I'm nothing like him. That's my whole point," Abel said.

"Daddy measures everything by money. He sums up a man by the size of his house, the size of his wallet. Turns out, so do you. But a mansion can't love, it can't dance, it can't do anything as wonderful as this." She held up her hand and flashed her cotton band. "You made this. You show me a fancy house that can do something as magic as that. You show me a house that can love me like you do."

Stella ran all the way up the hill. Abel watched her go and fought the urge to call her back. Her name stayed stuck in his throat like lint from the carding room.

The next week was filled with protests and demands. *Tell him to quit docking my pay, just cause I've got kids. I heard he's got three kids too. He want us to dock his profits?* Abel tried to soothe his workers, but he didn't tell them they were wrong. He remembered his mama and how she worried his pay would be docked. And he thought about Abraham Linton. He wrote that the Mayfield Mill was the only mill in the South that docked pay according to family size. *Maybe he's got a few good points,* Abel admitted to himself.

The spinners walked out at their lunch break and never came back. Soon the mill struggled to operate on less than half staff. Outside, lintheads threw cotton bolls at workers who dared cross their strike line.

Mr. Mayfield hired police to stand guard and ordered the mill to remain open regardless of the poor production numbers. He refused to be defeated by a fake-named Yankee. The bosses all wondered how long he could last without making any concession. Secretly, they hoped for a small raise.

The next Sunday, Abel scooped up the newspaper. This time, Stella smiled from the center of the front page. Abel gasped. It was a Mayfield family portrait, of Mr. and Mrs. Mayfield and their three girls. He ran to find a spinner who could read. He shoved the paper in her hands.

The spinner smiled. "This one's good," she said and began to read aloud.

A Linthead Love Letter
by Abraham Linton

Dear Mr. Mayfield,

One of your beloved daughters has chosen a linthead love.

I understand, even sympathize, that you and Mrs. Mayfield have dreamed of a son-in-law with lint-free hair and pampered hands. But love is made of fire, not manners.

I do not reveal this to shame you. When I learned of this predicament, I simply knew that it illustrated my previous letters perfectly. Your workers are a people of unseen value. They are much more than bobbins and bales. Your daughter knows this well.

Will you scour the mill for the culprit who loves your daughter? Will you call him a thief? Order his dismissal just like the widow with her seven children?

There is a better way. Your mill is nearly closed, and an olive branch is desperately needed. May I suggest that instead of relying on curses, you choose blessing instead? At the very least, allow the love to come to supper.

Times are changing, Mr. Mayfield. The first revelation of our modern age is that honor and worth are not defined by wage or education. The second is this: Love is a fire, and flames of equal match cannot be quenched by cotton lint.

Sincerely,
Abraham Linton

Abel struggled to remain calm as the spinner finished reading.

She grinned. "How 'bout that?"

"Bunch of lies," Abel growled.

"Abraham Linton don't lie. Some have been whispering about the youngest one, the redhead. Seems she likes to come down to the mill more than the others. Seems she likes to be around lintheads. We're all guessing it's her. And I think the linthead is Mark Mallord. That's who I'd pick anyway."

Abel took the paper back. "Who is Abraham Linton?" he demanded. "If I find him I'll choke the life out of him."

The spinner laughed. "I know he's meant trouble for you bosses, but for us normal folk, he's our Moses."

Mr. Mayfield called another emergency meeting. He was purple-faced and cursing as he waved the newspaper around. "My granny always said the Yankees wouldn't stop till they bring us to our knees."

"What do you want us to do?" one of the bosses asked. "Bales are stacked up in the warehouses. We ain't got enough people to open 'em, much less get anything weaved."

"Maybe if you just raised wages a nickel...just gave 'em something to feel like they won," another boss suggested.

"Reward evil?" Mr. Mayfield shouted. "Never. You go house to house and deliver this message: No more *Linthead Letters.* For every new word from Abraham Linton, I'll cut wages by ten percent."

The bosses went through mill town delivering Mr. Mayfield's message. Sometimes they were met with sobs. Most of the time, they were met with anger. One boss was given a black eye.

Just before dark, Abel noticed a line of lintheads snaking down the road. He followed them from a distance, until they reached the mill. He smelled their whiskey and tobacco, as they yelled curses and tossed small rocks at the mill.

"Ain't you a boss?" one of them yelled when he saw Abel. "You here to spy?"

Abel shook his head. "I ain't taking names. I don't even recognize most of y'all."

"We're from the next mill town over," one of the boys said. "Them *Linthead Letters* are being passed around our parts too. We're here to show our support. We heard the owner is fixing to dock pay. Tonight's gonna be the biggest rally yet."

Soon, other lintheads arrived. A mob swelled. *He better not cut our pay!* they shouted to one another. They cheered for Abraham Linton. They demanded freedom for the Linthead Lovers.

A rock smashed into a spinning room window. A war cry broke out. More lintheads came, bringing quarts of moonshine. Soon the chants grew messy and the mood boisterous. Abel stayed in the shadows, watching, and was about to leave when a new cry caught his attention.

"There she is! It's the girl from the paper."

Abel ran into the crowd and saw Stella. The mob surged toward her.

"Your daddy wants to dock our pay," somebody yelled.

"I came to show my support," she shouted. "I came to say that it's not right..."

"I'll be your Linthead Lover," someone called out. The crowd answered with jeers and whistles. Someone dragged her up to the mill door.

"Open it," they yelled. "You own it, so open it."

"I don't have a key," she stammered. "I promise. I truly do support your cause though. You deserve better wages and better houses and gosh, it's so awful what happened to the widow with her seven kids... Honestly, I'm a huge fan of Abraham Linton."

"Open the mill! Open the mill! Open the mill!" the mob demanded.

Stella was flattened against the door as the mob pressed against her. A rock sailed up and smashed another window. She ducked and screamed as glass fell down on her. Abel pushed and swung his way to the front of the crowd. He threw himself in front of Stella and faced the mob.

"Your fight ain't with her," he yelled. "She didn't set your wage or build your houses."

"Then we'll keep her, until he raises our pay," someone cried from the back of the mob.

"Go home and sober up," Abel shouted. "Come back in the morning and we'll talk."

"We keep the cotton princess." The crowd cheered and surged toward Stella again. A man grabbed the hem of her dress and tore off a strip of silk. He waved it like a victory flag and reached for more.

Abel pulled his keys out of his pocket and dangled them high in the air. "You want inside?" He unlocked the two bolts and turned the knob. The door swung open and the crowd surged forward, screaming victory. Abel grabbed Stella's hand and jerked her through the crowd.

"Run," he yelled. "Run!"

He watched her run down Linthead Road until she disappeared. Then he stepped inside the mill. Bobbins were thrown like baseballs against the wall. Bales of cotton torn open and slung.

BOOM! came a noise from somewhere in the mill and the ground shook. BOOM! It was nearly dark now, and Abel had to peer through the moonlight as he tracked the noise. He made his way down the hall toward the spinning room, but just as he turned the corner something crashed against his head. Everything faded.

When he woke up, he was alone. The sun was just beginning to rise. Warm, sticky blood dripped from his head. He sat up slowly. The spinning machines were smashed into thousands of pieces all around him.

"What have you done to my mill?" someone asked.

Abel recognized the voice before he saw his face.

"What have you done—" Mr. Mayfield repeated, as he stepped into the light.

"I came to see but then ..." Abel mumbled, confused.

"You let them in. Your key is still in the door."

"I had to," Abel said. "They had Stel—they had your daughter."

"Why were you here?" Mr. Mayfield demanded. "Surely my bosses don't protest."

"I followed 'em."

Mr. Mayfield stepped around the broken spinning machine pieces and into the hall.

"My weaving room," he shouted. He ran to the next room and screamed again.

He returned to Abel, screaming with rage, "*You* let them in."

"They had Stella!"

"A man's work is his life. Some of these machines can't ever be replaced. They don't even make 'em anymore."

Another boss walked in. Mr. Mayfield turned to him, shouting and shaking his fist in the air. "Get the sheriff!"

Abel returned to his shack, cleaned up his wound, and laid across his bed. He tried to sleep, but kept thinking about Stella. He kept seeing her panicked face as she stood pressed against the mill. He wished now, alone in his shack, that he had done something bigger and braver. He wished he had punished the men who terrified Stella instead of giving into their demands.

Just as he began to imagine all the things he could have done, his door burst open and Stella rushed inside.

"What are you...," he began. "If somebody sees you—"

She flung herself into his arms. "Daddy's sending the law for you."

Abel pushed her back. "What... why?"

"He says you organized the mob. That you wanted the lintheads to destroy his mill."

"Did you tell him what really happened?" Abel asked. "How they scared you? How they threw rocks... how they wanted to keep you? Did you show him your dress?" Abel slammed his fist against the wall. "I wish I'd have—"

"I told him," Stella whispered. "He said you were only pretending to save me. That getting them in the mill was the plot all along. Daddy just wants to punish somebody, and the only name on his lips is Abraham Linton."

"Well good luck finding him," Abel scoffed.

"He says it's you."

Abel laughed loudly.

"Daddy swears you're pulling the cotton over everybody's eyes. Making it look like you're a good boss. Meanwhile, you're writing articles and letting the lintheads destroy the mill. He's talking with his attorney now. They're making a whole list of things to arrest you for."

"But what about the other lintheads?" Abel asked. "The ones who destroyed the mill?"

"He blames you. He's offered a twenty percent pay raise to every linthead who comes back to work once the mill is fixed, as long as they never speak of Abraham Linton again. *That* is his olive branch."

"Sheriff won't arrest me."

"Daddy runs mill town," Stella cried. "He pulls any thread he wants."

She nestled back into his arms again and this time Abel didn't push her away. He felt her trembling as his mind worked to make sense of everything.

"I'll catch him," Abel said. "I'll find Abraham Linton for your daddy to punish. That Linton's been snooping where he don't belong."

"You can't catch him."

"Watch me," Abel grunted. He stood to his feet and stepped toward the door.

"It's me."

Abel stopped still.

"I'm Abraham Linton," Stella said.

Abel shook his head slowly, but Stella nodded. "Me."

"Why?" Abel shouted. "Why would you ever—"

"Remember that Sunday we met and you kept talking about being a thief? You think I didn't know where you were headed with that junk? I kept talking about Sally falling down the banks so you couldn't finish and ruin things. When I went home, I started thinking about how nobody sees you the right way. Abel, you are smart in ways that most aren't. You are trustworthy and dependable. You're the best man I know, but you just see yourself as a poor linthead. And you were right, my daddy would just see you as a thief.

"For years, he's been worried about the times changing, about people organizing over workers' rights. For years, he's been worried about Yankees coming down here and giving his lintheads ideas that they deserve better. Until you, I always thought that'd be a bad thing. Daddy said the Yanks would steal our business if they got their way. But if it was money, the fact that I had too much and you had too little, that was keeping us apart, then I decided that it was wrong to hold back change. Maybe I should even help it."

"You took Paul's picture?" Abel asked. "You got the widow kicked out of her home?"

Stella's lip trembled. "I didn't mean for that to happen."

"What about the mob? What about them grabbing you like they did? You mean for that to happen?"

"Of course not. After I wrote that first letter, things took on a life of their own. People started making demands. I thought it was wonderful at first. I was changing our story, Abel. I was changing how people see us. I thought Daddy might finally realize that lintheads are people, not just workers. And even if he didn't, I thought surely *you* would change. Surely you would listen to Abraham Linton and understand that you got the same right to love as anyone. But no, you kept talking about money and Daddy kept talking about money, so I wrote that last Linthead Love Letter. It was a final effort at changing your minds. I meant what I wrote. Every word. My love is fire, and cotton lint can't quench it."

"Well how about jail then?" Abel asked. "If I'm in jail, will that quench it?"

"No." Stella began to sob. "I'm sorry. I never dreamed the lintheads would destroy the mill. I just wanted you to feel good about loving me. I wanted Daddy to change, for the world to change all around us."

Abel sat down on the edge of his bed. "Of all the crazy things to do..."

"I wasn't wrong about you. You saved me last night."

"And now the Sheriff is coming for me," Abel replied.

"Not when I tell Daddy it was me. I got a whole stack of linthead pictures I can show him to prove it. Last year, for my birthday, my aunt mailed me a camera from New York. I told the lintheads I was doing a report for *Beautiful Madame's* Magazine on working fashion."

Abel remembered the way Mr. Mayfield didn't flinch when Abel told him about Stella being held hostage by the mob. He remembered the way Mr. Mayfield cried when he saw his smashed up mill. *A man's work is his life.*

"I can't put you at his mercy," Abel said. "I don't trust him not to—" Abel stopped when he saw the pain across Stella's face and knew she had reached the same conclusion.

"I'll leave," he finally said. "I'll be gone before he gets here."

"Me too?" Stella whispered, desperately twirling the cotton thread across her finger.

Abel took a deep breath, as he realized everything he was about to lose. His good job, all the years he'd spent working his way up through the mill ranks. His home, the fields and woods he loved. He looked at Stella. Saw how her skin burned with panic and passion. Saw the fiery hair piled on top of her head like a crown.

Redbud, Abel thought as he looked at her and remembered the lesson the woods had taught him. It always takes a little cold to make the good things bloom.

"You'll never have another silk dress," he told her.

"I'm a cotton woman now."

"I'll never be able to buy you a big house."

"I belong with you."

"I'm the first branch on the Weaver family tree."

"We'll add to it."

"There won't be many feasting suppers."

"You promised to teach me how to fry catfish."

"Stella, I can't give you—"

"Do you love me more than money?"

Abel nodded.

"I'm richer than ever," she whispered.

Abel circled her in his arms. The only money he had was in a half-empty tobacco can beneath his bed. But there was something he could give her after all, something she didn't have on Mayfield Hill. It was the way he looked at her, like she was the shiniest jewel. It was the way he wanted her, like no money could ever compare.

There was nothing poor about that linthead love.

XX

Boom. Boom. Boom. It was my heart, pulsing fear and defiance.

Boom! Boom! Boom! It was my fist, pounding on Loretta's door.

As I waited for her to open it, my mind franticly rehearsed the story that I had plotted the day before. My plotting began soon after Loretta left to move her sister into the old folks' home. I was packing my getaway bag, trying to figure out the best place to run, when I heard strange noises. It was the soft sound of things being ripped apart.

I followed the noise down the hall and slowly opened the door to the Oriental Room. Katie was standing in her Eskimo coat, weeping. Torn paper snowflakes were scattered everywhere. She grabbed another handful of snowflakes from the ceiling and ripped them down.

"Katie?"

She turned and faced me. Her mouth opened in stunned surprise. "You're out of jail? I seen it on the news where you got arrested. Something about a riot. What happened? Loretta would only moan about her heart whenever I asked."

"Somebody got hurt at the talent show. They say it's my fault."

"Was jail like it is in the soaps? With prisoners sneaking knives and singing old hymns?"

"It was—" I stopped and shuddered. "Nothing like that. I'm in a lot of trouble."

Katie shrugged. "But you got Loretta. She'll never let you go to jail because—What's wrong?"

"Loretta's getting somebody new to raise me. She won't help me."

Katie closed her eyes and screamed. "Everything's gone crazy! Tomorrow, I'm getting shipped off to Vegas where I'll be forced to obsess over tans and stripper clothes. And now you're going to jail."

"No," I said. "I won't go back."

Katie stepped forward and grabbed my hands. "Pearl ... where are you gonna go?"

"Someplace different," I answered. "I'll start at the bus station tomorrow while Loretta's seeing you off at the airport."

Katie ran across the room, swishing through the few remaining snowflakes that dangled from the ceiling. She kneeled by her bed and pulled out a box. I was surprised to see that she had hidden treasure of her own. When I looked inside, I saw stacks of brochures on Alaska.

"You want different?" she asked. "You could look the whole world over and not find anywhere like it."

I picked up a brochure and traced the mapped lines of Alaska. There were other papers. Airport schedules. Ferry departures. Vegas bus routes, going all the way to Canada. *Katie was planning something too.*

"I got a spot nobody would ever look for us," Katie promised. "We could be free forever. But one big problem stands in the way. Tomorrow, Loretta's taking me to the airport and putting me on a plane to Vegas."

I repeated her words under my breath. "Yeah," I whispered. "Loretta will put us on the plane. We don't need the bus station. Your mama's credit card number is still pinned to the fridge. We can call and order our tickets ... and I got the combination to Daddy's safe. He always kept a thousand in emergency cash."

"But how will we ever convince Loretta—"

"We can't," I said. "We've got to trick her."

The next morning, I stood with trembling knees and a heart full of tricks and pounded on Loretta's door. Finally, the door opened a crack, and Loretta peered out.

"Pearl?" she croaked. "It's barely dawn. I've got another few hours before Katie's flight. Unless I misread ... it's not sooner, is it? In all the fuss over moving Edith, maybe I—"

"No, ma'am. We don't have to get to the airport yet."

"Well, leave me be then," she said as she started to close the door. "Yesterday was hard, and I tossed and turned all night."

I put my hand out to hold the door open. "Today's a hard day too."

Loretta leaned against the frame. "You got yourself in more trouble?"

"The old folks' home called. Your sister got confused during the night and wandered out. Made it down to the bus station."

"Merciful heaven ... Is she all right? Is she back in her room?"

"She took the bus to Asheville. She's there now. They gave me this address." I handed her a slip of paper. "They got a security guard sitting with her, but she refuses to leave with someone she doesn't know. They called to see if you would bring her back."

"Oh," Loretta wailed. "I knew it. Katie's mama is my blood kin, but I got no pride in her. I knew she hadn't picked a decent home. All they're worried about is tax returns. They didn't write down her diabetes diet like I told 'em. They didn't write down which soap operas she can't miss. They just kept on me for them tax returns. And now they done lost Edith on the first night!"

She wheeled around to get dressed. She was whisper-yelling the entire time, cursing Katie's mama.

She gasped. "Oh, Katie."

I stepped into the room. "What are you gonna do? Can't be in two places at once."

Loretta held her hands out, groping for a solution. "I got to get her, but there ain't no way…"

"The thing is," I said, "she's real addled. The security guard says Edith tried to bite him. He's threatening to have the cops come and get her. If you wait much longer, you might have to bail her out just like you did me."

Loretta sat down on the bed and sobbed. I sat down next to her.

"There's still a way to take care of everybody," I said softly. "Drop us off and tell the airline lady you have an emergency. Sign us over, and they'll make sure we're taken care of. I saw kids left alone at the airport with stewardesses all the time when I flew with Daddy. I'll wait with Katie, so she won't be lonely. You head to the

Asheville bus station and get your sister, and then come back and get me."

Loretta studied me, weighing my words and worthiness. I remembered a warning Katie had given, and began to tremble again. *If she smells even a hint of a lie…*

But then I thought of Daddy's confidence in my imagination. He swore I could make anything I wanted come to life. Courage surged.

"It's not too late for me to start being good," I pressed. "I know I'm in trouble, but that doesn't mean I can't help you and your sister, and Katie. Besides, Edith needs you. Take it from me, you don't want her going to the holding tank. I don't think an old woman like her could survive it."

Less than an hour later, a wide-eyed Katie and I followed Loretta as she stormed into the airport. Loretta had never flown or visited an airport before. She crouched and covered her head as she heard the roar of a plane taking off.

An airline employee walked by, and Loretta grabbed his sleeve. "I've got a bad emergency!"

"How can I help, ma'am?" he asked.

She started wringing her hands and mumbling. I caught Katie's eye and winked because everything was going perfectly. Another plane took off and she crouched lower, almost to the ground. The man waited for her to stand.

"My sister's got old-timers," she said. "She gets too mean and they'll call the cops. And the girl's plane leaves before I can get back."

I stepped forward and spoke in a calm voice. "She needs to leave us here to wait on our flight. Bless her heart, she's in the midst of an awful family crisis."

"Are the tickets purchased?" the man asked.

"Yes," I answered. "I've got the credit card information to confirm." I glanced at Loretta. She was twisting her hands the way she did when wringing out her mop. Twist and squeeze, twist and squeeze, until the mess is flushed away.

"I need you to fill out a form," the man said to Loretta.

He had her write the names of the children she'd be leaving in the care of the airport. She wrote Katie's name. I pointed to the blank line under it.

"Me too," I said. "We can't leave Katie alone."

She wrote my name. The man showed her where to sign at the bottom and then checked her license. He signed beneath her name.

"That's it," he said. "I'll take them to the ticket desk."

He stood to the left while we said our good-byes. Loretta hugged Katie tightly. "Gonna miss you. Nobody loves my cooking like you do." She patted me on the back. "Be good. No more trouble. I'll be back in four or five hours ... hopefully."

"Take your time," I said. "Make sure you get Edith settled nice and cozy. I'll be fine. I brought a good book." I pointed to a waiting area. "I'll be sitting in front of that window, reading and waiting on you." I hugged her. I could count on one hand the number of times we had hugged. Loretta was a need-to-only kind of hugger. She only gave them away for the big deals: funerals, Joan-of-Arc tree tying tears, and Vegas departures.

She stiffened in my arms. "All right now. Let me get to Edith."

As Loretta walked away, the man motioned us over to the ticket counter. I pulled the pink slip of paper from my pocket.

"We need to pick up our tickets," I said. "Here's our order information and card number."

The ticket lady typed for a few minutes and then smiled. "That's nine hours to Anchorage. Good thing you've got each other so you'll have some company." She handed our tickets to the man supervising us. He led us to the waiting area and introduced us to the stewardess.

I sat by the big window that I showed Loretta. Katie leaned close. "She said nine hours."

"L-o-o-ng flight." I nodded.

"But Loretta's coming back in four. When she sees you gone, she'll be onto us. She'll track down where we went. If our flight is nine hours, we won't even make it off the plane. They'll just turn us right around and fly us straight back to Carolina."

I rolled my eyes. "Did you really think, after everything, that I wouldn't take care of that? Remember how I told Loretta I'd be by this big window, reading this book?" I flipped the pages and pulled out an envelope with *Loretta* written across the top. Katie opened it and began to read.

Dear Loretta,

Once you read this, I'll be two hours toward Tennessee.

It's time I stopped being a character. I want to know who I really am, who I was born to be. I think that starts with Mama. She was born in Tennessee, had a whole history there. But I don't know much about her besides birthright pie. So I'm going to go see where she grew up, see my mama's setting. I hired a man in the parking lot to drive me to Tennessee for two hundred dollars plus a tank of gas. Don't worry, I didn't steal that money from anybody but Daddy. When you go home you'll see I emptied his safe. I know the money is for emergencies, but lately my whole life has been an emergency.

Don't go to the police. I will be back before my court date. If they think I've skipped out on bail, I'll go to jail forever.

I will call in a couple of days. Hopefully, by then I'll know who I really am. Maybe I'll even become an iron skillet.

Love,
Pearl

P.S. Of course I stayed and watched Katie fly to Vegas. I wouldn't have left her alone. She said she'd have her mama call sometime tomorrow once she is settled.

Katie folded the letter back into the envelope. "Wow. You're so ... smart." Her words were flattering, but her eyes were cold and the corners of her mouth turned down.

"What's wrong then?" I asked.

"Nothing. It's just ... I guess I understand what you meant when you were telling me about Gretchen and the tree. Being smart isn't the same as being good. Loretta's heart is weak and—"

I shook my head. "She's an iron skillet."

"You sure she'll believe it?"

"She'll suspect I'm playacting some myth," I said. "So she'll go home and make sure I'm not there. Then she'll check the safe, see the missing cash, and realize I'm gone. I don't think she'll call the cops because she'd rather drive to Tennessee and haul me home herself. She knows the way, and she knows Mama's town. She won't figure out where I really am until after she talks to your mama and finds out you didn't get off the plane in Vegas. They can track our tickets with the credit card, but Alaska is a big state and...you know, I'm not even sure Loretta will want me back." I exhaled slowly. "You're right. I'm not good. I tried to be good once. It just didn't take with me."

"Are you ladies ready?" a stewardess asked. "The flight is boarding now."

Katie grabbed my hand. She was trembling. "We can be good in Alaska," she whispered, as we followed the stewardess. "Pearl, this don't feel real. Feels like a story."

"It is," I answered.

We were straight out of a storybook, two girls with Circus Room eyes bound for Alaska. I glanced over my shoulder, saw the large airport window offering one last look at Carolina, the setting of my people.

I remembered my final good-bye with Daddy. I wouldn't make that mistake again. There'd be no back turned, dismissive wave. Because when you really love something, an easy good-bye won't do.

I turned and held my arms out in a wide embrace, tears stinging my eyes as I saw my land like a storybook page, in watercolors with a burning sun smudged across the top.

"Everything okay?" the stewardess found me and asked. "Afraid to fly?"

This was the moment a writer would pause. If I had soaked up Daddy's lessons, I would have considered the consequences before boarding that plane. But I was just a fish, hooked on the line, desperate for a chance to swim away.

I forced a smile at the stewardess and followed her onto the plane. I took my seat and closed my eyes as my heart cried its new wish.

Alaska. Alaska. Alaska. Alaska!

Part Two
Settings

XXI

Finding food and shelter is never a runaway's greatest challenge. It's grown-ups, and all of their questions. Within the first minutes of arriving in Alaska, we realized we had to make more than one getaway. We had to live the art of escape.

And so, we plotted stories.

They're making Granddad's funeral plans today. They must be running late, we told the stewardess when she asked why our family wasn't waiting for us in the lobby. As she chatted with a coworker, we blended in with the crowd and hurried away.

Our parents took our baby sister to the hotel. It was a long flight, and she hasn't stopped screaming, we told the cab-driver when he asked why we were alone.

We asked the driver to take us to a wilderness store so that we could buy warmer gear. We bought everything the store clerk said we needed to survive an Alaskan winter—long wool underwear, parkas with negative degree ratings, boots, gloves, and a backpack for me. When she stared oddly at our pile of gear and watched us count out hundreds in cash to pay, we gave her an interesting plot to distract her.

Our parents are out testing the lighting conditions. If they get the right photos, they might land a spot in National Geographic. Oh... and they wanted us to ask, is it always this cloudy?

The cabdriver took us to a Holiday Inn that we had passed on the way to the store. We joyfully waved at a random couple in the parking lot. *Thank goodness,* we said. *They must have gotten our sister to nap.*

But the greatest challenge was convincing the hotel clerk to rent two kids a room. She raised an eyebrow as we approached. Katie carried a duct-taped duffel bag, and I had a backpack so crammed with wool underwear it was peeking out the top.

"We need a room for three, please. Our mama's in the car on crutches," I said.

The lady didn't budge, so I continued my story. "We went off the trail and she fell and broke her ankle. Took forever for the rescuers to get her back down. Maybe you saw something on the news? A crew with a camera came and said they might run a lunch hour piece about how tourists keep putting local rescuers at risk. She's in awful pain, so she sent us in with cash to pay."

"Daddy always said she's got more guts than brains." Katie laughed as she laid a stack of cash on the counter.

"And you all were hiking with her?" the lady asked.

"Yes, ma'am," Katie said pitifully. "My legs ache something fierce."

The lady glared. "Children should never be dragged up the mountains this time of year. Bear are sure to be looking for a last snack before hibernating." She sighed and shook her head. "Tourists should only come to

Alaska to see things from a distance. Look, but don't touch."

Katie mumbled a weak, "Yes, ma'am."

"She'll need a ground level room?" the lady asked.

I smiled. "That's real thoughtful, ma'am."

Victory. We had escaped Loretta and Vegas, gotten our gear, and now had a place to rest. We raced out to the parking lot. Katie ran to find our room, but I stopped. It was finally safe to pause, breathe, and see my new setting.

I only saw mountains. Sure there was a McDonalds, a bowling alley, and a line of traffic snaking into the Kmart across the street. But these were invisible blemishes. Because the mountains loomed over all, and they were everything Katie had promised—a totally different land. I'd hiked the Appalachians dozens of times, but these giants didn't rise from the mist of gentle foothills. They launched from the ground like warriors bent on conquering. Their tops didn't roll in sloped circles, but sliced through the sky like a shattered milk glass.

Katie yelled from across the lot and pointed to our room. I joined her, and once inside I collapsed on the bed. I had been running on will and adrenaline since the night of the talent show.

Katie unfolded a map.

"Here's where we were," she said and pointed to the lower right corner of the map. "And look at where we are." She pointed toward the upper left corner. "We made it to the top of the earth."

"But we can't stop," I mumbled as I worked to keep my eyes open. "People are the most dangerous thing... always asking questions..."

Katie pulled the covers around me. "You did real good, Pearl. Get some rest. You got us here. I'll keep us here."

When I awoke the next morning, the first thing I saw was a snow globe on the nightstand next to me. In the center was a little girl wearing pink ice skates. I picked it up and shook it, watched the glitter swirl. Faded letters were written on the bottom. *Happy Birthday Katherine!*

"Hey," Katie said as she held out her hand for the snow globe. "Give it."

I handed it back. "Where'd you get it?"

"Nowhere," she mumbled. "C'mon, get up. We slept past check-out time. Any minute they're gonna knock on our door and start asking questions."

Katie dressed and hurried out the door to stuff her bag with food from the free breakfast buffet. She returned smiling and opened her bag for me to see. There were apples, mini boxes of cereal, several bagels, and cartons of milk. She tossed me a bagel. "Eat up and let's go. Odds are Loretta and Mama are tracking our flight. Hotels will be the first place they look. I know somewhere safe. Getting to it though ..." She rummaged through her bag and pulled out a small canister.

"Pepper spray?" I asked. "Are we getting mugged?"

She handed me a printed flyer. *How to Survive a Bear Attack* was typed in bold letters across the top. "I'll never be the smarty-pants you are, but I've been studying up on this place for years. Trust me, this pepper spray might save our lives."

She called a cab while I read about the advantages of standing tall over playing dead, and about singing loudly to warn bears away. If all else failed, we had pepper spray.

When the cab came, I climbed in the back while Katie spoke to the driver. She handed him an envelope and pointed to the address at the top.

He traced a line on a map taped to his dash. "That's toward Denali, hours away. I'm a city cab."

"Name your price," Katie said.

The driver studied the map again, "Five."

"No way," I shouted and scrambled out.

Katie took the envelope back and walked over to me. "Get in."

"Five hundred dollars?" I whispered through gritted teeth. "After all we spent yesterday? We'll be out of money."

"We can't stay here. Even if Loretta didn't track us, we gotta get out of this city. You said it yourself, people are the most dangerous thing."

"Where are we going?" I asked. "What's that envelope?"

"He said it's just outside Denali—"

"*He* said? But what do *you* know?" I persisted.

"That you sound more like Aunt Loretta than my best friend."

Katie grabbed my backpack and tossed it in the cab along with her duffel bag. She climbed in the back seat and scooted over to make room. "Besides, we're headed straight into them mountains that you kept gawking at yesterday."

I bit my lip and crawled in next to her.

"Where are your parents?" the driver asked. His eyes were round and opaque, like dark brown beads. I saw misery and meanness floating in them. Katie must've seen it, too, because she didn't try and spin a story. You can never out-lie misery and meanness.

"You want five hundred dollars or not?" she barked.

As he drove us out of the city, Katie leaned back and dozed. But I was wide awake, staring at the mountains. I traced their jagged lines and my heart pounded. They were the most beautiful thing I'd ever seen. I wondered if that meant they were also the most dangerous.

Eventually, the road soared upward and we drove into a small town with just one street and a handful of stores. The driver parked and I nudged Katie awake. He pointed to a little cabin.

"That's not it," Katie said. "That's a post office."

The driver nodded. "Mail don't carry up. Roads neither. You'll have to hike."

"Where do we start?" she asked as we climbed out of the cab.

He pointed to a wooden trail marker and grinned meanly. "See you later, bear bait."

The cab disappeared back down the mountain, and we stood, awkwardly shuffling our bags and staring at the trail.

"So, this was the big plan, huh? You read about this place in one of your magazines or something?"

Katie turned toward the trail with determined steps.

"Hey," I called. "That paper said to sing."

She belted out one of the Top Forty songs that she had memorized back in the summer, and we hiked up and up until our calves throbbed. The trail was steep, winding, and poorly marked. Enormous trees crowded around us so thick that sometimes we could only hope we were still on the trail. My eyes searched for something familiar, but there were no maple, oak, or hickory trees. It was a wild Christmas forest with huge patches of giant evergreens.

Katie stopped and leaned against a tree. "You think that's bear scat?" she whispered and pointed to the ground.

"Maybe," I guessed. "You think it's nearby?"

The answer came from the woods below us. Something moved and rustled. I crouched low, like Loretta at the airport.

"Stop," Katie ordered. "Stand tall. If all else fails, play dead." She started hiking with a quick pace. When I didn't follow, she yelled back, "Move it and get to singing!"

I knew a few choruses from our summer lessons and hummed them off-key, but I couldn't string together more than a few words.

Katie groaned. "Bears ain't scared of humming. Don't you know a single real song?"

Daddy had a collection of folk and bluegrass songs that we listened to on road trips. He said working people used to tell their stories with songs instead of books. When I asked why, he talked about money and education, but I guessed another reason. These were stories about love and famine. The only way you could tell them without crying was to sing.

Katie sneezed and cursed the pines around us, and immediately, I knew the right song.

In the pines, in the pines,

Where the sun don't ever shine,

And you shiver when the cold wind blows.

Something crashed in the woods near us. We jumped and clutched each other.

"In the pines!" we shouted.

"In the pines!" we screamed.

But the noise came again and we bolted. Up and up, screaming about pine trees, until I collapsed to my knees. Katie leaned against the tree next to me.

"Not much farther," she gasped. "We passed marker five a while ago."

We caught our breath as we listened. We hadn't learned yet, that the wilderness is never silent. We jumped at every little noise. And within minutes we heard a crunching sound. This time it was closer than ever. Katie gripped her canister of pepper spray.

"Hey, Bear," she yelled. "I will burn your eyes out!"

The noise came again. I peeked around a tree and searched the woods behind us. "Don't spray," I cried.

I saw antlers, arced as wide as the tree trunks around us. I'd seen plenty of deer by the Yadkin, even a twelve-point buck once. But I had never imagined a creature so large and proud it wore a king's crown.

Katie peered around the tree. "Moose!"

He turned his head and looked in our direction. His antlers were larger than I first thought. More than a king's crown, they were the very castle itself.

The moose turned and walked deeper into the woods until he disappeared. But I didn't stop staring, hoping to see him again. That's when I noticed a faded piece of wood lying on the ground.

"What's that, a trail marker?" I asked. Katie stepped closer to examine it.

"Seven," she yelled. "It had fallen down. We had walked right past it."

Katie ran into the woods behind the marker. I followed her, but stopped when I noticed what had to be more bear scat.

"C'mon," she yelled from somewhere up ahead. "Hurry!"

As I pushed through the last stand of trees, I entered a clearing and saw a cabin built on the side of the mountain. It was shabby, but the view was rich. Milk glass mountains stretched in the distance and a brilliant sapphire sky was at our fingertips.

I asked Daddy once why Carolina colors weren't the gem-like blues and greens of the outer space earth. Daddy guessed it was shadows, blocking our view and dimming the brilliance. He said only those who traveled the far limits, like astronauts, could enjoy unobstructed beauty. As I stood on that mountain and stared at the view, I knew that he was right. And that I had traveled the far limits.

How did Katie know about this place?

"You've been here before," I guessed. "All that stuff about wanting to go to Alaska one day—you already had. You just wanted to come back. Right?"

Katie ignored me. She jumped up and down, her face pink with excitement. "This is it! This is it," she yelled. She ran around the cabin twice. "There's a shed of wood out back," she called. "And an outhouse and a well with a hand pump!" She ran to the front door and turned the knob. It was locked. "No worries, Mama taught me how to jimmy these." She dug through her duffel bag and pulled out her old school lunch card. She slid the card's edge into the space between the lock and the doorframe. "If I can just get this card under the bolt..." But thirty minutes later the door was still locked and the card was too bent to slide easily. She launched her shoulder into the door.

"I felt it budge," she said. "Help me."

We kicked and pushed the door until we were breathless and sore. It didn't open, and there were no windows to try. The sun was setting and the wind began to cut through our layers.

Katie swore under her breath and walked around to the back of the cabin. When she returned she carried a large ax.

"Found this by the woodpile," she said.

"You can't chop down the door. Let me have a shot at that card trick."

She handed me her bent card. I worked to ease it into the crack of the door frame. I slid it up and down carefully while Katie tried to twist the knob. It never turned.

"Pearl," she whispered. "You read that part about how bears are nocturnal? You know what that means?"

I dropped the card. "Start chopping."

She picked up the ax, but it was too heavy for her to lift high or swing hard. The wood above the knob barely dented after the first blow. She swung five more times and managed to carve a small line in the door.

She handed me the ax. "It's like trying to bust rock."

My mind flashed with memories of Loretta's hammer and skillet lesson. *I'll break you,* I promised the door. Over and over, I swung while chips of woods began to fly. Katie took another turn. We switched back and forth as the door began to give way.

It was completely dark now, except for a bit of moonlight. The air around us was freezing, but we were sweaty from our work. We stopped being careful where we aimed and swung wildly at the door. With one final blow, the wood split and a huge section busted out. The doorknob fell off and the door crashed open.

Katie dropped the ax and we stepped inside the dark cabin. We bumped and scooted our way around, feeling blindly for anything that might be useful. After several minutes of rummaging, Katie squealed and a beam of light glowed. She pointed the light toward the fireplace. "There's another one."

She handed me a flashlight and shined hers around. There was only one room with a couch, a chair, and some shelves in the back. There was no electricity, but the fireplace was large and had skillets hanging around it. A box of matches was on the hearth.

I shivered. "Let's get a fire."

With our flashlights in hand we went back out to the woodshed. We each carried in as big a log as our arms could hold and heaved them into the fireplace. While I shined the light, Katie lit a match and tossed it into the hearth. The flame immediately went out.

"We need some kind of starter, like paper," I said, remembering Daddy's fires. Far from an outdoorsman, he had few wilderness skills. But he loved to write by a glowing fireplace, and often began his fires with disappointing pages.

Katie went to her duffel and pulled out the *How to Survive a Bear Attack* flyer. "You need to read this again?"

I shook my head. "I got it down."

She twisted the paper, laid it beneath the logs, and held a match to it. Beautiful orange flames lit up the hearth.

"Ahhh," I said. "That's it."

But the paper burned to ash in seconds. Thick white coils of smoke twisted off the logs and filled the room with an even muskier scent, but there were no flames or warmth. We searched the room and found an old magazine in the corner. We packed several pages around the logs and lit them all. They burned bright and warm for seconds, but always twisted into ash before the wood caught fire. I shivered again and looked up to see the front door still swinging open. Arctic wind poured into the cabin.

"We've gotta fix that," I said.

We pushed the couch against the door to hold it closed. Then we sank to the floor and leaned our backs against the couch. I pulled down an old blanket and covered us with it. With the door shut and the blanket around us, the cabin felt warmer. But the door was still busted, and the outside air would always creep in.

"Wish we could have a fire," Katie whimpered. "Never knew it was so hard." She started laughing.

"What's so funny?" I asked.

"Nothing... it's just... maybe we ain't as smart as we thought. You can quote Shakespeare and I know what's cool, but we can't start a fire with matches and wood."

She reached into her duffel and pulled out two apples.

"Let's save the batteries," she said, nodding toward our flashlights. "Can't be much longer before morning."

I switched off my light and the cabin turned black. Katie ate her apple quickly, ravenously, but I held mine to try and warm it first. My mind wandered to dangerous thoughts. About my old warm bed. About barbecue and hushpuppies.

"Katie," I whispered, to distract myself. "Tell me about this place. I know you've been here before."

When she didn't answer, I switched on my light to look at her. She was asleep, with the apple core still gripped in her hand. I was wide-awake and miserable. I tried to focus on making plans for the next day. I imagined new strategies to build a fire. I planned ways to repair the door. But instinctively, I knew Alaska would not submit to my plots. It wrote its own poem.

Look but don't touch. Look but don't touch, the hotel lady had warned. We had done much more than touch. We had plunged headfirst. I raised the apple to my mouth and took a bite. My teeth sank into frozen flesh, and the cold pierced my teeth with pain. A gust of wind burst through the door and another chunk of wood fell to the ground.

I crouched under the blanket and tried to distract myself by remembering the glory of the milk glass mountains all around me. But instead of feeling soothed, an old memory surfaced.

Of all Mama's dishes, milk glass was my favorite. It was an opaque white, but not dull. Without any glitter or obvious sparkle, the glass glistened. Once, I dropped a large pitcher. While Loretta ran around fussing about the mess, I laid flat on my tummy and stared eye-level at all the pieces shining across our walnut floor. I cupped a milky triangle, glowing in my palm.

"You can't replace your mama's things," Loretta huffed. "You get careless and break 'em all and you'll have nothing to remember her by." I gripped my glowing triangle and started to leave the room. "Watch out," Loretta warned. "This glass will gouge you." I carefully stepped around all the large, jagged pieces. But some hidden, tiny sliver sliced my foot. A trail of blood smeared across the floor. Loretta screamed and startled me so that my hands curled into tight fists. I cried out with pain as my palms flung open. My milk glass triangle tumbled to the floor.

I reached to pick it up but stopped when I saw it. Instead of pearly beauty, it glistened with my blood.

The Heart-Shaped Museum

Stella dreamed in black and white, the accidental colors of her wedding.

As a girl, she'd imagined a pink wedding in spring, when the trees were covered in a mist of baby green instead of a full frock of leaves. She'd carry pink rosebuds and bloom like an Easter lily in white silk, with a veil that trailed the length of the church.

But Stella's rosebud dreams stayed on Mayfield Hill. Abel hitched a ride south to a new mill town. They rode for hours in the back of a cotton delivery truck, until they came to a little church.

As the driver parked along the road, he yelled back to them that he'd only wait twenty minutes. Abel ran and knocked on the parsonage door and paid a small sum for the preacher to quickly marry them. But when the preacher and his wife led them to the front door of the church, Abel stepped back.

"How about we go to that field?" he asked, and pointed behind the church.

The preacher laughed. "That's our graveyard. Don't reckon you want to marry among the dead."

Abel shook his head. "Then how about the one across the road?"

"Ain't church property."

"Oh, come on now," the preacher's wife said. "You know that's ol' Roby's field, and he won't mind at all. Come Sunday morning all the little ones play hide-and-seek in it after church and he's never said nothing. Let me run get a lantern." She grabbed Stella's hand. "You come with me, honey."

She led Stella inside the parsonage and rummaged through a closet until she found the lantern. "Wait here," she said and left the room. When she returned she carried an armful of white flowers.

"From my snowball bush." She smiled. "Biggest blooms we've had in years."

The flowers were shaped in round, heavy clusters. They weren't delicate like lilies and rosebuds, but they smelled of summer. The preacher's wife pinched individual blooms from a cluster and tucked them around Stella's hair until she wore a snowball crown.

She handed Stella more snowball clusters to carry, and they hurried out to the field. Abel pressed down a barbed-wire fence with his boot and helped Stella climb over it. The preacher pointed to a dirt path.

"I know a pretty spot," he said and led them deep into the field until they couldn't see the road or church anymore. The preacher's wife held the lantern up when they stopped, and Stella held her breath as she looked around. She'd climbed in the back of that delivery truck, excited and determined to marry Abel. She knew he'd be a wonderful husband, and that was all she focused on. She'd never imagined that her runaway wedding could be beautiful.

But cotton bloomed all around them, like a field of a thousand wedding bouquets.

The night was deep black, but the sky was dotted with stars shining like cotton bolls in the sky. The flame of the lantern shimmered off the snow buds tucked in Stella's hair. It was a black-and-white wedding. It was starlight and fire, cotton and snow, in the middle of July. *Pink* could never compare.

For the first time in his life, Abel didn't notice the fields. His eyes stayed on Stella and her crown of snow. He'd lived his whole life having less—eating less, learning less, expecting less. Somehow he'd won a love that was *more.*

"You step back twenty paces," the preacher's wife ordered Stella. "And I'll sing you down the aisle. Is there a hymn you prefer?"

Stella shook her head. She knew Mozart far more than church hymns.

"That's all right. I've got one that suits my voice best."

As Stella walked away from the group, a soft soprano voice broke the silence and began to call her back. *It is well, it is well, it is well with my soul,* the preacher's wife sang. Abel wondered at the choice. He'd only heard it at funerals before. But then Stella stepped toward him and his heart shouted, *It is well with my soul.*

Their vows were simple. They promised to love in good times and bad. Then the preacher placed his hands over theirs and asked them to repeat a Psalm.

"The Lord is the portion of my inheritance and my cup; You support my lot. The lines have fallen to me in pleasant places. Indeed my heritage is beautiful to me."

Who would have ever thought *lines* could be pleasant, Abel wondered, as the sweet words tumbled from his mouth. He thought about the lines that once sliced through his life. Even there, in the middle of his cotton field wedding, painful memories from Jack's funeral flashed inside him. But as he looked at Stella, he knew the Psalm was true. Without him ever expecting it, his lines had fallen in pleasant places.

Somewhere in the dark distance, a horn honked. The preacher quickly pronounced them husband and wife. As the horn honked again they thanked the preacher and ran back to the truck.

Within the hour they were settled in a mill shack. Since they'd come "fresh off the road," the Boss said they couldn't be picky. They had to take the house as offered, without fuss or inspection. The ceiling was mildewed and the floor had rotting boards. Abel promised a better house soon. "Boss probably thinks we don't plan to stay more than the night," he explained. "So he gave us a shack that ain't fit for living." Even with the mildew, Stella had no regrets. She believed Abel's promise of a better house. She was young enough to think that because she had chosen love, one day she would win it all.

That was the night Stella began to dream in black and white. As she slept, she saw piano keys and sheet music, the treasure she'd left behind. She saw newspaper print, black words stamped across a white page. She saw a black sky dotted with cotton stars, snowballs in her hands, and Psalms in her mouth. She saw lint, falling down from a burned up sky. She had laughed and called it Dixie snow. *No*, her mama said. *Ashes.*

She woke to the sound of the mill whistle, opened her eyes, and sat up. Abel came, bringing a mug of coffee.

"Lady next door was kind enough to share a cup," he said as he gently stroked her back.

Stella drank it quickly, the Boss had been clear that if they were going to ask for a free house after suppertime, they had better not be late to the morning shift. She followed Abel out the door and down a new Linthead Road to the mill. She stood in the new hire line with him, waiting on the Boss to inspect her and assign her a room.

Abel coached her on what to say. "Don't say you don't got skills. Remember, you spent part of your childhood in the mill."

The Boss ordered Abel to the weaving room once he heard his experience, but Stella was assigned to the carding room.

"She's got nimble fingers, sir," Abel protested. "She plays piano like nobody else. She could tie those threads quicker than anybody in the spinning room."

"She ain't ever worked the new machines though," the Boss replied. "She'll start as a carder."

It's fine, Stella mouthed to Abel, as the line moved forward. She was surprised to be hired at all. They stepped inside the mill and parted ways down different halls. Stella grinned as she walked to the carding room.

She felt free, even though she would work for the next ten hours. She felt rich, because the money she earned would be hers. She wasn't a silly garden party girl anymore. She was a Weaver. She was linthead.

Stella had been taught that working women were to be pitied. Yet growing up, she played waitress and maid far more than princess. She lined her best dressed dolls in a row, and instead of hosting the tea party, she served it. Sometimes the dolls were rude and had impossible demands. But little Stella persevered, and her labor was rewarded. Two pennies, a fine tip pulled from her piggy bank, always magically appeared beneath the scattered stack of plastic dishes.

Let's play pretend, was the only experience that Stella had with hard work. Inside the carding room, she quickly learned that while earning a living might make her free, sometimes freedom is miserable. She knew there'd be lint. Stuck in her clothes and in her hair. What she hadn't expected was carding room lint. Clouds of lint filled up her nose and throat, choking her, making her hoarse. By the end of the first week she had learned to breathe through gritted teeth, swish, and spit the lint onto the concrete floor.

She hadn't expected the heat either. With motors running full blast in July, the room was ninety degrees by noon. She couldn't take a break just because she needed one. She had to take her breaks when ordered. Every afternoon she'd become so light-headed she'd fall down on the nasty floor while lint stormed down upon her.

Her hands cramped. Her fingers twisted in painful knots from the repetitive motion and dehydration. She could play any musical masterpiece from memory, but by late afternoon she struggled to push a sheet of cotton in the carding machine.

It's not supposed to be like this, she thought a hundred times that first week. She'd spent her childhood going to the mill, to bring her daddy a message from home or when he gave tours to a congressman. She'd seen grim faces and discontented eyes, but this level of misery was shocking.

Hadn't she chosen love? Surely love, all those sweet nights with Abel, would eventually make her work an easy thing to bear. But the hard days didn't end, and Stella learned that love does not stop misery. In her case, love had beckoned it.

Life outside of the mill was as sweet as her little girl dreams. In the evenings they scouted out fishing holes and Abel taught her how to cast a line. Soon Stella learned the joys of a poor man's summer feast, with fresh-caught fried trout, killed greens, and hot blackberry dumplings splashed with milk. They went to mill church on Sundays. It was Stella's idea, and Abel watched her more than the preacher. He saw the way she leaned forward and gripped the pew whenever the music began.

Stella had grown up attending the downtown Presbyterian, where the organ wailed while the congregation chanted lines from an embroidered hymnal. She'd been trained to say *How beautiful* after every service. Anything less was sin. But secretly she worried that God didn't have an ear for music.

Inside mill church, people gave their music like an offering. There was no embroidered hymnal. There was just a movement that swelled, leading them through one old song into the next. As soon as Stella learned most of the words, she joined the choir. She sang "I'll Fly Away" every Sunday, and for a few precious minutes wondered if she already had.

Abel paid a half-dollar and his best fishing rod in trade to a mill church deacon for his old violin. Stella had never had a lesson or touched a string, but soon she started running home from the mill, instead of trudging from exhaustion. She'd kiss Abel, put a skillet on the stove to heat up grease to fry supper, and sit on the floor and play her fiddle. More than one mess of fish was burned black, but Stella was mapping out all sorts of melodies. Mozart and Beethoven danced with "I'll Fly Away" and "It is Well."

As summer ended, Stella began to cough. Abel insisted that she quit the mill. But Stella always ended up back in the carding room. Abel was panicked with worry of lint lung. *It's the curse of the carding room,* his mama had chanted as his daddy lay dying. He bribed a boss with a week's worth of free overtime to have Stella moved to the spinning room. Stella only spent one day there though, and then asked to be moved back to the carding room.

"Don't you know it's cursed," Abel shouted. "That room kills people. Why did you go back? I had you moved out, free and clear. Why, Stella?"

She almost lied and said *it's easier.* She even thought of making an Abraham Linton workers' rights speech. But of all the instincts that pulsed inside her, the most basic was her trust in him. And so she handed Abel her secret and watched his eyes to see the truth of what he thought.

"The music."

"We go to church for music. I bought you a fiddle. The carding room ain't no dance party."

Stella shook her head. "I'm not dancing. I'm listening."

What Stella longed for, maybe her whole life, was something all her own that could rise above a disappointing earth. She had tried before. Had a whole notebook of stops and starts on the shelf back at her daddy's home. Nothing ever made it past an opening line or two. She could play the work of any other, but she could not compose.

But inside the carding room, things began to change. It was something about the frenzy of sounds. The wail of the whistle announcing lunch, the clicking of the gears, the hum of the motors, the whir of the cotton being torn and stretched. As her hands fed cotton into the machines, her mind mapped each rhythm, each pitch. She wasn't just finding music. She was living in it.

"I've never been able to write," she confessed. "I've always felt this urge to, and sometimes I'd try, but every time I'd end up pulling out Mozart. Why work hard to make something new when I had the best at my fingers? But in the carding room, I can."

It's easier, would have been the simpler speech. *Workers' rights,* a more noble one. But Stella wasn't a little girl playing pretend. She dreamed in black and white now, not blush pink. And she had learned that pain and survival, love and misery, could be twisted together as smooth as a bobbin of cotton.

Inside the carding room, as Stella sat coughing and light-headed on a nasty floor, she found a reward far more precious than two shiny tea party pennies. Love was not going to kiss her wounds. It was going to make a song from them.

XXII

"Mornin'," Katie said as she gently shook my shoulder. "Guess where you're at, sleepyhead?"

I blinked my eyes open and stared at the room around me. The night before, the cabin had been a dark cave to hide in. In the morning light, it was much more. Katie began surveying everything and calling out her discoveries.

"Some cans of food and a can opener. I'll open some soup."

She found two mugs and divided the soup between them. She handed me a mug and I took a sip of icy soup.

"Bleh." Katie grimaced. "I went to a restaurant once where they served this fancy cold soup. People all around me ordered it, and I thought they were crazy. Now look at me." She sighed. "We have to get the fire going. Eat up so we can get started."

"You've got a story that needs telling first," I said.

Katie raised her eyebrows, in *Who me?* fashion.

I nodded. "You told me Alaska was your storybook, and that you knew of a place, but you never said you had a home here."

She took a long, slow sip of her soup, like she was hiding behind the mug.

"Katie," I pressed. "I've got to know."

She went to her duffel bag and pulled out the envelope that she had showed the cabdriver.

"I found this when I was seven. Along with that snow globe and a dozen other cards. They were hidden inside a shoe box at the bottom of Mama's closet. I could barely read, was just in first grade and sounding out letters. But I loved that snow globe, and my name was on the bottom so I knew it was mine. I set it on the nightstand by my bed and took this one letter too. I put it under my pillow hoping I could figure out the words before second grade. Mama saw that snow globe, yelled at me for snooping, and next time I went into her closet that shoe box was clear empty. But I kept this. She don't know I ever had it." She handed me the envelope and I pulled a letter out.

Dear Katherine,

I can't believe you are four! I remember the day we brought you home from the hospital. You nearly fit in the palm of my hand. And now you are a big girl.

Hopefully your mother will let me fly you out here this summer. If she does, Katiebug, we'll have a real Alaskan adventure. Me and Uncle John bought a cabin in the mountains where we can vacation during the summer. I am writing you from the cabin right now. It's far away from the city, and I have the best view. On a clear day, I can see Denali.

When I first got here before the thaw, there was a frozen wood frog by the front door. He was gone the next morning, and I can't help but wonder if he came back to life. I've heard that they can. If you come to visit, I'll let you name the wood frogs.

I hope you have a wonderful birthday.

I love you,
Daddy

I handed the letter to Katie. "But you said your daddy ran off with another woman and lives in New Hampshire."

Katie shrugged. "Mama's a liar."

"You never got any more letters?"

"No. I asked Mama about him a few times. She said he'd run out on us, and I needed to quit trying to drag him back." She walked to the back of the cabin. "I'm gonna dig through this trunk. There's a pair of snowshoes laying on top."

Katie's a liar, same as her mama, I thought. The first time I met Katie she declared she had her own storybook page framed in icicles and sparkling with snow. But her story wasn't about Alaska. It was about a long lost daddy.

I imagined Katie's daddy sitting in the cabin, writing by firelight. A memory of my own daddy sparked inside me. *We're all liars,* I thought. Spinning stories around our daddies, but never about them.

"Can you go study the woodpile?" Katie called.

"Study it?" I asked, confused.

Katie nodded. "It's gonna take more than just any piece of wood. Find the driest pieces you can." She was kneeling at the hearth, with her hand on the logs we only managed to smoke the night before. "These are damp."

I stepped outside. The view was shiny with beauty and something more. Like a great secret was just beyond my reach.

"You okay?" Katie called from the door.

"Yeah."

I walked to the woodpile, and in the daylight, discovered all the logs were soaked through and covered with a spongy fungus. We were going to have to chop our own wood. I went back to the cabin and grabbed the ax by the front door and headed to the edge of the woods. My muscles were sore from chopping the night before, and I struggled to lift the ax above my hip. I found a low branch and took a weak swing.

"Defense! Defense! Gooooooo defense!" came a cry behind me. I jumped and turned around. Katie was standing with her arms raised and her fingers waving with cheer spirit.

"What are you doing?" I groaned as I tried to lift the ax again.

"I'm tired of singing away bear." Katie grinned. "But I can cheer all day."

I kept chopping and managed to bust up a small pile of wood while Katie cheered for me to *Be Aggressive!* Katie scooped up the chips of bark that flew off while I was chopping, and some small sticks that were already on the ground.

One hour and several wasted matches later, we had our first fire. We learned that soaking wet logs will never burn. Green, fresh chopped logs will, eventually. Dead wood, the smaller dry sticks that Katie scooped off the ground, catches quickly. And nothing sparks a flame as well as dried out pine needles.

We jumped and yelled in celebration. Soon, the cabin was filled with warmth, and we took our coats off for the first time since crawling out of the taxi. Katie opened a can of beans and poured them in a skillet to lay in the fire. We scooped hot beans into our mouths with our hands, since we couldn't find spoons. They were unseasoned, but they filled us with rich warmth. Loretta's pintos and cornbread never seemed so delicious.

With our bellies full and our bodies warm, we curled up on the ends of the couch and slept. When I woke up, the sun was setting and the fire was just glowing embers. Katie was still asleep, but I hurried and tried to rekindle the fire with the few small sticks we had left. There wasn't enough wood to get a lasting flame though, so I put my coat back on, grabbed the ax, and shuffled back to the edge of the woods.

I couldn't get a firm grip on the ax handle with my gloves on, so I chopped bare-handed. My palms throbbed as a row of blisters swelled across them. Night was coming, and the front door wasn't fixed. We needed lots of wood.

I was an angry woodchopper. Mad at the ax for how heavy it was. Mad at the cold for how unrelenting it was. Mad at Katie for sleeping soundly and not taking a turn. Mad at the fire because it would always be hungry, always need feeding. Mad at the tree for how hard it was to break.

So many times I had pretended to be a castaway, a lost pioneer, or starving Persephone. These were pretty daydreams, where misery—being cold and hungry—was a beautiful, noble plot.

The blisters on my palms burst and began to bleed. It became difficult to grip the bloody ax handle. I kicked the tree in frustration, and with a roar of anger and pain I swung wildly. Bark began to fly from the force of my blows. I chopped enough branches to last the night and then looked at my scorching palms. No matter what the pretty stories insisted, misery was not beautiful. It just hurt. I held my palms into the wind. Alaska kissed and cooled them. I looked at my pile of split branches on the ground. *That* was beautiful.

We spent a week focused on fire, with our days anchored by chopping wood. Katie chopped wood in the morning and I chopped in the evening. In between, we carried off the rotting woodpile and began a fresh one. Katie kept her gloves on, so that her hands were never hurt like mine. Soon my wounds were replaced with thick calluses, and my hands gripped the ax handle firmly. I chopped twice as fast as Katie.

We worked to keep the fire burning so that we wouldn't use any more matches. I slept fitfully at night, scared that I wouldn't wake to tend the fire.

I found a hammer in the cabin and searched for nails to repair the front door. When I didn't find any, I draped the patchwork blanket from the couch over the busted boards. It made a decent barrier, but when the wind blew strong it danced in the air like a patchwork flag.

We counted cans of food and matches, but we didn't count days. We let them blur in a mix of exhaustion and celebration. Each day was an accomplishment. Every day that we didn't use a match, that we increased our woodpile, and that we didn't get eaten by a bear, was a victory. We didn't speak of the things we missed, like a bed, television, or pizza. We were not heroes blazing across the pages of an Alaskan storybook wilderness. On a good day, we were fire-building runaways. On a hard one, we were scared little girls.

"We've got to talk about food," I said, once the danger of freezing seemed conquered. "We can make the matches last, but we're eating four cans of food a day. I'm always hungry, but at this rate we only have enough for a few more weeks."

"We could go down the trail to that town. See if we can buy supplies," Katie suggested. "But we'll get asked a bunch of questions."

I nodded. "What about the fishing rods in the trunk? Whoever left them, must know there's fish nearby."

"We'd have to go back into the woods."

"Which do we fear more, people or bears?" I asked.

The next morning, we woke up, split a can of peaches, and dressed in all of our winter gear. I packed a flashlight, some matches, and two cans of beans in my backpack.

"Where do you want to go?" Katie asked as we set off into the woods.

I pointed up the mountain. "Farther."

Katie walked behind me cheering "Two bits, four bits, six bits a dollar! If you're a Gamecock stand up and holler!" But I focused on mapping the new setting all around me. The first thing I noticed is that we weren't only in the pines. Just like the trees in Carolina had different shapes and textures, so did the evergreens of Alaska. Some of their needles were long and sharp, while others were short and silky. Some had a few large cones while others had hundreds of tiny ones. I collected small branches and cones from half a dozen trees and tucked them in my backpack.

A huge bird swooped above the trees. I grabbed Katie's sleeve and ordered her to hush. We'd seen similar birds soaring by Seven and guessed they were eagles. We heard its call, more like a shout, so different than the mourning dove's song in Carolina. Katie tapped my shoulder and handed me a long brown feather. I tucked it in my backpack next to the evergreens.

It wasn't long before the sun started to dim. The days were quickly getting shorter and we turned back so that we wouldn't get lost in the dark. Back at Seven, we had to use a match to build a fire. While we heated a can of beans, I laid the eagle feather and evergreens in a row across the shelf. I peeled the label from a bean can and used a pen we'd found in the trunk to record my samples. I didn't know their real names, so I gave them new ones. *The Green Soldier* for the leaves that looked like little swords. *Thirty Shekels* for the tree that had little clusters of tiny berries tucked beneath the leaves. *Stella's Pine* for the tree with the silkiest leaves, because Grandma Stella loved cotton best, but she'd been born for silk.

Katie stared at my bean can label. "You writing poems 'bout these twigs?"

I shook my head. "Labeling our setting."

"It's just a bunch of pines. What's the big deal? C'mon, let's eat."

The big deal was that on the morning I met Katie, she promised Alaska was totally different than Carolina. I was discovering—documenting—how right she was.

On the third day, after hiking deep into the woods, we heard the sound of water. We followed it down a slope until the trees cleared and revealed a wide stream. The water was deep but clear to the bottom. It moved quickly and caps of white churned around the rocks.

"Two Bits, Four Bits, Six Bits, a Dollar," Katie screamed.

I startled and shoved her on the shoulder. "Hush ..."

Katie scowled. "Streams are the most dangerous place of all. Bear love fish more than anything." She pointed at the ground. "See that?" It was a pile of fresh scat. I turned and looked uneasily into the woods.

"I thought they'd be hibernating by now," I said.

"The meanest always hang around for a last-minute snack. This stream is where they'd get it." Katie raised her arms in a victory salute, ready to cheer. We trudged back to Seven for the night, but pulled out the fishing rods and tackle box from the trunk. I studied the collection of hooks, little tufts of feathers, and colored jelly bits.

I was worried. "We don't know what we're doing."

"We'll be fine," Katie assured me. "We're smart girls, remember?"

"That's what we thought about building a fire too."

Katie peered inside the tackle box. "Well I remember some of that stuff. I've gone fishin' before."

I raised my eyebrows. "Your Skatey Lady mama took you fishin'?"

Katie laughed. "Mama always goes crazy for her boyfriends' hobbies. When she dated a baseball player, she became obsessed with the Braves. When she dated a Nascar fan, she bought herself a bunch of *Number Three* shirts. And when she dated a man who liked to fish, she made me stay up late figuring out how to get a worm on a hook. We were all going fishin' the next day and she'd done told him that she loved it even better than skating. Putting that worm on the hook was gross, but we managed, and she thought we were prepared. Turns out fishin' has a lot more to it than worms. I don't know why folks like to talk like it's some peaceful thing. It's more like plates spinning in the air, there's all sorts of things to stay focused on. You got knots in the line, casting close to trees without getting tangled, and then how do you know if a fish is really nibbling your bait or if your hook is just caught in weeds? Twenty minutes in and Mama's mascara was running from all the sweating, and I was missing her Nascar days where all we had to do was sit on the couch, eat Cheetos, and pray for Dale to win. I think she missed it, too, because soon she was on to a new guy who loved golf. That was a fun one. I got to ride in the cart and Mama got to wear short skirts. But I remember this much from our day of fishin', of all of the plates spinning in the air, the most important one is if you feel a nibble, give it a jerk. That sets the hook deep in their mouths. Otherwise, you done lost your bait with no fish to show."

We spent days fruitlessly fishing. We burned through ten matches at Seven because the fire was out and the cabin freezing by the time we returned. We never thought of giving up though. We were too ravenous. The idea of fresh fish, the hope of having a full belly, stirred up a frenzied determination. Over and over we cast our rods and pulled tangled line from the rocks. All while singing and cheering as we kept watch for bears. Eventually we realized that we had to weigh the line down so that the current didn't drag it downstream and knot it. Once we were casting well and our lines weren't in the rocks, it wasn't long until Katie felt a tug.

She screamed, jerked the rod, and began reeling her line in with an awkward, desperate motion.

"I can't hold it," she yelled. "It's a fighter!"

I laid down my rod and ran to help hold hers steady while she reeled. The fish flopped out of the water a few times.

"Get it!" I cried.

Instead of reeling, Katie ran backward, dragging the fish toward land. Soon she was back in the woods, and the fish flopped near shore. I reached down and grabbed it, held it up for her to see. She ran to me, beaming and hollering.

"Wooohooo!" we screamed and jumped.

Katie cradled the fish in her arms, and I stroked it's smooth, slippery skin. It was like touching a rainbow. It had a dark green upper ridge, a silvery side flecked with speckles, and a shining white belly. I saw the metal hook slicing through its flesh, the fishing line stretching from its mouth. I watched it flap, so desperate to escape.

"What's wrong with you?" Katie asked. "Why are you blubbering?"

I wiped away my tears. "Nothing ... only ... it's so hard to be hooked ... and it's too pretty to eat."

"Everything is pretty here," Katie said. "We won't catch an ugly fish. Besides, I bet pretty fish are more delicious."

I carried our poles home to the cabin, and Katie carried the fish. She laid it by the fireplace.

"Found this stuffed under the couch cushion," she said as she pulled out a book. "It has all sorts of things about Alaskan animals. Let's see if we can figure out what kind of fish it is."

We turned to a section on fish and studied the pictures. We pointed to the same one.

"That's it," Katie said. "And, in my defense for dragging it in, read what it says right there, 'it's a very lively fish to catch.' I'll say, that sucker tugged so hard I thought I was catching a shark."

I looked at the name beneath it. "Dolly Varden. I know her! She's in a Dickens novel. A pretty girl, a flirt that likes flashy clothes." I looked at the fish with its green ridge and speckled side and laughed. "She wore a green dress with dots on it."

"Well, flirty Dolly, I bet you'll be delicious," Katie said to the fish. "Grab that knife on the shelf."

We carried the fish outside. My stomach tightened when Katie made the first cut.

"I don't know what I'm doing," she admitted as she stuck her hand inside the fish's belly. "But I know we don't want to eat guts."

I gagged and turned my back until Katie rinsed the blood away from the meat and her hands. With the fish rinsed clean, I scraped the scales from the skin. Then we laid the pink filets on our skillet and carried it to the fireplace.

The smell of fresh roasting meat, after so many days of canned beans and soup, was delicious. We had only allowed ourselves half a can of peaches for breakfast that morning. So we took the leftovers and emptied them around the fish. It made a lovely skillet of food, with strips of pink meat next to sunny peaches floating in juice.

I took a bite. "Oh, wow."

We scraped the skillet clean and tossed the fish bones into the fire. Katie grinned and pointed at the hearth. "See that?"

I looked closely and saw a can just inside the edge of the fire.

"Found that can of sweet milk on the shelf. Big Jamie, my grandma's helper, loved hot caramel and ice cream. He normally bought the jarred stuff at the grocery. But once, they were out, so he bought sweet milk. He said you just gotta cook it long enough ... and I put it in the fire before we cleaned the fish. Wanna see?"

We opened the can and saw golden, warm caramel. We each stuck in a finger and quickly popped it in our mouths. After so many days without dessert, it tasted better than any banana pudding I'd ever eaten. We passed the can back and forth, scraping out the caramel with our fingers. I leaned back on the couch and sighed happily. It had been so long since I had felt satisfied. The cabin was toasty warm, and my belly was content with fish and caramel.

I pulled three small silver scales out of my pocket and laid them on the shelf next to the evergreen samples. I scribbled *Dolly Varden* across the back of the canned peaches label and laid it beneath the scales.

Katie was on the couch, nearly asleep. I added wood to the fire and curled on the other end. I closed my eyes and as my body relaxed into sleep, I saw Dickens, knocking on our patchwork door. *Well done,* he said when I told him about our fish. He spied the can of hot caramel and asked for a taste.

I startled awake and jumped from the couch. I grabbed the peach can label and crossed out *Dolly Varden.* I wrote, *Supper with Charles Dickens.*

It didn't occur to me, yet, that I was writing. Daddy had promised that I was a writer, but I could never find my own stories in his library or classroom. Those places were already brimming with beautiful stories that belonged to someone else.

But I was beginning to find my own. They were sitting on my supper plate and knocking on my patchwork door. Alaska might kill me with its bears, its cold, and its daily hunger. But it was giving me a gift I never knew I needed. My own page.

XXIII

Our days settled into predictable routines. We chopped wood every morning and gathered dry pine needles to store in empty bean cans. Once we'd cut enough wood for the day, plus extra for the woodpile, we ate breakfast. Usually, it was leftover fish from the night before. We'd set the skillet with leftovers outside for it to freeze and stay fresh. In the morning we'd reheat it. We rarely opened a can of food. We saved those for the days we didn't have fish.

After lunch, we hiked to the stream. We never learned how to reel in our catch. Whenever we tried, we'd lose the fish. So we stuck with Katie's method of running backwards into the woods to drag the fish to shore. It was messy, haphazard fishing, but it kept us fed. We ate fish until we swore through stuffed mouths that one day we'd never eat another.

We weren't starving, but we were skinny and our legs cramped during hikes. Our bodies constantly yearned for foods out of reach. We forbid ourselves to speak of them, but my thoughts were filled with hushpuppy dreams.

We had lost all comfort—things like hot showers, beds, and a change of clothes. But we never spoke of going home, and we never whined about how difficult life was. We did whatever we needed to get through a day. I even took my precious eagle feather and cut it into little bits, like I found inside the tackle box, so that we could have extra bait.

The days were changing though, and I worried about the new challenges winter would bring. The woods grew strangely silent, and we rarely heard the calls of eagles. The sky became fickle. One minute it was bright and clear, letting us easily perform our chores. The next minute, the snow was so thick and pelting we had to blink swiftly to keep it from stinging our eyes. Katie started wearing the snowshoes, but I couldn't figure out how to walk in them without tripping. Each afternoon we turned back toward Seven earlier than the day before, as the light began to fade. Katie said that soon, there wouldn't be any light at all. We worried the woods would all look the same in the dark. So I carried the ax one day as we walked to the stream and stopped to chop *X*s deep into the trunks of trees to mark our path.

"Good news is, once the light is gone, the bears are definitely gone too," Katie said.

I was looking forward to not having to worry about bears. They had been on our minds since that first morning at the Holiday Inn. They were the reason Katie cheered and kept the pepper spray gripped in her palm. They were the reason we jumped anytime we heard a noise in the woods. But we had never seen one, even though the stream had piles of scat around it.

One afternoon as I stepped into the stream's clearing, Katie grabbed my arm and jerked me back. I started to wrestle free until I saw her face and what she was looking at. *Bear tracks.*

They were enormous, nearly twelve inches long, scattered down the muddy bank. I thought about how big the bear's jaws must be.

"Back... up...," Katie whispered.

We edged into the covering of the trees. A branch broke somewhere behind us. We both jumped and Katie grabbed my arm with a rough grip.

"*Do... not... run,*" she ordered through gritted teeth.

She flipped off the safety of the pepper spray can and raised it. "If anything charges I'm gonna spray and then we play dead."

Play dead? I shook my head. *I'm running.* She squeezed my arm so hard it throbbed.

Somewhere to our right, branches crashed together. Katie's eyes were wild and her thumb tapped the pepper spray trigger like she was anxious to fire. I looked in the direction she stared.

Fear, like lightning, pulsed from the crown of my head to my toes. My legs buckled and I sank. The bear was huge. From my spot on the ground he seemed as big as a car. How could we have ever believed a junior varsity cheer could scare it away? How could we think pepper spray could protect us?

The bear splashed in the stream like he was playing. He romped clumsily in the shallows, occasionally sticking his face in the water or spinning his body toward the rocks. Soon, he plunged his head beneath the water and came up grasping a large fish in his jaws. He tossed it on the ground. As he ripped into the fish, chomping its flesh, the ground turned red with blood. Fish guts trailed out of his mouth. Katie whimpered. Suddenly, the bear turned in our direction and stood on his hind legs. He sniffed the air.

"He ... smells ... us," Katie whispered as she sank to the ground beside me.

He stared into the woods.

"He ... sees ... us," I answered.

I wanted to run, but I had no control over my legs. My breath came in little gasps that I couldn't silence. The bear dropped to all fours and lunged toward us, then stood abruptly and sniffed again. He was so close I could smell his wet fur and see the blood on his snout. His eyes found mine. I swallowed a scream.

"*Play dead,*" Katie cried.

We curled our knees to our chests and covered our heads with our hands. The bear moved closer, sniffing the wind and grunting. I squeezed my eyes shut. *Go someplace different,* I ordered my mind. *You can be anybody, bring anything to life.* But as I lay on the ground waiting for the bear to eat me, I could not see Jane Eyre and I could not find Persephone. I was the one lost in Alaska—this was *my* setting.

I opened my eyes. The bear lunged again, testing for a reaction. I leapt to my feet, raised my hands high above my head and screamed bluegrass as loud as I could.

"In the pines! In the pines! Where the sun don't ever shine, and you shiver when the cold wind blows!"

The bear growled.

Katie jumped up and joined the battle. "Two bits, four bits, six bits a dollar!"

The bear circled around and slowly began to lumber away. I kept my arms raised and I screamed bluegrass until the song seared my throat. When the bear was out of sight, I looked at Katie. She was spraying the wind with pepper spray.

I coughed and touched her shoulder. "He's gone."

We sat on the ground in stunned silence until Katie finally whispered, "Hey Pearl?"

"Yeah?"

"We just fought off a bear with bluegrass and a cheer. I mean ... wonder why that worked?"

I hid the quiver in my voice. "Our accents. He must not like Southern food."

We started going over each detail of that bear, until we had turned him into more myth than animal. Now he was bigger than a car, with claws like a tiger and teeth like a shark. When the air around us turned as gray as the rocks in the stream, we picked up our rods to walk home. We were only halfway when the sun fully set. The trail was dark, but I'd marked the trees with *X*s that we could see by moonlight and even feel if needed. We went from tree to tree toward Seven.

We were tired, but we marched quickly and Katie kept trying to cheer. When her voice trailed off, I began a chorus of *In the Pines* to give her a break. A high-pitched moan joined my song.

I stopped. "Was that you?"

"Huh?"

"Singing?"

"I was humming along a bit. I like that part where it goes *And you shiverrrr—*"

It came again. Another high-pitched wail. Then another.

My eyes met Katie's. "Wolves?"

She nodded.

"What do we do? Any papers on wolves?" I asked.

"I only studied bears. I watched a TV show once that said wolves are real shy and might steal a farmer's chickens, but won't hurt a person."

The howl came again, then another, both of them much closer than before. We bolted up the mountain, falling over branches and logs, helping each other up and half dragging one another at times. The howls came close, accompanied by yelping that seemed to surround us. I knew that to hungry wolves, we looked the same as a farmer's chickens.

Katie stopped. "They're ambushing us! We're gonna run right into them!" She was sobbing and gasping. Yelps were all around us.

I grabbed Katie by the shoulders and shook her. "You didn't cheer off a bear to get eaten by a dog! Run, Katie Monroe, run!"

We ran up and up the slope. Branches slapped us in the face. Wolves hid in the dark, nipping at our heels. We ran and ran until finally the trees ended and we saw Seven. We tumbled inside, pushed the couch against the door, and collapsed.

A wolf howled outside. Katie sobbed.

"They can't come in here," I assured her. I found a flashlight and began building a fire. I was disgusted when I realized we hadn't brought in enough wood to last the night. We only had enough for a couple of hours.

A whole pile of wood was stored behind our cabin, but we wouldn't dare go back out until morning.

I found a soup can label and wrote *Pearl Weaver and the Bluegrass Bear* across the top. I drew a line and beneath it wrote *Pearl Weaver and the—*

Katie howled. Her head was tilted back, her mouth shaped into an O. Somewhere in the wilderness, a wolf answered.

"He sounds sad," Katie said. "Sad I wasn't his supper." She tilted back her head and howled again. "I'm telling him, *Sorry, Sucker*!"

I listened as Katie and the wolf howled back and forth. I looked down at my soup label and crossed out the bottom half. I wrote *Katie Monroe Sings with Wolves.*

"Can you believe this day?" she asked. "We're caught up in a string of miracles."

"Miracles? We almost got eaten. *Twice.*"

Katie stared at me. "Never mind. Someone from your kind of family...wouldn't understand."

"Oh yeah? My kind of family?"

"Trust me, it's not a bad thing. Y'all were too good to need miracles," Katie said and grinned. "But before my granny got the old-timers, she was always seeing miracles. Like if we got a good parking spot, or Mama got a bigger part than she tried out for, or my report card was better than I'd worked to get. 'What a miracle,' Granny would smile and say. One day, when I was ten, Mama didn't come home after work. Granny paced the floor that night wringing her hands with worry. I told her that Mama probably just went dancing, but Granny kept shaking her head, muttering 'Mercy...mercy.' Next morning, when I opened the door to catch the bus, there was Mama in a heap on the front stoop. Her face was bloodied, her body limp. Her hands were clutching the doormat like it might save her. I started screaming, and Granny came running and scooped her up. She had to pry Mama's hands off that rug. 'What a miracle,' Granny whispered. She carried her to the couch, pushed her hair back, and studied her bloodied face. 'What a miracle,' Granny sobbed.

"I'd had enough of it though. 'She's half-dead,' I shouted. 'Her tooth is missing. Her lip is busted. She don't know where she's at. You're talking like we found a good parking space. This ain't no miracle.' Granny held Mama's hand and stroked it gently. 'She's alive,' Granny whispered. 'After all the killing that's been laid on her, it takes a string of miracles to keep on living.' It made me angry then, but I get it now. You see, in families like mine, hard times are the daily lot. We expect our checks to bounce. We expect ground chuck to be a buck-fifty a pound when we only got a dollar. We expect doors to be locked, fires to not start, and fish to never bite. If we see a bear or get chased by a wolf, we expect we'll be supper. When those things don't happen, it's a miracle."

My family had a miracle story too. A sweet lullaby about a big brick house and young lintheads in love. As I listened to Katie's story, I began to wonder *why* Abel and Stella's house was a miracle. *How much killing had been laid on them?* Did life bring them to a heap, desperately clinging to the floor? Had Daddy edited their stories, just like Mama's, to feed me sugary plots?

I shivered. The cabin was freezing and it would only get worse. I switched on my flashlight and looked around, desperate for something to burn. Fear surged as I noticed what was missing. Somewhere in the dark, along a wolf-lined trail, were our fishing rods.

I thought of Katie's mama, lifeless at the door. *So much killing.* I thought of Loretta, swinging her hammer. *And the blows keep on coming.*

The Heart-Shaped Museum

Stella spent a year working cotton during the day and composing music at night. She began with carding room minuets, but found her way to lively reels. She messily jotted her favorites down on scraps of paper that she saved from mill flyers, ads, or labels peeled from boxes of grits. She rolled them up into little tubes and stored them in a tobacco can beneath their bed, next to the can filled with all their money.

Stella hadn't "won it all" like she once expected. She didn't have comfort or a cottage on a hill with a piano in the corner, but she had better things. Love, a dozen cotton wedding bands worn to shreds and always replaced. And music, an original tune always scrolling through her mind. She wouldn't ask for more.

But more still came. It brought her to her knees in the carding room, with a sudden rush of heat, her mouth watering and stomach heaving into the lint pile on the floor. She sat back on her heels and wiped her mouth, but soon plunged to the floor heaving again.

Stella was pregnant. And just like her first months in the carding room, growing a baby was a stormy mix of magic and misery. The only food that tasted clean, that she had a chance of holding down, was cornbread soaked in milk. She ate it for breakfast and she packed it in her lunch pail. She hid around the side of the mill to eat, so she wouldn't have to watch the other lintheads gnaw on nasty chunks of pork or fried fish. In the evenings, Abel paid to join another mill family to eat. Once, when he tried to cook, their home smelled so wretched Stella heaved into a bucket all night.

She became boney and pale. With her red hair, she looked more like snow on fire than a healthy redbud blooming in spring. She was always gagging, always on the verge of vomiting, yet still working cotton and breathing hot lint.

Stella had grown up around pregnant cousins who took extra naps and ate the biggest pieces of chicken. They floated through their season draped in folds of beautiful silk. But thoughts about pretty dresses and naps never crossed Stella's mind. The only thing beautiful, the only thing sweet about her pregnancy, was the baby. She held her tummy with wonder, even as she heaved. She loved her baby, and was wise about her misery. She knew love wouldn't chase it away. One day, it would sing her a song.

Abel nursed his own misery though, and it was getting worse every day. He woke before the mill whistle each morning, his mind searching for a solution. Since the stock market crash, pay had been cut and workers were spread across more machines for longer shifts. Most of their friends in mill town were leaving. Rumor had it, things were better out west.

Stella was willing to leave, but Abel refused. She was in no shape to travel, and he only had one skill he could count on to feed his family: cotton. He'd heard about the tent towns and he'd seen the bread lines. Every morning, men lined up to beg for his job at the mill. He couldn't walk away while so many other men begged for the work he already had. So he worked unpaid shifts to cover impossible mill quotas, and he promised Stella every morning that things would get better.

By Stella's eighth month, her belly was round and firm with little pink lines across it where the skin was stretched. Her sickness suddenly settled, and left her with an enormous appetite. No matter how much she ate, she never felt full. She was still boney, pale, and exhausted from months of building a baby with little food. But at least now she was able to think of other things. Like names.

She whispered them into Abel's ear at night. She played with the rhythms and sounded out melodies. She wanted a name that was built of more music than letters.

She finally agreed to move to the spinning room. She was slow and cumbersome, but there was a code among mill mamas to help one another. If someone needed to slip off to nurse a baby, others would step in and tie threads so that her absence wouldn't be noticed. And when Stella's belly slowed her down, the mamas on either side of her took over as much of her portion as they could.

But even with Stella's spinning room wage, there was never enough money. Wages were cut again. Workers bit their lips and didn't dare protest. Too many lint-heads were already out of work. At home, their roof was falling in and Abel was always rummaging for scraps to repair tiny sections at a time. They didn't have the money to buy real supplies and, even if they did, stores were closed all around. They didn't have a cradle, a smocked nightdress, or little leather baby shoes like Stella once wore.

But the hardest thing for Stella was that they didn't have the money to *feast*. Abel fished and hunted to round out their meager meals. But Stella craved something more than a linthead supper. She'd grown up on feasts. At night, she dreamed of them.

Weekday suppers at her daddy's house served two kinds of meats, chicken plus ham or steak and gravy, fried corn, stewed potatoes, deviled eggs, green beans shiny with pork fat, little bread and butter pickles, angel biscuits, and chocolate pie. Sometimes, the dreams were so real Stella talked in her sleep. Abel would wake up and hear her praising the pie, and then he'd spend the rest of the night worrying how to fix things.

Stella was ashamed that pregnancy reduced her to nothing but belly. Her first months spent heaving and rejecting food. Now she was controlled by a raging appetite. She was embarrassed to think that she left her daddy for a thing as big as love, yet dreamed of crawling home for pie.

She knew she wouldn't. Even if she did, her mama would have to sneak a plate out the kitchen door like she was a traveling hobo come for a charity bite. Since leaving, she had only seen her daddy once. She had gone to Raleigh for the day, back before the crash when money was easier and life could be fun. They had nearly bumped into each other on the sidewalk. He turned his head and walked to the other side of the street without speaking.

So Stella wasn't too surprised when her sister, Sally, knocked on her door one day, eyed her swollen belly, and announced that she had been disinherited.

"Mama's dying," Sally said. "Her feet turned black with the diabetes. I guess it got Daddy's mind to pondering, so he had his lawyer out to go over the will and such. But the only thing Mama owns is some bit of swamp and Daddy had her leave it to me. I spied that Betsy gets the big house. Can you believe that? Why, I'm the oldest one, if anybody deserves the house it's me. Mama says it's cause I'm marrying Dale and he's richer than Betsy's fiancé and already has a house bigger than Daddy's. I told her that's like punishing me for doing good. I do get the mill, though, which is what I really wanted. We split the contents of the house. I mean, me and Betsy split it. He made sure to write down that you get nothing. Betsy had the idea that once Daddy died, we should at least give you your old piano. You know I don't know why everybody calls that *your* piano? Nobody seems to remember that I took lessons too. I like playing a little tune now and then. Why do you deserve the piano just because you can play all the tricky pieces? Makes no sense at all. And Dale says it relaxes him something marvelous to hear me play. Besides, you don't have a place for a piano. I told Betsy the weight of it would crash through your floor. Anyhow, I brought you a chocolate pie. Well, part of one. I had the maid pack me a lunch. I'm on my way to inspect some mills with Dale that he's thinking about buying. With the crash and all, he says there are some truly marvelous opportunities. Won't it be something strange if I end up being your boss?"

"Pie?" Stella whispered. "You said something about pie?"

"I have some leftovers. You look like you could use it. Skin and bones except for *that*," Sally said as she eyeballed Stella's tummy. Sally rummaged around in her purse and pulled out a flattened paper bag. "Crushed, I'm afraid." There was a box of trash by the front door, filled with potato peelings and bean snaps for Abel to haul away. Sally tossed the bag into the trash and shrugged. "Wasn't Daisy's best effort anyways. The meringue was weepy. Well, sister, I must be off. Dale will be waiting."

As soon as Sally was out of site, Stella sank to the floor and grabbed the crushed bag. A potato peel had fallen inside it, and Stella stuck it in her mouth to suck every bit of chocolate cream off. Then she used her hand to scrape the smushed pie chunks into her mouth. It was delicious and so shameful. She giggled as she ate it, but her eyes were wet with tears.

If only the crash had never happened, Stella thought. *I could learn how to make pie.* She marveled at how something so far away in New York could hurt Dixie lintheads. She looked in the trash box. A piece of crust had fallen into the bean snaps. She picked it up and nibbled the edge. *If only misery wasn't so greedy,* she thought next. She had learned to live with lint. She had learned to live poor. Life was hard, but she was happy. But misery kept coming. It took her health. It took her beauty. It took her husband's peace. *It don't ever stop,* she sobbed, as she crammed the crust into her mouth.

That night, she was more restless than usual. Abel held her tightly and whispered stories in her ear. Old cotton talk, about the time a gang of little boys snuck into the mill and tied all the threads in knots, caused all kinds of haint worries, before they were discovered. And a fairy tale, about the time all the cotton turned to silk, and nobody knew why except for Abel. He was four-years-old on his knees catching a grasshopper, when he looked up and saw the butterflies. A cloud of them flying through the fields. They landed all over the north side of the mill until the wood glowed yellow. It takes a whole cloud of butterflies to turn cotton into silk.

Stella's breathing slowed, and she fell asleep. Abel's arms were wrapped around her, and he could feel his baby swirling beneath his fingertips. He laid awake all through the night, working to solve things. By the next evening, though, his time was up.

"It's your wife," a man said as he pulled on Abel's arm. "She fell by the spinners."

When Abel found her, Stella was in agony. The baby was coming quickly and the other mama's said she couldn't be moved. The shift was just ending, so the Boss ordered the women to finish spinning around Stella before they closed down the machines. Abel sat on the floor with her, as the machines clicked and threads whirred around them.

Stella delivered a screaming baby boy just as the final mill whistle blew. There was no blanket to wrap him in, so Abel took off his shirt to swaddle him. He looked at his son for the first time. A brand new Weaver, wrapped in his shirt and dusted with lint.

"Jack," Stella whispered.

Abel smiled as his eyes filled with tears. "You don't got to ... I know you were wantin' a music name."

But after months of whispering names, Stella only found two that she loved. *Anna Pearl* was like a song in Stella's mouth. *Jack* was a song for Abel's heart.

"Love is music too," Stella whispered.

Settled in their shack, Stella's milk was slow to come in and once it did, Jack still cried. Other mill mama's came to visit and fuss. They were all of the opinion that Stella's milk had no butter.

"You're feeding him blue john," the mamas told Stella. "You got no cream or butter in that milk. That's what grows a baby and makes 'em sleep."

Stella did anything suggested to add fat to her milk. She swallowed spoons of grease like they were medicine. She boiled chicken bones and ate the broth. She gave up eating onions and greens. But no matter what she did, Jack cried. When Stella wasn't nursing, Abel walked him up and down the tiny shack, trying to help him sleep. Stella had planned on taking Jack to work, like she'd seen other mill mamas do. But those women had fat, sleepy babies that yawned by the spinners and only woke when it was time to nurse.

She quit her job, stayed home, and nursed constantly. Abel stopped coming home when his shift ended. He stayed out searching for odd jobs in town. Winter was coming and their roof was falling down. If something didn't give soon, they'd have to leave. Even though Abel swore he'd never let them see a tent town, Stella expected it now. She closed her eyes and saw herself, clutching Jack inside a tent town where everybody was half-starved. *It don't ever stop,* she whispered as she spent her evenings alone, rocking a wailing baby.

Abel begged his boss for more work. He asked to sort the cotton bales as they came off the trucks, unskilled work reserved for new hires. But his boss mentioned the strikes and the riots and said he had to spread the work around as much as he could.

Abel had heard about the masses of men enraged at being unable to work. He felt the same riot in his heart, every time he saw the bones rising up in Stella's face and neck.

And then one day, Abel showed up for work and was told to go home. Cotton shipments were down, less workers needed, so they started at the top and cut the highest paid.

"I'll be a new doffer," Abel offered. "Just like a young boy. Don't need to be an old-time one."

But the Boss had already lined up his doffers, for less pay than one person could live on, much less a family. "You need to find something else," he told Abel.

There was nothing else. Stella said the newspapers talked about a New Deal, but what Abel needed was bread. He didn't come home for two days. Stella feared him dead, sat down on the floor, and wept right along with little Jack. During those two days, Abel stood for ten hours in a hiring line with a hundred other men at a pepper factory. The Boss hired eight. A riot broke out. Abel left and went to a bread line. He stood in line for three hours for half a loaf. Not enough to get full. Just enough to not die.

When he finally returned to their mill shack, he knew what they had to do. Stella would crawl back and beg her daddy. Not just for chicken and pie, but for Jack's future.

"I can't feed you," he growled, with his head low with shame. He slammed a fist into the wall. It went straight through and Stella stared at the blue sky on the other side. "Everything's ruined. Just cause of some Yankee accident."

Accidents. It was something Abel would ponder his whole life. How the unplanned, unknown, and far away could change everything. Like a crash in New York. Like a cotton mill fire.

After a week of fighting and weeping, the notice came that they had to move since Abel was no longer a mill employee. They were hungry, homeless, and Jack was coming down with a cough. Stella broke and agreed to Abel's plan. She tried to promise to return, but was crying too hard to speak. She was packing a bag when someone knocked on the door.

Stella guessed it was probably a new mill worker, come to claim their house. She sobbed and Abel gripped his fists to keep them from ripping the shack until it was nothing but splinters. But then the knock came again, this time louder and Jack began to howl.

Stella opened the door. There were two gentlemen in finer suits than mill town had seen in years. "Stella Mayfield?"

She shook her head. "I'm Stella Weaver now."

"Your birth name, though, is it Stella June Mayfield?"

"Yes."

"Ma'am, we're here on behalf of the federal government to inquire about the Forsyth property."

"I don't know..." Stella mumbled and began to close the door. "Don't know any Forsyth property."

One of the men put his hand up to block the door. "By the Yadkin?"

"Never heard of it," Stella whispered.

One of the gentleman took off his hat. "Maybe you haven't heard about the fire?"

Stella shook her head.

"You might wanna sit down. We have some unfortunate news. There's been a horrible accident."

Stella leaned against the doorframe as the men told her how her daddy died. There had been threats of riots at the mill. Her daddy spent his nights sleeping inside the mill to defend it. Somehow during the night, probably from a candle that he placed too near the cotton, a fire broke out. The mill burned to the ground as he worked to save the machines.

Her mama was already ill and died a month later. She had always followed her husband's wishes in planning her menus and raising her girls. But in her final hour, when her mind grew still and quiet, she wasn't thinking of her husband. She remembered how she once loved three daughters. She remembered her Songbird.

She called for a pen and her strongbox to be opened and a deed brought out. She had inherited one thing all her own. A piece of land and an abandoned house was given to her by a spinster aunt. Her husband had laughed when they went out to see it. It was on the river, marshy at the back, and the house was covered with so much ivy you couldn't see the windows. Her husband had joked that it was just thirty acres of swamp and an old barn. She had never cared for the property until the last chance, one final moment to cry out last words:

I, Delores Mayfield, bequeath my daughter, Stella June Mayfield, the thirty acre parcel of land and home located in Forsyth county, deed attached.

The gentlemen showed the deed to Stella. She passed it to Abel without looking at it. Her mind was spinning from all the news. *Her parents were dead. Sally's big mill burned down.*

"Why are you here again?" Abel asked.

"Because the land borders the river. We'd like it to be part of the New Deal. We have a plan to develop it for tourism. If you sell the back fifteen acres to us, that leaves you the house and the front parcel, and you'll know you've done a great service for your country. This project will put hundreds of men to work."

"You said there's a house?" Abel asked.

The man nodded. "Seems y'all haven't had a chance to look at the property yet. We'd like to move quickly, so if you're willing, we'll take you out there today to walk it. We'll pay five dollars for your troubles."

Stella sank to the floor, hid her face in Jack's tattered blanket, and wept. But Abel took her by the elbow and pulled her to her feet. "Can I be one of the men?" he asked.

"For what?"

"That works on the land."

The men shrugged. "Don't see why not."

On the way over, Abel was in knots wishing and begging the home to have a decent roof. He could make the five dollars feed them. What they needed most with winter coming and Jack's cough, was decent shelter.

When the car stopped, Abel got out and took off jogging toward a shed in the back field. It was leaning a bit to one side, but the roof looked fine and strong and Abel pumped his fist in the air with joy. His mind buzzed with a list of all the repairs that would make it more comfortable.

Stella tugged his hand and sobbed. "Abel?"

"I can fix that lean," Abel promised. "Don't cry Redbud. I'll only need to collect a pile of river rock. It looks small, I know, but that roof is tight."

"Abel ..." Stella sobbed.

He put his arm around her. "I know your folks died. I don't mean to ignore that. It's just ... this is our way to stay together, Stella. Our chance to keep Jack out of tent towns."

"But that's not our house."

Abel shoved his hands in his pockets and frowned. "Farther back then? Is it swampy? Why are you crying Redbud? All I need is a good roof—"

Stella covered her mouth with her hand and shook her head. She turned and pointed to the three story house that Abel had run right past. "That one."

Mill houses had two rooms, maybe three small ones for a boss. When Abel lay awake at night wondering how to fix things, he only thought about a shack with a good roof. Once, before everything seemed impossible, he had dreams for his family. He dreamed that Jack would learn to read. Stella would have new dresses. And when he let himself imagine the very best, he dreamed of a home like the one he'd lived in before his daddy died. It had three rooms and smooth pine floors.

So the first time that Abel walked and stood before their three story house, he didn't see the ivy that was matted and tangled from decades of overgrowth. He just saw the beautiful brick beneath the vines. He'd never been inside a brick home. He didn't see that the windows were all broken or missing. He just counted where they should be, and it seemed the house stretched into the sky. Abel didn't notice that the front door fell off the hinges when he opened it. He only saw past it to all the rooms, more than ten mill houses combined.

Big houses weren't for lintheads. Big houses weren't for babies born by the spinning machines. Abel had never once dreamed of them. His eyes didn't even know how to see them.

XXIV

We were scared to go more than a few steps from Seven. We'd only walk the small circle from our busted door to the woodpile, outhouse, or water pump. Finally, as the woodpile diminished, I stepped to the forest's edge and chopped fresh wood.

We were ravenous. Our bodies had become used to the fat and protein of fish. We split two cans of food a day and the gnawing pain in our bellies never left. I was desperate to find our fishing rods. I gathered a bag of rocks and tucked the ax under my arm.

"We can't cheer away wolves," I said to Katie as I handed her the bag. "From now on, we go armed. I'm the best chopper, so I'll take the ax."

Katie balanced a rock in her palm and hurled it against a tree. It smacked the trunk with a loud whack before falling to the ground. She slung the bag over her shoulder. She was a long way from the middle school dance, where she had looked so pretty with her smoky eyes, red lips, and black dress. Now she wore a thick parka, oversized snowshoes, and had a bag of rocks swinging across her back. Her hair was wind-whipped and matted. Her buttermilk skin was raw and chapped. She looked more like a hobo peddler than a cheerleader.

"They could be anywhere, watching us," she said. "We didn't know about them until they were all around."

I had spent the past two nights listening for them and didn't hear anything. "They've moved on," I told her.

But we weren't as confident as we used to be. We understood that in the wilderness we looked more like supper than runaways. We walked until we heard the stream. I tried to remember the spot where I dropped my rod.

"Around here," I said. "We probably tossed them into the trees. They might even be caught in a branch." I leaned my ax against a trunk and started pushing back branches and searching the ground. We looked in the trees and dug under the snow. We walked up and down the stream. But we never found our rods. I stared at the water's edge and saw a glimmer of silver scales.

"We're starving," Katie said. "Soon we'll be too weak to chop wood. We only have a few cans left and it's all I can do to not eat them all at once." Her eyes filled with tears. "And we don't have enough money to buy food to last the winter. We'd have to beg or find odd jobs. We spent so much on our gear and the hotel..."

"And that crazy taxi fare," I grumbled.

Katie sighed. "The facts are, we're running out of food, we don't have any rods, and we're out of money."

I knew what Katie was hinting. "I'm not going home," I yelled.

"I'm not saying that's what I want," she whispered as she twisted her hands together. "But I don't wanna starve."

"Then I'll catch us some fish," I promised.

I took our patchwork flag and tied it into a loose net at the end of a long branch. I stood at the edge of the water, dragging and scooping the quilt through the stream. But it was difficult to stretch my arms out to reach the deeper water. Most of the time, the quilt swished aimlessly.

I took a slim branch and whittled the end into a point. I stood by the stream, tossing it into the shallows, hoping to spear a fish. It was a blind and clumsy effort, and I had to wait for the water to drag the spear back to the banks.

I saw a row of rocks like a bridge across the stream. I held my breath to steady myself and stepped onto a rock. I took another step, and another, felt the rocks become wet and slippery beneath my boots. The stream gushed in a circle around me. I leaned over the water and saw a glimmer of silver. I plunged the spear with all my might. An arc of water splashed up as silver scales swished and flopped in the air. Dolly with her green spots. Dolly with her dancing dress.

We fell together. The fish and I passed each other in the air, both of us flopping with alarm. We sank. Dolly swam away unhurt, but I had jumped through a forbidden window. My skin was pierced by a thousand cuts of cold.

I ordered my body to move. I commanded my legs to kick, but they were disobedient, rebellious things. They felt separate from me, like another out of reach fish. Katie was on the rocks and screaming. She grabbed hold of my collar and dragged me to shore, like she had once dragged the fish. My net and spear floated away.

"Fire," Katie screamed. "Fire!"

Yes! I agreed as Katie pulled off my soaked gloves and parka and the air touched my skin. Everything burned like I was trapped in a fire. Katie took off her dry parka and forced it on me.

She started dragging me again. "We've got to get you back to the fire."

My feet were heavy and numb. I kept falling, so Katie grabbed my hands and pulled me up the slope. When we were finally back to the cabin, she worked furiously, using match after match, to build up the fire.

I held my hands near the flames, but had to pull them back quickly. My skin was red, like it was sunburned. My fingertips had blisters across them.

"You've gone crazy," Katie shouted. "You've lost all good sense. We're leaving this place tomorrow."

"But I hit one," I argued. "I just didn't throw the spear hard enough. Next time I'll get it."

"Pearl! We're starving and now you're hurt. Look at your toes ... they're covered in blisters. I'm not saying they'll get chopped off, but ..." She wiped tears from her eyes and looked away.

"If I go back I could go to jail for years," I cried.

Katie put her arms around me in a tight hug. "*Shhhh,*" she whispered. "If we stay, we'll die. I know there's hard things waiting for both of us back home. And it hurts something awful to leave this place, but maybe ... maybe that's a good thing. We've had something worth weeping over."

I couldn't stop sobbing. Katie pulled back and studied my fingers. "Does it hurt that bad?" she asked.

Yes. My skin tingled with a pins and needles pain, but the thought of leaving, of going home to Carolina, burned worse than the blisters across my skin.

"I'm going back to the stream," Katie said. "We left your coat and gloves and the ax. It's going to be a long trip down the mountain. We'll both need a coat and gloves. And we'll need the ax in case we run across those wolves."

"Wait till the morning and we'll go together."

She shook her head. "I doubt you'll be up for extra walking. Don't worry, I'll be back soon." She grinned and nodded toward the little bit of food we had left. "Then I'm opening all of it."

After Katie left, I sat by the fire to warm up, but a deep chill had settled in my bones. I couldn't stop shivering. My hands and toes ached, and I felt dizzy and out of breath. My eyes kept closing. Soon, I was asleep.

I dreamed of Katie. She held a rock in her hand. A wolf howled nearby and she screamed and ran. I followed her. Pines slapped me across the face. Something grabbed my feet. I sank to the forest floor.

I looked around to see what monster grabbed me. Was it a bear? A wolf? Some ancient Arctic creature? I gasped. *It was the king's castle.* An enormous set of antlers, nestled among the pines.

I touched them. They were the color and feel of cleaned bone, but beautiful in a way that ordinary bones couldn't be. They weren't built for hidden support. They were designed for display.

Somewhere nearby, Christmas music began to play. Daddy called through the woods for me to help host his holiday open house. A group of his friends gathered behind me, eager to see shiny one-of-a-kinds.

I pointed at the evergreens. I pulled Dolly Varden scales from my pocket for them to touch. I told them about the Bluegrass Bear. And then I stood to the side and let them stare with eyes full of wonder at my king's castle.

Who's the artist? they asked.

I sucked in my breath as I searched for an answer.

Who's the artist? they demanded.

I startled awake, coughing and gasping for air. My skin burned but my bones trembled with cold. The fire had died and the cabin was dark. Katie was still gone.

I staggered outside. "Katie," I called. I hurried toward the trail in the woods. "Ka-a-a-tie!"

Just as I was beginning to panic, Katie burst from the woods. "Run!" she yelled, as she grabbed my arm and pulled me back toward the cabin. "He hunted me. I kept hiding, but every time he'd track me down. He *hunted* me!"

"A wolf?"

Something stirred in the woods. Katie screamed and pulled me into the cabin. She slammed the front door and started pushing the couch against it. I leaned down to help her. The couch surged against us. We pushed back with all our might, but inch by inch, the couch scooted toward us and slowly, the door opened. We sank to the floor and clutched each other. Katie buried her head in my shoulder and closed her eyes, like she didn't want to see the monster that would eat us. But I did.

The fire had died long ago, but against a backdrop of blazing stars, I saw a man with a long, thick beard. I searched for his eyes, to see what thoughts swam inside them, but became too distracted by his hands. One gripped a large rifle. The other carried my ax.

XXV

"Mister," I said, forcing my voice to be even and calm. "You've got the wrong cabin. My daddy won't like you being here. You best walk on up the trail." There was a fireplace poker near my feet. I picked it up and held it in the air. "You got a gun. But I'm little and quick. I'll cripple you."

The man started to speak, but his voice broke off as he wiped his face with his sleeve and cussed. He propped the ax against the wall behind him, pulled a flashlight from his coat, and switched it on.

"Katiebug?" he asked.

I looked at Katie, still huddled on the floor. She raised her head slightly, and the man shined the light on her face.

"How about we set our weapons down," he said to me as he leaned his gun against the wall and motioned toward my fireplace poker. But I gripped it tightly with my numb hands.

He reached up and slid off his toboggan. He had long dark hair the same color as his beard. "You're alive," he muttered and shook his head. "How on earth—"

I coughed so suddenly and forcefully that it left me gasping and dizzy. The man shined the light on my face. Then went to the fireplace and pulled two small rocks from his pocket. He struck them together and soon had a fire warming the cabin.

I couldn't stop shivering. I coughed again and moved toward the fire, even though he was still near it. He stepped back to the front of the cabin and motioned for me step closer to the fire.

"I figured I'd find bones or bodies. But you've made out all right." He nodded toward me. "You're real sick though."

"She fell in," Katie said. "Her hands ... they got blisters all over."

He walked to me and roughly grabbed my hands. He frowned. "You need a healer."

"We're going to a doctor tomorrow," Katie said.

The man scoffed. "Up here?"

Katie blushed. "That little town at the bottom of the trail."

"Closed up. This is a summer season place. Sane folks don't spend the winter up here."

"Daddy," Katie whispered. It wasn't a question, and it wasn't like she needed confirmation. She whispered *Daddy* like she wanted to hear the sound. Like she wanted to know how it felt to call someone that.

He gave a subtle nod. "What are you doing up here?"

She found the letter in her bag and handed it to him. "You invited me."

He scanned the letter quickly. "This was ten years ago."

"I've just been waiting for my chance."

He smiled sadly. "I sold my share of this cabin. It's been ages since I've been up here."

"No way for me to know that. Weren't any other letters. Weren't no phone calls. No visits. Mama said it was cause you lived in New Hampshire with a new wife and her daughters. But I had this. I knew different."

He stared at the ground. "Things between your mom and I were ... difficult. She thought it best if I leave the two of you alone so you could move on and make a new life. She said you were happy. After a while, I figured you'd get along better without me interrupting things."

Katie shook her head with disgust.

He tried a different explanation. "I was four thousand miles away."

"And yet here I am," Katie said, grandly. "Just a kid and made it on my own." She grabbed the letter back from him. It was their first moment together and I knew later, once it was over, they'd wish they could edit it, just like my good-bye salute.

"You're asking for the wrong thing," I said to him. "It's easier to forgive a hurt than excuse one. When you've missed out on your girl's life, when you've left her to be raised by a mean mama, you don't blame geography."

There was a moment of stunned silence, followed by a deep breath. He held his hands out, palms up in surrender, but he didn't speak. Katie sat down on the couch and put her head in her hands.

"She's a mean mama?" he asked.

"All she wants to be is a Vegas showgirl." Katie smirked. "Ain't much mama in her."

"She got a call in to me. They pulled me off the rig to tell me my daughter had gone missing. She accused me of arranging it all. Said you and a friend had flown to Anchorage, and there's no way you could have pulled it off without help. Took me forty-five minutes to convince her I'd been on the rig for the past three weeks without a break. No way I had time to set up a couple of runaways. I searched the city. I tracked down every cabdriver until I found one that knew you. When he showed me on the map where he'd taken you, I thought there was no way you could still be alive." He cleared his throat and shook his head. "But here you are, Katiebug."

Katie stared at me intently, like she was trying to send some secret message.

"And we ain't ever going back," she said.

"Your mother's got the law looking for you too. She'll have them come up here and drag you out. You're too young to live on your own."

"We'll live with you," Katie answered.

He laughed loudly. "In Barrow?"

Katie nodded.

"You'd hate it. Dixie belle like you—"

"Let's get one thing straight," Katie interrupted. "Don't *ever* call me that. Belle means pearls and mimosas. It means golfing daddies and country club mamas. That's more fairy tale than truth for my part of the South. I'm cutoffs and Cheerwine and Friday nights down at the Skatey Lady. I'm the girl that buys her lip gloss from Kmart, not the counter at Parks Belk. I'm the girl who never met her daddy and whose mama can only get into the country club when she waits tables there. I'm no belle."

He cleared his throat. "Do you know anything about Barrow?"

She nodded. "It's here in Alaska."

"At the top of the earth. Temperatures are far below zero during winter. There's no road in or out of the town..."

"You got a new wife and daughters there?" Katie asked.

He smirked. "No."

"Then there's nothing you gotta warn me about."

"I can warn you that Barrow is the reason your mother left me. If we had settled farther south, maybe even here, where things thaw and trees grow, she might've stayed. But Barrow is different. I moved a Dixie bel—" He stopped and swore under his breath. "Look, your mother liked it when I called her belle. And I moved her to the most northern city possible. I was an idiot. You can't transplant a belle to the Arctic. She said being even a little bit cold actually hurt. I never understood that. Cold feels cold to me. But a nice thirty degree day was downright painful to her." He looked at Katie and smiled sadly. "You were born in Barrow, but you're a Carolina girl now."

Katie nodded. "Sure, I like sweet tea and chopped pork plates, and I've been coached to yell for Dale. But you've been blaming the wrong thing all this time. Mama's not a belle. She's a snake. You moved a snake to the Arctic. My blood don't freeze when it gets cold."

He stared at her for a minute. "The dark drags on for months. Nearly drove her crazy. I'd come home from work and she'd be curled next to the reading lamp, as close as she could get, trying to soak up the light."

"Mm-hmm. Snake."

"Maybe if we'd stayed in California things would be different, but the job was off Barrow. Oil and gas were booming and you were on the way so—"

"Wait. California?" Katie asked.

"She never told you?"

Katie shook her head.

"I'd never been to the lower 48, and California was the place to go according to my brothers. I could get work at a port, same as here, only much warmer. So one summer I went with a buddy. He knew a guy in San Pedro who was looking to hire deep sea fishing instructors for tourists, and just like that, we had summer jobs. San Pedro is outside LA, where your mother was. She had run off the minute she turned eighteen to take her shot at modeling. She waitressed during the day and posed for pictures at night. She was the prettiest girl ever. Girls up here are all wrapped up in gear and toboggans and scarves. And most of the other girls in LA were too made-up. But your mom was as glossy and golden as a stack of warm pancakes. We tried to stay and make California work once you were on the way. But her tummy got covered in these little pink marks. She'd spend hours rubbing cream and hoping they'd go away so that she could model again after you were born. I lost my job when the tourists stopped coming. My dad called and said he had good work lined up for me working rigs off Barrow. We needed the money and the insurance. She said she was willing to go anywhere, except home to Carolina. She lasted one winter. You were born in the spring and we nestled down in Barrow through that first summer. We fought all the time. We were just getting to know one another, and she didn't like to hike or fish or hunt. She said all she wanted was a nice mall and a Shoney's salad bar. Come fall, when the temperatures dropped again, she packed all your things. She said she wouldn't spend another winter holed up in Barrow."

"You try and stop her?" Katie asked.

He sighed and shook his head. "I was relieved. I figured I could still do my part by you. I sent money. I called. But it was hard. She was so angry, like I was the one who made Alaska cold. Or like I was the only one responsible for those pink belly marks that ruined her modeling." He glanced at me and looked back at Katie. "I *am* sorry."

Katie put her hands on her hips and raised her chin. "Sorry means you've changed, don't it? It means you wish you could get another chance?"

His hand went to his beard and he shook his head. "She won't allow it."

"She wants to do shows more than raise me," Katie insisted. "Besides, if you say no, we'll just run again. We'll find a map and see how far another four thousand miles will take us."

He nodded in my direction. "What will her family say about all this?"

"She's *my* kin. And her guardian's looking for somebody new to raise her anyways. Looks like you just volunteered for the job."

"Well, first thing, we need to get her to a healer," he said. "I know somebody in Barrow who'll fix her up."

"Isn't there a doctor that's closer?" Katie asked.

He shook his head. "They might start carving on her. I know a lady that'll know what to do. Besides, it'll give you both a chance to see how you really like Barrow." He turned toward me. "I'm Eric, by the way."

"You ever been on any glaciers?" Katie asked.

"Lots."

"I wanna catch an ice worm."

"You are not your mother's daughter," he mumbled under his breath.

Katie laughed. "I've been telling you ..."

The room began to spin. I made my way to the couch and fell in the corner. I listened as Katie told her dad all about our journey. She began with our flight and moved on to building our first fire, catching the Dolly, and outrunning the wolves.

"If we hadn't lost our rods," she said, "we could've stayed forever. That's why she fell in. She was trying to fish like a bear."

I sat up to defend myself. I was *not* trying to fish like a bear. Hadn't I carved a spear? Hadn't I fashioned a net? I wasn't blindly pawing the stream. But my voice broke and my eyes felt so heavy. I sighed and collapsed back onto the couch.

"We were gonna leave tomorrow," Katie said. "I was looking for her coat when I heard you tracking me."

They sat by the fire and chatted while I dozed. As I listened to them, I remembered all the nights I once curled by the library fire with Daddy.

"We survived so many things," Katie exclaimed. "A whole string of miracles happened."

No, I moaned through frozen, chattering lips. Loretta was right. It was all just a reprieve, a short stay of execution. There were no miracles.

Later that night I opened my eyes and saw that Katie and Eric were asleep. My skin blazed with the burn of a thousand suns, but I couldn't stop shivering. I stood up, felt my weight sink against numb feet. I shuffled outside into the dark night.

It was my last night at Seven, and the most beautiful one. The stars kissed the mountain tops.

"Who's the artist?" I begged the sky.

The wind blew cold, as fire crawled across my skin.

"Who's the artist?" I yelled into the dark.

The cabin door opened and Katie screamed for me to come back. But I stretched my palms toward starry milk glass. *Who?* I cried. Who dreamed up this strange canvas, where killing and beauty are swirled with the same brushstroke?

XXVI

I left Seven wrapped in Eric's coat as he carried me down the mountain. His gun was strapped against his back, and I fell asleep staring at the long black barrel pointing into the trees. When I awoke, I was slumped against the window of a plane.

No roads lead in or out of Barrow, but Eric had a bush pilot brother who flew supplies into tiny villages all over Alaska. For our flight to Barrow, we sat knee to knee inside his plane.

We flew for hours through a snowy day. Once we began our descent, I could see the ground below. There were no mountains or trees, only miles upon miles of lakes and flatland.

"The tundra," Eric said when he saw me staring out the window.

After we landed, Eric carried me off the plane and into the airport parking lot. There were only a handful of airport workers. They all knew Eric and whispered excitedly about him finding his runaway daughter. They peeked at me with worried faces while I shivered inside Eric's coat. A fierce wind blew bits of icy snow into my eyes. *This* was arctic cold. It made the weather at Seven seem warm.

"It's freezing!" Katie whined through chattering teeth.

One of the airport employees laughed. "In another month everything goes dark for weeks. That's when it gets cold."

Eric gently laid me inside his truck. "Let's head home," he said.

My skin alternated between burning and feeling numb. My lungs ached, and I shivered even when I wasn't cold. I hadn't eaten since the morning I fell. Eric had offered beef jerky and packs of peanut butter crackers out of his backpack to squeals of delight from Katie. She ravaged hers, so Eric gave his portion to her. But I was too exhausted to eat. It was a struggle to hold my eyes open, but like strange torture, I couldn't sleep deeply either. Every time I fell asleep I woke up aching or coughing.

But even as my body failed, my mind didn't. I leaned against the truck window and studied my strange new setting. I was at the top of the earth. I had imagined tall drifts and snowbanks. But the road only had a white dusting, and beneath it I could see patches of dirt. The yards and roofs were covered with inches of snow, not feet. The houses were beaten and weary. Most were built on poles and pilings. It reminded me of a worn out beach town where homes are designed with hurricanes in mind. Eric said that the poles kept the houses from melting the tundra and sinking into the ground. We turned down a different road.

"How come they're all dirt roads?" Katie asked.

"Can't pave permafrost," Eric answered. "That should help you feel at home, huh?"

"What do you mean?"

He winked at her. "Aren't dirt roads common in your part of the South?"

Katie rolled her eyes and Eric laughed loudly. "I'm teasing. This road leads straight to the Chukchi Sea, part of the Arctic ocean." He pulled into a driveway. "And this is home."

Eric's house was rundown and faded like the others, but it was an A-frame, a near perfect triangle with a roof that sloped to the ground. He carried me inside and I saw that the triangle shape wasn't hidden by walls and rooms. It was the main feature of the house.

He carried me up a set of stairs to the second floor. "There's just this one room and the bathroom up here. My bedroom's on the main level next to the living room. Then there's one more out back behind the kitchen for Noatak. You all can have this one."

He opened the door. The room was in the very tip-top of the A-frame. The walls sloped sharply together. Eric had to stoop to fit inside the room. If Katie walked anywhere but the very center line of the floor she had to stoop too. Tucked against each wall was a neatly made twin bed.

"My brothers sleep here when they visit," he said. "That's not as often now that they don't work oil or gas." He laid me on one of the twin beds and pulled a quilt over me.

My body relaxed into the support and warmth of a real bed. Just as I began to close my eyes, a small woman shuffled in the doorway. Eric stepped near her and they whispered together and exchanged serious looks.

"This is Noatak," Eric said. "She lives back and forth between here and the tundra. When she's here, she keeps the place running while I work the rig. She's a healer. People come to her from all over. She's a fine cook too. She'll give your Dixie dishes some real competition." He winked at Katie. "I'm gonna take a quick shower."

Noatak had black hair that fell to her waist, with one streak of gray above her left ear. Sharp cheekbones rose to meet her small, black eyes. Her skin was the same cinnamon shade the Yadkin turned when it flooded. It was perfectly smooth except for one deep crease above her brow that shattered into tiny wrinkles when she smiled.

"You're a real live Eskimo!" Katie said joyfully.

I cringed at her rudeness. But Noatak smiled, and her eyes nearly disappeared with the rise of her cheekbones.

"Inupiat," she said.

"Huh?" Katie asked.

"Ee-nyoo-piat," Noatak repeated slowly. "I am Inupiat." She stepped into the room, grabbed Katie, and hugged her. "Welcome, Katie-the-bug." She leaned over the bed and patted my shoulders. "And you, Nukka Pearl." As she stood, she rattled and jingled. That's when I noticed that she wore a purple-striped apron that was covered with a dozen wide pockets. She pulled the quilt back and examined my hands. She took off my socks and studied my feet.

Katie grimaced. "We've gotta get her to a hospital."

Noatak tossed her head from side to side, like she was considering it. "Maybe."

"The longer we wait the worse she'll get," Katie insisted. "There was this one time I had strep throat but Mama didn't take me to the doctor for a few days and—"

"They'll cut her," Noatak interrupted. She leaned close and examined my hands. "There is still time."

"And if you're wrong?" Katie asked.

Noatak shrugged. "We take her and they still cut."

"NO," I cried. "No!"

Noatak laid her hands on my head. Not to feel for fever, and not to tell me to hush. She laid her hands on my head like she could give me her warmth.

"I will help you," she said softly. "For thousands of years my people have treated snow sickness with no doctors. We don't know about cancer or heart attacks. We still don't understand why sweets give us diabetes. But snow sickness? Ahh ... that we know."

She sat down on the edge of the bed, laid her head on my chest, and told me to take the deepest breath I could. I started coughing. She sat up and solemnly pronounced her diagnosis.

"Your lungs, bones, and muscles are still frozen. In order to heal snow sickness, you have to thaw from the inside out. I'll be back soon. We will fix you." She turned to Katie. "Say good-bye to your friend and come with me. You must sleep on the couch for the next few days and not come back here until she is well. Your mouth is never quiet and Nukka needs silence to focus on her thaw."

Katie put her hands on her hips and jutted out her chin, but Noatak tugged her gently out of the room. I could hear Katie protesting the whole way down the stairs. When Noatak returned, she was alone. She turned me so that my feet dangled off the bed and then pushed my feet down into a bucket. I expected a warm, soothing foot bath, but my feet plunged into icy water. I screamed and tried to pull them out, but Noatak was strong. She grabbed my legs and held them down. My whole body lurched with chills. Noatak watched as the cold overwhelmed me and nodded like she approved. After several minutes in the bucket, she lifted my feet out and dried them. She laid a bowl across my lap and shoved my hands into the icy water.

I tried again to twist away, but Noatak was too strong.

"Your skin had thawed," she explained. "But you are still frozen inside. That's why you have blisters and numbness. That's why your lungs hurt. We have to re-chill your skin. You must thaw from the inside out."

"But cold water is what made me sick in the first place," I cried. "This will just make it worse."

She clucked her tongue. "No, no. This is not just cold water. *This* is the Chukchi Sea. Home of the whale and the seal. They swim in this beautiful water. It keeps their skins perfectly healthy."

After soaking my hands for several minutes, Noatak lifted them out and gently dried them. I reached for my blankets, but Noatak pulled them away and laid them on the other bed.

"You must get warm from within first," she insisted.

She switched off the light and carried the seawater out of the room. I lay in darkness, violently shivering, my breath coming in gasps as I worked to calm my body. At some point, Noatak returned. She lifted my chin and held a spoon to my mouth. I pressed my lips together tightly and turned my head.

"*Shhh*, this will help you thaw," she coaxed.

I expected freezing seawater, but the liquid was piping hot and tasted of spice and pine. It was like drinking Christmas. I opened my mouth for more.

"This is labrodor tea," she said. "Made from a furry leaf that grows on the tundra. I harvest it at least once a year. Then I dry the leaves and keep them to make this tea. It is good for warming and for coughs. It also fights infections."

I finished the mug and my body grew calm. Noatak tucked the quilts tightly around me. "You are thawing. You will sleep good."

I slept for three days, only waking when Noatak came to spoon more tea into my mouth or feed me bits of toast and crackers. I dreamed thick, confused dreams that whisked me from one setting to another. I was at Seven, eating a Dolly Varden. I was in the hospital. They were chopping away at my skin. I was on stage, reading *Jane Eyre.* Yellow wizard dust choked me and made my lungs burn. I was in the Chukchi Sea. My hands were flippers. My feet were as blue as the whale's tail.

I sat up, sweating in bed. I shoved the quilts off and looked at my feet. They looked worse. The blisters had popped and the skin was peeling the way a sunburn does.

"Noatak," I cried. "Noatak."

She ran into the room.

"I'm gonna have to be cut."

Noatak studied my feet for several minutes and then examined my hands. She grinned. "You are beginning to heal." She pulled a dark flask from an apron pocket and uncorked it. The room was filled with the rancid odor of rotting fish. She poured a palm full of dark oil into her hand and began to rub my feet while I gagged.

"It's turned rotten. I'll get infected."

Noatak laughed. "This is seal oil. Like Inupiat penicillin. Heals most anything. Once, when I was a little girl, a starved wolf attacked me. My *anik* chased it off, but I was badly bitten. Three of my toes dangled by the skin. A hospital would have chopped them, but my *anana* swaddled my foot in seal oil."

I leaned over the edge of the bed and looked at Noatak's bare feet. Her cinnamon toes were straight and well. She pulled fur-lined socks from another apron pocket and tugged them over my feet.

"Caribou," she said proudly. "Warmest possible."

She repeated the same treatment with my hands, and I bit my tongue to keep from gagging. I was grateful when she tucked my hands down inside caribou gloves because it helped contain the scent. She pulled a spoon from her pocket, filled it with oil, and held it to my mouth.

"Please, I can't," I begged. "I'll vomit."

But Noatak pressed the spoon firmly against my lips. I opened my mouth and she dumped the wretched liquid into my mouth. I swallowed and collapsed gagging.

"Where's Katie?" I asked, once I could speak.

"Hiking glaciers. If you feel like it, you can get up and move about the house today."

I did feel like it. My cough was nearly gone, and my hands and feet were sore but not numb. I felt suddenly curious and excited to be at the top of the earth. When Katie came home, she caught me up on all that I had missed. Eric had called Carolina. He didn't tell Katie what was discussed, but he hadn't mentioned anything about sending us home.

"He wants to get to know me," she said with a shy smile. "He takes me all around town and introduces me as his daughter. Almost like he's proud of me."

"Tell me about Barrow," I begged.

She began with the whalebone arch, where two whale ribs stand together like a gate to the Arctic Ocean. She told me that riding a snowmobile was more scary than fun. She was working up the courage to keep her eyes open during her rides with Eric. She tried her best to describe the glacier in a way that could help me see it.

"It was big," she said. "Maybe as big as the mall. And really white. Maybe as white as a Barbie doll's teeth."

"You find any worms?" I asked.

She sighed. "No. Next time, I'm taking an ice pick and digging deeper."

But of all the things that Katie had enjoyed in Barrow, the thing that surprised her the most was her visit to the grocery store. "*Nothing* is a good deal up here," she swore.

Over the next few days, she coached me to enjoy each meal more than I seemingly did.

"Don't you dare gulp that orange juice," she shouted during supper. She picked up the carton and pointed to a price tag on the side.

I was stunned. "Sixteen dollars? Is it magic juice?"

"Florida is so far away," Eric explained. "In fact, everything is very, very far away. Potato chip makers, dairy cows, candy bar factories ... so most of the grocery store foods you were raised to love and crave are very expensive here. Things like caribou, seal, and whale fill our bellies much cheaper." He turned to Katie. "Your mother drove me crazy whining for fresh salads and blueberry yogurt when she was pregnant. Do you have any idea how hard it is to get fresh lettuce up here? Or blueberry yogurt?"

He looked at Katie suspiciously, like he was waiting to see if she'd end up begging for salads and yogurt. Katie must have noticed, because she took a long, slow sip of orange juice.

"It *is* magic juice," she said. "And I think caribou and whale sound much more delicious than yogurt."

Eric laughed. "We'll see about that." He looked at Noatak. "Any flags? Or any news from your family?"

Noatak frowned. "Nothing. And this week is our last chance."

"For what?" I asked.

"Hunting whales," she replied.

"Only Inupiats can hunt them," Eric said. "And whenever a family makes a kill, they share portions with all their people. They raise a flag to let everyone know."

Noatak sighed. "It's been five years since my family has raised their flag. My brother is very old. This is his last hunt. It would be a great honor for him to have a final strike."

That night, after supper, I obediently took my oil and tea doses. Noatak examined my skin and was pleased.

"You can explore Barrow tomorrow if you like," she said.

My healed skin was a blanched grayish-white, compared to the skin on my arms. Noatak noticed me studying it and assumed I was worried.

"The skin is new. The scars will soon fade," she assured me.

"I hope not," I replied. "These scars tell a great story, about the time the icy water almost killed me."

Noatak stared at me. "Come with me."

Like Loretta's room, the door to Noatak's bedroom was kept shut. But that's where the similarities ended. Noatak's room was bursting with interesting things to look at. The walls were lined with shelves filled with jars and bottles, skins and furs, and dried clusters of evergreens and mosses. The room was more than a place to sleep. It was a pharmacy and a study. It was the healer's museum.

I noticed a small black-and-white picture, framed in rusted tin. *Cotton.*

"Where is this?" I asked.

"The tundra."

I shook my head in disbelief and picked up the picture for a closer look. The stems were longer, but the same puffy tuft of white fuzz dotted the ends.

"But that's cotton," I said.

"Cottongrass. It feeds the caribou. Grows all over, like a weed. I like it though. Reminds me of being a little girl, playing so carefree."

"Cotton needs a hot sun," I protested. "No way it can grow up here."

Noatak laughed. "And yet, there it is, on my tundra."

Alaska had confounded me. It had shown me dangerous beauty—milk glass mountains, outer-space greens and blues, the bear and the wolves. And now, after all of that, the old comfort of home?

Noatak took my hand and held it. She gently ran her old, leathered palm across my skin.

"Nukka," she said. "Tell me the story of your scars."

I shrugged. "We'd lost our rods and were starving. I made a spear and a net, but I couldn't reach the fish from the banks. So I walked across the rocks into the middle of the stream. I threw my spear and hit one. It flopped up, startled me, and I fell. The water was cold and deep and I never learned to swim. Katie dragged me out by my collar. I was soaking wet, and we had to hike up the mountain to get to a fire. By the time we did, the damage was done."

"But why did you go into the stream in the first place? Especially since you can't swim?"

I began to feel uncomfortable. "I was crazy hungry. We were living on two cans of food a day."

Noatak walked to a shelf and pulled off a stained leather journal. "I became a healer when I was thirteen. I was the very last child in my family, just like my *anana*, and that meant I was born to heal. When my *anana* died, it became my duty to harvest the evergreens, the mosses, and bottle the seal oil. For most of my life I had stayed by her side, so I knew what to do. I soaked frozen limbs. I spoon-fed oils and teas and spread mosses across sick skin. I swaddled feet in caribou. But the ways of my people began to disappear. Tundra children stopped becoming healers. They were leaving to become teachers or rig workers or commercial fisherman. People brought me their sick from all over. Even the white men working rigs began traveling to visit me. *It's the ice,* they all cried. Just like you. Yet, there are so many of us living in this cold, loving this cold, still unharmed." She flipped through the pages of the journal and sighed. "I am eighty-four years old."

I gasped in surprise as I remembered her strength when she held me down in the Chukchi water. She smiled. "Yes, very old. But it's given me time to understand that I'm not usually fighting the ice when I treat the wounded."

"What is it then?" I asked. "Infection?"

Noatak chuckled. "I have treated hundreds of cases of snow sickness. Only a very few have been truly accidental. Like a hiker that thought he packed his matches, but had forgotten them. Or the toddler, too young to have any sense, that wandered out the front door. Usually, the people I treat put themselves in harm's way. We know to wrap up in the cold. We know to wear gloves and build fires and seek shelter. We know not to walk into a rushing arctic stream. All of this is instinct, even for a girl from Carolina. So what makes a person stop doing this? What makes a beautiful girl that doesn't know how to swim, climb into a frozen stream when her best friend wants to call home and be rescued? You knew that stream could kill you. If Eric had not found you, Nukka, you would have died. So tell me, was it the ice that hurt you?" She pressed the journal into my hands. "I've never shown it to anyone before."

"Why me?" I asked.

"Katie talked of you nonstop while you were sick. I imagine Eric knows as much about you by now as he does her. One thing she kept saying was how smart you are and how many books you have read. *Pearl knows stories,* she said over and over. And it struck me as very sad that maybe ... maybe you don't know your own."

Her words pierced me, but I pretended to shake them off. I carried the journal to my bed and began to read. The paper stunk of seal oil and Christmas. The handwriting was faded and scrawled. Each page was written like a list, with numbers lining the far margin. A diagnosis was in parentheses, along with treatments given. Most of the illnesses were snow sickness, but there were coughs, boils, broken bones, and a strange thing called snow blindness. The treatments were seawater, teas, mosses, seal organ meats, and oils. Occasionally mother's milk and urine were listed too. I could have shrugged it off, like a dry nonfiction read. I could have flipped through the pages quickly, appreciated the years of history recorded, and turned the light off to sleep. But there were stories too.

Or rather, there were quotes. Just a sentence or two, scribbled after the diagnosis. As I read them, I remembered how Daddy said one sentence sometimes summed up a whole book. Clearly, in her brief scribbles, Noatak believed this too.

34. "It's not that far to the liquor store."

212. "I'm the last one."

389. "He promised."

Months ago, the quotes would have seemed sad, but also mysterious and romantic. I would have daydreamed about them and spun fanciful plots. Now, I knew better. And soon I grew weary of the pain behind the words. I flipped back to the first page of the journal and read what was written on the inside cover, where a dedication might be.

"God is Light, and in Him there is no darkness."

Once, those words were the only comfort offered after a string of horrible nightmares. I dreamed of my drowning pond, a monster that pulled me low, and all the bits of swimming dead things that surrounded me. I woke with a scream and Loretta came running. She patted my back and shushed me. She said that I had weak legs, and that's the only reason I nearly drowned. "There are no monsters," she promised. When she started to leave the room, I begged her to leave my light on.

"Girly," she said. "Think of the electric bill."

"Daddy won't mind."

"Well he's traveling, so it's up to me now."

"Don't leave me in the dark," I begged. "The monster ... please give me some light."

Loretta's face hardened. "God is light," she said with a stony whisper.

I stared at those words inside Noatak's journal, baffled that my drowning dreams and my near-miss with an Alaskan death, were now connected by one line about light and darkness. The first woman who whispered those words to me was an iron skillet. But the second, was a healer.

Katie came to bed and switched off the light. In the quiet darkness, Noatak's question chased me.

Was it really the ice that hurt me?

XXVII

A bright light flashed in my face. I blinked my eyes and shielded myself from the glare. Someone grabbed my shoulders and shook me.

"Hurry!" Noatak urged, waving the beam of her flashlight across my face. "He's changed his mind. He's going to take you."

"Huh?" I mumbled. "What's going on?"

"Hurry," Noatak repeated. "They won't wait!"

I looked for Katie. She was already getting dressed.

"All your gear," Noatak ordered. "The caribou socks and gloves. And you must not take anything off even if you feel hot. Your skin is too new."

I dressed and walked down to the kitchen. Noatak pressed a thermos and a bag of granola in my gloved hands and hugged me. "Lord bless you," she whispered. "Eat on the way."

I went outside to the truck and Katie scooted over to make room for me. *I'm dreaming,* I told myself. I was dressed in full gear at the top of the earth, speeding down a dirt road with a bag of granola in my hands and a thermos of coffee between my knees. I unscrewed the thermos and took a slow sip. I hadn't tasted coffee except for those nights with Daddy, when I'd sip his lukewarm drink and make a funny face so that he would laugh. Loretta insisted that even one cup would stunt my growth. Noatak clearly didn't share this opinion. The thermos was filled to the brim with steaming, black coffee. I smelled it and took another sip. I felt the warmth spread through my body and knew that I was awake.

"Where are we going?" I asked.

"Whaling," Eric answered. "I go with Noatak's family whenever I can. It's a big honor for people like us to go, but it's illegal for non-natives to shoot the whales. I called earlier in the week and asked Captain if I could bring you all. He said no, but for some reason changed his mind. Call came at five o'clock this morning that he wanted you to come. They sail at seven thirty. It's the last day to hunt till spring, and most likely Captain's very last hunt altogether."

"But he hasn't got a whale in five years, right?" Katie asked as Eric made a sharp right turn and parked in a row of other trucks.

Eric nodded. "For three years the boat kept breaking. One thing after another. Captain would scrape the money together, get something fixed, and then something else would break. So last year, the fourth year, he got a new boat."

"Well thank goodness!" Katie said. "I thought you were gonna take us on some lemon-boat."

Eric chuckled. "This boat's brand new. And *that* is why they think we can't strike a whale. There's a lot of tradition and respect for ancient ways, a lot of superstition. They believe the whale chooses whether or not to give its life for them, as a gift, to feed the community. So their guns have to be perfectly clean because you shouldn't kill a noble creature with a dirty gun. Some of them paint their faces for luck, the way their grandfathers taught them. And they bring the tips of fox tails, or eagle feathers, as good omens."

Katie took a slow, deep breath. "I spent years hoping to hunt worms. Now I'm hunting whales."

Eric opened the truck door and motioned for us to follow him. "Sit tight on the boat. Don't touch anything, especially not the harpoon or shoulder guns. They have bombs attached to them. Captain said your job is to spot whale spouts. It'll be a big stream of water shooting up from the ocean."

We followed Eric through the dark, and as my eyes adjusted, I realized we were walking toward a wharf. There was a boat docked there, with men loading it. As we climbed on board, I felt the rocking of the Chukchi beneath us. An old man stepped out from the dark and shined a flashlight in our faces. We squinted into the light.

Eric stepped forward. "Girls, this is Captain Apannugak."

He looked ancient. Noatak was surely his baby sister. His face was deeply wrinkled, his black eyes piercing. He handed the flashlight to Eric and stepped closer. His right hand reached and touched my face. I flinched, but did not pull away. He traced a diagonal line from above my left brow to below the bottom corner of my right lip. Then he did the same to Katie.

"*Hmmpph*," the Captain grunted as he studied our faces. "Runaways." He pointed a bony finger at us. "The whales are running too. Escaping the coming ice." He grunted again and walked away. Eric showed us where to sit while the men loaded and inspected the gear. Katie and I huddled together and looked at each other with wide eyes.

"You have—" I started to say.

"So do you," she said.

Captain Apannugak had done more than trace a diagonal line across our faces. He had drawn it, with an ash-like smudge. We noticed the same black lines were drawn across the faces of some of the men working on the boat.

"What's this about?" Katie pointed to her face and asked Eric.

"It means that today you are Apannugak. I told you there's a lot of superstition that goes into this. I think maybe that—"

"He's counting on us," I said. "He thinks we'll find the whales because we're runaways like them."

"Right," Katie chuckled. "I can catch a Dolly but that's as far as my fishing experience goes."

Somebody called for Eric's help. "I've got to go. I'll come back and check on you."

Katie leaned in close as he walked away. "So ... we're supposed to be whale magnets? How will we do that?"

"Think like a runaway," I said.

The boat started with a roar and after a couple of minutes of slow maneuvering, we sped out into open water. Everything was black. The air around me, the sky above, and the sea stretching out in front. But my eyes continued to adjust, and light from the boat illuminated the details near me. Like the way Katie sat with perfect posture, her hands gripped together, her face turned sharply toward the water. I could see the dark streak dividing her face, marking her Apannugak.

The boat slowed and stopped. That's when I began to realize the darkness was rapidly changing and soon the sun would rise. In Carolina, watching a sunrise meant that I focused on the sky. It meant that I traced the slow fade of black, as pinks and oranges appeared. But on top of the earth, I watched the water as it divided itself from the sky. It grew shinier, richer, a deep oily black while the sky melted into something milky and pale. It was like night plunged into the Arctic's depths to escape the rising sun. I raised my hand and traced the line between the dark water and pale sky.

"Welcome to a fall morning in the Arctic," Eric leaned close and whispered.

And that's when I began to think like a runaway. As I stared at the black water dotted with chunks of floating ice, I remembered home. In Carolina, fall was a blaze of red and gold and orange. Cars full of tourists headed to the Blueridge to revel in the mountains' show. But on that morning, I only saw stark shades of white, gray, and black.

It was not boring. A world where color is missing sounds bleak and dull, but it was a crisp black-and-white photo. A place where the lines are sharp and obscure details shine. A place where you can hear a whale, before you even see it.

Katie would always say it sounded like a sigh. Eric called it a puffing noise. But to me, to my runaway ears, it was a proclamation. *I am here! I am here!* A giant stream of water shot up, like an exclamation point bursting from the sea. All the men yelled excitedly and pointed toward the spout. The boat turned and sped toward the place where the water had shot.

"That was a bowhead spout," Eric told us.

"So we got one?" Katie asked.

"Not yet."

The whale was more like a part of the sea than a separate being. It was an enormous dark wave rising and rolling from the depths. It did not swim away. Even as the shoulder gun bombs were raised. Even as the harpoonist launched its deadly blow. Lines were attached, smoke rose in the air as the bomb went off. All around me, men roared with urgent calls and shouts. The whale rolled to its side, and I bit my lip until I tasted blood.

"Honey, it's not in pain," Eric whispered. "They used a grenade that explodes inside the whale, killing it instantly. It's already dead." He was speaking to Katie. Tears rolled down her face.

"I'm glad they got it," she sobbed. "I don't know why I'm crying."

I knew exactly what she felt, and what she was trying to say. Watching that whale die was sad and powerful, beautiful and mysterious. All of these things rushed inside us.

The men were busy working with lines, hooks, and floats, attaching the whale to the boat. One man was on a radio repeatedly calling other boats and announcing the strike. My eyes found Captain Apannugak. He gave a slow nod before turning to call out orders.

In the distance, other boats approached. Three more came and circled the whale to attach their own lines and hooks. Eric put his arm around Katie and gave her a squeeze. I saw the way she leaned into him and didn't stiffen or push against his affection.

"Why are all the other boats here?" I asked. "Isn't this ours?"

"There's a firm limit on how many whale strikes Inupiats can make, and the strike counts whether or not we get the whale to shore. It's a sad thing to strike a whale, but not be able to feed anyone with it. So other boats help drag it. This whale belongs to the whole community now."

The boat began to move, this time much slower, and in unison with three other boats. The whale had lines stretching from its body, and the water divided around its hulking mass.

Back at shore they attached the drag lines to a bulldozer to help haul it onto the snow-covered beach. It was larger than the bus Katie and I used to ride. Its skin was still as black and shiny as the Chukchi. It had tiny eyes and an enormous mouth. But it wasn't beautiful. I *remembered* it beautiful, when it rolled and swam in a marriage with the sea. But dead on the snow, it was like a large, black slug.

The beautiful thing now was the people around it. An Inupiat crowd gathered. They cheered and hugged as they organized into teams for work. Three men climbed on top of the whale's back and started slicing lines that wound around and down the sides of the skin and blubber. The flesh was pulled off in long strips and arranged in neat rows on the snow. Older men sat nearby, sharpening knives and handing them up to the carvers. Red prints, where children and workers stepped in the growing puddle of whale blood, were scattered along the snow. I saw Noatak, surrounded by other women. They were laughing and wiping away tears. I wanted her to see my face and know that I was Apannugak.

After a couple of hours, most of the meat was laying in large slabs across the snow. Soon the innards of the whale glistened as the men began to carve into them. Someone called out to ask for the liver.

"Yuck," Katie muttered. "I can barely stand chicken livers. Imagine whale liver."

Noatak appeared behind us and laughed. "He'll use the liver skin to make drums."

By sunset, all of the meat had been divided into shares. Every family that helped catch, haul, or carve the whale received a portion. The largest share went to Noatak's family. We dropped Noatak off at her brother's house. When we pulled up two young boys were hoisting a flag in the front yard.

"My family's flag," Noatak said. "Tomorrow we serve the whole community."

The yard was lined with cardboard, and the truckloads of whale meat and organs were unloaded on it. Women gathered around the meat discussing what they would be responsible for. Some would carve meat, some would clean the intestines, some would dice the flipper or kidneys, and some would make dinner rolls. There were propane tanks lined up in the driveway and garage. Multiple kettles already on a full rolling boil.

Noatak hugged me before she stepped out of the truck. She traced the ashen line across my face. "Tomorrow, you will help serve."

Serving meant feeding the whole town. Around noon the next day, the feast was announced over the radio and lines began to form outside. As they came through the garage where the food was arranged, Katie and I held open Ziploc bags. Each one was filled with a roll, some heart or kidney, skin, flipper, intestines, and whale meat.

I'd never seen women so proud of their banquet, as the ones standing behind the serving table. I'd been to Thanksgivings served on china plates and eaten with engraved silver. I'd dined on tenderloin and even stolen a sip of champagne at academic banquets. But the feasts of Barrow were different. They were whale parts floating in plastic bags. Family flags raised for decoration, for honor. And an open invitation to anyone willing to stand in line. The joy was electric.

When the lines slowed, a woman gave Katie and me our own bags. We stared into them and wondered if we could just snag some leftover rolls. Noatak came and mercifully took away the bags. She handed us paper plates filled with long, wafer-thin strips of meat. Each strip was perfectly divided into two halves. One half was translucent pink, the other dark black. Next to the meat was a dinner roll and a little dipping bowl filled with dark, watery sauce.

I looked at the pink and black rectangles of meat. They reminded me of the sunrise on the Chukchi Sea, when the sky fades pale and the water turns a rich black.

Katie stared at her plate. "What is this?"

"Muktuk," Noatak said.

Eric joined us. "Whale skin and blubber. *Raw.* Remember how you said whale sounds better than blueberry yogurt? Well ... now's your chance to test it."

He grinned as he reached for a piece from Katie's plate. As he chewed, his eyes were filled with the same *dare-you-to* challenge that I'd seen in Katie's so many times.

Katie raised her chin, picked up a strip of muktuk, and folded it into her mouth. She gave me a nod to tell me to do the same. I took a small bite. It was slightly sweet, but not slimy like I had expected. It was firm and so chewy I wondered if I'd ever be able to swallow it.

"Keep chewing," Eric said and laughed at Katie's stuffed mouth. "It's Eskimo bubble gum." Eventually, the texture broke down and the fat and meat melted in my mouth. Katie's face was red as she struggled to chew.

Noatak touched my hand. "Try it like this," she said, as she dipped a piece in the dark sauce. "Wasabi and soy."

I picked up a piece, dipped it in the sauce, and took a bite. The salt and heat of the sauce mingled nicely with the sweetness of the skin. "That's good," I said and dipped another bite. The muktuk was rich, and I began to feel warm and content.

"This will help your skin, too," Noatak said as she took our empty plates. "Muktuk has everything your hands and feet need to become smooth again."

As the last of the diners finished their baggies, Katie and I carried in kettles to be washed and dried in the kitchen. We chatted happily about the boat, the whale, and all the things we planned next. Nothing seemed impossible anymore. We'd hike the biggest glaciers. We'd visit the tundra and run through arctic cotton fields.

The doorbell rang and Noatak laughed. "Now come the late diners."

She was carrying a large kettle and Katie's hands were sudsy with dishwater, so I answered the door. I opened it with a smile and came face-to-face with a police officer.

"You have the right to remain silent."

Katie screamed *Run!* Noatak sobbed. Eric yelled that I was just a kid, and couldn't we work something better out?

The officer waved a warrant in the air for his answer, and the bombs exploded inside my heart. The hooks set deep.

Hoist your flag. Call a Carolina party. The runaway whale is caught.

The Heart-Shaped Museum

The sale of the land to the government happened quickly. Abel and Stella had money to begin repairing their home. Abel did most of the work at night. He took his time, carefully restoring everything. During the day, he joined the men working by the river behind his house. They were digging a lake, with plans to develop it into one of the largest tourist attractions in Carolina. But the land was full of boulders and rocks that had to be shoveled out and dragged away by mules. It was slow, hard work, guaranteed to keep the men employed.

Stella had grown used to working hard too. She could no longer abide floating aimlessly through her days, like she once had on Mayfield Hill. She made platters of chicken and rows of pies, and eventually worked her way through the entire *Sycamore Baptist Recipe Book.* Jack still wasn't a fat, sleepy baby. But he became content, finally, the moment he was able to move. He was a born scooter, and he happily rolled, pawed, and crawled his way across old walnut floors. With her hands free, Stella had the idea to cook for the men. She wrapped biscuits, hunks of ham, fried pies, and jars of tea and carried them down to the river. She shifted Jack around on her hip as she handed out sack lunches for a nickel each. The men were ravenous from their work, and Stella turned a double profit each week. She handed the money to Abel to help repair and finish their house.

But something else happened far away that changed everything one more time. War broke out. And now the government didn't need shovel-diggers. They needed bullet-makers and soldiers. The mules and wagons disappeared. The men stopped showing up. There would be no tourist resort. Instead, there was a torn up river parcel and a one acre dust pit. The government had no use for it, and Abel bought the land back with the money they were paid for it. He spent weeks digging a shallow trench from the river to the pit. Slowly, whenever the river rose from rains, water ran back and flooded the pit. A dark pond was born.

Abel was looking for work when he heard about the church a few miles from his house. It had caught fire in a lightning storm and nearly burned down. The preacher needed men to rebuild it. Abel stepped into a sanctuary full of dust and ashes.

"I'm here about a job," Abel said to the preacher. "Heard you were hiring."

The preacher sighed. "I wish. I run out of money to pay."

Abel saw an ash covered piano in the corner. "Does it still play?" he asked.

"Mostly. But we were planning to switch to an organ anyways."

Abel walked to it, ran his hand across the keys, and listened to the mishmash of sounds coming out. "What do you say I fix the roof for you, in exchange for this piano?"

The preacher frowned. "That ain't fair to you."

But Abel shook his head. "It's a good wage."

It took five men to lift the piano up the front steps into Abel and Stella's house.

"Where do you want it?" one of the men asked.

"This way," Stella said as she led them to the kitchen. She pointed to the long counter, the one she used for prepping meals. "Right against there."

The men snickered.

"Stella," Abel whispered. "What about your cooking?"

"I cook on the stove," Stella snapped.

"Yes, but we got that whole big room with the fireplace in it. And that big window, looking over them fields. Wouldn't a piano be pretty there?"

The men snickered again.

Stella glared at them. "That *is* a beautiful spot for a piano. Why don't you buy one and put it there?"

Abel frowned and Stella sighed. "Look," she said. "A woman spends most of her time in the kitchen, either fixing supper, washing up, or waiting on something to finish and making sure it don't burn. I don't want to lose any more time. I want to be able to sit down and play while the potatoes boil and not have to worry about burning the roast because I'm away. The room with the big window and the fields feels miles away from where I do most of my work. I don't want to wait another second to play."

Abel motioned to the men. "It goes in the kitchen."

And so the old church piano found a new home among custards and kettles. It would always smell of smoke, especially when Stella played a rousing tune that caused her to bang the keys. But Stella loved it. She still managed to burn the meat and let the potatoes boil over numerous times. Whenever she sat down to play, she escaped the kitchen. Her piano became its own hidden room.

One evening, just before supper, while the gravy simmered and Stella softly played an old carding room song, someone banged on the front door. When Stella opened it, she gasped and began to smooth her apron. Her hair was in the messy braid down her back that Abel adored. Her sleeve had gravy spotted across it.

"Sally?"

"Hello, Stella."

"What are you ... I mean ... why are you—"

"Are you going to invite your sister in, or are you going to leave me standing here in the wilderness?"

Stella glanced behind her sister. There was a car parked along the road with a man sitting inside.

"Does Dale want to come?" Stella asked. "It's awful muggy out and—"

"He's fine."

Sally stepped past her with the same older-sister-arrogance that Stella always despised. She turned a circle in the foyer, her eyes inspecting each wall carefully.

"Not much for decorating, are you?" Sally smirked. "The structure's solid though, and the rooms well shaped. My my, it certainly is quaint."

"Are you hungry?" Stella asked. "I've got roast chicken, gravy, and dressing."

Sally shook her head.

"How about some pie then? I've got a chocolate pie. You remember that picnic by the river with all our cousins? How you snuck a whole chocolate pie under the table? Sat there and ate the whole thing." Stella laughed. "I thought Mama would have a fit when she found you. And Daddy got to laughing so that he—"

Sally held her hand up to stop Stella's story. "Pie will be fine."

Stella and Sally took pie and coffee into the big room, *the pretty room*, as Stella called it when she showed Sally. Sally grunted and looked out the big window.

"The view is nice, I suppose," Sally said. "You sure could use some drapery though. These naked windows would have made Mama blush."

Stella watched as Sally took a bite of pie. Then three more.

"Made it myself," she said proudly. "Think it's as good as Daisy's?"

Sally smirked. "You're quite the domestic now. Doesn't your husband earn enough to hire you some help?"

Stella blushed. "We have plenty."

Sally nodded. "So I've heard."

"Why did you come? Is Betsy all right? Did she marry? Does she have any babies? I've got a little boy ... oh, Sally, you've got to meet him."

"Betsy is fine. After all, she got the house and it wasn't her mill that burned down. That was mine."

Stella noticed the way Sally's teeth gritted when she said the word *mine*. A chill began to creep over her.

"Dale, your husband, he's richer than Daddy ever dreamed about being though," Stella reasoned with her. "That's why Daddy gave Betsy the house. He knew Dale could run the big mill for you, and that he already had a whole string of houses."

"Yes, Dale could have run the mill for me. But of course, *it burned down.*" Sally took a deep breath and laid her pie on the window sill. "There's a richness to your pie, sister. It unsettles my stomach. I think you should consider hiring help after all. Might I have a glass of tea?"

"I'll get you some."

"I'll come along. I'd like the full tour," Sally said.

Stella cringed. *Now* she wished the piano was in the pretty corner. She started the tour upstairs, hoping Sally would forget about the tea. There were entire rooms still unfurnished, and she held her breath as Sally sneered. But she loved showing off Jack's room with the little blue and yellow patchwork quilt on the bed, and the rug stitched with a circle of rabbits.

"My baby boy's room," Stella said as she opened the door. The doorknob fell off in her hand as she opened it, but she smiled proudly. How could any room that cradled such treasure, ever fail to shine?

"I'd like to see the kitchen now," Sally said. "My throat is parched. I surely need that glass of tea."

As Stella led Sally into the kitchen, she waited for the stinging insults about her decorating skills. But Sally didn't speak, she shrieked with laughter. She laughed until her face was red and tears pooled in her eyes. When she finally caught her breath, she leaned against the wall and rolled her head from side to side.

"This proves everything," she said with a triumphant smile. "Everything I've been telling Harold. Just wait till he hears about this."

"Who is Harold?" Stella asked.

"My husband."

"What about Dale?"

"What do you think happened to Dale? I was left without a mill or a house, with only the clothes on my back and Mama's china and pearls."

"Daddy had money for you all to split," Stella said.

"Of course he did, but that wasn't nearly enough to snag a man like Dale. He's an entrepreneur after all. I don't know if I could have respected him if he had stooped to marrying a girl like me, without any real wealth of my own. He married Betsy. After all, her inheritance didn't burn down."

Stella gasped. "I'm so sorry."

"Yes. Betsy ran off with my fiancé. And *you*... you ran off with the rest of my inheritance," Sally said bitterly.

"What? What do you mean?"

"I mean this place. Daddy always joked it was a swamp, but Harold and I drove out here last month. We looked it over. Saw how nice it is. You know river-bottom land sells for quite the good dollar these days."

"It's nice because of Abel," Stella said. "He hasn't stopped working since we got here. When we first came, every window was broken, but he—"

Sally held her hand up in the air. "You know this would have been mine. Should have been. Daddy wrote in the will that I get the mill and any other unnamed properties. He insisted that you get nothing. You chose your linthead over Daddy."

"But this... this house was Mama's," Stella stammered. "She's the one who decided."

"When she was out of her head with grief," Sally yelled. "In her right mind she never would have crossed Daddy. She didn't even budge when I came home and told her you were pregnant and slumming."

"But she changed her mind. The men came and told us. She signed her name and everything."

"Harold sees things different. He's an attorney, you know, and he sees how Mama was so sick with the diabetes, out of her head with grief, and not thinking straight. He says maybe she didn't even remember how you had disgraced us. Maybe she didn't even remember that you weren't really me. I mean, Stella and Sally aren't such different names. Maybe she meant to write Sally all along."

"You don't really believe that," Stella whispered. "There's no way for you to know—"

"Now that I've seen that," Sally interrupted as she pointed to the piano, "I know you don't deserve this house. It doesn't really belong to you."

"Because of the piano?"

Sally laughed. "Because you're linthead! You'll be just fine living in an old mill shack. Nice houses belong to real ladies who don't disgrace their daddies. Ladies who hire help to make their pies. Ladies who marry schooled attorneys instead of cotton-talking doffers. Ladies who would know pianos shouldn't smell like smoke and ought to be set in front of large windows. You may be a lot of things, but you'll never be the lady of *this* house. And my Harold will see that you quit pretending otherwise. He knows all the right laws, he knows all the right judges. He works for the biggest firm in this state, and his daddy is the new senator."

"What are you going to do?" Stella said, as she clutched Sally's arm. "My family lives here ... my baby boy ..."

Sally shook her head bitterly. "All I got was ashes. *Ashes!* And I'm not the one who ran away. I'm not the one who broke Daddy's heart."

"But you love living in Raleigh," Stella cried. "You'd hate living out in the country."

Sally gritted her teeth as her hands curled into fists. "You have no idea what it's like to see our old friends and have them ask me where we summer. And I have to make up some lie about how Harold's work is so busy, and he misses me too much to let me go anywhere. The truth is, we haven't got any place to summer. We only have the one house because neither of us inherited another. But that's all going to change. We're going to sell this place to the highest bidder, buy us a pretty mountain estate, and the next time somebody asks me where I summer, I'll have a better answer. I'll tell them—"

Stella slapped Sally. It happened in a blink, like instinct, before she had a chance to restrain herself with ladylike manners. Sally's face burned with insult and injury while her mouth gaped open in shock.

Secretly, Stella was equally shocked by what she'd just done. But she didn't regret it. She felt wildly unleashed as she grabbed Sally by the elbow and dragged her toward the door.

"Get out," she screamed. "Get out!"

Sally, pink-faced and bewildered, walked out the front door. Stella braced herself against the wall as she tried to calm down.

Abel appeared around the corner. "That thing come off again?"

Stella looked down at her hand. She was still clutching the doorknob from Jack's bedroom.

"I'll bolt it," Abel said. "Wood must be going soft inside. How's your sister? Didn't she wanna hold Jack?"

Abel looked up from the doorknob he was holding and saw Stella's face. It was the same look she'd given him long ago, when he told her to go home because he couldn't keep her and Jack fed.

"What's wrong?" he asked.

"She's come to take our home. Cause she got nothing but ashes and has no place to summer. Cause my pie is too rich and my piano is in the kitchen."

"Because your pie ... what?"

"Daddy said I get nothing. But here I am, standing in the big house making my too-rich pies and playing songs while the chicken fries. So Sally's come to take it back. She's got some husband-attorney. Says he knows all the right laws and judges. And so I smacked her across the face and—"

Abel held her and pressed her head down on his shoulder. "This is your home. This is Jack's home."

Later that night, when Stella guessed that Abel was sleeping, she crept out of their bedroom and hurried to the kitchen. Dirty dishes were scattered across the stove and counter. The half-eaten pie was sitting on top of her piano.

But Stella didn't wash dishes, and she didn't clear the pie. She sat down among the gravy mess and began to play. Every rolled up grit box label. Every Mozart masterpiece. Every bit of hymn she'd ever learned.

Abel lay awake and listened. His hands gripped their cotton sheets and twisted them like the cotton bolls that covered his brother's grave. He heard something new in Stella's music. There was joy of course. There was always joy in her music. But that night there was something else that he recognized from his own darkest hours.

Grief. It was in her urgency. It was in the way she played song upon song, chord after chord, without pause. She was soaking it up, every possible minute with her smoky piano. On and on, all through the night, Stella played her long good-bye.

Part Three
Endings

XXVIII

I was transported directly to the Piedmont Justice and Rehabilitation Center for Juvenile Girls. I was fingerprinted again and dressed in a beige jumpsuit with the word *Juvenile* stamped across the back. I was given a pillow, a thin blanket, and taken to a room with a set of bunk beds.

"All yours," the officer said as I stepped into the room. "No roommate yet." She grinned, like she had given me a present. "Things are organized by halls here. You're on Hall B. You all eat together, have classes, and work duty. Halls compete to earn privileges like movies, so best look sharp so as not to bring your crowd down, all right?"

"How long will I be here?" I asked.

"Somebody'll come see you about all that. Right now, Hall B is finishing up breakfast. I heard you took yourself a big vacation ... some kinda globe-trotter, huh? Well things are different here. This ain't no vacation resort. There's no talking at meals, in the bathroom, or during work duty. The only time you talk is at recess or during lights on time in your bunk. You ain't got a roommate, so I guess you can just talk to yourself. You keep the rules, you don't throw no fits, and you'll do fine. You hear?" She leaned close and pointed to her ear. "I asked you a question Juvie."

"Yes, ma'am."

A whistle blew.

"That's the Hall B alert," the officer said. "When you hear that whistle you need to line up. It's time for morning work duty."

Hall B's work duty was sanitation. If I had been assigned to Hall C, I would have had recreation related chores. I would have helped organize the library and maybe taken a moment or two to read a quick page. Or if I had Hall D's, first impression duty, I would have helped clean windows and rake leaves, stare into freedom and pretend I was someplace else. But sanitation meant that I was handed a pair of rubber gloves, a bottle of bleach spray, and told to scrub. Not just showers and toilets. We did those first, and I assumed we were done. But there was a whole list of things the officer ordered us to clean, like trash cans, rubber doormats, and the buttons on the TV remotes in the media hall. If people touched it, if a flu germ could possibly live on it, then we scrubbed it. We worked for three hours before the officer blew the whistle again. I followed the other girls as they put away their cleaning supplies and lined up.

"Academics," the officer barked. The girls turned to march down the hall. The officer grabbed my arm. "Not you."

She led me to a long gray hall that was lined with doors. When we passed an open one I peered inside and saw a tiny room, not more than six feet across, with a small table in the center and two chairs on either side. At the very end of the hall, the officer pointed toward a door.

"That's yours," she said. "I'll be back in thirty."

I expected to see Loretta, maybe even Katie, waiting inside the room. But instead there was a woman with cropped curly hair and long, dangly earrings that brushed the tops of her shoulders. She had an open folder on the table and flipped through it.

"Come in," she said cheerfully, without looking up. "Have a seat. I'm just wrapping up a few things and then we'll get started."

She didn't wear a wedding ring, didn't file her nails, and wore an uncomfortable blouse. I guessed this from the way she kept reaching behind to tug at her collar, like the tag was scratching her. Her hair had gel in it, the kind that holds curl but also makes hair crunchy. Her eyes were puffy and ringed, and the corners of her mouth twitched slightly as she read. I tried to guess what all those little details meant. Was she a tired woman? A kind woman? Would she help me?

She looked up, noticed a tear falling down my face. She reached into a bag at her feet and pulled out a tissue for me. She did not say, *Don't cry.* She did not say, *It will be okay.* And that's how I knew things were really bad.

"I'm Marcia," she said. "I'm not a therapist, but I'll listen to your problems. I'm not your attorney, but I'll talk about the legal process. I'm your social worker. It's my job to move you through the system, help figure out the best place for you to grow up healthy and stable. Understand?"

I nodded.

"Here's the deal. Loretta Mason has relinquished all legal rights to you. She has provided us with a list of your remaining next of kin, but it's not long. So far, I haven't had much luck contacting anyone who knows you. Currently, the state has custody of you. And you've got multiple criminal charges filed against you."

Of course. Even though I had expected this news, I slumped forward and wept. There's such a difference between *thinking* something, and *knowing* it. One threatens to cut, the other carves and slices.

Marcia waited for a minute before speaking again.

"We don't have much time...About that list of possible guardians," she said. "I was wondering if you might have any suggestions? A relative you remember? Someone that you had a special bond with, that might be sensitive to your case? Like I said, the list I have isn't very long and the judge will handle the custody issue before the criminal matters. So, do you know of anyone?"

I shook my head.

"If I can't find someone suitable, you'll remain a ward of the state. Depending on the outcome of your criminal case, you might eventually be eligible for foster placement."

"How long will I be here?" I asked.

"Let's see, credit card theft, running away while out on bond, reckless endangerment, vandalism, grievous bodily harm..." She sighed and shook her head. "Let's focus on what we can fix. You need a new guardian."

"Everybody's dead."

Marcia handed me another tissue. "Well, on the bright side...it's not all jail here, not like you think.

There're different levels. Hall E has field trips, movies, and nail polish nights. You're starting out on Hall B, like most new girls do. Work hard, behave, and you'll be promoted." She leaned back in her chair and crossed her arms, satisfied with the good news she'd given me.

"Was there a boy?" she asked. "Were you in love?"

I startled. "What?"

"Or bullies at school? I have to put something in your file. I'm supposed to make sense of this for the judge." She tried to run her hands through her curls. The stiffness of the gel stopped her, so she settled for just scrunching them in her fists. "But sometimes things won't make sense. Take you, for example. Straight-A-trust-fund kid...what on earth are you doing using someone else's credit card to buy a ticket to Alaska?"

I didn't answer and she leaned forward and grinned. "You know, I feel like we've met before. I read your father's book. He mentioned you in the acknowledgments. Called you his favorite character."

"You don't strike me as a reader," I muttered.

She shrugged. "I like historical romance. And there's this whole Community Read program at the library each fall that I participate in. Three years ago, his book was the pick. It was pretty good. I mean, I don't know about the ending. Open endings aren't my thing. It takes so much work to get through a book that size. And then to have to guess what happens at the end feels, I don't know, like I've been cheated."

"If you didn't care at all, that'd be much worse," I whispered, a perfect echo of something Daddy said to a complaining reader.

Marcia stared, waiting for me to explain.

"He didn't want the last page to be the end," I said.

"Oh, so he planned a sequel?"

"No. That last page was an invitation for *you* to keep the story going. He wanted you to love those characters and always wonder how they're doing. To walk around still holding your breath for them."

Marcia's eyes widened. "Ahh, I see. That's what you were doing, right? Disappearing to Alaska, making us all hold our breath over you, your father's favorite character?"

I shook my head with disgust. "I *hate* my story."

Marcia pointed her finger at me. "Bingo." She flipped open the file and started writing furiously. When she finished, she sat up and tugged at her collar.

"That's almost always the reason," she said. "Sometimes it's pure meanness. But most of the time, it's what you said. Other girls don't put it as poetically, but they say it in their own way. And it's why places like this exist." She leaned forward and patted my hand. "Your father might even call you ... cliché."

I winced at the word, just as someone banged on the door and yelled, "Time's up!" Marcia slapped my file closed.

"You'll see your attorney tomorrow," she said hurriedly. "I'll finish calling my list to see if I can come up with a guardian before you see the judge."

The door swung open and an officer stuck her head in. "I'm sorry, but if I don't stay on schedule ..."

"She's ready now," Marcia answered.

But I wasn't ready. Marcia had talked stories with me, when what I wanted was instructions: Be good for ten days and then you'll go home. Or, say you're sorry to Loretta and she'll take you back.

The officer led me back to my cell and told me to wait there until someone came to get me for Academics.

"Marcia know how long you're in for?" the officer asked. "Always curious as to which ones are here for the long haul."

"She wasn't sure," I said.

"Ah, that means maybe till you're eighteen." The officer smiled. "Welcome home, globe-trotter."

XXIX

At six a.m. the lights in my cell blinked on. I dressed in my beige jumpsuit and joined the girls from my hall as we walked single file to the cafeteria for a silent breakfast.

Trays of burned sausage and soggy toast surrounded me. I choked over my first bite, but everyone else devoured their breakfast. I had planned to make a burnt porridge joke later, when we could talk during recess, but it seemed that everyone loved the food.

After breakfast came work duty. Hall B was assigned to sanitation for the full quarter. We would disinfect the same showers, toilets, floors, sinks, remotes, and doorknobs every morning for three months. I gagged when I scrubbed a toilet. I heaved when I pulled a clog of hair from a shower drain. My eyes were pooling with tears from the burn of bleach in the air when the Hall B whistle finally blew. It was time for academics.

I was assigned coursework based on my age. There was no record or concern for prior test scores. Before, I was mastering geometry. Now, I was given pages of multiplication memory facts. There was no art class. There was no creative writing, no poetry assignments or fiction prompts. Worst of all, there was no library. Library time was an earned privilege for girls on better halls, just like movies on Friday nights. Instead, I was assigned a reading comprehension book that had been specifically approved for delinquents. The pages were filled with plodding plots designed to teach me a lesson in morality. The stories had no runaways, no thieves, or open endings. They were about young girls making wise choices and reaping all the benefits.

After a three hour block of academics came lunch. We were served turkey or ham sandwiches, an apple, cold tater tots, and watery lemonade. Once again, everyone devoured their meal. I received odd looks when I threw away my nearly full tray.

Outdoor recess followed lunch. There were jump ropes and balls scattered around a fenced yard, but most girls huddled and chatted over top of one another for the whole hour. The older ones pined after boys they left behind. The younger ones missed their mamas. One girl told a long tale of her shoplifting adventures. She noticed me listening and gave me a nod.

"How about you, newbie?" she asked.

"Huh?"

"What got you in here?"

"Alaska."

The girls in the group raised their eyebrows and looked at me.

"I ran away to Alaska," I explained.

"Yeah right," one laughed and rolled her eyes. "You probably just made it across the Yadkin."

I shook my head. "All the way to the top of the earth."

Most of the girls had the same *whatever* look on their faces as the girl who had challenged me. But none of them walked away.

"Yeah?" the shoplifting girl asked. "How'd you manage?"

I took a deep breath. "There was this girl named Katie Monroe..."

I told wild tales. About ice worms as long as jump ropes, writhing through the glaciers. About an arctic storm that capsized my boat and threw me into icy waters. I held up my hands and showed them my snow scars.

When the whistle sounded, we returned to another block of academics, followed by another round of chores, or for lucky girls, visitation. But my name wasn't called to go to the common hall and receive a guest. I had a string of apologies rehearsed for Loretta, but I was sent to do laundry. As I folded a stack of beige jumpsuits, I exchanged my apologies for curses.

After laundry and visitation came supper. It was a pasty meat, soggy potato, and a limp salad. I was ravenous now. The food was disgusting, but I chewed it quickly and knew that I'd never bond with Hall B girls over burnt porridge jokes. Girls in jail eat what's served. There's no barbecue supper coming later. There's no Snickers bar hidden in a school locker. No Capri Sun to sip on the bus ride home. The only way to get the gnawing out of my stomach was to eat what was served. And so, like every other girl, I pushed passed the gagging and did it.

The day ended in the recreation room, where we could talk again, play with board games that were missing most of the pieces, or scribble at the table with scrap paper and broken crayons. When the whistle came, we filed back to our rooms to wait for lights out. At six a.m. the exact same routine began all over again, day after day, whistle after whistle. I was like a doffer, changing spools. Or a spinner, tying up broken thread after broken thread. It was a maddening routine.

I met with my attorney. He scanned my file and complimented my grades. When I pressed him for how much longer I would have to stay in jail, he spoke of getting me a "good deal." Like I was buying a used car. A "real good deal," like I was a couponer, waiting for the J.C. Penney's clearance sale.

"I don't want a good deal," I told him. "I want out."

He chuckled. "Honey, the state won't just wink at what you did and call it cute. Louise Lawson is still in physical therapy for her hip. And if that one boy hadn't gotten to his inhaler in time after all that sulfur dust got tossed around, things would be a whole lot worse. Look, we'll get you before the judge, get things settled with Marcia and your custody, and then get your criminal case moving along. I'll do my best by you. I won't accept anything less than a real good deal."

As I waited for my first court date, my hands stayed busy with the Hall B routine. But my mind simmered with excuses, a whole long list of eloquent reasons for why the judge shouldn't hold me responsible. During the day, I had hope. I convinced myself that I was a sympathetic case—I was young, confused, orphaned.

But at night, once the scrubbing and multiplication pages were all finished, I lay in the dark and panicked.

I was guilty. I built my pomegranate prison with my own hands.

Marcia met with me again on the morning of my court appearance.

"I wanted you to hear it from me first, before I tell the judge today," she began. "I spoke with Loretta about her decision to relinquish her rights to you, and I agree with her. Her health isn't the best, and she's raising her niece now. I don't think she has the physical or emotional resources needed to give you the proper care. Since I haven't found an appropriate substitute, I'll be recommending the judge award permanent custody to the state."

"I won't go home?"

Marcia sighed. "Until the judge sees fit, your home is here. And until you're eighteen, you'll be in state custody. You'll have to live wherever we place you." She flipped through my file. "Your behavior charts look great. I bet you'll be promoted to Hall C next month!" She stopped and smiled proudly. "Pearl, you could be cold and hungry in Alaska right now. One day you might look back and say this place was the best thing that could've happened to you."

The best thing? What a small life Marcia had lived. To call the Hall B daily drill, the *best* thing. I looked around at that tiny concrete room, with its gray walls, gray floor, and flickering fluorescent lights. I looked at the tired circles under Marcia's eyes.

"I've seen milk glass mountain tops. I watched a muktuk sunrise. I saw a whale give its life to the Inupiats," I said.

Marcia raised an eyebrow. "And?"

"You don't know how good the *best* can be. Sometimes you have to run away to see it."

She waved her hands through the air to swish away the idea before it got close. "It's time for court."

She signed me out of the Justice Center, and we rode together in a Honda that smelled of fries and mint mouthwash. Fast food wrappers were crushed in a pile on the floor. A tube of mascara, a wand of concealer, and a travel size bottle of Scope were crammed into the drink holders. She noticed me staring and laughed. "It's a busy life being a grown-up. Everything's on the go. I eat on the go, work on the go, sometimes I have to get ready on the go."

We drove down the same roads that I once traveled with Daddy. We passed a magnolia tree, like the ones he loved from his campus. Then we passed the doughnut shop. And it struck me, as I rode in the car with my social worker on my way to see the judge, how disappointed Daddy would be.

"Don't be scared," Marcia said as she noticed my tears and handed me a tissue. "You don't have to do a thing. You just sit where I show you and stand when the judge enters. I'll do all the talking."

As we stepped inside the courtroom, someone shouted "Pearl!" and I turned to see Katie wildly waving. Loretta scowled and pulled Katie's arm down by the sleeve. Loretta's eyes found mine, and I tried to burn her up with hatred. She never looked away.

Katie desperately tried to send a message. I couldn't understand her, and she finally grinned and gave me a thumbs-up. *Always the cheerleader.*

Marcia led me to a table at the front and nudged me to stand when the judge entered. I looked around the room at all the solemn faces and overdressed strangers. It was all so similar to that lonely morning in the campus chapel, when a crowd of sad, overdressed strangers gathered to mourn Daddy.

The judge flipped through my file, then motioned to Marcia and she began to speak. As words poured out of her mouth, I recalled the drone of organ music.

"She has excellent potential," Marcia declared. "A true scholar, with a trust fund available for college. There's a lot of hope with this case. For now, I recommend she remain at the Piedmont Justice and Rehabilitation Center for Juvenile Girls. Once her criminal case is concluded, we will review her placement status again for further options. It is my opinion that this arrangement promotes her best interest. She's already established a positive behavior track at the Center and is likely to be promoted and granted further privileges soon."

I remembered that lying song. *It is Well, It is Well,* they all sang at Daddy's funeral, even though nothing was.

"This is the *best thing* for her right now," Marcia purred.

Pearl is Well. She is Well. She is Well.

My spine began to roll crazily against the back of my chair as I remembered the wooden pew from the campus chapel. I reached down and scratched my legs. They itched like I was wearing panty hose.

"Very well," the judge said in lofty tones. "Since we have assembled ourselves today to determine what custodial arrangement is in this minor child's best interest, prior to the adjudication of her criminal matters..."

I blinked my eyes and saw Styrofoam hearts bloom. I pounded my fist against the table. Didn't I write this story? Shouldn't I be the one to tell it?

"But I thought this show was supposed to be about me!" I cried out.

Marcia gasped in bewilderment.

The judge glared, and his eyebrows raised into angry peaks across his forehead. "This *show*?"

"I mean..." I stopped and took a deep breath. *Pause for emphasis,* I heard Daddy whisper. "This is my story, Judge. Y'all aren't telling it the right way."

The Heart-Shaped Museum

A stranger knocked at the front door and handed a sealed envelope to Stella. She opened it with shaking hands and began to read the complaint to Abel. But she sobbed so hard that Abel couldn't understand much after the part where Harold and Sally contested the validity of the last will and testament of Delores Mayfield.

Abel scanned the complaint. He wanted to know everything it said, but he didn't want Stella to keep reading. He tucked it in his toolbox and went to work early the next morning. He asked the preacher to read it to him.

They sat together on a half-burned pew as Abel learned the details of the complaint. Harold and Sally claimed that Mrs. Mayfield was too incompetent, due to her state of grief and advanced diabetes, to make a new will. They demanded the disputed property be returned to the original Mayfield estate where it would pass to Sally. They demanded payment of any moneys received from the government's use and easements of the land, and any profits made from the sale and repurchase of the back acreage. They demanded the Weaver family vacate the premises immediately.

The preacher folded the complaint and handed it back to Abel. "That's some kinda trouble for a sister-in-law."

Abel kicked a burned pew until a cloud of soot began to billow around him. The preacher put his hand on Abel's shoulder. "Gonna wear out your boots doing that."

Abel slumped into the pew and put his head in his hands. "Always goes like this. Every good thing gets broken."

"How do you reckon?" the preacher asked.

Abel told him about finally making it to the spinning room and then Jack dying. About finding Stella after all the numb years and having to run off like a thief. About making a good life together, until after the crash when he couldn't keep his family fed.

"The day after we buried my brother, I punched the man that picked out his tombstone. *All things work together for good* was etched in big letters over his grave."

The preacher nodded. "That's in the Bible—"

"It's a lie!" Abel sat back and studied the preacher to see how shocked he was by his blasphemy.

"Surely you won't just hand the house to your sister-in-law?" the preacher asked.

"Gonna get a downtown attorney."

"Good. Then quit hanging your head like you done been whooped."

The next day, Abel planned out all the things he'd tell the attorney. "We didn't go asking for it," he mumbled as he practiced his speech. "We never hoped on any kind of inheritance."

But when he showed up at the attorney's office, he didn't get a chance to make his first point. After a handshake and a quick introduction, the lawyer announced he could not take Abel's case.

"It's a personal conflict," the attorney said. "I helped Harold's daddy run his senate campaign."

"You don't know why I'm here. You haven't even heard what my problem is."

"I had a phone call this morning," the lawyer said. "I'm up to speed on it."

"What about the other name on your door? Can he do it?"

The attorney stretched and slowly shook his head. "Harold's daddy won that campaign. You don't get to be a state senator without being a very well connected man. Do you understand what I'm saying?"

"You're all in cahoots," Abel said.

The attorney laughed. "Well it's not like this is a matter of great justice. You don't need an attorney to keep you off death row. It'd be foolish for any of us to fight over some bit of swamp Harold has set his eye on."

When Abel returned to the church the next day, the preacher asked him how the meeting went.

"He won't take the case. Says nobody else will either. Says Harold's a senator's boy and it'd be foolishness to stand in his way." Abel threw his hands up. "It's over."

"Well now, wait a second. Don't seem like there's no big legal mystery here. And any man can tell his own story the same as the next."

"So you think *I* should..."

"Sure I do. You tell the judge your history with that house... why you moved there, how you fixed it up, what it means to your family," the preacher said.

"But these other men got all kinds of money and been to years of schooling. I been poor my whole life and never gone to school. A man like me don't count for nothing. Especially not in a courtroom."

The preacher stared at Abel with a surprised look on his face. "You don't—"

"Know how to read?" Abel interrupted. "Never had a chance to learn. I can recognize some words, but if I ain't seen 'em before, I don't know how to figure 'em out."

"But you don't got to be able to read stories to tell 'em," the preacher said. "I hear you swapping 'em with the crew all the time—about haints and cotton and fishin'." He pulled a Bible from the back of a pew. "I got a story you need to hear." He dusted the soot off the cover but didn't open the pages. "A long time ago there was a man who built stuff with wood, just like you do now, named Joseph. And his wife Mary was gonna have a baby boy."

Abel frowned. "Preacher, I ain't up for singing Christmas carols right now."

The preacher held up his hand to hush Abel. "Hang on a quick minute. It's rude to interrupt a storyteller." The preacher cleared his throat. "A law came down from the big men in charge that everybody had to go pay a tax in their family's hometown. That was quite a trip for ol' Joseph and Mary, especially with her pregnant. But they weren't in cahoots with nobody that could help, so they had to make the long haul to Bethlehem. While they were there, wouldn't you know it, her pains started comin'. Joseph tried to find her a decent spot, tried to do right by his family, but nobody would make room for 'em. Mary gave birth in a barn." The preacher stared at Abel for a moment. "You reckon a man like Joseph counted?"

Abel felt embarrassed and confused, but the preacher persisted.

"Did he?"

"Sure," Abel grunted, unwilling to let the preacher trap him into more blasphemy. "He's part of the holy family. I ain't completely ignorant."

"He was like a linthead after the crash," the preacher said. "He wasn't a king, wasn't a boss, and his daddy sure wasn't a senator. Joseph and Mary were poor, worn down, out-of-towners. And you and I know the world don't make room for folks like that."

Abel had never heard the story this way. Before, it was a *Silent Night, all is calm and all is bright,* kind of story. But now Abel wondered if Joseph punched the barn wall in anger when he couldn't do better by his family. He thought about the first time he held baby Jack by the spinning machines, how he wiped away the lint sticking to his head. He imagined Joseph, picking off bits of hay that clung to Jesus.

"Forget what you think you know," the preacher said. "What did you just hear?"

Abel shrugged. "It was a hard night more than a silent one."

The preacher nodded. "God could have chosen a senator's son or a man with lots of schooling. But he chose Joseph, a man who wasn't in cahoots, and that the world didn't make room for."

Abel stayed quiet and stared at his boots.

"There were other men like him," the preacher continued. "A pack of boys who worked the sheep, but never owned the big farmhouses. These guys were so poor and grubby they probably weren't allowed inside a church. But that night, during the late shift, an angel showed up. I reckon they started shakin' so hard the lice jumped off 'em. 'Don't be scared, boys,' the angel said. 'I'm bringing y'all the best news. The Savior is born! Run on and take a gander. You'll find him lying in a feed box.' " The preacher grinned. "On that first night, God looked down on a world filled with kings on their thrones, learned fellas in their libraries, and preachers in their pulpits, and the men he picked to join his party were too dirty for church."

"Look at me," the preacher said softly.

Abel raised his eyes from his boots.

"No matter what else this world has taught you, I'm telling you now, God counts men like you. He chose men like you to be first in line. So don't be scared. Your story, your right to be heard, counts the same as any rich man's."

A crew of men ready to work on the church stomped through the door. The preacher pressed the Bible in Abel's hands before he stepped away to discuss rebuilding the steeple.

That night, Abel couldn't sleep. When that happened he usually told himself old cotton stories. He played with endings and inserted new twists until his body and mind relaxed. But tall tales wouldn't work. He kept thinking about Joseph pacing the barn floor.

He went to the mantel and pulled the Bible down. He flipped through the pages, stared with wonder at the thousands upon thousands of words that he would never read. Stella stepped into the room. Her face was pale and her eyes panicked. He knew she needed a good story too.

"Read us a bit," he said as he showed her the Bible.

"Wouldn't you rather me read the almanac about spring planting signs?"

Abel shook his head.

Stella took the Bible and thumbed through the smoky pages. "Mercy sakes, where do I even begin?"

"There's a real good part about some dirty shepherds. I think it begins with how them boys don't have any kind of farmhouse," Abel said.

Each night, when they couldn't sleep for the fear and dread that filled them, they curled up as Stella read from the biggest story either one of them had ever heard. Stella had been raised in church far more than Abel, but this was the first time that she had read the stories for herself. More than once, her mouth opened in astonishment.

"Well now... that is not how my mama told it," she'd whisper. Sometimes she laughed softly as she read. "More blind men and lepers."

Abel's heart recognized those blind men and lepers. They were linthead, too, with lines drawn to keep them separate from the rich, the clean, the owners of the day. He loved how Jesus saw through their misery to the hidden field inside them. Over and over, he planted his story there.

And the story was so different from what Abel expected. Before, when he marked off mill church like another chore on a checklist, Jesus' story was pretty and *safe*. But those soot covered pages revealed something fierce. Jesus didn't tiptoe around the lines the world marked off. He burst through them. He didn't just take notice of the filthy, the crazy, the most wretched of all, he fed them too. He healed broken hearts, broken bodies, broken spirits and lives, all while his story built toward the wildest plot twist possible. *Jesus broke himself.*

Abel held up his hand for Stella to stop reading. He'd heard the story preached before, but he'd never thought about a line-crossing, linthead-loving Jesus, being nailed to a piece of wood.

Abel's mind swarmed with old, hard memories. *Every good thing gets broken.* It's what he learned when he stared down into the ground as they buried his brother. *Every good thing gets broken.* It's what he believed, when his mama turned her back on him, as he waited in the long mill line. *Every good thing gets broken.* It's what he screamed as he punched the wall of the mill shack when he couldn't find work and couldn't keep his family fed. *Every good thing gets broken.* It's what he knew as truth by the time Sally came to steal his house.

And now Abel listened about how Jesus broke himself.

"Why'd he go and do a thing like that?" he asked.

"I learned a verse for a pageant once," Stella said and flipped pages until she found it. " 'For God so loved the world, that he gave his only begotten Son, that whoever believes in him shall not perish, but have everlasting life.' I think this whole story fits right inside that one word, *love*." Stella, still the love-hungry-pretty-girl, traced the word with her finger over and over, like she could lasso love for keeps.

Abel watched her trace the marks on the page, but it wasn't love that he lingered over. The word that he repeated under his breath, that echoed inside him, was something that he'd always hungered for but never believed possible. And it wasn't to learn to read or to own a solid roof. Those were good things, but fragile and weak. Abel craved something *everlasting*.

Stella turned back and started reading again. And once more, the plot twisted. A stone was rolled away. A tomb was emptied. And the lie—that every good thing gets broken—was defeated. Because the God who broke himself, could not stay broken. There was no line he could not cross. His death was the price, and *everlasting* was his gift.

Abel and Stella didn't bow their knees, they sank to them. And that night, inside a linthead's house, a miracle occurred. Abel opened his clenched fists and gave his broken life, all his broken dreams, to a linthead-loving Jesus.

When the morning arrived for Abel to face the suits and ties inside the Carolina courtroom, he didn't punch the wall and scream the old lie as he dressed in his overalls. He trembled and his heart raced, but he knew now that he was no longer an abandoned boy standing in a long linthead line.

Abel Weaver counted.

XXX

"Young lady," the judge boomed. "My courtroom is neither a show nor a story. Outbursts are not allowed."

I collapsed in my seat, raised my hand, and waved it in the air.

"What are you doing now?" the judge demanded.

"Hoping you'll call on me, so I won't have another outburst."

The judge slowly exhaled. "Very well, Miss Weaver, you may stand and tell the court what it is that you feel you must say."

I rose to my feet. "Marcia's lying. Jail is a miserable place. It's the worst setting. There's nothing to learn and nothing to read. The food is rotten potatoes and burnt porridge, but everybody still has to eat it. I'm not thriving. I'm dying. And if you're the one who decides what is best for me, I think you should know the truth."

The judge stared at me in silence for a moment. "For a young girl, you speak with a great deal of passion and clarity. And although I'm sympathetic to your plight, you must understand that if you are miserable, and I happen to believe that you are, it is the result of your own choices. Loretta Mason has relinquished her custody rights to you. The state has custody of you, and foster care is not allowed, given your upcoming criminal proceedings. Marcia isn't lying when she says that jail is the best option. Quite frankly, it's the only option. There is no one else who will be your guardian."

"Oh!" called a voice from the back. "Do I speak now? Or maybe ... I don't know ... later?"

I turned to see a woman standing in the back of the courtroom. Her hand was raised halfway in the air, like a student afraid to ask a question.

The judge groaned. "State your name."

"Ivy Rutherford."

"Miss Rutherford, do you have information that is pertinent to the matter currently before the court?" the judge asked.

"I think so, Your Honor."

"Proceed."

"I've come to get Pearl."

"Marcia?" the judge said in exasperation.

Marcia held her hands out, palms up. "Your Honor, this lady has never contacted me or anyone that I—"

"I am just so sorry about that," Ivy interrupted.

And the first detail that I collected about her was her accent. Her syllables were one beat slower than Carolina words. She sang "sorry" rather than spoke it, her voice rising and falling in sweet soprano tones. *S—o—r—r—y.*

"I don't know one thing about how this is done," she continued. "I mean, I called and called the Justice

Center, and they took messages. Finally, I got someone to tell me that she had this court date, so here I am. I've come to get Pearl."

Who is she? Who is she? More details began to rapidly spin inside my mind. She had red hair, with soft curls swirling across her shoulders. Milk glass skin and a sugar pink mouth. Her hand was still halfway raised in the air. Her fingers trembled.

"What is your relation to this child?" the judge asked.

"I'm her mama's first cousin."

"And why are you just now showing up in this child's life?"

The woman's faced turned as pink as her lips. "Christine died nearly fourteen years ago. I didn't know Tom enough to stay close. A few years ago we began exchanging Christmas cards. But I didn't know he had died until Loretta told me about what happened and all of Pearl's troubles. And well, here I am."

"Troubles? She is in state custody for serious matters," the judge said.

The woman nodded slowly. "She's made a real mess."

"Alleged *crimes*," the judge corrected.

"Yes, sir. But you heard her, jail isn't in her best interest. I think I am."

"The court can't just turn over a child to you. Before you can begin to be approved, you must submit the proper paperwork to Marcia, set up appointments, have a home study, perhaps take a parenting class."

"Yes, sir."

She was losing her courage. I could see it in the way her trembling hand began to lower. In the way her voice didn't sing her syllables nearly so clear or loud. The judge noticed too.

"Miss Rutherford, right now this child is being reformed by behavioral modification experts. I mean, what is *your* background? What can you offer a troubled child?" he asked.

"She can take me home. I want her to," I cried out.

The judge pointed his finger. "One more outburst and I'll have you removed."

"Your honor," Marcia spoke up. "I'd actually like to ask Miss Weaver a few questions if I may."

"Proceed," the judge barked.

"Do you even know Miss Rutherford?" Marcia asked.

I glanced over my shoulder at the woman. She gave me a slight nod, like she was eager to hear my lies. *Mark of a villain,* my heart whispered. In stories, when a stranger shows up out of nowhere, claiming to be a hero for no apparent benefit to themselves, it's almost always because they have an ulterior motive.

"Well, Miss Weaver?" the judge prodded.

I forced a big smile. "She's wonderful! Daddy told me so many stories about the fun times she and Mama had. And she always sent me the best birthday presents. She knew just what to get a little girl, almost like a mama would. I know that Ivy Ruther... Ruther—"

The judge leaned back and crossed his arms. "Rutherford?"

"Yes sir, she's going to look out for my best interest."

The judge held up his hands. "All right, here's what we have to do. Marcia, meet with Miss Rutherford. Make sure she understands she's not just asking for custody of a sweet little girl. Miss Weaver is a criminal defendant. And regardless of *where* she awaits trial, there is a high likelihood that she will return to the Justice Center upon sentencing. The court is not ignorant, though, of the benefit of having a relative oversee a minor's progress through the criminal system, even if they do not always reside together. Therefore, court is postponed until this matter can be further sorted." He looked at me and raised his eyebrows. "Good enough show for you?"

I nodded.

"Only in juvie court," he said and chuckled before he banged the gavel and hurried out.

From the corner of my eye I saw Loretta still in the back of the room. Her chin was raised, her eyes blazing. Ivy Rutherford was next to her. *Who is she? Who is she?* my mind demanded. Why had she come? Was Loretta paying her? Was she after Daddy's money? Who was this unknown cousin, with her sing-song Southern syllables?

Of course she'd never sent me presents. I had no memories of her at all. I thought about her comment about exchanging Christmas cards with Daddy. And then suddenly I remembered the cards with the pine trees and squirrels wearing Santa hats. It was the same card for the past five years. Like she'd bought a jumbo box and was trying to use them all up. *Wishing you a Merry Christmas and a Blessed New Year* was printed inside. There was never a personal message, or even a signature.

Instead, the bottom of the card was rubber-stamped *I. K. Rutherford* in red ink, block letters.

Suddenly, I remembered something. It was bitter and burning, and I rolled the powerful omen across my tongue.

Ivy Rutherford was illiterate.

XXXI

Abel was our illiterate hero, a smart man who was too poor to attend school. Ivy was just a dropout. Daddy said she'd gone to school for ten years, never learned to read, and then quit.

"What happened to her?" I asked Daddy.

"She… drifted. Your mama's whole family was red-faced over it. Your mama though, spoke tenderly about her. She tried to help her, but…" He stopped and shook his head.

I kept Ivy's secret as Marcia questioned me about my memories and thoughts. I noticed that the stack of paperwork that Ivy had turned in was filled out in Loretta's handwriting.

"It's sure odd," Marcia said. "I mean, usually I'm begging folks to show an interest in their kin. But this lady has gone and hired a lawyer to hurry things up and make sure you get a pre-trial release. And most amazing, she actually turned in all of her paperwork. I mean, look at this stack. I'm intimidated by it, and I've been going through these papers for years." She laughed for a moment before her mouth turned down and she cleared her throat. "My first worry is your inheritance of course, but she's leaving your trust with Loretta and paying your lawyer fees herself. And she's a successful chef. She's already found work at one of the best local restaurants."

Lies! I laughed to myself. *She can't read a recipe.*

"I'll keep in touch, of course," Marcia said. "So if anything odd were to come up, anything at all, just call me. But unless you have any last bit of information you want to share, you'll be released, temporarily, into her custody."

"Temporarily?" I asked.

"You're criminal proceedings are in two weeks. Ivy—er, the attorney, insisted you be released now so that you all can establish an orderly household routine. This will help prove to the court that your criminal rehabilitation will be better accomplished at home with her instead of the Justice Center." Marcia leaned in close. "Listen to me. It's really important that you don't get into more trouble during these two weeks. If Ivy can't keep you out of trouble, there's no way she'll get to raise you. Okay?"

I nodded.

"Good. Follow me to the lobby. Ivy's waiting."

Ivy signed me out of the Justice Center and drove me home. She made stiff attempts at conversation about the weather and how she liked my curls and wished she had curly hair. I stole a sideways glance and noticed that she kept biting her lip. I wondered what it was she was holding back. What did she really want to say?

When she opened the front door, I wiped my feet on the foyer rug even though I'd never bothered to do so before. I stood there awkwardly, wondering what to do.

"Katie's at a yearbook meeting and Loretta's gone to the store," Ivy said. Then she gasped. "The tenderloin!" She laughed and rushed past me. "I've killed the fatted calf!"

I stood, holding my plastic bag of possessions from the Justice Center, and looked around. The house had new residents and rhythms. Strange curtains were swinging low in the dining room. Henry's paintings were still in the hall, but so was a vase of fake flowers. Daddy hated fake flowers.

I remembered how sad the house was after Daddy died. It was as though people inhabit more than skin and bones. Lives reach beyond bodies, to fill the very rooms that surround them. Our home had grieved Daddy, right along with me. And as I stared at the cheery vase of fake flowers, I knew the bitter truth: The house had moved on without us.

Someone had replaced the light bulb in the hallway that had burned out nearly a decade ago. I didn't remember the hall ever being lit by anything more than a window. Now, everything glowed. There was a picture on the hall table of Katie, Ivy, and Loretta. Katie was wearing a party hat and there was a cake in front of her. But what really caught my attention was Loretta laughing. She was bent over with her hands on her belly trying to hold back her glee, but her mouth was wide open and smiling. Underneath the picture, in Katie's handwriting, was a small caption. *The Birthday Joke.*

Who was this new family? How had they managed to take over my home? Why were they filling it with themselves, with inside jokes and private parties? Didn't they know that lines had been drawn, whole histories preserved?

I sought out something familiar and unchanged. I stood in front of Mama and Daddy's wedding picture that was hanging in the foyer. Everything was just as I remembered. I took a deep breath. *I'm home.*

"There's me," Ivy said, suddenly. Her hand reached over my shoulder as she pointed to a blurred red head in the background. "It was the most beautiful day. There's never been a bride like your mama. I bet one day you'll get married here too."

I ran up the stairs toward my room. I stopped suddenly on the middle step. My beautiful soldier stared back at me. "We gotta defend our ground," I urged him.

I went to the Linthead Room. The bed was messed up and there were pajamas in a heap on the floor. Ivy was sleeping in Abel's sacred room. I glanced at the dresser and saw scattered makeup and perfume bottles. She was taking it over. I grabbed the pajamas and slung them out in the hall. I opened a dresser drawer and crammed the makeup inside. I looked at the walls. The pictures were still there, black and white and full of stories. I stepped close to the picture of Abel and Stella and young Jack in front of their home. "This is your house!" I told them.

I ran to my room, and the walls were the same great green as always. Katie yelled for me but I slammed and locked my door.

"Pearl?" she called through the door.

"Go away!" I shouted.

"Geez, what's your problem? I thought you wanted to come home."

I did! Only, so much had changed and it wasn't ever supposed to. That was the promise—the one constant of my life. The whole world could look the same, but my home was the Weaver museum. It would stand untouched and unchanged.

I heard Ivy urging Katie to give me some space.

"It's gotta be a shock, after so much time away and all she's been through," she whispered. "It must be so hard to adjust."

The hallway became quiet. I found the box hidden beneath my bed and thumbed through its wonders. I kissed Daddy's coffee mug. I pressed my hand against his unfinished novel. *Come back, Daddy. They're stealing our home.*

I fell asleep curled around my treasure. In the morning, I opened my eyes to sunlight beaming off green walls instead of the sharp Hall B whistle. Someone knocked at my door. I crawled from bed and opened it. Ivy was grinning and pretty. Her hair was tied back in a loose ponytail, with chunky pieces straying down around her neck and face.

"Mornin'," she said.

I scowled.

"You sleep well?" she chirped.

"If you had read more," I said, subtly prodding her secret, "then you'd know this isn't how these things are done."

Ivy winced, but brought her eyes to meet mine. "Tell me how these things are done."

"You've taken over my home. Made me the stranger here. So you don't ask *how I slept* at a moment like this.

You say something to keep me from running away again, because you've set out fake flowers and tacked up gross curtains and had parties and made jokes and now your blurry head is ruining my parents' wedding picture and I won't stand by and—"

"French toast."

I snapped my mouth shut.

"Best you'll ever eat," she continued. "And I sure do hope it makes you feel at home. You'd be a fool to run away without trying a bite."

I *was* hungry. I had skipped supper the night before and been too nervous to eat my lunch at jail. So although I didn't smile or answer how I slept, I followed Ivy to the dining room. There was a potted violet in the middle of the table. I sat down, leaned forward, and tugged a leaf to see if it was real. The stem snapped, and the leaf broke off in my hand.

"Tuck it in the dirt," Ivy called as she skipped into the kitchen. "It'll sprout and make a whole new plant. I'll just be a couple more minutes."

I laid the leaf on the table and listened to the sound of pots and pans banging in the kitchen. Clearly, Ivy did not cook like Loretta. Loretta was an orderly, one dish at a time kind of cook. She would fry the chicken, get the dirty dish soaking, and then warm the green beans. After which she'd butter the rolls. With Ivy, the kitchen sounded like a mechanics shop. Metal was banging, glasses were clinking, and water was rushing from the sink.

Ivy carried in empty plates, glasses of orange juice, and two jam jars filled with warm syrup. Then she hurried back into the kitchen.

"I'm so excited about these pots and pans," she yelled back. "Your mama had such classic taste!"

She was tearing down Mama's mausoleum kitchen. Didn't she know we did more than just remember the dead in our house? We gave them a room, their very own exhibit.

I was rising from my seat, ready to instruct her about our house rules, when she walked in carrying a platter filled with food. The sweet and salty scents of syrup and bacon filled the air. My mouth watered.

"Don't get up," Ivy said. "I'll serve you. Loretta said you liked sausage better than bacon, but I made this because…well, you'll see. Some foods are meant to be together."

She laid two pieces of golden toast on my plate, and then sat across from me. She didn't put any food on her plate, but picked up the violet leaf and tucked its stem in the dirt.

"Go on," she said as she sat down and pushed a jam jar of syrup near my plate. "Try it."

I picked up the jar and poured the syrup over my plate. It wasn't clear like normal syrup, but was creamy with little flecks of deep brown swirled through it.

I frowned. "I like Aunt Jemima."

"This is my own thing. Try it."

I dipped my finger in the jam jar and cautiously tasted it. It was sweet and warm, with flavors of spice, butter, and brown sugar. I dunked my finger again.

Ivy smiled. "I only make this for French toast. It doesn't work as well for waffles or pancakes. But something about the cinnamon and nutmeg work so well with the flavor of yeast in the bread. Try it."

I cut a corner of the French toast, rolled it through the syrup, and took a bite. *This was not French toast.* French toast was leftover hamburger buns that Loretta dipped in milk and eggs and browned in a skillet until it was soggy in the middle and burnt on the edges. But Ivy's toast was crusty and golden on the outside, moist and sweet within, and swirled with spicy sweet syrup. I ate an entire piece before I looked up.

Ivy was watching me instead of eating. She pushed the platter of bacon near me. "Put a piece of bacon on top, cut it together for a bite. Try it."

"You say that a lot, you know," I mumbled with a full mouth. "Try it. Try it. Try it."

Ivy laughed. "Picky eaters are my worst fear. I can have the best recipe in the world, but if people don't taste it, who cares?"

I reached for another piece of toast and Ivy smiled.

"Mama's kettles must have magic in 'em," I huffed.

"Nah," Ivy said. "Loretta had a fit the first night I pulled them down from the rack. She had to take two aspirin! But then she ate my braised short ribs and began to soften to the idea. Once she realized I wasn't just gomin' and that I intended to clean every pot that I dirtied, she relaxed."

My stomach was just full enough to remember the lecture I was going to give her about tearing down Mama's kitchen.

"It's the way we do things around here," I said dryly. "In this house, we respect the dead. We don't make messes with their things."

Ivy winked at my empty plate. "Was that a mess?"

I wished I hadn't eaten so much. My appetite was giving her far too much satisfaction. I wished I wasn't looking at the last piece of toast on the platter, with greed and longing. Ivy laid it on my plate.

"Why are you here anyway?" I asked, as I made a vicious slice into the toast. "I lied in court about knowing you because I wanted out of jail. But you never sent me presents. I don't know you."

"You have a theory about me though, don't you?" Ivy countered.

"You're a villain," I said coolly. "You're after Daddy's money, or to take over this fine house and let people think you own it."

"I'm not a villain anymore."

I grunted. "Anymore? Once a villain, always a villain."

Ivy smiled with amusement. "For a girl that prides herself on reading so much, you should know from stories that is not true."

I blushed. How did she know stories, anyway?

She nodded toward my plate. "Bread changed me."

I scoffed. "Bread?"

"You think there's magic in your mama's pots and pans," she said. "I think the magic is in the bread."

I took another bite of toast and chewed it slowly, trying to sense the magic. I shook my head.

"But imagine tasting it, after days of eating out of a trash bin."

"Gross," I muttered.

Ivy chuckled. "I'd been hitchhiking for a week, trying to make my way home. I got kicked out of my ride and spent the day walking a tiny mountain road. My thumb was up, but nobody wanted me, and I don't blame 'em. I was a wreck. I'd spent a decade gomin' up my life."

I held up my hand to stop her. It was the second time she had said *gomin'*. I dismissed the first out of generosity. But in Daddy's house—in *my* house—words were as real as rooms. If Ivy couldn't read them, she ought to at least know how to speak them.

"*Gomin'* isn't a word," I said with my best professor's voice. "If you're going to tell stories, you should at least use real words."

Ivy blushed. "It's a mountain word. If your mama had lived longer, you'd know what it means. Bet you'd even say it too."

"Is it in a dictionary?" I smirked.

"It's in the mouths of thousands of mountain people."

I started to give a sharp answer, but remembered Daddy and the linthead tongue he refused to shed.

"It means making a mess," Ivy explained. "And I was a champion mess maker. As I walked that mountain road, evening came. I didn't have a place to sleep or any hope for supper, when I came to a little store. It was closed, but I peeked in the window and saw loaves of bread lined up on the counter. I punched my fist through the glass of the door, unlocked it, and stepped inside. I ate a whole loaf before I noticed my arm was all cut up. I reached for a second loaf and saw an old lady watching me.

"I figured she'd already called the cops so I bolted out the door, blood streaming down my arm. That's when I heard her yell, 'Try it!' She held out another loaf. I could see the steam rising from it and melted butter dripping. I walked back and ate the whole thing. Then she led me into her kitchen to wash and bandage my hand. 'Now you gonna bake some new bread,' she told me. 'To replace the one you stole.' I told her I didn't know how, but she promised to teach me. I'll never forget what it was like seeing my first loaf of beautiful bread. Knowing that something I touched hadn't failed. As we cut the bread to taste it, the woman told me that she needed somebody to help her bake. She offered to let me sleep in a little cot in the kitchen if I would stay. I told her I never cooked anything other than warming a can of soup. 'But look what you just made,' she said.

"Night after night, we worked together. I learned how to make all kinds of things. Bread showed me that I was good for more than gomin'. I had beauty too. So yeah, I came to that store a villain, but I didn't leave that way."

She took a long drink of orange juice, and I noticed the flush across her cheeks. She stacked the dishes and handed me the plates. "Let's get these in some soapy water before the syrup dries."

I followed her to the kitchen and saw that every one of Mama's kettles was off the hanging rack. The rolling pin had been moved. The only thing that was the same was the framed picture of birthright pie.

"You've stolen Mama's kitchen," I whispered as I looked around.

Ivy frowned. "Kitchens ain't for owning. They're for wearin' out." She tossed me a dishrag. "Wash the plates up and I'll wipe down the counters."

I'd scrubbed toilets and floors in jail. It was prisoners' work. But I'd never done dishes inside my own home before.

"Where's Loretta?" I asked.

"She and Katie are giving us the morning to get settled. They'll be back soon, so let's get this place sparkling."

I rolled up my sleeves and scrubbed the plates and set them on the clean towel laid across the counter. Ivy nodded toward the broom, and I grabbed it and began sweeping all the bits of sugar and toast crust scattered on the floor.

"You know this is Loretta's job, right?" I asked. "She's not really family. She came here to clean. Daddy was a true scholar. He didn't waste his time with stuff like this and he wouldn't want me to either."

Ivy stopped wiping the counter. "We clean our own messes now."

"I'd rather spend my time reading."

Ivy nodded to my scattered dust pile. She pulled a roll of duct tape from the drawer and taped a small square on the floor. She took the broom from my hands and showed me how to use the square like a target, and pull all the bits into it instead of just pushing them around.

"Well clearly," she said as she handed the broom back, "some things can't be learned in books."

My face burned with heat, and I longed to shout her secret shame. When the square was full, Ivy took the broom and used a dustpan to gather up the mess. Then she pulled the tape from the floor.

"Run shower and get dressed," she said. "We've got a lot to talk about. We have to get a plan in motion before your next court date."

I was out of the kitchen, almost to the stairs, when I heard Ivy speak again.

"More juice ... eggs ... oatmeal ... oooh and chocolate chips, don't forget those ... peanut butter."

I crept back toward the kitchen and peeked around the corner. Ivy was speaking into a handheld recorder.

"Some chicken thighs ... fennel ... Nilla wafers ..."

She was making a dropout's grocery list. One that she recorded instead of wrote. I sneered and turned to leave when I heard something else.

"Oh!" Ivy gasped. "Would you just look at that spice grinder ... like a work of art. Christine, you stocked a fabulous kitchen. Cousin, I am truly grateful for your fine taste."

She really is a thief. Underneath all the pretty details about midnight kneading and loaves rising in the moonlight, the truth was, Ivy Rutherford took what she wanted. Even if she had to break a window. Even if she had to raise a crooked kid.

XXXII

There was a sheet of paper and a pen on the dining room table.

"Take notes," Ivy said. "In two weeks, we're back in court. But right now we're trying to work out a good plea deal for you."

I laughed bitterly. "A good deal? I'm supposed to just admit guilt? This attorney is ripping you off."

"You admitted in your police interview that you booked the tickets to Alaska with Katie's mama's credit card. The state has interviews from a dozen witnesses about what happened the night of the talent show. Our battle is over sentencing, not guilt. And we can't ask for mercy, we can't say that you've changed, unless you admit that what you did was wrong."

Of course she wanted me back in jail.

"Listen, if you have to go back to jail, I'll come visit," Ivy promised. "And I'll be waiting for you, right here, when you get out. Maybe that's the first thing you should write down."

I slumped over the paper and jotted a quick line.

"Good. Now, so far the state has offered two years of jail, followed by post-release conditions. I turned that down, and our attorney counter-offered probation for as long as they want, community service, and a hefty fine. Now draw a list with little stars or points."

She looked over my shoulder as I filled the margin of my paper with numbers and dots.

"The first point in our plan is education. You're expelled from Jefferson for the rest of the year. Your old private school won't discuss readmission."

"That just leaves Gunthry," I said. "The alternative school for mess-ups."

Ivy shook her head. "We'll hire private tutors, to finish the current year at home. If you work at your own quick pace, you can complete the full year's requirements. If you establish a good record of behavior and grades with your tutors, you'll be eligible for public high school in the fall. No way the judge can't see that's better than juvie. Okay, the next dot is household structure. Did you write all that down?"

I smothered a laugh as she smiled and said, "Good job."

"We have to establish structure," she continued. "So, we'll keep a schedule. Breakfast at 7:30, lunch at 12:30, supper at 6:30, bedtime at 9:30. You make your own bed and help me clean the kitchen. You show respect to all members of the household. The attorney said we needed a discipline plan to show that we have set consequences. So, every time you stay up too late or talk sassy to Loretta, you get a point. When you have three points you lose a privilege like TV time. Got it?"

I nodded. I could cuss Loretta twice, without any consequence.

"Next is community service. You'll volunteer to tutor at the library Homework Help Hour. I talked to the librarians and they are thrilled to have you...they remember your daddy so fondly. Also, we'll gladly accept probation and all of its terms. For now, it's the only way to keep you out of jail. Eventually though, we'll work to have your records expunged. Finally, you need to apologize. You'll have to write an essay."

"An essay?" I asked.

"The attorney says writing something in your own words will establish you as a person, instead of just being a list of crimes. He wants you to write what you were thinking and feeling before you ran away. How you feel now that you are facing the consequences. Write about how this whole thing has changed you, and why you would never do anything like this again. C'mon, write that part down so you won't forget."

I scribbled more lines on the paper.

"One more thing. Loretta told me how much you love stories, and I know how much your daddy did. She told me about how she tried to get you to—"

"I know, I know. Be the iron skillet," I interrupted.

Ivy stopped and stared at me strangely. "What?"

"She wanted me to quit stories and be a skillet. That way I won't ever bend or break."

Ivy cleared her throat and shook her head. "How about, instead of using them to escape, we enjoy them together."

"I'm supposed to talk stories, with *you*?"

"Well I love stories too and—"

I held my paper out. "Will you read this over and make sure I didn't leave anything out?"

Ivy's pinched her lips together.

I tossed her my pen. "Or since storybook time is your big idea, why don't you write down the details."

Ivy sighed. "You know I can't."

I sucked in my breath and tried to ignore the flat feeling inside my heart.

"But," Ivy said softly. "I *can* make the best banana puddin' in the world. It will be on this table tonight. It'd be a pity to miss it. And if you come for puddin', you'll get what you really crave—the story about why I'll never be able to read." She exhaled slowly. "Run get to work on your essay. For a superduper reader like you, that shouldn't be hard at all, huh?"

I hurried to my room and read all the secret lines that I had written. My own plan, so much safer than Ivy's. I would never risk going back to jail.

"Pearl?" Ivy's voice called down the hall. "You working on your essay?"

"Yes."

"Great!" Ivy stuck her head in the door. "Got a title for it yet?"

I nodded and wrote it across the top. *Pearl Weaver's Great Escape.*

XXXIII

If burnt porridge and rotten potatoes can unite awkward middle schoolers, then imagine the spell that delicious food casts, especially after living on the brink of starvation. Supper was pot roast, but not an ordinary pot roast. Far more than tender, it was delicate, falling apart with the slightest pressure from my fork. And it was seasoned differently than Loretta's brown-gravy-packet recipe.

"What are these little pine needles?" I asked.

"Rosemary. There's fresh thyme too," Ivy answered.

To a girl trained to crave barbecue, rosemary was exotic. Next to the pot roast were roasted vegetables and a large hunk of Ivy's magic bread soaking up broth that oozed from the meat. I took a bite of the bread, curious about whether it would be as delicious as the French toast. It was a bit sweet, with a strong yeast flavor like a soft roll, but with the texture and weight of bread.

Before I finished my second bite, Katie and Loretta walked in.

"I was wondering where y'all were," Ivy said. "Lemme grab you a plate."

My spine stiffened and I laid down my fork. But Katie hugged my neck, plopped down, and howled, "I'm so starved I'd eat muktuk without whining." Then she grabbed my hunk of bread and took a bite.

"Katie," Loretta snapped. "Get yourself some manners. Ivy will bring you bread." Then Loretta nodded to me, with a stiff smile on her face like I was special company. "It's surely good to see you. I trust you're settling in well?"

I considered marching to my bedroom and slamming the door for an answer. I could not sit across from my betrayer and eat supper. *Or could I?* It was so good, and I'd only had a couple of bites. *Maybe I should carry my plate with me,* I thought as I picked up my fork and swirled a piece of a potato through the broth.

"Hey," Katie nudged me. "I know you're worried about all this...believe me I was too. I thought Loretta had lost her mind for a couple of weeks. She drove us all over Tennessee searching out your family. Loretta would show them your picture, tell them about you being in jail, and then just flat out ask them to come and help raise you. Everybody looked at her like she was bonkers. One man chased us off his property. But Ivy invited us in, gave me a cookie, and listened to everything we told her. Loretta just kept saying the word criminal, over and over. So I told Ivy you were probably a genius, a somewhat talented singer, and had hair good enough to be in a shampoo commercial. I'm not bragging, but I'm the one who sold her on you. Ivy said to give her a few days to think things through, and the next thing I know she shows up here with a suitcase announcing she's come to get you out of jail. Now, I know what you're thinking—you and your storybook mind—and believe me, I thought she was crazy too. But then she made these ribs that fell off the bones, and a glazed coconut cake that tasted like heaven had come down. And then she started calling the Justice Center and hired an attorney. And look, you're home for supper. So yeah, she's helping us even though she doesn't know us and that seems crazy. But you'd be in jail right now so ... who cares if it's crazy?"

Katie leaned in close and stared at my face.

"What are you doing?" I asked and pulled away.

"Stop it," she said.

I startled. "What?"

"That thing you're doing. I can see it in your eyes. Where you always think you're smarter than everybody else and nobody knows the real story like you do. I'm telling you, Ivy is okay. Trust me."

I took a bite without answering. *Mercy, it was good.* I took another, and then laid my fork down slowly, purposefully. *The spell is in the food.* Hadn't Katie just admitted it? She thought Ivy was crazy until she cooked ribs and cake. Wasn't Snow White's doomed apple the shiniest of them all?

Ivy carried in plates for Loretta and Katie.

"Extra potatoes for you, Loretta, because I know you love them. And extra carrots for you, Katie. You're hoping to avoid the glasses, remember? I've heard this might help."

Katie nodded to me. "Doc says I'm borderline, and we'll check again in six months. I don't know how I'll take pictures for the yearbook with glasses on. But if I do get 'em, I'm thinking hot-pink frames in that cool cat-eye shape."

Ivy and Loretta started chatting about their days. Loretta complained about traffic, and Ivy chirped about the beauty of the roast and how the local butcher knew his art. Loretta grunted that "dead cow will never be art" and Ivy laughed. Loretta was as gruff as ever, yet less wooden. Every once in a while she would pause and ask something that hinted of a compliment, like "How did you get the potatoes browned all over but so soft inside?"

Ivy would answer and then Loretta would tuck back into her meal. Katie started talking about the difficulty of taking the school orchestra picture.

"There's no way to get all the instruments in the photo. I can have the woodwinds pose with their flutes and clarinets ready to play, but the violins would block everybody's face. And then there are the people in the back row, like the timpani player and the bass players. I can only get them from the neck up."

"Maybe you could group them into smaller pictures?" Ivy suggested. "A woodwinds picture, a strings picture, and so on?"

Katie turned her head to the side. "If they'd give me a two-page..."

It was as though I watched them from outside a window. Like a street bum, looking in at some cheerful scene. I was separate from them, jealous of them, but couldn't help but marvel at the strange, happy family.

"Pearl and I'll do the dishes tonight," Ivy said as she began to clear the table. "Katie, you have the night off."

But Katie wasn't taking the night off from *me*. She came and leaned against the counter, slowly drying dishes while I washed, and prattled on about how she had found her calling with the yearbook staff.

"There's still so much drama though," she said with an eye roll. "I mean, you expect cheer squad drama. If you get on the squad you're supposed to look cute and throw some fits. But yearbook nerds?"

"Katie!" Ivy scolded.

"I'm allowed to say *nerds* if I'm one of 'em. My point is, you'd think that working with smart kids, we'd act smarter. But nope. There's constant bickering over who gets to check out the fancy lens for the day or who gets their name under the photo for credit if two people worked on the layout."

"Wow. Sounds like you've had it real tough lately," I muttered, but Katie didn't catch my sarcasm.

"Yeah. But I wanna do this. It's not about yearbooks or capturing school memories. Every picture I take is really for Alaska."

I dropped the dish I was rinsing into the sink.

"There's so many pictures I need to take there," she continued. "Pearl, do you remember those mountains? And the moose ... even the wolves, if I ever get another chance. The whale captain with that war paint. And the whale. Every picture of woodwinds and violins, I count as training for all the pictures I'll take in Alaska. You understand ... you've seen it."

I nodded. There were a thousand pictures of Alaska, scattered in precious piles across the floor of my heart. "Have you heard from your daddy?" I asked.

"He calls every Sunday when he's not on the rig. He's thrilled you're out of jail. Noatak cried she was so happy. Daddy says we can come visit this summer. He's waiting to get his June work schedule and then he'll let me know the dates."

We finished wiping down the counters, and Katie and I went to the Oriental Room—*her room* as she called it now—and continued to catch up. Only I had nothing to say. I didn't want to talk about my time in jail folding laundry and reading value stories. Katie had no problems filling the void.

"Mama's show won a Vegas award for best costumes. She seems happy. And have you noticed Loretta? She still scowls all the time, but it's like she don't mean it anymore. Like she scowls for the habit of it, but not the message. It was bugging me, you know? So I asked her about it in the car today. I said, 'Auntie are you dying?' She got this real mean look on her face. So I told her, 'You don't seem nearly as irritated with me as usual. And I've heard that people get real sweet if they know they're about to die.' She said that she'd just had a powerful burden lifted off her, and that she couldn't help but feel lighter because of it."

I was the burden. Daddy had saddled her with me, and she had abandoned me to jail. Ivy had lifted that burden of guilt and responsibility right from her shoulders.

"I know you hate her," Katie said. "But she's so old. How was she ever gonna raise the two of us without some help?" Katie turned and looked at the clock on the dresser. "Dessert!" She bounced off the bed and headed to the door, stopped and looked back at me. "Ain't you coming?"

It had been a long first day home, and I craved the silence of my room, the protection of my great green walls. But… *banana pudding.*

"Yeah."

In the center of the dining room table was a large trifle bowl filled with banana pudding. Spoons and parfait dishes were next to it. Ivy walked in carrying two large candlesticks with taper candles glowing. Loretta stepped in the room and switched on the lights.

"Don't wanna eat if I can't see what I'm eating," she grunted.

Ivy pointed to the candles. "Thought we could enjoy some candlelight, since we're celebrating Pearl being home."

Loretta frowned, but switched the lights back off. "Well I reckon this way we won't see how brown the bananas get inside the puddin'."

Ivy served us each a bowl. She was purposeful with her spoon, making sure to give each of us a nice balance between wafers and bananas. I took a bite. *How did she do it?* How did she take simple foods I'd known all my life and reintroduce them?

"*This* wasn't the box recipe," Katie said as she licked her spoon.

"Nah." Ivy grinned.

Katie winked at me. "A puddin' worth defending your lines over."

Ivy smiled. "Glad you like it. Now, tonight we're celebrating Pearl being home. Stories are one of her favorite things. So in her honor, does anybody have a story for the night?"

"I do," Katie announced proudly. "The story of my first kiss."

Loretta scoffed. "No need for hussy talk."

Katie flashed her best vixen grin. "He was wild, so strong and muscular, and also ... *a bear*!"

"No way," I yelled and laughed.

"Oh you know everything, don't you? What if I said I went out one night without you?"

"You were too scared."

Katie shook her head. "You were snoring away, but I was feeling pent up and couldn't sleep. I thought maybe if I went out, I'd see the northern lights. So I bundled up and walked around the yard for a bit. The sky was black though, nothing special. I turned on my flashlight and pointed it toward the woods, and out of nowhere, there was the bear. He was standing on his hind legs like the one by the stream. I bet he was ten feet tall."

"Why didn't you scream for me?" I asked.

"In my panic I forgot about standing tall and screaming loud and just skipped to playing dead. I fell on my side, curled up in a ball, and hoped with all my might that he wasn't interested in having a cheerleader for supper."

"Clearly he wasn't." Loretta groaned. "The. End."

Katie glared at Loretta and took a deep breath. "So there I am curled up, and that bear starts sniffing the ground all around me. Then he starts sniffing me. He started nudging my face with his nose and I felt how cold and wet it was. Then everything got quiet. When I opened my eyes, he was gone. I got up, ran back to the cabin."

"Where you were safe and warm for the night. Meanwhile, your mama and I were losing our minds with worry," Loretta said. "The end!"

Katie shook her head. "No, Auntie, the end is this: I think that bear knew I wasn't dead. He knew I belonged in Alaska the same as him. I've wished a hundred times that I could go back to that night and open my eyes."

"And then he'd eat you for sure," Loretta said. "And it would have driven me and your mama to the grave."

I laid my spoon down. "Katie Monroe, did that really happen? I have to know..."

Katie smiled. "Don't you always say the best stories leave you wondering?"

"It's a wonderful story," Ivy said and glanced cautiously at Loretta. "I've never been to Alaska, but would love to go. How about you, Loretta?"

Loretta shook her head. "My joints could never abide such cold."

"Well then," Ivy said. "Who's next?"

Loretta and I exchanged matching scowls.

"I'll go," Ivy offered. She paused as she looked at each of us and held our gaze. And I knew, right then, exactly what she was doing. That pause, the gaze, the look around the room were ancient tricks of my inheritance. Whatever else she might turn out to be—villain, illiterate dropout drifter—Ivy Rutherford was also a storyteller.

"Once upon a time," she began. "There was a girl born in the Tennessee mountains. Life was simple. She played in the creek behind her house. She collected acorns in the fall, had whole mason jars full of them lined up on her bedroom window. But then the little girl grew and started school and things changed. She never finished her papers, even the coloring sheets, on time. By the end of first grade she still couldn't write her name. She couldn't even point out the letter *A*. She was in trouble all day long. Acting out in awful ways to hide the fact that she couldn't do her work. She never got to go to recess. She never made friends."

Katie smirked. "Sounds like a real dummy."

"Katie!" Loretta scolded.

"What?" Katie asked. "The girl can't learn the letter *A*."

"Yes," Ivy said. "And no one understood why she just wouldn't focus and work harder. Everyone said she was lazy. Dumb. Or worse, rebellious and needed more punishment. The little girl roared through school like a tornado. Finally, when she was sixteen, to the relief of the school and the shame of her family, she dropped out."

"Well I hope somebody told her that there's always the GED," Katie said. "I mean that's what my mama had to do, and it's not exactly the same but—"

"That might have been an option," Ivy agreed. "For someone who could read or write. This girl still couldn't."

"How could she go to that much school and never soak up anything?" Katie demanded.

Loretta shushed Katie. "Don't talk about things you don't understand. You need to show more compassion, and understand that in the good Lord's wisdom, not everybody is made the same and—"

"She's asking the right question," Ivy interrupted. "It's what everyone wanted to know. But in her heart, the girl knew the reason. She was cursed."

"Did she die of it?" Katie whispered. "Or go crazy and kill somebody? Stories like this always end up with somebody dying."

I laughed and could not contain myself anymore. "*It's her!* She's talking about herself."

Katie's eyes grew wide and round. "You didn't know how to read during school?"

Ivy shook her head. "Still can't."

Katie gasped and Loretta frowned. "Well now, there's no point in shaming ourselves," Loretta said. "Kids today think they got the right to know everything and I don't think—"

"I spent many sad years feeling ashamed. I didn't know that there is something very different inside my brain that makes me unable to absorb the code of letters and words. The alphabet never meant more to me than random drawings. It never connected into a system of sounds and words. It remains a mystery. And I didn't grow up in an area that had resources to test for such things, or even awareness that it was possible. It wasn't until many years later, after I had found my calling with bread and was learning how to cook other things, that I received my accidental diagnosis."

"Accidental?" Katie asked.

Ivy nodded. "I was a dishwasher in a four-star restaurant by day, and a student standing in the kitchen corner at night, learning by watching. One day I was on my way to clear a table when a diner stopped me. 'I'm sorry,' he said when he looked at me. 'I thought you were my waitress.' Then he pointed to two different lines on the menu. 'But since I've already stopped you, which would you recommend?' I pretended to look and then said, 'I'd always get beef over chicken.' He seemed confused and then tried again. 'But between these two, which would you get?' 'Oh,' I said. 'The fish for sure. It's always fresh.' He frowned. 'This is the dessert menu, dear. Why can't you read?' I bolted from the dining room back to the kitchen, but that man chased me down. He was a brain doctor and convinced me to come to his office for a free evaluation. A few days later, and I had a big list of fancy science words for what was wrong."

I struggled to hide my shock. All this time I had believed she was too lazy, too *bad* to be a reader. But Ivy really was cursed.

Katie turned to Loretta. "You knew?"

"She had to fill out my guardianship paperwork for me," Ivy said. "And Pearl knew because her daddy must've told her."

"Haven't you heard her making lists on her voice recorder?" I asked Katie.

"I just thought she was like me, with a hand that aches from too much writing. I was thinking about asking for one of them recorders for Christmas."

"Well, now everyone knows," Ivy said.

"Hallelujah, the end!" Loretta barked with a grin. "Let's get seconds."

"Wait a minute," Katie said. "How do you drive? How'd you find this place all the way out here?"

"After my diagnosis, I returned to that doctor's clinic for lessons in life skills. Just because I couldn't be cured, didn't mean I couldn't adapt. Like learning to drive. I worked really hard to be able to identify road signs by their shape and color. If I need to read a map, I talk to people—stop at as many gas stations as I need—and use the landmarks they describe to me."

"How have you become such a good cook when you can't read recipes?" Katie persisted.

"I make phone calls."

"What do you mean? Like you call your mama and she reads you stuff out of her recipe box?" Katie asked.

Ivy laughed. "I call *anyone* that might have a good recipe. I've even called the White House for a salad dressing. I can't research cookbooks like other chefs. I can't dig around in old recipe boxes, but I can always talk to people. I can tell them I love their food or I've heard they make a great dish and ask for the recipe. You'd be amazed at how many secret recipes I've been told, just because I'm willing to ask. I've called famous hotels for their cheesecakes and chocolate mousse. I've called people's grandmas. This puddin' you're eating right now came from a man in a restaurant who made the passing comment that nobody would ever make a banana puddin' like his grandmother. I got her number and called her the very next day. I'll hunt down anybody that has a good recipe. Instead of thinking about all the cookbooks I can't read, I've made the world my cookbook."

"And look at you now," Katie grinned. "After all those years, with people calling you dummy, you're working at the classiest restaurant in town. So the jokes on them suckers."

"It never felt like a joke. I hated my life for a long time. But it wasn't really a new brain that I needed."

"It was a new attitude," Loretta said with an approving nod. "A person can overcome anything if they just chin-up and keep a good attitude."

Ivy reached under the table and pulled out a velvet bag. She loosened the top and turned it upside down. A stone rolled out of the bag. "This was my real problem. My real curse."

"A rock?" Katie asked.

"A tombstone," Ivy said.

Katie's eyes widened. "Spooky... Guess we're moving on to ghost stories."

Loretta was confused, which always brought out her most furious scowl.

But I set my spoon down, leaned forward, and studied the rock. The candlelight flickered across it and cast odd shadows around the table. What was the tombstone story?

"Enough from me tonight," Ivy said as she leaned forward and blew out the candles. She switched on the lights and pulled a paperback *Jane Eyre* from beneath her chair. "I had Loretta pick this up. I've heard it's your favorite." She slid the book over to me. "Your turn."

"Skip that whole part about the birds," Katie coached.

"But what about the tombstone? Aren't you gonna finish?" I asked.

"Yes, please, get to the end," Loretta said. "That hunk of gravel might scratch the varnish off the table."

"Oh, Loretta," Ivy laughed softly. "Your favorite thing to say about a story is always *The End.* Can you guess what mine is?" Ivy winked at me. "To be continued..."

XXXIV

Katie and Ivy returned to school and work, and I spent my week planning my escape. I made sure the brakes on my bicycle were working, and the chain wasn't in danger of slipping. I took it for several spins around the driveway.

Loretta stood with crossed arms, studying me. "You sure have taken a liking to that bike since you've been home. Used to have to order you to ride it. You always preferred make-believe to healthy exercise."

"I missed having fresh air," I explained.

"Just make sure you get that court essay written," she reminded me. "Like I've always taught you, work before play."

But I wouldn't write a single word. Not for the attorney. Not for the judge. Certainly not for a cousin who couldn't read. I didn't despise Ivy for being illiterate anymore, but I didn't think it made her wonderful either.

Katie couldn't stop gushing about it. "People book reservations to eat her food. And she can't even read recipes."

I shrugged. To me, the strangest thing about Ivy was not that she had a successful career. It was that she understood stories. She had mastered the magic, with her perfect pauses and her cliffhanger endings. How?

I guessed it was because of food. Ivy knew how to drizzle chocolate or sear a filet, to make a person crave *one more bite.* I stared at her pretty plates and discovered that a story isn't so different from a beautiful meal. Full of layers, twisted flavors, and surprises. Ivy understood what roused hungers and what satisfied them, and that is what made her a storyteller.

She left *Jane Eyre* on the dining room hutch during the week, but it was the velvet bag that held my interest. I peeked inside it every day, staring at that rock and wondering how it was a tombstone. When it was finally Saturday night again, I spied a chocolate cake on the counter. I was at the table, waiting, before anyone else. Ivy came in carrying the candles, only this time she set them on the hutch behind her. The room was darker that way, with the candlelight hugging the walls instead of us. Loretta carried plates of chocolate cake, and Katie brought mugs of milk.

"Reckon you can set them candles on the table?" Loretta asked. "You know I just hate when I can't see what I'm eating."

"There is nothing in that cake that you wouldn't want to eat," Ivy answered.

Katie stuffed her mouth with a huge bite and grinned at me. "Told you chocolate is better than banana."

Loretta took a modest bite and nodded stiffly. "Reminds me of a chocolate glazed Coca- Cola cake my mama used to make. I never managed to get the recipe."

"How do you remember all your recipes?" Katie asked. "Since you can't write them down?"

"I use these," Ivy said, as she tapped her ear. "I listen close when someone tells me a recipe. I record it if needed in my tape recorder so that I can listen until I've got it down. But desserts and breads are the only things that need recipes. That's why I'm not a full-time pastry chef. Meats, vegetables, soups...these are all cooked by instinct and taste, not words." She looked at my untouched plate. "Don't you like chocolate cake?"

I nodded toward the velvet bag. "I'm here for the story."

"Of course." Ivy reached behind her and brought out *Jane Eyre.* She slid it over to me and flipped the lights on. "There you go, Loretta. You get some light after all."

Was Ivy toying with me? Did she know much I wanted to hear about the stone? Was this a case of dueling storytellers? If so, didn't she realize whose daughter she'd challenged?

"Turn the lights off," I said. "I'll read by candlelight." Because I knew how to set a mood too, I took a long pause, locked eyes with Ivy, and called my favorite line from memory. *"I resisted all the way..."*

I read without pause until I got to the part when Jane's aunt banishes her to the orphanage. I became suddenly conscious of Loretta, sitting rigid and smug across from me. Judging me. Judging my stories. Memories of all the times she tried to banish me and my characters, began to blur with Jane. My face flushed and my voice trembled as unexpected, raw emotion swept over me. I looked up at Loretta and cried old words, written long ago, but born fresh in my wounded heart.

"I am glad you are no relation of mine. I will never call you aunt again as long as I live. I will never come to visit you when I am grown up; and if anyone asks me how I liked you, and how you treated me, I will say the very thought of you makes me sick..."

I wiped a single, hot tear from my face and laid the book down.

Katie whistled lowly. "That's one way to let it all out."

I expected Loretta to excuse herself and take an aspirin. But she cleared her throat and nodded. "I reckon it's my turn to do this show. And my story starts by saying that I just didn't know what to do for you, Pearl. That's why I signed over custody of you to the state. That caused you a lot of extra hurt, and I wish I'd done it different. I ain't gonna ask you to excuse me, not for my pills nor my pains, because no reason is good enough. But I am asking you to forgive me, cause you'll always be my girly." She sighed and laid her fist across her heart. "The end."

I wrapped my arms around myself, suddenly empty and tired. I had been at war with Loretta for so long. And I thought she expected me to say, *It's okay you abandoned me. I'm too wicked, and you're too old.* But Loretta only asked for forgiveness. There was nothing left to fight about.

"Well now, somebody else needs to go," Loretta huffed. "Never liked everybody looking at me. Ain't easy being a storyteller."

Ivy reached for the velvet bag and set it on the table, but she didn't empty the stone.

"My story begins with bread," she announced.

I let out a disappointed sigh. "Already heard that one."

"Sit tight," she replied. "Every storyteller needs a bit of leash to roam, right?"

I slumped forward and nodded for her to continue.

"I'll never forget my first loaf. I watched it rise, but waited for it to collapse. I smelled it baking, and expected it to burn. When I finally tasted it, I wept. I had spent so much of my life being hungry, and gomin' up every opportunity that came my way. In just one evening, an old lady named Myra, taught me how to make something beautiful.

"She offered me a job and a cot to sleep in. I never told her that I couldn't read. She was the kind of teacher who showed me what to do and watched over my work, giving gentle instruction. I depended on her calm, kind voice to call out instructions for how to shape the loaves. I relied on her to hand me the right measuring spoon, the right bag of flour. She never knew that I was practically blind, unable to read a single label, as I followed her around.

"Meanwhile, as we worked, she told stories. About her childhood in the mountains, about her family and building the store. And then there was a story about bread. It must've been her favorite, because she told it every time we had a large order and the counters were covered with loaves. It was about thousands of hungry people who needed bread. But they were in a desolate place, with no way to feed themselves. So Jesus fed them. *'Imagine what it tasted like,'* Myra whispered, as she held a slice of fresh bread for me to sample. *'Imagine making bread for thousands, all from five loaves... '*

Katie set her fork down. "Oh! I know this story. Learned it the time Auntie dragged me to bible school. I even made a little paper plate craft about it."

Loretta nodded proudly. "See, I managed to get some folks to church."

"I only went for the Oreos," Katie confessed with a shy grin. "They served cookies and Kool-Aid at the end of every lesson."

Ivy laughed loudly. "I've been bribed with Oreos to go to church, and I've also been dragged there. But Myra's story wasn't cookies-and-crafts, and it wasn't about me getting my act together before some invisible God stomps me. Myra told about a God who made the whole world, but still saw the beauty of a simple loaf. He wasn't angry or hiding. He met people in desolate places. He fed them. This was a God with his hands in the bread.

"Myra began to have confidence in me. She'd step out to run the store register and not hurry back to check my work. She'd have long conversations with her customers while I shaped and baked loaves. I was nervous, but soon realized that although I couldn't read, my hands knew the feel of good dough. My eyes recognized the golden crust of a perfectly baked loaf. One day she announced that she had to visit a sick family member. She didn't know how long she'd be, and she needed me to begin baking the bread for the next day. She told me she left the Thursday baking list on the counter. I knew the list by heart. It was the biggest of the week—the store's busiest day was Friday, when restaurant owners picked up their orders for the weekend and wives came to buy all sorts of pastries to serve at their homes. I decided to begin with blueberry bread. I was so proud of myself when I was able to recall the shapes of the cups and spoons that I needed to measure ingredients. I made a large batch of dough, and measured it into eight loaf pans. I popped them in the ovens to bake and began work on the farmhouse yeast bread. But by the time I had kneaded it for the first rise, smoke filled the kitchen. I opened the ovens and saw the smoldering tops of charred blueberry loaves. I pulled them out, coughing and cursing. I had no idea what I had done wrong. I turned to the farmhouse dough and saw that it wasn't rising. It was just a lump.

"The sight of that flat dough, all those burned loaves, filled me with rage. I felt so stupid for thinking I could do anything good on my own. I hurled the loaves against the wall. Burned blueberries and wet batter exploded everywhere. I ran to the cash register, pressed the green button and the drawer full of cash slid open. I grabbed fistfuls of money and headed toward the door. Just like that, I was done with bread forever. I wasn't a baker. I was a thief. And deep down, even when I baked good bread, I never forgot that. I always knew that was... my end."

Ivy took a deep breath, picked up her fork, cut a corner of cake, and took a bite. She watched us while she chewed. We were silent and spellbound.

"Anybody want more cake?" she asked brightly.

Katie frowned. "You didn't really steal it. Some of that money was yours, you know? Myra gave you a cot and food, but that ain't much of a paycheck, not like what she owed you. And besides, that money got you off the mountain and into a restaurant where the brain doctor found you. So it all worked out, right? I mean, you're not a thief anymore. You're a chef. People make mistakes, and they grow from them and move on."

Ivy stayed silent, so Katie turned to Loretta for reassurance. Loretta shook her head sadly, and pinched her lips together to measure her words carefully. "I've been the one left behind in the batter-covered kitchen, while some wild girl breaks my heart. I just wish Myra knew the truth about your struggles and why you acted like that. It's so hard to be the one left behind, with all the mess and questions and not understanding what happened." She cast a sideways glance at me. "But sometimes people act out of their pain instead of good sense. I'm sure Myra knows that... I'm sure if she saw you today, all the skills you have in the kitchen, she'd be so proud."

Ivy looked at me. "And you? What do you think about my story?"

I looked at the candlelight shadows creeping up the walls. I saw the velvet bag still sitting on the table. I met Ivy's stare. "I think that night wasn't the end at all. It was a plot-shift. You're just turning the page."

"Pearl... knows... stories," Ivy said softly. "That's the first thing Katie told me about you back in Tennessee. She was right and so are you. I never made it out the door that night. Myra was standing in the way, watching me. She hurried toward the kitchen and stopped when she saw the mess. 'Wonder why it burned?' is all she asked. She stepped inside and I heard her call out. 'Oh no! I left the ovens on 500 instead of our normal 350.

I should have told you. I baked a batch of pretzels this afternoon. Pretzels need high heat and I never turned it back down.'

" 'It wasn't your stupid pretzels,' I yelled. 'It's me! I can't read which flour is which ... can't read what scoop or spoon to use. I can't read any of your notes. The only way I can bake is if you're in the kitchen telling me what to do. I'm cursed!'

"Myra returned to me. 'Of course you are,' she said. 'But your curse ain't got nothing to do with reading words on a flour sack.'

" 'But if I could read, everything would be different,' I sobbed. Myra reached up to the counter and grabbed the rock that she used as a paperweight for order slips. She handed it to me and my hand sank with its weight. 'Wouldn't fix your tombstone heart,' she said."

Ivy pushed her cake plate out of the way and reached for the velvet bag. She pulled out the stone and handed it to Loretta, who quickly passed it to Katie, like a game of hot potato. But Katie didn't set it down or pass it to me. She cradled it in her hands and leaned forward, waiting for Ivy to speak.

Ivy pointed at the stone. " 'You got bones stacked inside your heart,' Myra told me. 'All the bad things you've done and all the killing you've had to survive. Child, you're a walking graveyard. You could read a whole library and not be healed. You could rob a dozen banks, and never be full. You don't need books or money. All you need is bread.'

"I followed her back into the kitchen, but Myra didn't reach for a cookbook like I expected. She reached for her Bible and read about the hungry thousands. Only this time, the story continued as Jesus told the crowds, *The bread of God is the bread that comes down from heaven and gives life to the world.* And so the crowds cried 'Give us this bread!' And Jesus answered, *I am the bread of life; whoever comes to me will never go hungry.*

"I glanced around the room and knew exactly what it felt like to be one of the hungry thousands. The only bread I was able to make on my own, the only loaves that I could multiply, were burned and ruined. My mess, my life, disgusted me. 'Would you…would you read some more about bread?' I asked Myra.

"She read about Jesus' last supper. How he broke bread and said *This is my body, given for you.* I held my breath, because I remembered what came next. Only this wasn't another Easter sermon that left me squirming and wondering if Mama's ham would be dry. This was the God with his hands in the bread, letting those same hands be nailed to a cross. The God who fed people in desolate places, going to the most desolate place of all. The graveyard.

" 'Why?' I asked her. Myra flipped forward in her Bible. *'This is love,'* she read. 'Not that we loved God, but that he loved us and sent his Son as an atoning sacrifice for our sins.'

"The words hung in the air around us. They were pretty words, lofty words—words that were difficult for a dropout to grasp. 'But what does it mean?' I finally whispered. Myra smiled. 'Jesus loves you. He died to take your graveyard.' "

Ivy paused her story and took a long drink from her mug of milk. My eyes burned as the echo of the lines I had written in Daddy's class surfaced in my mind. *You are wrong about the love,* I wrote. *Maybe it is just one note. It's still the whole reason for the myth.* Hadn't Mama said the same thing about her story?

Katie handed the stone to me. I lifted and lowered my hand as I tested its weight in my palm.

"I gripped that rock," Ivy continued. "As Myra began to read again. 'I will give you a new heart and put a new spirit in you. *I will remove your heart of stone,* and give you a heart of flesh.'

"And as she read those words, I felt the full sinking weight of my tombstone heart. I was so worn out, being a walking graveyard. I didn't understand how it worked. I'd never prayed anything besides the God-is-Great chant. So my prayer wasn't fancy. It wasn't something you'd learn in Sunday school. But they were the truest words I've ever uttered. 'Jesus, take my graveyard. I want a heart that lives.'

Ivy took the stone from me and slipped it back into the bag. "That prayer was the new start that wasn't supposed to be possible for someone as broken as me. And it didn't mean that I could suddenly read, or that people would instantly stop seeing me as a dropout thief, or that I'd escape all the consequences of years of bad choices. It meant hope that beauty was possible. It meant mercy, that I could try again and again. It meant the old, lying bones, the ones who told me I was worthless and unlovable, were cleared away. In their place—" Ivy turned around and lifted the candles to the center of the table. The soft glow of the flames glistened across century-old wood. "Light."

I remembered Noatak's journal. I could see the line written on the inside cover. *God is Light, and in Him there is no darkness.*

Ivy reached back to the hutch and pulled out two Bibles. One was deep purple and one was magenta pink. "For you," she said as she slid them toward me and Katie. "Check out Psalm 19, Katie. See if you recognize anything."

Loretta grunted. "Well good luck getting them to actually read 'em. But at least they've heard the story. And my, my, you have a way of telling it. All these candles and tombstones remind me of a big show the youth put on at church. And I don't know that the Lord abides by shows inside a church, but I can't see why he'd mind one at our dining table especially when it ends happily. You had me worried when you nearly ended it with you thieving that money. Like I always say, and I warned Tom about this, too, but he'd never listen—a story can't be good without a satisfactory ending. Tom liked complicated endings. But folks prefer sweet and simple and happy."

I leaned forward and blew out a candle. "But that's not real, Loretta. Especially in our family. Was Daddy's ending simple and happy? How about Mama's?"

"But what if...what if their story didn't end?" Ivy asked gently.

I laughed bitterly. "No matter how much you wish on it or make-believe it, every story ends. You got Jesus. I had Jane. Mama had some curse-breaking word. But Jane didn't work for me, and Mama's word sure didn't work for her. And even your Bible has a last page."

"What was your mama's word?" Ivy asked.

"Don't know. Daddy was going to tell me and then he died. Some curse-breaker, huh?"

Loretta reached out like she wanted to touch me, but wasn't sure if she should. Her withered hand hovered in the air. "Girly, your mama didn't get a chance to tell you, but she would have ... And your daddy, he got so hurt when he lost your mama that he shut down and—"

I stood up. "Don't you act like you knew them more than me. Don't act like if I believe in a dropout's bread-and-butter fairy tale, that they won't be dead and everything will be okay." I turned to go, and left my Bible and cake untouched. "C'mon, Katie, let's go watch a movie."

I was almost through the doorway when I realized that Katie wasn't following me. She was reading, her finger tracing the lines.

"You're not buying this junk, are you?" I called to her.

She looked at me, speechless for a moment, and then she began to read. Only now her voice and expression weren't the Dixie-vixen of our *Jane Eyre* readings. Katie read poetry like a lullaby, full of silky Southern syllables.

"The heavens declare the glory of God, the skies proclaim the work of his hands. Day after day they pour forth speech; night after night they reveal knowledge ... Their voice goes out into all the earth, their words to the ends of the world."

She looked at me with wide eyes. "Don't you see, Pearl? This is my storybook page. This is Alaska!"

XXXV

I returned for the cake. Once everyone was sleeping, I crept down to the kitchen to cut a slice. But as I walked past the dining room, I noticed my saucer of cake was still on the table. So was the Bible. Loretta had a firm rule against food in the bedrooms, but I simply did not have the willpower to resist sugar, or a big book of stories. I balanced the cake on top of the Bible and carried them to my room.

As I took a big bite, I skimmed the table of contents. It was a whole new library. I began with page one and read until I fell asleep.

The next morning, I woke up to a knock at my door. "Just a minute," I called, as I hid the Bible and saucer under my bed.

"The attorney is here," Ivy said. "C'mon down when you're ready."

I met them in the Circus Room. The attorney discussed my plea offer of probation, community service, and an apology essay.

"But the state hasn't agreed," he said. "You drew a jail hungry prosecutor that believes kids never learn a lesson without being locked up. But given your age and lack of prior record, I'm gonna fight to keep you out. I can't make any promises, but try not to worry too much."

Ivy squeezed my hand.

I wasn't worried. I would never go back to jail.

"I know you're plottin' something," Katie whispered, once the attorney left. "But let's chin-up and get this behind us. Then we can plan our next trip to Alaska. Besides, if you runaway again, who will teach me more about stories?"

"You have Ivy."

Since that night with the tombstone, Katie had followed Ivy around listening to her stories. She told tall tales about tumbling walls, wedding wine, and unruly seas. I'd hang near them, secretly listening.

I spent my nights chasing down Ivy's stories. Visiting with kings and warriors, harlots and lepers. And the more I read, the more I wished the story was real and would never end. But I remembered how flat *Jane Eyre* felt on the night of the talent show. Stories were just ink and paper.

On the night before my court date, I selected things to pack from Daddy's memory box. I might never return home, and there were some things that could not be left behind. Like Daddy's galley. And the unfinished novel, his *last new thing.*

"Pearl?" Katie called through my door. "What are you doing? Why don't you come join us?"

"I'm trying to finish this stupid essay," I lied. "I've got court in the morning, remember?"

"Well, take a break. Let's have one more dessert night."

One more. Everybody expected me to return to jail. I wished I could go ahead and make my escape. But I had to play it cool and pretend to go along with Ivy and her desserts, stories, and good-dealing attorney. I opened my door and followed Katie to the dining room.

The candles were on the table, but there were no books or velvet bags. I sat down as Loretta came around the corner, grinning and carrying a pink lemonade cake. She proudly set it before me.

"You know how I feel about traditions, Girly," she said with a firm nod.

Ivy arrived carrying a stack of Mama's milk glass saucers and a pie covered in whipped cream. She set the pie next to the pink lemonade cake and began to slice and serve. I saw that underneath the pie's whipped cream was a soft custard, topped by a rich golden layer. Ivy passed out our portions, and each milk glass saucer held a pink square and a silky triangle. It was a pretty and tempting plate.

Everyone was quiet and somber. I sensed the weight of the coming morning hanging over us. I took a small bite of pink lemonade cake. It was my first taste of it since Daddy died.

Loretta watched me, but didn't act smug like I expected, as I took a second, larger bite. "Your mama and daddy fell in love over cake," she said softly.

I didn't hate it anymore. Daddy always wanted that cake to mean something to me, and it finally did. It meant disappointing birthdays that now glowed in my mind with perfection.

I ran my fork through the pie and studied the custard, trying to guess its flavor.

"Birthright pie," Ivy announced.

I gasped. "Mama's? The one in the picture?"

"Yes! Her famous pie."

I took a bite. *Banana cream.* All along, Mama's secret recipe was banana custard, layered with golden caramel.

"Well, Pearl, you've won," Katie declared. "This pie is truly better than anything chocolate."

Ivy smiled. "Christine had a knack for pairing flavors. One day, when she wasn't much older than you, Pearl, she decided to layer a banana cream pie with a caramel one. Birthright pie was born. It's a real legend in our family."

"Why'd she call it that, I wonder?" Loretta asked. "Seems to me it'd be more fitting to call it Caramel Banana Pie."

"There's this story about two brothers," Ivy explained. "One sells his birthright, his whole inheritance, for a bowl of stew."

I had read that story, during my night of Bible and cake. I hadn't thought to draw a line between the words I was reading and Mama's treasure.

"When my grandfather took his first bite of this pie, he said 'I don't see how anybody would sell their birthright for stew. But for this pie...well, I don't reckon I'd blame 'em too much.' Ever since then, it's been birthright pie."

I accepted a second piece. And I knew for certain that it wasn't fiction after all—Mama really was our Sugar Queen. The pie was perfection. After I finished, I pushed the saucer back and excused myself to leave. "I've got to get back to work on my essay. No time for stories."

"*You* are the story tonight," Ivy said. "This cake, this pie ... even your mama's dishes ... we chose them because they're a part of you. And yes, there's so much pain, but it's not all gomin'. There's real love, even here in the desserts. There's beauty woven all through your story."

Loretta twisted her hands and her eyes had an urgent look. "Maybe I forgot who you are ... or maybe I never bothered to know. But even if you land in jail, don't try and be a skillet. I guess, nobody really is. You just go on being our Pearl."

My face burned with heat, and the only thing I could think to whisper was, "Why are you here, Ivy? I don't want to know about tombstones or bread. I want to know why you came. To give me pie? To serve my last supper, before I'm sent away for good, so you can steal my inheritance? Why?"

"We have the same bones," she said. "Our graveyards look a lot alike. And you can't be rescued from a graveyard as dark and crowded as mine and not want to share that, especially with *family*. I don't know what's going to happen tomorrow, and Lord knows I don't want you to go to jail, but more than anything, I want you out of that graveyard."

I would not be baited back to jail by sweet words and pie. I reminded everyone that I needed to prepare for court, and returned to my bedroom. But after midnight, I crept out of the house, grabbed my bike, and pedaled with a steady pace. I would arrive at the bus station well before dawn.

But it was a moonless night, and I could barely see anything, much less the lines on the road. More than once I drove into the ditch. I had to guess at the depths of curves, because I couldn't see them. It was freezing too. I shivered as the winter wind whipped around me. I wished that I had worn my Alaskan gear.

I pedaled for hours, through the cold and the dark, up the hills and around blind curves. The only thing that kept me from turning back was the thought of jail. Finally, I could see the bus station just down the hill, with fluorescent lights glowing in the dark. There was an empty field next to me, and I dragged my bike into it. I didn't want to look like a runaway, arriving alone on a bike. I sat down on the cold ground and took a few deep breaths. I needed to collect myself and get my story straight, like at the hotel in Alaska.

"Mama's in the car on crutches. She broke her leg, so I'm going to my grandma's," I rehearsed.

My voice was tired and shaky. I took a deep breath, wiped the sweat from my brow, and tried again. Once I felt calmer, I picked up my bag and walked toward the station. But the dark was out to get me. It concealed more than curves, and my eyes missed something low and hard on the ground. I walked straight into it, fell forward, and smashed my head. I groaned and reached my hand up to my forehead. It was sticky and wet with blood. *The blows keep on coming!*

I searched my bag for a shirt to press against the wound. My head throbbed with pain. *What could I have hit?* I was in an empty field. Were there boulders around me? Maybe old tree stumps? It was too dark. I would have to wait until there was at least a bit of light to clean myself up and walk to the station. I started to cry, and I cursed myself because tears were no help at all. *Such a baby thing to do.* But I could not stop shivering, my head would not stop throbbing, and all I wanted to do was walk toward the light.

It was the waiting that caught me off guard. I had left in a fury. I had escaped and pedaled with fervor. But now, I was stuck in the dark with all my thoughts and memories. My mind searched the details of the past two weeks. French toast and learning how to sweep a dirty floor. Katie's first kiss, and the acorn collecting, Tennessee girl with the tombstone heart. I thought about Loretta, how she was sorry after all.

Stop it! For once in your life, be an iron skillet. But a trickle of fresh blood rolled down my forehead, and I remembered Loretta's words. *Nobody ever really is.* No, when Daddy died, I broke into a million tiny pieces. I wrapped my arms around myself and squeezed and squeezed. *How do I hold myself together?*

As my eyes adjusted to the dark, I began to see things—strange, terrifying shapes, blacker than the night, looming around me. I tried to focus on the distant light of the bus station, but all I could think about was the day the canoe sank, that endless pit where bits of swimming scum thrived, and the light that stayed far off and broken. I sat, shivering with terror as more black shapes rose around me, and I realized there wasn't just one dark pond. It was a pit-filled world. Sometimes people are born in them, like Ivy and her broken brain. Some pits we fall or are even shoved into, like when Daddy died, and I was left orphaned. But the darkest pits of all, the most horrifying, are the ones we jump into.

Like my night in the holding tank. Like that moment, trapped in a black field of terrifying shadows.

The sun began to rise. I peered through the first hint of light as the shapes began to brighten. *What were those things?* Dozens of them ... no, hundreds. One was there, right in front of me. The boulder I had tripped on, or was it a stump? I reached out and touched it. My hand traced letters etched in frozen stone. A tombstone. I looked around and saw rows and rows of dark tombstones. *I was in a field of dead things.*

I leapt to my feet and ran. But in the new light, I saw the bus station wasn't nearly as close as I had thought. There were acres of graves to run through. In my panic I hadn't closed my bag, and as I ran, out fell my purple Bible. A slip of paper was sticking out the top. It was a note written in Loretta's squared handwriting.

"Dear Pearl, You mentioned a story your mama loved. Maybe this is it. Only you will know. Love, Ivy."

Any other day, any other moment, I would have tossed that Bible back in my bag with an angry, *You don't know me or my mama* shout. But there's something about being alone and hurt in a field of graves that makes a handwritten note compelling. It makes the single word, *Love,* feel less like a standard closing and more like a true pledge.

So I didn't scowl over Ivy's bravado or assumptions. I pulled aside the note and read the first lines on the page beneath it, aching for anything beyond that field of graves.

"In the beginning was the Word."

I read it again. I whispered it to the dawn.

"In the beginning was the Word, and the Word was with God, and the Word was God...

"In him was life, and that life was the light of all mankind. The light shines in the darkness, and the darkness has not overcome it."

At last, I knew Mama's Word. And I realized, everyone's Best Part pointed to the same story. Noatak's Light. Ivy's Bread. Mama's Word. As I tucked the Bible in my backpack, I noticed how badly my hands were shaking. I needed to compose myself if I was ever going to convince anyone to sell me a bus ticket.

I desperately needed comfort, a distraction to soothe my burning nerves. So I fell back on old tricks, and I did the thing that Weavers always do. I reached for a story. I pulled out Daddy's half-finished novel, and traced the title for the hundredth time.

The Heart-Shaped Museum
By
Jack Thomas Weaver

I turned the page.

Dear Pearl,

Remember the Best Parts party? When writers tried to outdo one another with wise and witty quotes? After that night, I've been thinking about the best parts, what they are and how many I've edited out.

So many times I've told you, so many times you've whispered along with me, "Our house is a linthead miracle." But the real miracle was never made of brick and ivy. I edited it out, even though, like your mama believed, the story is all around us.

It's all through our best literature too. It's the heart of "Tiger Tiger," and it's in Jane Eyre. *Jane's very last line is… well, I'll let you read it for yourself.*

I deleted the miracle because I was angry and hurt. I gave you stories, but not the truth that Abel taught me. You've never heard the real linthead miracle.

Here it is. Not a novel for the world, but my gift to you. Pearl, I've learned that truth is the greatest darling. And as it turns out, darlings don't deserve to be killed.

Love you,
Daddy

It wasn't a novel. It was a gift. Daddy had finished it. He'd not left behind a half-written book after all. But didn't I know everything? About love among the cotton bales and the piano in the kitchen?

I turned another page. Read the first line of chapter one, so familiar and sweet. Daddy's voice echoed all around. *Abel Weaver was born Abel Thomas Cunningham.*

Everything was just as expected, comforting and perfect. I read all the old details about the mill, Abel's grief, and him and Stella dancing among the cotton. I loved Daddy for writing it all down. I loved Abel and Stella for living it all out. But soon, the story was so much harder than I had been told. *So much killing* was laid on my great-grandparents, bringing them to their own heap upon the floor. Stella was starving and baby Jack had a cough. Abel was standing in a bread line and thinking about sending his family to crawl up Mayfield Hill.

I breathed a sigh of relief, when finally, there was the piano in the kitchen. Only this time it came from a burned out church. There was a preacher with a smoky Bible and a different kind of Christmas story. I fell headfirst into the pages, nodded along with Abel as he whispered, *Every good thing gets broken.* I held my breath as I saw Jesus through Abel's linthead eyes. I felt my own knees shaking as Abel sank to the ground and whispered Mama's Word. I wondered—I worried—over what other differences I would find as I turned the page. I bit my lip in suspense, because Abel was about to enter the most frightening pit. A Carolina courtroom.

The Heart-Shaped Museum

Abel wore his best pair of overalls to court, the ones that weren't torn in the pockets from carrying around too many tools. Stella handed him a freshly ironed shirt. She had wanted to buy him a suit, but he wouldn't hear of spending money on clothes when they didn't know where they would be living the next day.

He knew how strange his overalls seemed inside the courtroom. Harold and two other gentlemen sat at a table next to him. They wore three-piece suits and shiny shoes. Abel tried to smooth down the corners of his collar. Stella had never gotten the hang of ironing, and whenever she made a real effort, the corners of his collar stuck up like little wings.

The judge announced that Harold was the plaintiff, and would speak first. He talked and questioned witnesses for hours. He used charts, land surveys, maps, and a timeline of dates with births, marriages, and deaths. Abel listened as Harold rattled on in lofty lingo. He tried to think of what he would say when it was his turn. He had practiced some with Stella the day before, but there in the courtroom he couldn't remember his main points. Panic choked him.

How about them shepherds, was the thought he tried to soothe himself with. God picked them to join the holiest story, in spite of their dirty hands and smelly clothes. Maybe because of it. He thought about the fishermen too. Working men that Jesus gave his story to, told them to cast it far and wide.

What was it about Jesus' story that made it so powerful? Abel wondered as Harold rattled on. Why was Jesus' story such a line-crosser?

"Your Honor, this defendant," Harold said as he pointed a finger at Abel, "was an outlier to the respectable Mayfield family. A nobody, born with a thieving heart. Raised in a shack and set on stealing the mill owner's mansion. He spied an opportunity in Stella. He took advantage of her blushing youth. He ran off with Mr. Mayfield's baby girl because he thought he could weasel his way into the Mayfield fortune. He didn't bother to ask for a blessing. He didn't have enough respect to tell Mr. Mayfield his intentions. And now that he's laid claim to that river-bottom land, he thinks he's accomplished his goal. Only this court can set it right. Only this court can help undo the devastation to the Mayfield family that this man has caused."

And that's when Abel knew what he would say. He wouldn't talk about the house and how hard he and Stella had worked to fix it, how many hours he'd spent polishing the old staircase, how many bricks he'd laid around the crumbling fireplace. He wouldn't even mention how badly they needed that home. He would talk about the love. He thought of Stella, and how she wanted to lasso love for keeps. It was the best part of his story. Isn't love what gave any story its power?

"My name is Abel Weaver. And I don't know what an outlier is, but if it means a nobody linthead, then Harold's right to call me that. I wasn't born for mansions or river-bottom land."

"Uhm, Mr. Weaver, do you understand your purpose today is to present your defense?" the judge interrupted him.

"Yes sir, that's what I'm fixin' to do."

"A strange way to begin, Mr. Weaver," the judge mumbled. "Proceed."

Abel told the court about growing up in the mill. About the first time he saw Stella, swatting at the lint as he swept the halls. He told them about finding her asleep inside the cotton warehouse, and how he convinced the other lintheads that she was the Mill Granny. He told them about how love bloomed among the bales. About how he married her with a string of cotton for a ring, and how she still refused to wear anything but a cotton band.

"This is all well and fine, Mr. Weaver," the judge said. "But perhaps it would help clear things up if I asked a few questions during your statement. Do you have any objection to that?"

"No, Your Honor."

"Very well, the plaintiff has accused you of eloping with Stella because you wanted to weasel your way into the Mayfield fortune. You knew there was no Mayfield son and none of the other girls had married yet. It does seem like a prime opportunity for a young man to marry into. How do you respond to the accusation? Why did you elope with Stella instead of asking her parents to bless your union, or perhaps work and prove yourself to them?"

Abel caught a glimpse of Harold sneering at him as the judge questioned him. He told the judge about Abraham Linton's letters, and how he let the protesters into the mill to protect Stella.

"Mr. Mayfield was so angry with me. I told him about how they had Stella, but he kept screaming, *"A man's work is his life!"* He sent for the sheriff. Was going to pin the whole thing on me. That's why I decided to run. And Stella wanted to come too. I knew she was leaving behind her whole world of pretty dresses and rich parties. But I also knew she was worth far more than any cotton mill. I don't reckon nobody else up on Mayfield Hill knew that. Except her mama, there at the end when she wrote that will."

Abel paused and took a deep breath. "I never run off with Stella because I was trying to weasel my way into the Mayfield family. I didn't like it one bit that she was a Mayfield. Life would have been a lot easier if she'd been born linthead. I ran because I'd lost my job, might've been losing my freedom, and because I loved Stella and would give my life to take care of her. That's the reason I'm here today."

The judge silently stared at Abel. Then he cleared his throat. "Perhaps you have some evidence of your own ... maybe some surveys?"

"No, Your Honor."

"Then you should present your summation."

"I should ... what?"

"Your final thoughts, Mr. Weaver. Any last words?"

Last words. Abel paused to collect his thoughts, but his mind returned to his brother Jack and that final punch Abel landed on his shoulder. He remembered Jack's very last words. *Where'd my little brother go? Who's this strong man standin' here now?*

Abel smiled for the first time ever over that memory. He thought about what Jack would think, what he would say, if he saw him standing in his overalls inside a Carolina courtroom.

"Mr. Weaver? A summation?"

"I'm no thief. I wasn't back on that night when I opened the mill and I ain't now. I don't want a house that's not ours by right. I can't say I know for certain what was in Mrs. Mayfield's heart when she wrote that will. But I don't think Harold and Sally can either. Me and Stella, we'll never believe it was grief or diabetes or that big word Harold keeps saying. We choose to believe it was love. That's why she changed the will. Love is why she gave us the house."

The courtroom was silent as Abel took his seat.

Harold rose. "Your Honor, if I may rebut?"

"Quickly, counselor."

"Your Honor, the issue before the court today is simple. In whose house does this man belong? And we contend, considering the status of his birth and—"

"Gentlemen?" the judge interrupted. "I've actually heard enough. I'm going to withdraw to my chamber to ponder my decision. Court is adjourned for two hours, at which point I'll make a ruling on the ownership of the disputed property."

Harold grinned like he'd already won. Like he knew the reason the judge interrupted him was because a rebuttal wasn't even needed, since the evidence was so clearly in his favor.

Abel thanked the judge and smoothed the wings of his collar down one last time. He walked out of the courthouse and down the street, his mind buzzing with thoughts.

In whose house does this man belong? Harold had asked. Hadn't Abel always wondered that too? When his mama made him hide his true last name ... when he eloped to a strange town and a new mill with a new wife ... when the crash happened and the shack was falling down and Stella was so skinny.

The sidewalk ended but he walked until he came to a large, open field. There was no fence locking him out, so he stepped into the grass and took a deep breath as he wondered what the judge would decide.

He felt like a shepherd, with no farmhouse over the hill. Like Joseph, with no senator daddy and no motel for his wife. But he knew that he belonged to the house of Jesus. In that home, there are no abandoned boys.

Yes, Abel longed for victory. Yes, he dreamed of his grandchildren romping in the fields behind the house one day. But Jesus had weeded out the lie that *every good thing gets broken* and planted a new story, deep within his heart. Brothers die, mamas won't claim you, and sisters might try to steal houses, but Jesus broke himself to give every poor linthead their very own inheritance. Everlasting life. Unbreakable love.

When it was time for the judge to announce his verdict, Abel carried this truth inside him, straight into that Carolina courtroom. His very own treasure, locked inside a heart-shaped museum.

XXXVI

As I turned the last pages, I stood with Abel inside that Carolina courtroom and pondered dirty shepherds. I cheered for him as he told the judge his story. I believed him, of course it was love inside his mother-in-law's heart. I stepped with him into that field and heard him repeat the question of his whole life. *In whose house does this man belong?*

It wasn't three stories of weathered brick with a burning sunset smudged across the top. That was just another faded storybook page. *Abel belonged to the house of Jesus.*

Someone called my name. I looked up to see Ivy running through the graveyard. Her arms were open and reaching, though she was still far away. I couldn't keep myself from stepping toward her.

"You're hurt!" she cried.

She folded me in her arms, and I leaned into her and wept. I thought of all those graves around me as I named the bones piled up in my heart. *Daddy.* Because he'd died so young and no matter how many times I begged, he wouldn't come back. *Mama.* Because I didn't know her, and that's a hard kind of loss all its own.

I cried and cried and I did not edit a single tear. I did not try and become a different story, or be an iron skillet. All my pieces fell apart.

"You all have the same story," I sobbed. "You wanted bread. Mama wanted the word that could lift the curse. Noatak wants light instead of darkness. Abel wanted something that couldn't be broken."

"And you?" Ivy asked.

"I want…I want…" I was about to say *to escape,* as my eyes stared longingly at the bus station in the distance. I was about to plead with Ivy to buy me a ticket and help me hide. But I remembered all my other great escape attempts. My night in the Red Room and the ghosts I crossed out. My flight to Alaska. None of them worked.

"Your heart was a graveyard," I finally whispered. "Mine's a holding tank. I hate my story, but it's got me hooked on the line. I've done too much…now I can't stop running. Loretta was right all along, every lawless deed gets judged."

"Isaiah 55:7," Ivy answered as she reached for my Bible. "Try it."

I flipped through the pages until I found the right spot.

Let the wicked forsake their ways and the unrighteous their thoughts. Let them turn to the Lord, and he will have mercy on them, and to our God, for he will freely pardon.

And like Abel, I was confronted by the one word I didn't think possible. If normal words were as real as rooms, then inside *pardon,* I found a whole new house. A safe one, where my story wouldn't have to be deleted to find healing. Where I wouldn't have to outrun my guilt to know mercy. And for the first time in my life, an apology felt like the perfect place to start.

I'm sorry. I've locked myself inside a holding-tank heart. Jesus, will you set me free?

An hour later, after racing home for a quick shower and a change of clothes, we met my attorney on the courthouse steps. I told him I didn't have an apology essay and had never started writing one.

The attorney scrunched his face up then flipped open his binder and started writing. He walked away and yelled back that he had to make a quick call. When he returned, he looked relieved. "Your apology just got a lot more complicated, young lady," he laughed stiffly. "But this job has taught me to expect curve balls. For the past several years the state library system has sponsored an annual memoir contest. I know about it because my wife is helping her grandma put something together for it this year. I called, and there is no minimum age requirement. They just want work that reflects the unique experiences and heritages of our state. I'm going to propose to the court that you be required to write a memoir of your criminal experience for this contest."

I gasped. "A memoir... like a whole book?"

He nodded. "Not only will it be punitive, because it will require a great deal of effort from you, but it will also enrich the arts culture of our state and serve as a warning for other youths about the dangers of reckless choices. I think, given your literary heritage, I can convince the court that you want to write more than a simple essay. You need a memoir to explain what you did and how you've changed."

"How long will I have to write it?"

"I'll suggest it shouldn't be due until the end of probation, which at minimum will be a year, but likely much more."

Ivy nodded. "Maybe you can start thinking about how you'll write it, if court drags on today."

We walked up the courthouse steps together. I stopped and tugged on Ivy's hand. "I'm scared."

Ivy took my face in her hands. "Me too. But he will feed you in the desolate places."

That day in court, I felt the circle, the full circle of my family's story, as I sat listening to attorneys debate the question of the day: *In whose house does Pearl Weaver belong?*

And I knew the answer, though nobody bothered to ask me. Because what began inside a pomegranate prison had bloomed into a new linthead miracle. I belonged to the house of Jesus, the house of peace and pardon. In that home, there are no holding-tank hearts.

Think about how you'll write it, Ivy had encouraged.

Daddy's writing lessons bubbled inside me. And though I didn't have my first line, I remembered how good stories end. Always, with wonder.

So maybe, right now, I'm sitting by the Yadkin telling stories with a linthead tongue. Maybe I returned to tall-tale dreams inside a cinderblock cell. Did I find my way back to the end of the earth? Are my Dixie born feet running through arctic cotton?

Hold your breath over me. Carry me around in your heart. Because this apology ends, but my story does not.

Only now, instead of dry bones rattling or prisoners wailing in the dark, my pages sing: *It is well. It is well. It is well.*

Such treasure, living inside my heart-shaped museum.

I love discussing books with groups of readers. Below, I have included some questions that I enjoy thinking about. If your book club would like to discuss *Pearl Weaver's Epic Apology* with me, please visit my website at www.rachelkeener.com for more information on how to set up an author chat.

Discussion Questions

1. Pearl's father valued eccentricity and personal story, above social ease. Was Loretta right, that he hadn't allowed Pearl to be normal? Or was he simply gifting Pearl with a beautiful family legacy? If her father had not died, do you think Pearl's efforts for a fresh start at school would have been successful?
2. Stella tossed away money, comfort, and a secure future to marry Abel. Besides her marriage, what did Stella gain in exchange for the things she gave up? Have you ever sacrificed a "sure bet" to pursue a greater passion?
3. Pearl's father taught that a great setting can save a sinking story. How did Pearl's escape to Alaska change her story? Did it help save it? Have you ever needed to change your own setting in order for your story to progress?

4. Ivy and Loretta read the same Bible and prayed to the same God. Yet their faith was radically different. What was the key difference between the two, and how did each woman's faith impact Pearl for either good or bad?
5. Who, or what, represents the unwritten outcome of Abel's courtroom battle over the disputed house by the Yadkin?
6. Why did the hymn "It is Well" repulse Pearl at the beginning of the novel, but become her anthem at the end? Pearl's grief was still present, and her circumstances bleak. What had changed?
7. What do you believe happened to Pearl after her day in court? How important is it to you, to have every detail of a story wrapped up and revealed?
8. What is Pearl Weaver's epic apology? Is it the book you are holding? Or is it something else?

Made in the USA
Columbia, SC
04 July 2018